Every Second Counts

EVERY SECOND COUNTS

DAVID DONACHIE

McBooks
Press
Essex, Connecticut

McBooks
Press

An imprint of Globe Pequot, the trade division of
The Rowman & Littlefield Publishing Group, Inc.
4501 Forbes Blvd., Ste. 200
Lanham, MD 20706
www.rowman.com

Distributed by NATIONAL BOOK NETWORK

British Library Cataloguing in Publication Information available

Library of Congress Cataloging-in-Publication Data
ISBN 978-1-4930-6064-1 (hardcover)
ISBN 978-1-4930-7063-3 (ebook)

♾™ The paper used in this publication meets the minimum requirements of American National
Standard for Information Sciences—Permanence of Paper for Printed Library Materials, ANSI/
NISO Z39.48-1992.

BY DAVID DONACHIE

THE JOHN PEARCE ADVENTURES
By the Mast Divided • A Shot Rolling Ship
An Awkward Commission • A Flag of Truce
The Admirals' Game • An Ill Wind
Blown Off Course • Enemies at Every Turn
A Sea of Troubles • A Divided Command
The Devil to Pay • The Perils of Command
A Treacherous Coast • On a Particular Service
A Close Run Thing • HMS Hazard • A Troubled Course

THE CONTRABAND SHORE SERIES
The Contraband Shore • A Lawless Place • Blood Will Out

THE NELSON AND EMMA SERIES
On a Making Tide • Tested by Fate • Breaking the Line

THE PRIVATEERSMEN SERIES
The Devil's Own Luck • The Dying Trade • A Hanging Matter
An Element of Chance • The Scent of Betrayal • A Game of Bones

HISTORICAL THRILLERS
Every Second Counts
Originally written as Jack Ludlow

THE LAST ROMAN SERIES
Vengeance • Honor • Triumph

THE REPUBLIC SERIES
The Pillars of Rome • The Sword of Revenge • The Gods of War

THE CONQUEST SERIES
Mercenaries • Warriors • Conquest

To the memory of

Sarah Grazebrook

My partner and inspiration for

forty-four wonderful years.

To jaw jaw is always better than to war war

WINSTON CHURCHILL

CHAPTER ONE

Wednesday, July 24, 1940, 4:40 a.m.

Billy Houston had no idea what was in the stolen briefcase. He did know he'd been required to kill to get it. Unable to sleep and still fully clothed, he rolled out of bed to quietly ferret in the toolbox in the hall cupboard, only to find it took a chisel and a four-pound hammer to break the lock. Pulling out the mass of stuff inside, he threw the brief-case, along with the still attached handcuffs, under his bed and made his way to the kitchen.

The dim bulb, combined with limited early morning light, was little help in a basement flat damp and chilly even in midsummer. So Billy pulled on his raincoat and lit the cooker, hoping to warm the place. Shivering at the table by the heavily barred window, he began to study what he'd acquired.

Top of the pile was a large, lined pad, listing a series of hand-written numbers, underneath a set of folded maps, twenty in all, covered in symbols, each one broken into squared and numbered sections. The first showed the east coast of Kent from Dover to the Thames Estuary. Others went all the way past Portsmouth and Plymouth. The rest covered the inland areas, the various towns and cities of southern England, from East Anglia to Bristol.

Concentrating on the one covering the beaches to the north of Dover, he studied the mass of neatly inked signs, these overlain with thick, scribbled pencil marks, arrows and numbered circles which made no sense to him. As the sun rose, to shed light into the street of five-storey houses, he focused on the permanent markings.

Tiny skull and crossbones denoted minefields and these he recognised, symbols he had seen in the Great War as a sergeant in the Highland Light Infantry. This pointed him to the probable meaning of the others, like the trench systems on the heights overlooking Dover Harbour. He felt a growing sense of excitement at what he might have, though it was mixed with frustration. Even after an hour, he had failed to solve the mystery of the pencilled notations, which matched the figures on the pad.

At the sound of movement from the next-door bedroom, he flipped over the topmost map, shoving it underneath the folded pile. Gingerly, he ran a hand over the painful patches on his face, wondering how bad they looked. It had been a ferocious scrap in that narrow hallway, as tough as any he had fought as a youngster in the streets of Glasgow or his more recent battles against the East End Jews. As a fight it had been more like the cramped and murderous 'kill or be killed' struggles he had experienced in the desperate closing battles of 1918.

His victim had been fit for his age, but the briefcase attached to his wrist had hampered him as he tried to match Billy blow for blow. It took time to create enough space to swing the lead pipe and get a whack to the cheek, then finally to fell his opponent with one to the forehead.

Having already carried out the planned burglary, the briefcase looked like a bonus until Billy, just getting his breath back, couldn't find any keys in the groaning victim's pocket. Livid and feeling thwarted—he'd always had a red-mist temper—he cracked down on the man's head to shut the sod up. A search of the garden shed yielded only a small pruning saw which proved to be useless in getting the briefcase off the arm. It tore the skin, but the bone he had to stamp on to break.

The saw, lead pipe and blood-stained gloves had ended up in the River Thames as he made his way back across the Lambeth Bridge to Pimlico. Only when he got back did he realise the bloodied instruments, hidden inside his Mackintosh, had left stains on the lining. Now, folded on the back of his chair, these marks were hidden.

Bettina Wyvern pottered out of her bedroom, frowning at the still-lit cooker. Ever the tidy one, she lifted the coat to hang it in the hall, eyes wide with hurt when he snapped at her to leave it alone. Having examined the scratches on his face, her eyes moved to the objects on the kitchen table, by size and shape, unmistakable. Bettina, clearly troubled, rubbed her hands nervously down her sides and shook her head several times, her fleshy jowls quivering.

To her clandestine lodger the reaction was typical. How different people were when they ceased to babble about "doing something for the cause" and were actually required to act. He'd seen it too many times to be surprised when they turned out to have lily livers.

The "cause" had been an excuse. Billy, on the run, needed money and robbery had looked like a way to get some. Bettina, who cleaned houses to make ends meet, had let slip one of her regulars was something in the military. More importantly, he kept a large amount of cash in a bureau in his spare room, all this really a boast to let Billy know how much she was trusted.

'He'll have missed them by now.'

Billy patted the topmost map, his tone confident. 'He will, Bettina.'

'I hope it's worth it?'

'Of course it is, lassie. We struck a blow.'

'I should never have given you the key. He's bound to know it was me.'

He looked up at her, seeking to convey reassurance, even as he felt his anger rising. Her hands were clasped under a substantial bosom, which matched her pudgy body. The broad, pink-cheeked face, under a knotted turban was creased and unhappy, making her even less attractive than usual and that was pretty unappealing to begin with. No wonder she'd stayed a widow.

'He will not, Bettina, cause ah've made it look like a proper break-in, so he'll reckon it's a burglary. You can turn up on Friday looking innocent and shocked. Now, what about a cup of tea and a wee bit o' toast?'

'Someone might have seen me in the phone box.'

'Who's going tae see you in the blackout? And even if they did, the chances of it being a body tae recognise ye is slim.' He smiled at her and added in his most seductive tone. 'Come on, make us some breakfast, hen?'

Bettina's task, her "aid" to the cause, had been to occupy the phone box at the corner of the street and alert Billy with two rings on the house

3

phone should her employer show up. But he never got the warning. Had the old cow even stayed there as lookout? He could ask her, but he doubted if she'd admit to having panicked and fled, which she must have done to get back to the flat ahead of him with time to get in bed.

Upstairs, rifling and pocketing the contents of a carved wooden box, Billy had heard the rasping of the owner's key. Given his only possible exit was blocked, he'd knew he'd have to fight his way out, a bloody resolution being the inevitable outcome.

As Bettina began to fill the kettle, it was clear what he had was of value, so he must decide what to do next. The sharp crack of the letterbox, followed by the slapping sound of the morning paper hitting the lino, made Billy jump. He rose to fetch it, leaving Bettina to slice the bread with her worn, bone-handled knife.

Unfolding the paper, his heart lifted at a headline and he ran his eyes over the article it covered. This delayed him too long so, by the time he came back to the kitchen, Bettina was at the table, standing over a map, face up and fully open. His raincoat had been turned inside out as well, the lining now on show.

Her eyes flicked towards the coat, before she looked directly at him. 'Billy, what you have done?'

'What was necessary for the cause,' he replied. 'That's what ah've done.'

Gently he edged her away from the table, murmuring reassuringly about the cause they both supported and how his actions had made what they both believed in possible. But Billy was really reflecting on the way she'd betrayed him the night before, and he knew she might do so again, which had him slip the breadknife into his hand.

CHAPTER TWO

Wednesday, July 24, 5:00 a.m.

Unbroken sleep didn't come easily to the deputy director of Counter-Espionage at MI5. For weeks now, Adam Strachan had rarely been able to get through the night without tossing and turning to eventually wake up. Tasked with keeping the nation secure, it had been hard enough following the outbreak of war. How much more difficult would it become with the Germans holding the coast of Europe from the tip of Norway all the way to the Spanish border?

The last two months had been especially hectic. In May, MI5 had finally been given the green light to move against adherents of all the right wing and anti-Semitic groups, a sweep against organisations which had been a curse to the country throughout much of the last decade. Nearly all the outright fascist sympathisers were now either behind bars or barbed wire on the Isle of Man. Few had escaped the net, though it had proved impossible to arrest everyone with extreme right-wing views.

Adam knew, for every high-profile detainee, there remained thousands in the country who secretly sympathised with National Socialism, not least in the upper reaches of British society, and such people lurked elsewhere. Pre-war there had been one or more propping up the bar in every pub and golf club in the country. They would be less vocal now, but their views would not have changed.

The rounding-up of enemy aliens followed, arrests carried out with too few operatives, in an effort to crack a problem next to impossible to solve. How to sort the bad from the good? For the escapees from Nazi tyranny, the good had to be in the majority, but there was no certainty.

The action had been especially harsh on German Jews already uprooted to avoid Adolf Hitler's thugs.

Then Mussolini had invaded the South of France, an attack which, even if it had been a military fiasco, led to the detention of legions of bemused Italians—hotel staff, restaurant and café owners, many of whom had lived in Britain for decades. Even the maître d'hôtel of the Savoy had been hauled off, which had led to howls of protest from his well-heeled clientele.

Neither had it been a pleasant assignment, even for him, supervising matters at arm's length, not in face-to-face contact with those taken into custody. And it did nothing to solve the central problem; where there still active spies in the country? Dozens of enemy agents had been rounded up since the previous September, but you could never be certain you had them all.

The Abwehr was reckoned to be a model of efficiency, which made suspect such ineptitude when planting spies in Britain. Some agents had struggled to speak decent English and knew nothing of the British way of life. Others had made simple mistakes, like using their radios in static locations, making them easy to track down, perhaps too much so.

No one believed Admiral Wilhelm Canaris, who ran German military intelligence, was inept; if anything, the opposite was true. Thus, the suspicion existed he was prepared to sacrifice small beer and in quantity in order to protect his more valuable intelligence assets. Gnawing on this, Adam lay awake, teeth clenched. Each time his concerns faded and he was going under, his wife would turn in bed, groaning and murmuring.

When he did eventually drift off again, it was to the image of messages being sent to Berlin by people as yet undiscovered, intelligence which would ensure much of what he and his department had done since the outbreak of war had been totally wasted.

CHAPTER THREE

Wednesday, July 24, 5:14 a.m.

Rudolf Graebner arrived home in fitful morning light, fresh from the bed of a new amorous conquest. He'd spent the previous evening at a Mayfair nightclub, mixing with the society he'd been tasked to monitor. It was a place frequented by the well-heeled and the well-informed, and it had turned out to be an especially productive night. The chatter was full of whispered hints a change was imminent at the top of the British government. On his way to the lift, he'd picked up the early editions of the morning papers, to discover, in the stop press, such gossip was based on fact.

Reich Chancellor Hitler's speech from the stage of the Kroll Opera House, delivered the previous week, offering an olive branch to the British Empire, had been followed by a diplomatic note sent through Sweden. It suggested an immediate armistice as a precursor to peace talks. Churchill had responded in his usual bellicose fashion, determined to go on fighting, even with an invasion threatened and, after endless evacuations following on from Dunkirk, an army that had abandoned its equipment and was now in tatters.

Wiser heads at the cabinet table had prevailed and the Bulldog had resigned, his replacement as yet unnamed, news which Rudi absorbed with mixed feelings. Ever since Germany had been forced into launching a pre-emptive attack on Denmark and Norway, he had been obliged to read about the stunning successes of the German armed forces while he was twiddling his thumbs in the enemy capital.

His presence in London, as well as his induction into the Abwehr, had come through an early upbringing in Madrid. Born into the Spanish nobility, he naturally possessed complete fluency in his native tongue and

7

had a good command of French. An infancy spent under the hand of a British governess, employed by his widowed mother, had also provided him with an ability to speak fluent, albeit grammatical, English.

Such advantages had not been lost upon moving to Germany with his stepfather, Karl Graebner, the Kaiser's assistant naval attaché in Spain. That was the country he now considered home and in whose navy he served. Recruited by Admiral Wilhelm Canaris at the outbreak of the Spanish Civil War, to act as an interpreter for the German military mission, his task had been to keep Berlin informed of the currents of feeling on the nationalist side, which were not always pro-German.

Following the end of the civil war, the Spanish diplomatic corps was now full of new people, the previous Republican diplomats, those on the losing side, not being perceived as sufficiently ideologically sound. Thus, victory for General Franco had allowed Canaris to slot his man into the London Embassy before the outbreak of the European war. Known in London as Rodolfo de Bázan, his Hidalgo birth name, only the intelligence officer and the ambassador knew his real identity.

To everyone else he was Spain's cultural attaché, a post which opened up a stream of invitations to society events. Questioned on the origins of his blond good looks, he would claim descent from the Visigoths who had conquered Roman Iberia many centuries past. With a diplomatic passport and the immunity it conferred, he had for several months, been relatively free to travel around Britain, albeit he was obliged to share his destination and journey details with the Foreign Office.

Country houses had been opened to him, while his skill with the rod had led to an invitation to fish for salmon on a private stretch of the River Tweed in the borders of Scotland. Grouse shooting also brought him into contact with people of influence, including those who held political views considered dangerous by their government. Many of these notables were prepared to air them to a man taken for what he claimed to be.

He was viewed as a well-born Spaniard from a noble family, who shared the values of the upper strata of European society: extremely anti-Bolshevik and inclined to see developments in Italy and Germany as a political template not to be despised. Graebner had thus been able to supply Canaris with a great deal of the social gossip which buzzed throughout the upper reaches of the British establishment.

The link to the admiral was through private letters which travelled in the diplomatic bag. This went back to Spain once a week, now, since the fall of France, routed by air through Lisbon. Supposedly inviolable, it had been rendered less secure since Graebner had become involved with the activities of a US Embassy cypher clerk called Tyler Kent. This fellow had traded what he thought was valuable intelligence, copies of sensitive cables between Churchill and Roosevelt, communications eventually and embarrassingly made public in the German newspapers.

With a suspicion of Spanish involvement in getting them to the enemy, MI5 would be intercepting personal correspondence. Not that the decoders would succeed in reading his missives, they being based on a book used only by three people; himself, Canaris, and the postman the admiral had working for him in Madrid. Without the source text, it was impossible to decipher his correspondence.

But the Tyler Kent affair had seriously strained his relationship with the Spanish ambassador. The arrangement was he should act as no more than a listening post, not an active agent; a listener, not a provocateur. This was not what he had set out to achieve when he followed his stepfather into the Kriegsmarine. Added to that, what seemed glamorous in peacetime, when Canaris first placed him in London had, despite compensations, morphed into dull routine following the outbreak of war and the restrictions on travel this imposed.

As ambitious as any of his comrades, he longed to be the originator of some stirring achievement, or to participate in a great naval victory, one that would elevate his name in his adoptive country. Such a thing was never going to happen in his present posting. He would, as usual, go to the embassy this morning, to see if anything had come in with the diplomatic bag, instructions being strict that letters with the de Bázan name should come directly to him. Yet the feeling of deep frustration, already acute, was growing day by day. It was time for a change.

On his way to bed, with the sun now risen, he began to mentally compose a letter to Wilhelm Canaris. It would say he had done enough in his present situation. It was time to allow him to return to the naval duties for which he had been trained.

9

Wednesday, July 24, 5:59 a.m.

Detective Chief Inspector George Naylor peered down the narrow hallway. 'Who found the body?'

'Milkman, sir. Saw the smashed lock and looked inside. Knew he was dead, right off.'

'Regular delivery?'

'Pint every two days.'

That was relevant. Had it had been like that yesterday, the smashed-in door would have been spotted. Whatever had happened, it had occurred in the hours of darkness.

'Touch anything?'

'He says only the door and with his elbow.'

'What about you, Constable?'

'Checked for signs of life, though there weren't much doubt, then went to phone in. Milkman stood guard while I was away.'

'Where's he now?'

'Finishing his round, sir, says he'll come back when he's done.' Seeing the look, the constable added. 'He's local like me, sir, and I know him well. Besides, I didn't see he could run far with a carthorse, never mind a couple of hundred milk bottles rattling on the back.'

The man looked to be an experienced copper, greying hair, perhaps retired but brought back to fill in for those younger fellows who'd be given permission to join the armed forces. You had to trust his judgement and suffer the mild sarcasm which coloured any exchange between uniformed tit-heads and the detective branch.

'Seen bodies before?'

'Too many, sir.' He gestured over his shoulder. 'In the trenches and a lot worse than chummy in there.'

Naylor went into the house, his nose registering the pungent smell of fresh polish, stepping over a scattering of wood splinters and walking warily along the hallway, ensuring, as he examined the linoleum floor, he wasn't messing up the crime scene. The body, in a blue, belted raincoat, lay face down. The back of the head was split, the blood where it had seeped out onto the matted grey hair, picking up the early morning sun streaming through the front door.

Smashed glass and a broken wooden frame came from a picture that looked to have been knocked off the wall, while close to it lay a trilby on edge. Squatting down, Naylor could see enough of the victim's face to establish it was heavily bruised. The left arm was under the body, the other stretched out rigid, the amputated hand inches from the ragged stump, jacket sleeve rucked up, shirt cuff tight against the forearm, leaving a larger pool of congealed blood.

Edging to the foot of the stairs, Naylor elbowed open the door to the front parlour, well furnished with a bay window. The tile-surround fireplace had been laid with scrunched up newspaper, some faggots and unlit coals, with more in a brass scuttle. On the mantle above stood a clock showing it had just gone six, as well as a trio of framed photographs, one of a group of young men in uniform standing before a Sopwith Camel biplane. The others looked to be parents and possibly a girlfriend or a sister.

The room was dominated by a three-piece suite in pale cream cloth and a marble coffee table with two large ashtrays. Behind stood a limewood veneer sideboard, bearing various glass objects and a white telephone. There was a snazzy gramophone-cum-radio in an all-in-one unit, which must have cost a mint, as well as a padded cocktail cabinet in the alcove, with opened bottles and an array of sparkling glass on the shelves behind.

A second door led to a dining room which was very different. There the walls were dotted with hunting prints, with a dresser and highly polished table, both mahogany, the latter with six tucked-in chairs. Both dresser and table bore several brightly polished silver objects; an ice bucket, salt and pepper cruets, two heavy candelabra and a statuette of a naked boy. The contrast between the two rooms he noted: one very modern, the other traditional, but both tidy.

A familiar voice echoed down the hallway. 'Guv?'

'In here, Ben.'

'Shall I come through?'

'Might as well, but watch where you put your size tens.'

'Christ!' Detective Sergeant Ben Foulkes had obviously come far enough to see the severed hand. 'Do we know who he is?'

'There's no name on the door and I don't want to touch the body till the forensic wallahs show up. There should be something in the house.'

Ben moved to fill the doorway. 'Nothing from the neighbours. No reply next door and, on the Westminster side, there's an old fella deaf as a post. Drew a blank at most of the rest. Those who did answer heard nothing unusual.'

'There's a kitchen down the hall and a back yard most likely. Do that while I have a shufftie upstairs.'

The place was a typical two-up, two-down terraced house, with a box room converted into a bathroom on the upper floor. Each room had a double bed, both made, windows screened with net curtains framed by heavy velvet drapes. In what Naylor took to be the main bedroom, a walnut-veneer dressing table, with a triple mirror, backed on to a sash window overlooking a row of back gardens and yards, all walled and several with Anderson shelters.

The dresser had on it a set of silver-backed brushes, a spray bottle of eau de cologne, and a couple of dishes containing odds and ends, as well as an open and empty carved wooden box. Interestingly, as he rubbed a knuckle over a bit of the surface he reckoned safe, there was no dust, but again the smell of polish was prevalent. He couldn't resist glancing into the large central mirror at his own face, which seemed to have more lines on it every time he looked, caused by too little sleep and too much work. The war had left the Metropolitan Police severely short-handed at a time when the blackout favoured a whole host of folk with criminal intent.

The wardrobe was mainly oak but was also inlaid with a variety of wood veneers. Art Deco in design, it was one of those pieces made for the modern gentlemen who, lacking a valet, required advice on how to arrange their belongings. Naylor read the ivory-etched list inside the door, which counselled the owner on what to pack for various occasions: shooting weekends, country house parties and foreign travel.

What brought him back to his task was the blue uniform with four rings on the sleeve. This, added to the peaked cap on the shelf above with its gold wings surmounted by a lion and a crown, told him it belonged to an RAF Group Captain and two things connected. The uniform of a probably high-ranking stiff lying in the hall in civilian clothes and the severed hand.

The temptation to immediately phone the Air Ministry was strong, but it would be better to have a name. He found one in the other bedroom, in a writing desk crammed with papers, letters and bills. The drop flap was down, showing a mass of things, including an empty cash box and a folder of bank statements.

'Ben!' he shouted, 'you there?'

'Sir?'

'There's a phone in the parlour. Use your hankie and a pencil. Get on to the Air Ministry. Ask them if they know of an officer called Group Captain Peter H. de Vries and, if they do, find out if he was in the habit of bringing work home.'

Wednesday, July 24, 6:22 a.m.

Eleanor Strachan had never liked the idea of another phone in the bedroom. Adam also knew full well, in what had become a vastly expanded organisation, and Eleanor regularly reminded him, she didn't like her husband's job much either. It meant late nights and indeterminate hours, which played havoc with their once active social life. Before he got the phone off the hook, he heard her curse the 'Bloody thing!' Spinning furiously, she pulled the sheets and blankets back over her head.

'Duty officer here, sir,' the voice said. 'Bit of a flap on. It was felt you were needed. There will be a car outside shortly.'

Adam was on the pavement by the time it arrived, under the clear blue sky of a late July morning. Muttering a greeting, followed by a yawn, he climbed into the back where lay, in a pile, the final editions of the morning papers. He rifled through them, occasionally distracted by a car being passed, not that there was anything cheerful to read. Churchill was out of office which meant he would now have new political masters.

The *Daily Mirror* and *Manchester Guardian* were far from thrilled, but the *Times* called for sound judgement and a pragmatic realisation of the dire situation the country faced. The *Telegraph* went big about getting home the huge number of soldiers taken prisoner, while the *Mail* carried an article on the folly of Britain getting involved in adventures on the continent, full stop.

Such a view was hardly surprising. The *Daily Mail* had been the lead pre-war appeaser, both the paper and Lord Rothermere, its proprietor, backing Neville Chamberlain as well as praising Oswald Mosley and his Blackshirts. The *Daily Express* wondered what the Empire would think if the war was not pursued until Germany was defeated, which seemed rather beside the point and a damned long way off. Naturally all were speculating on the formation of a new government, given Churchill's successor might well seek an accommodation with Hitler.

All made much of the note from Berlin offering an armistice, but there was one surprising addition which seemed to be confined to the *Daily Mail*. They saw Hitler as being magnanimous, citing his proposal the talks should take place on British soil. Adam wondered if the dictator was just being sly. He'd humiliated Neville Chamberlain at the Munich Conference; asking any successor to travel to Germany again would be rubbing noses in the same ordure.

Adam entered his chief's office in a far from cheerful mood, his superior's early presence a sure sign the "flap" was important. This was rapidly confirmed when he heard what had occurred at the home of Group Captain Peter Henry de Vries.

'He had a series of large scale maps in his possession, Strachan, the entire National Defence Plan. They show the layout of troop and artillery dispositions, minefields and wire, underwater obstacles, every pillbox and strongpoint overlooking the beaches of Southern Britain from the Wash to Falmouth, as well as the location of those still under construction.'

Brigadier Oswald, "Jasper" Harker, paused and chewed on the stem of his empty pipe to let the import sink in, fixing Adam with a cold stare, as if he was somehow responsible.

'Inland the maps have the locations of fuel and ammo dumps, tank traps, anti-aircraft emplacements, not to mention the prepared defensive positions supposed to blunt an enemy attack.'

'What the hell was the dozy sod doing taking them out of the Air Ministry?' Adam demanded. 'Come to think of it, what were the maps doing out of the War Office?'

'The flyboys needed to know where to go after the enemy. De Vries was given the task of designating which squadrons were to cover which sectors and what target areas they had to avoid. No point in their strafing or bombing our own minefields and setting them off, what? He was under some pressure too it seems, getting the maps ready for a conference at Fighter Command HQ later this morning.'

'He should have asked for help.'

'Very likely, but that's by the by. Should Jerry breech the shore defences, once their route of advance has been established, the RAF would have to know where to concentrate their attacks, as well as any positions our troops would be told to hold. Don't want them shooting up our own lads now, do we?'

'Too late to make changes, I suppose?'

'Do be sensible,' Harker snapped. 'It's taken over two years of digging and building to get to where we are now.'

Adam still found it strange to find Harker occupying this office. Ever since the creation of MI5 during the Great War, it had been home to Sir Vernon Kell. Churchill had kicked him out following the exposure of a US Embassy cipher clerk, who had been caught passing secret documents to the Germans. Kell had refused to expand the investigation to include people he'd known for years and whom he considered naïve, not traitorous.

Tyler Kent was connected to the Fascist Right Club, and MI5 had suspected for some time he was engaged in clandestine activities, without knowing what it all added up to until the enemy made it public, which actually exposed their source. While the cables contained no vital secrets, the traffic between London and Washington, to do with arms shipments and equipment orders, was highly sensitive.

'Do we consider de Vries might have been a traitor?'

'No real reason to,' Harker grumbled. 'Family's been here for generations and he has a blameless service record.'

'The maps might still be in the house.'

'Doubtful, but I've roused out a couple of our newly-recruited Cambridge Johnnies to go down and look. Special Branch have been informed and I'll ask for a D Notice to be sent out to keep the news editors away from any details.'

'Who discovered the body?'

'No idea, but the police were called. It was they who phoned the Air Ministry to ask if de Vries might have had a briefcase with him. When they checked his safe and found only one of the two keys—.'

'I take it they're wetting themselves?'

Harker winced. 'Undoubtedly true Strachan, but people soiling their underwear won't get us very far.'

'It could be just a burglary.'

'We can't rule it out, but neither can we base how we react on such an assumption. It could be a clever ploy to get us chasing the wrong fox. We have to find the de Vries briefcase or at least the contents and damn quick! There's no time for pussyfooting around. Anyone who even smells suspect will have to be pulled in.'

'Pick up everyone on the Grey List?'

'Precisely! And we'll have to step up the search for anyone we missed from the original round-up.'

'Some of those we have in custody might have a clue.'

'They might but, given the numbers, how long will it take to question them?'

'I was thinking of Mosley?'

Adam posited this suggestion gingerly, it being a sensitive area to Harker. He'd known the leader of the British Union of Fascists, now incarcerated in Holloway Prison, as a social acquaintance for many years. An ex-MP who'd held a junior government office, Oswald Mosley had been part of a social group that tended to move in a constricted circle of private clubs and residences, often country houses. Adam's own mother-in-law, being part of the same lot, was an added complication for him.

Harker's reply was terse, proof that the enquiry had touched a tender spot. 'Whatever you think of the man, I can assure you he's as patriotic as you or I. He'd never do anything to harm his country. If Mosley knew anything about espionage being carried on, so would we.'

'I'm sure you're right, sir.'

The reply obviously lacked sufficient enthusiasm. The look he got was even more severe.

'Let's do the necessary sweep and see where it gets us, but I don't want you bogged down, given it's work for our newer recruits. Word has come from on high that the mood has shifted substantially. It looks as if we might be coming round to talking with the Hun.'

'Which would be a mistake in my view, sir.'

'You may be right,' Harker replied, without conviction, leaving Adam to wonder if he approved of the idea. 'Ours is not to reason why, but to do as we're ordered by the government of the day. Those NDP maps would be just as useful to the Germans talking peace as making war, so their recovery is paramount.'

Harker's adopted a grave expression to emphasise the point, but it was wasted. Adam had required no prompting to reach the same conclusion.

'As to the Grey List,' Harker added, 'I would advise any notions of gentility would be misplaced. It's possible that lot had a hand in what happened to de Vries. If people have to be coerced into revealing what they know about those missing maps, so be it.'

Wednesday, July 24, 7:15 a.m.

Bettina Wyvern had always been a meaty lady, this driven home when Billy tried to move her dead weight. He'd finally managed it by rolling her onto a carpet, then dragging it into her bedroom over the polished linoleum. The death had been messy; the blunt point of the bread knife couldn't penetrate her corsets so, to stop her screaming, he'd had to cut her throat. The serrated edge had sent a fountain of blood in all directions, drenching him and everything he had on. It was time to have a very necessary bath.

Soaking in the pink-tinged water, wireless playing band music through the open door, Billy wondered how he was going to deal with the maps. Surely, they had to be genuine; why handcuff the case to a wrist and fight so hard to keep them otherwise? To the people he admired most in the world, they could be priceless.

As he stroked his unfamiliar moustache, Billy mind wandered, to conjure up the dream he had lived with since National Socialism had become his religion, with Adolf Hitler as its high priest. A one-time member of the British Union of Fascists, he had ended up a sneering critic of Oswald Mosley and his Blackshirts. They failed to see, if you wanted to fight Bolshevism and the machinations of international Jewry, you couldn't muck about. You had to go the whole hog, not prattle on about peace.

How many times had he stood on a soapbox at Speakers Corner, praising the exclusive Right Club, telling the world the truth about how Zion was plotting to take over the world, ever willing to get down and use his fists against those who disagreed with him. It bothered him not this risked arrest, a night in the cells and a fine he could rarely afford.

Not that he'd been much loved in the organisation he was raucously extolling; his working class background and a chippy attitude, in an outfit with too many snobs, had often seen him treated with disdain. Yet he had one asset the toffs lacked, the ability to do the day-to-day work, without which no disruptive group could prosper. It was Billy who had got the leaflets printed and out to the clubs and sympathetic newsagents.

His social superiors had been happy to recruit in their West End boltholes, collecting cheques with noughts on the end. He was the man who did the pubs and snooker clubs, who travelled the country around London talking to sympathisers in other places, extracting donations from folk who could only pay in shillings and pence and in cash.

Nearly discovered in the Right Club office when an MI5 dawn raid was organised—unknown to the top members, he was sleeping there— he'd only got out in time through a call from a sympathetic mechanic who'd overheard where the cars were off to. Billy had made sure he grabbed his personal receipt book, which had the names and addresses of all those low-value contributors. Lost, it would have seen dozens more people rounded up.

For all the condescension he had received, he'd found in the Right Club a proper spiritual home, so much nearer to his beliefs than the useless ranting of Mosely's Blackshirts. Them he cursed out loud, the words rebounding off painted bathroom walls, now running with condensation.

'British Union of Fascists, my arse. A bunch o' bloody Jessies.'

Too extreme for the BUF and sure he could lead it better, an opinion not kept hidden, Billy Houston had eventually been kicked out and, in his more fanciful moments, he plotted his revenge. Once Britain had the National Socialist government it needed, he would become a proper somebody, in payment for his tenacity. Boy, would he make those tossers jump!

Right now, he had more pressing problems. He might get away with the murder of de Vries, but he would struggle to avoid being had up for Bettina, who'd taken him in and hidden him to avoid his being interned. She'd bought the hair dye that had toned down his carrot-coloured mop, allowing him to go out occasionally after dark for some fresh air. Even at night though, he had to be careful.

Had she told anybody about her secret lodger, because she'd been a gossipy biddy? Whoever Bettina was supposed to be cleaning for today might be annoyed at her failure to show up, but there was a war on. They would certainly wonder why she failed to turn up in the Russian Tea Rooms in South Kensington. Given she always went there after work, to curse Bolshevism, if she missed two days in a row, someone might call round to see if she was sick. Best not to stay.

Bath over, dried and rummaging in the wardrobe, he helped himself to some of her late husband's clothes, he and Billy being much of a size, choosing his Sunday suit and flat cap, both smelling of mothballs. From a dresser he also got out the man's best shirts, collars and a tie, cramming them into his own battered old suitcase. They went in along with his raincoat, the blood-stained handcuffs, still attached to the briefcase, all the maps bar the one of the Kent Coast and his subscription book. Cleaning the dried blood off his shoes, he polished them to a gleam, like the one-time soldier he was.

A cheap hotel would be best and Billy now had the means to pay. He'd found just short of sixty pounds in the cash box, while the stolen chequebook would fetch a few quid. The box in the main bedroom had yielded gold cufflinks and mother-of-pearl shirt studs, which he could also trade. For change he raided Bettina's purse.

But those maps? They had to be put where they could do some good and for Billy there was no barrier of patriotism to impede the notion. If a German takeover of Britain was needed to achieve the right kind of government for the country, so be it. Unlike the silly sods now interned on the Isle of Man, he could see clearly what needed to be done.

But how could he get the information to the right people, with the English Channel sealed off? Now the Italian embassy was closed, the Spanish were a possibility, but he would need to show caution, given what had happened with the arrest of that stupid bugger, Tyler Kent. The news of his detention had ripped apart the Right Club, because the Yank had in his possession the book listing the main membership, which had led to a spate of arrests and the raid which sent Billy into hiding.

Frustration fought with caution. Having been active in the right-wing movement for years Billy had many times given way to near despair at the lack of progress towards that golden future for which he was so desperate. Now he had a chance to make an important contribution, to achieve something which would make everyone with whom he had ever shared his resentments green with envy. Added to that, the rewards could be fantastic.

'There's a risk, Billy,' he said out loud, 'but, by Christ, it's got tae be worth it.'

Stood in front of the long mirror on the inside of the wardrobe door, to check his appearance, Billy closed his eyes, for once allowing himself to imagine a vision in which he rarely indulged. Instead of the knot of listeners and hecklers he'd attracted at Speakers' Corner, he imagined himself addressing huge rallies at Hampden Park or Wembley Stadium, a sea of admirers who'd roar with approval at every point he made.

If an ex-First World War corporal, a seeming nobody, could rise from obscurity to become the absolute ruler of a nation like Germany, was it impossible for that to be repeated in Britain? Still visualizing those delirious crowds, Billy lifted his right hand in a full fascist salute.

CHAPTER SEVEN

Wednesday, July 24, 7:42 a.m.

From being the only car in the street, DCI Naylor's Riley had been joined by the medic's Austin Seven, the photographer's motorbike as well as the Bedford van from the Scenes of Crime section. The police doctor was examining the body, testing for the level of rigor mortis to try and establish a rough time of death. As soon as he'd finished, the fingerprint and forensic teams would go in to start dusting for clues. The milkman had been and gone, his horse leaving a large steaming pile of manure which, to George Naylor, was worth just about the same as what he could give in evidence.

The phone call to the Air Ministry set off alarm bells, which had rung all the way to domestic intelligence. They had rushed people to the scene, in this case two keen young chaps who looked, all floppy hair and pink skin, as though they should still be at school. They also spoke in accents that made the detective think of striped blazers and chinless wonders in punts. So, given they declined to ask his rank and treated him like a lowly beat copper, he applied all the stubbornness he possessed to keep what he called the hobgoblins out of the house.

'Look, friend,' said one of the youths, flashing an ID card under Naylor's nose, his tone full of mockery. 'This is not a job for plod, this is about the security of the nation.'

Naylor examined the card, registering the name Sefton Avery. 'It's a crime scene and if you think I'm going to let you trample all over it, you've got another thing coming.'

'You looking for a posting to the Shetlands, chum?'

'Got a dictionary, Sefton?'

'What the bally hell has that got to do with anything?'

'The proper use of the English language, cock! Look up "friend" and "chum" for a start. The pathologist is in there now and when he's finished and I'm finished and when everyone else has finished, you can go in the house, but not before!'

Avery called over his shoulder to his companion. 'Jocelyn, go to the car and get on the radio to the Commissioner of the Metropolitan Police. Tell him one of his officers is obstructing us in the pursuit of our duties.'

DCI Naylor raised his eyebrows in wonder. 'Blimey! I didn't know they had phones on the golf course. Must be hell trying to chip over the obstacles on the fairways to stop Jerry landing. You probably know, Sefton, how many penalty strokes would you get if you hit a German paratrooper?'

The doctor, cigarette in hand, came out behind Naylor, his arrival killing the puce-faced youth's chance of a reply.

'We'll have to get him on the slab, George, but I'd say he's been dead about eight hours. We're looking at about eleven last night. Cause of death, a massive blow to the back of the head. Judging by his knuckles, there's evidence of a proper punch-up, but it must have been a blunt instrument that finished him off.'

'Was he dead when his wrist was severed?'

'Heart must have still been pumping, but he'd have been on the way out.'

'So, the assault could have taken place earlier?'

'Not much earlier, but we can be more precise when we do the post-mortem. When do you want the body moved?'

'Not yet.'

A beeping horn saw the crowd at one end of the street part, to allow in a black Wolsey. This disgorged two large men in slouch hats and crumpled double-breasted suits, one with a belly extending way beyond his belt and straining shirt buttons.

'Watcher, George,' the first man greeted Naylor. 'Just heard on our radio you've been upsetting our security bods?'

'Can't help myself, Eddie.' He turned to the other Special Branch officer. 'How's the slimming going, Alf? You still cutting down as part of the war effort?'

'You should work with him, George, all he thinks about is food.' Eddie Banks ordered Alf back to the car, then turned to a furious Sefton Avery. 'DCI Banks, Special Branch, Guv, here to help.'

'That'll be a first,' Naylor grunted.

'Now, now, George.'

'Why should I worry if you get more money for less work?'

'What's the SP on this?' Eddie asked.

'Excuse me,' Avery snarled, 'while you are exchanging pleasantries, it might be that the whole security of the country has been compromised.'

'Can't help if we don't know what's goin' on, can we?'

'You'd best have a look, Eddie.'

'Why him?' demanded a very miffed Sefton Avery.

'He's a copper,' Naylor snapped, 'that's why. Not much of one I'll grant you, but unlike you, he might just have a clue what he's about.'

'Lighten up, George. Poor sod's just doin' his job. I'll babysit him if you like.'

'I am not a baby!'

Naylor's nose twitched. 'Funny, I can smell talcum powder. Eddie, make sure he doesn't touch anything till the evidence lot are through. What are you like with dead bodies, son?'

'I'm glad to say I have no idea, granddad.'

'Then make sure you're not sick, because you'll have to mop it up.'

The sight of the body, as they edged past it, then the ragged, severed wrist with the separated hand, both trailing strands of blood-soaked skin, had its effect.

'Oh, my giddy aunt', Avery gasped before turning to Eddie Banks. 'I need to see if there are any papers in the house, as well as a key.'

'I take it he had something on that arm?'

'He would have had an attached briefcase, yes.'

'Important?'

'Too important for me to answer.' A jaundiced look from the Special Branch DCI told Avery he was gilding it. They were both ignorant of the contents but the young man added quickly. 'But I've a slim hope what it contained might have already been removed before . . . you know.'

'Let's have a look.' Eddie slipped into the drawing room, his eye drawn to the cocktail cabinet. Removing a glove from his pocket, he slipped it on his right hand, then pointed to the array of bottles. 'Fancy a quick snifter?'

'No, I do not!' was swift and clipped response.

A grin from Eddie Banks told Avery he was ribbing someone he knew lacked experience. It did nothing to elevate the youngster when he quietly asked.

'By the way, old chap, what is the SP?'

'Starting price, Guv, just like in a horse race.'

Chapter Eight

Wednesday, July 24, 7:49 a.m.

George Naylor was examining the door where the lock had been splintered off, exposing the bare wood, nearly white. 'Pretty obvious, Ben. You couldn't just walk past it with the door ajar.'

'Blackout, boss, pitch black and no light on in the hall.'

'There was a moon last night.'

'Wouldn't be too many folk about,' Ben reasoned.

'Doin' this would have made a noise.'

'Everyone indoors, wireless on—.'

'Excuse me, sir,' a voice interrupted. 'There's a lady at the end of the road. Says she lives next door.'

'Fetch her in,' Naylor ordered.

The policeman went back to the little knot of people, signalling she should be let through the rope. Naylor observed her as she approached, carrying a shopping bag, smart-looking, high heels and long hair, a good quality light raincoat, open over well-cut clothes, early thirties in age he reckoned. His eye automatically went to the left hand as he tipped his hat, looking for a wedding ring.

'Good morning, Mrs.—?'

'Relph. I live at Number Seventeen.'

'Alone?'

The response was slightly defensive. 'My husband's in the navy.'

'Did you know the gentleman who lived here?'

'He's dead then?'

'Did you?' Naylor repeated.

'Not really, nodding acquaintance.'

'Were you in last night?'

'I work at the Admiralty. It's my week on nights.'

'Doing?'

'I'm not at liberty to say.'

The detective nodded. 'Bit late to be coming home?'

'Have to do the shopping. If I wait till the afternoon there's nothing left. Not that there's much in the morning either—'

George Naylor interrupted; a moan about food rations would get him nowhere. 'So, what can you tell me about the man who lived here.'

'Brylcreem boy, wasn't he?'

'He was a Royal Air Force officer, yes. Anything else?'

'Not really. Kept himself to himself. Liked to play loud music from what I heard when I was home. Classical stuff.'

'Visitors?'

'I don't twitch my curtains every time I hear voices.'

'Nobody says you did.'

'He had a lot of visitors.' She yawned, covering her mouth with her hand. 'The walls of these houses are pretty thin.'

'Ladies?'

'Not that I saw and not that I was looking, but most of those coming and going seemed to be chaps. The only lady was the one who did the cleaning. Saw her a couple of times doing the front step.'

George Naylor looked down at the bright red, unmarked front step. Everyone had avoided putting a foot on it because of the wood splinters from the smashed lock.

'Can you describe her for me?'

'Big woman, blond or grey. She wore a turban.'

'You talk to her?'

'Said good morning.'

'How often did she come?'

'Twice a week, Tuesdays and Fridays.'

'Thank you, Mrs. Relph. You'd best get your head down if you're working tonight. We'll try not to make too much noise.' She was just passing him when he said. 'By the way, who in the street *does* twitch their curtains?'

The anger that evoked was reward in itself. Here was a good-looking woman, living on her own, with a husband serving at sea. She would be a matter of interest for the kind of Nosy Parker who existed in every street George Naylor had ever known.

'Number Twelve, the dirty old bugger.'

'We might want you to answer a few more questions, Mrs. Relph. I'm sure you won't mind?'

'Would it matter if I did?'

Naylor tipped his hat again.

'Ben, get the forensic boys to look for tins of Cardinal and beeswax. There should be some prints on those. Did you do the back yard before the phone call I asked you to make?'

'I was still in the kitchen.' Naylor raised a critical eyebrow, which got a hurried explanation from his sergeant. 'Victim has a refrigerator, chock-a-block with rationed grub. Classy, don't you think?'

'Do the back yard now. I'll try Number Twelve. I take it you rapped on that one earlier.'

'I did. If his curtain twitched, I didn't see it.'

Wednesday, July 24, 8:18 a.m.

The opened door of Number Twelve let out an odorous blast common to elderly men who live alone. Unused gas, a whiff of stale food, a trace of an unclean lavatory. His collarless shirt was grubby, the woollen pullover had holes in it and his sparse hair was slicked over a pink head, with a parting just above one ear. He'd not shaved for a couple of days.

Naylor held up his warrant card. 'Police, Mr. . . . ?'

'Flitcroft,' the man mouthed, his lower mandible near to touching his nose; no false teeth in, if indeed he had any.

'My sergeant knocked on your door earlier, sir. Why didn't you respond?'

'Was in bed, wan' I?'

'We're making enquiries about the owner of Number Fifteen.'

'Ain't seen him since the outbreak.' He dragged a sleeve across his nose. 'Gone to Torquay, the lily-livered sod, hiding away while the rest of us face the Hun. Should be strung up, the lot of them—'

'So the gentleman who lives there is not the owner?'

'The fly-boy? Naw, he just rents it.'

The ritual had to be gone through. Had he seen or heard anything suspicious yesterday or in the days leading up to today? Every response had to be dragged out, until George Naylor finished with the obligatory, just before he turned away.

'Thanks, and we may require to ask you a few more questions.'

'Suppose you know he was a pansy?'

'Sorry?'

'The RAF fella. He was a shirt-lifter an' so was that sod, Sheridan, the one who rented it to him. Got in his motor and legged it down the bleeding Great West Road as soon as war was declared. They stick together that mob. Like I said, should be shot—'

'Thank you, Mr. Flitcroft,' Naylor snapped, before making his way back across the street to find his sergeant alone. 'Where are our cheeky chums, Ben?'

'Flown with Special Branch. Fat Alf got a message to say it was all hands. Asked if you would say nothing to the press at this stage and send them your findings. DCI Banks also wants us to search the streets around for a briefcase.'

'Lazy sod.'

'I found the cleaning stuff and gave it to Scenes of Crime.'

'Anything else?'

'Lobby leading out to the back. Found a box with all the bits and bobs, screwdrivers, pliers, putty knife that sort of thing, as well as some gardening tools.'

'Anything that could have done the dirty on that arm?'

Ben shook his head, waving to a lad in brown overalls to come over, another one who looked like a schoolboy.

'One of the SOC lads has spotted something.'

'Bit odd this, sir, the splintered door.' The youngster leant down and pointed to the shards of white shattered wood littering the step. 'Anyone doing that, if they'd smashed it in the dark, would have stepped in it and got those splinters on their shoe, stuck like. Some sign of them would have turned up inside the house.'

'But they didn't?' Naylor asked. The lad shook his head and went back to his tasks. 'Ben, we need to find the owner of the place, name of Sheridan. Apparently, he's fled to Torquay, so get a message down to the locals. He'll have to be registered. Our stiff rented it and it seems he and the landlord were both poufs. They are a bit social, so we might look for some of his mates in their dives and show them his photograph, so we'll need the one in the sitting room. This cleaning lady, did she come with the place or did de Vries hire her? I don't want to wait till Friday.'

'If she reads about it in the papers, Guv?'

31

'She might not turn up. Get on to the Midland Bank. The poor bugger's bank statements are there but his cheque book is nowhere to be found. There's an empty box open on his dressing table that might have had something of value.'

'You think it was a robbery gone wrong, Guv?'

'The door was kicked in *after* our man was killed.'

'So the robbery was a blind.'

'There had to be some kind of case handcuffed to his wrist and something in it to excite the sod who cut his hand off, our two young hobgoblins as well. Find that local bobby and ask him if there's a decent caff round here. We've not had breakfast yet.'

'Got a lot of prints,' said the head of the SOC team from just within the doorway. 'Different ones. Easy to eliminate the dead man, at least.'

Naylor found himself staring at the severed hand, which was being dangled right in front of his face. Suddenly breakfast didn't seem such a good idea.

For all the nosing about by MI5, to Scotland Yard this was a murder enquiry, and George Naylor had no desire to fish in the murky waters that spawned the weird ones. Alerted to a D notice muzzling the press, he was under no pressure, so the fingerprint and evidence bods could go about their searches in leisurely fashion. He had enjoyed a canteen fry-up and would now wait at the Yard for the doctor's written report.

Ben Foulkes had phoned the Devon police, then got through to Torquay once their Central Records Office confirmed that a Roger Sheridan, registered at the address of the murder, was living in the resort. The desk sergeant had picked up the phone and, once given the name, his response was immediate, if delivered in a painfully slow Devonian drawl.

'Our Mr. Sheridan, what's he been up to, then?'

'You know him?'

'Only too well, my old dear. We had to give him a caution for importuning in a public lavatory. A number of those sorts of gentleman have moved into Torquay. Place is bursting at the seams with London folk, every hotel and guesthouse packed to the rafters and raking it in. Can't get a room for love nor money, even if Jesus, Mary and Joseph turned up themselves. It's an ill wind, eh?'

'I need him questioned,' Ben interjected, not wishing to hear about the prosperity the West Country was enjoying from wealthy, panicky Londoners.

'Regarding?'

'A charwoman cleans his London house. We need to know if he employed her or the fellow who rented the place took her on.' Thinking on the slow way in which the desk sergeant spoke, Ben sought to gee him up a bit. 'This is an enquiry of a very serious nature, but it might not be an idea to let this Sheridan know.'

'Suspect, is he?'

'Right now, everybody is, mate, but I would appreciate a bit of hurry.'

'Get right on to it, me old dear.'

So slow was the desk sergeant's Devon burr, Ben thought it would be lucky if he got a response next week.

Wednesday, July 24, 9:26 a.m.

Rudi Graebner had arrived at the embassy, to be told the bag just arrived from Madrid contained a letter for him. The envelope he recognised, likewise the long gossipy missive inside. Apparently from a female second cousin, it was in truth a coded communication from Admiral Canaris, who was also fluent in Spanish. Had it already been opened? How might it have been done without leaving any trace?

Not trusting, even of those who worked in the embassy, and assuming his office would be searched, he'd filled a set of shelves with books in four languages. All were second-hand and well-thumbed, so no one could tell which one he used as a code source. He also destroyed the messages once read, rarely taking them out of this room and never out of the embassy. Being Spanish sovereign territory, entry to the building was denied to British intelligence.

The letter took time to decode, not that it contained any surprises after Dunkirk, the collapse of the French military and their subsequent armistice. Canaris wanted to know what the British would do in the event of continued war or a cessation of hostilities. The last part of the message was a reminder of Rudi's position within the embassy and the repeated stricture he must respect Spanish concerns.

Such information was easier to demand than provide. Gossip was one thing, fact another, made harder to uncover because the British had finally done, at the beginning of May, what any German government would have carried out on their first day in power. They had arrested anyone of importance voicing extreme radical opinions and put them beyond contact. The best of those, in amongst a host of rickety organisations, had been the Right Club. It contained, within its membership, people of real influence. They were now either threatened into silence, in jail, or in camps on the Isle of Man.

'Señor de Bázan, His Excellency is asking to see you.'

The arrival of the letter had obviously been reported. Rudi thought about immediate destruction, but to do so would fuel, not allay suspicion. Gathering up it and his deciphering, he made his way down to the ambassadorial office, where the Duke of Alba was waiting for him in the company of the only other person who knew his real identity.

'Good morning, Rodolfo.' Alba indicated Rodriguez, the fellow in charge of intelligence, who ostensibly held the lowly office of Passport Officer. 'Carlos informs me you have been in receipt of a communication. We would be interested to know its contents.'

'I have it with me. It asks only that I keep my ear to the ground, more important than ever now there is the possibility of negotiations.'

'Would I be allowed to see this communication,' asked Rodriguez, 'as well as what it says decoded?'

Hesitation was for effect. 'If you could agree to give them back to me as soon as they are read.'

Rodriguez nodded. He would need the source book to figure out the code, which Graebner would naturally deny him. He could search his bookshelves till doomsday and never be sure how to locate the right one. Taking the letter and the decoded message, Rodriguez studied them intently, watched in silence by Alba and Rudi. Finally, he handed them back, nodding to his superior that the necessary warnings about any overt action had been repeated.

The older man didn't ask for the contents to be explained. The less he knew the better, which would allow him, should he be challenged, to claim ignorance.

'You know I must be cautious,' Alba insisted. 'Our position here is even more delicate now your armies have enjoyed such success.'

'Mine more so, Your Excellency,' Rudi reminded him. 'I'm not about to take risks with your office or my obligations. In fact, I'm longing to return to my naval duties.'

'If Germany gets peace, such skills will not be needed.'

35

'I think I know my Führer well enough to be sure there will be opportunities in the future. However, I need to be sure my line of communication will remain open and I can still send information to Berlin.'

Alba's ambivalence was obvious, given he harboured warm feelings towards the nation to which he had been accredited. Yet he was still bound by instructions from Madrid and, provided the man before him kept to his brief, he would allow him to operate. The man had transgressed once and it had taken considerable pressure from Canaris to keep him in place, so it was incumbent on the Duke to remind him of the political fallout.

'As long as what you do does not compromise my position. The previous occasion in which it was under scrutiny proved exceedingly uncomfortable.'

Called to meet with the Foreign Secretary, Alba had been submitted to a lecture on his responsibilities. He had also been obliged to deny his embassy had been involved with a fellow of whom he never previously heard, one named Tyler Kent—he sought to shift the blame to the still neutral Italians—as well as any knowledge of who could have been the contact. Both statements, he had to assume, had been treated with suspicion.

'My instructions, as you know, oblige me to be very careful, sir.'

Alba nodded politely in dismissal and Rudi went back to his office. The message, plus his decoding, were soon dust in his ashtray.

CHAPTER ELEVEN

Wednesday, July 24, 11:07 a.m.

Special Branch spent the morning driving to addresses all over London, calling at the homes and workplaces of those on the Grey List, people who had axes to grind but were not deemed dangerous enough to be interned. Billy Houston got out of Bettina's flat before they knocked on her door, not that he would have answered. But since no one responded, a man was left to keep watch and pick up Bettina Wyvern when she came home.

Billy's first stop was Victoria Station, to drop off the battered suitcase in Left Luggage. Using Bettina's ration book and the loose change he'd taken from her purse, he had a late breakfast. To that was added a leisurely read of the *Daily Mail*, allowing him to relish the news about Churchill. Then, with the one map he kept separate stuck tight inside his shirt, he set off on foot for his first destination.

A man who'd done a lot of jobs in his life, few of them respectable, Billy was part of the flotsam that exists in every big city. Folk living on the edge, doing bits here and there but never settling into anything: labouring, occasional backstage work in the West End theatres, a bit of portering and dishwashing had kept body and soul intact.

If anyone had told him he was an itinerant worker he'd have laughed in their face, or possibly punched them for their cheek. Billy Houston held himself to be different from those he mixed with, a man with a purpose in life, one too important to allow him to be tied to any kind of permanent employment. But he knew a lot of places where low-lifes gathered outside the strict licensing laws: illegal gambling clubs and drinking dens, where no one asked your name and purpose.

His first stop was the Barracuda Club in Little Newport Street, a damp basement with a distinctive smell creeping up the staircase, a combination of poor drainage, inadequate urinals, unwashed bodies, cheap perfume and stale drink. The club was a haunt for out-of-work actors, stage hands, buskers and bums, where telling which from which was not always easy and had nothing to do with how they dressed.

Quiet now, the club's clientele was predominately male, but there were woman who used the place. As the day wore on, the puffy-faced female drinkers—ageing actresses and models, some of whom still had a trace of the beauty which had previously kept them employed—would be joined by the working girls of nearby Soho. They needed a rest by just staying on their feet for an hour.

Maltese Mary ran the Barracuda. A small, capricious woman, she wore enough make-up to paint nearby Leicester Square twice over; pancake on the cheeks, rouge thick on her lips and eyes heavy with mascara. Mary had a fierce reputation, being a woman of strong likes and dislikes, not based on any rational process.

For reasons unfathomable, she liked Billy. He was one of that charmed circle who could get a drink from her when they had no money. Catching sight of him, she registered no surprise at his appearance: too many actors used the place for it to be something to comment on. It was not unknown for a customer to have jet black hair one day and near white the next.

'Billy, *darlink*,' she cried, in her best Marlene Dietrich impersonation. 'Come, give Mary a *kees*.' Billy obliged, using his sleeve to wipe the make-up off his lips. 'That moustache you got tickles. You want drink?'

'I'll have a pint and a double dram, Mary.'

The pinhole eyes narrowed and the long false eyelashes fluttered. Mary wasn't that generous. Finger and thumb rubbed together.

'You holding, Billy?'

A ten-shilling note, taken from Bettina's purse, rapidly disappeared into Mary's waiting hand. The debt he had run up was nowhere near that much, but it would be inflated by the price of her credit.

'Take it out of that, hen, and have one yersel.'

'Big cheese eh! Won the football pools, maybe?'

'Bigger than you think, Mary. Just you wait.'

'Ah you, Billy? Still want change the world?'

The drinks arrived and Billy grinned. He always paid Mary back if he owed her, overpaid even. This was the only place he could get a drink when he was right on his uppers.

'Water?' Mary asked, nodding to the whisky, passing over a scrap of change.

'No thanks, hen. There's enough in yer spirits already.'

She responded with a high-pitched cackle and a get-away-with-you wave. If other people had said the same—true, as it happened—it would have got them thrown out on to the street.

The man Billy had come to see was sitting in the usual corner of what he called his "office" the Scotsman having clocked him as soon as he entered. Wally Burrell was a sad-eyed, sallow-faced ducker and diver, but one who dressed well in a shirt and tie under a beige, velvet-collared covert coat. This he topped with a brown bowler, the weather having no effect on his attire.

He made his living from a variety of shady practices: a bookie's runner, a bit of fencing, sometimes helping folk who were dodging the law or in need of a forged ration book, many on the run from their call up. The man approaching now was more serious and Wally shifted around on his backside as he approached, signalling he was wary.

'I thought they would have had you up by now, Billy.'

'Call me slippery, Wally.'

'Mouthy, more like. Nice 'tache, though, and the dark hair. You up for a part in a film?'

Billy ran a finger along his hairy upper lip. 'I need a new ID card, Wally, an' a good one. Shit-proof. Ration book, too.'

'Cost ya.'

'Will ye trade for these?' The gold cuff links and mother-of-pearl shirt studs were pressed into Wally's hand. He separated them so he could weigh the gold. 'Reckon that would cover it wi' change. Ah've got a near full cheque book to trade as well.'

Lips pursed, air hissed inwards, Wally produced the universal sound of perceived difficulty. 'Times is 'ard, Billy. The Old Bill is clamping down, what with old Adolf near to paying us all a call.'

'Come on, Wally, don't bugger me about.'

'Think of the stuff on the market. Everybody's unloading since Dunkirk.'

'Some Yid will still buy those an' you know it. That cheque book's worth good money tae a kiter working Oxford Street.'

'Then why not go to one?'

The response was no longer friendly. 'You ken why.'

'Some of my best friends are Jews.'

'Then ye should choose yer friends more carefully, pal.' Billy's voice was biting as he slipped over the identity card, one he dare not show the authorities. 'How long?'

'Tomorrow.'

'Today, otherwise I might have tae sleep out.'

'Good weather for it.'

'Too risky!'

'Ups the ante, old son. Got a new moniker in mind?'

'Brian Harris? Same initials.'

'Address?'

Billy wondered if he should tell Wally to make one up, but that had its own dangers. He gave him the Glasgow address where he'd been born. Wally nodded, his lower lip well out, hand weighing again.

'Earl of Shaftsbury, Snug Bar, round nine.'

'I'll take the cuff links back, Wally. Ye can keep the studs on deposit.'

'It's dangerous out there. You might get picked up by the Old Bill.'

'Have a care, Wally?'

Burrell knew a threat when he heard one, just as he knew who would follow through and who would not. Billy was the kind to belt you first and wonder why afterwards. The cufflinks were passed back.

'See ye at nine.'

'Don't be late, Billy, or you'll miss last orders.'

Wednesday, July 24, 1:15 p.m.

George Naylor, back from lunch in the canteen, was looking at the path lab notes on a different murder case when the phone rang. He answered in the affirmative when the caller used his name.

'Adam Strachan, Ministry of Information.' Tempted to chuckle—MI5 being domestic intelligence was never openly mentioned—Naylor held his amusement in check. 'I want to know, Mr. Naylor, what you've discovered regarding the murder of Group Captain de Vries.'

'Have your Baker Street Irregulars not told you?'

'Sorry?'

'Sherlock Holmes's urchins?'

'I'm still not with you.'

'The pair of gormless young gits that turned up this morning flashing ID cards so new the ink wasn't dry.'

'A bit intense, were they?'

'Rude, more like.'

'You'll have to forgive them, Mr. Naylor. We've been subject to a very rapid expansion. It's brought in people with a great deal to learn. They're just new and rather keen to impress.'

'You, perhaps. Not me.'

'Well, I've apologised and I'm not prepared to do any more, so can we get on to the reason for my call?'

Naylor saw no virtue in continuing to be irascible, and besides, the caller was probably quite high up, so it would do no good to rile him. 'You have to take most of what I say as deduction. We don't have enough facts yet.'

'Fair enough, but did you find any keys that would unlock handcuffs?'

'His possessions are still being logged, Mr. Strachan.'

'So, what *do* we know?'

'We're sure the door lock was smashed after the group captain was killed and mutilated, though he was clearly also burgled. His bank statements indicated that he drew out large sums of cash at monthly intervals, some fifty pounds a time, and the bank confirmed he had done so this week.'

'That's rather a lot?'

'He could well afford it. He had quite a healthy balance.'

'Not just his service pay then?'

'I'd say no. We found the cupboard under the stairs full of wine and it looked like pricey stuff. The house had a refrigerator stocked with the kind of food de Vries could only have got on the black market. Our victim comes across as a man who took good care of himself and one who entertained regularly.'

'What about the money?'

'Gone. Apart from the possibility of missing cash, there were certain items absent from the house I would have expected to find there, like his cheque book. There was an open box in the main bedroom that might have contained valuables but it was empty.'

'But if the lock was smashed after the murder?'

'It means the culprit either had a door key or he was the cleverest burglar I've ever come across. We looked at the windows back and front, as well as the back door. There was no sign of a forced entry.'

George Naylor could hear the pencil scratch as Adam Strachan scribbled down what he was saying, until the detective added quietly, 'Did you know he may have been a homosexual?'

Adam found the point of his pencil had snapped as he said '*Christ.*'

'Needs to be confirmed, of course, but we have received information he rented it from the owner, a Mr. Roger Sheridan, who is of the same persuasion. It means de Vries may well have invited his killer into the house.'

There was no need to explain the ramifications and it might even clarify the need for lots of cash. Sex didn't always come free. Had de Vries picked up someone on the way home, or maybe arranged to meet a person he already knew? Whatever, it opened up a can of worms because, whatever anyone's private feelings on the subject, such sexual proclivities did make those who indulged extremely vulnerable.

Yet the man was engaged in work of the highest national importance, carrying documents so secret they should never have been taken out of the Air Ministry. Would he have allowed lust to supersede his duty? Adam had the man's service record in front of him. Commissioned into the Sherwood Foresters, he was with the British Expeditionary Force in 1914 and fought at Mons, le Cateau and in the First Battle of Ypres, where he was wounded.

De Vries had volunteered for the Royal Flying Corps in 1916 and had six kills to his credit flying Sopwith Camels. Post-war he served in Iraq and on the North West Frontier of India. Took over a squadron in the early 30's, then a wing, before moving on to a job with the Air Staff.

'I take it that doesn't help?' George Naylor said, after a significant period of silence.

'No.'

'I know what you're thinking, but that makes no sense. Gut feeling, but he didn't know his killer. If he was indulging himself, whoever was after that case wouldn't have assaulted him so soon after the door'd been closed. Judging by his knuckles he went down fighting. If he was going to do the business, he would have taken what he had off his wrist first.'

'So, your conclusion is?'

'It's too early for conclusions, Mr. Strachan, because I'm speculating. Best wait till all the evidence is analysed and start from there. We put in a request to the RAF police to give us details of his office and information from his colleagues. Naturally they weren't keen to let us in. Said there were other folk interested.'

'It was my people who went in to ask the questions.' Adam paused for several seconds then, before continuing. 'Look, I can't tell you what this is about, but it's important.'

'And you want my full cooperation, yes?'

The quick deduction slightly threw Adam. 'I do.'

'My experience, Mr. Strachan, is whenever anyone asks me for that, it's a one way street.'

'Believe me, this is too serious for games. I'm aware in any investigation facts are not always available and certainly not in the time they might be required.'

'So, there's a time factor?'

'I would say yes, but then now I'd be speculating. The contents of the group captain's briefcase are important. Very.'

'Saleable?'

'It's unlikely this was done for financial gain.'

Ben Foulkes came into his boss's office holding up a piece of paper. The Torquay policeman might have sounded slow, but he had acted with commendable speed. Mouthing the words 'cleaning lady', Ben put the paper on the desk.

'Mr. Strachan,' Naylor said, 'I have just received the name and address of the lady who cleaned for the group captain and before the man called Sheridan. She's a Mrs. Bettina Wyvern, who lives at—'

'I know where she lives,' Adam interrupted, reaching across his desk for the list he and Harker had been discussing that morning. It was hard to forget the last name on it. 'Can I suggest that we meet you there?'

'We're on our way.'

Wednesday, July 24, 1:45 p.m.

The message having been radioed ahead and the door broken down, Naylor arrived to find MI5 men, including the two adolescents he'd encountered earlier, ransacking the place as if there were no dead body in the bedroom. His anger fell on deaf ears; he was told the 'stiff' did not matter. When Adam Strachan turned up, the DCI's mood was not the most welcoming.

'What they're looking for is vital, as I've already explained to you,' Strachan insisted while trying to be emollient. 'National importance.'

Which got him a glare from Naylor. 'Where have I heard that before?' That biddy in there is a big lady, but do you think she killed your group captain in a violent punch-up?'

The pause from Adam was minimal. 'Everyone stop and stand still.'

'Thank you, Mr. Strachan.' Naylor growled. 'There's a very good chance whoever killed de Vries, also killed Mrs. Wyvern who, I assume, is the person lying in the bedroom with her throat cut.'

'For the house keys?'

'Possibly, Mr. Strachan, but you knew who she was, so I'm bound to ask how?'

'She was on a list of potential Nazi sympathisers, a Grey List, people more anti-Bolshevik and not considered much of a threat.'

'Who broke the door down?' Naylor demanded and a couple of hands went up. 'So, taking into account this is a basement flat with barred windows, whoever killed her did not, as far as we know, force an entry.'

'Will we ever know?' Ben Foulkes moaned, looking at a kitchen floor covered with the contents of the cupboards and drawers.

'And I'd speculate,' Naylor added, 'what you're looking for is unlikely to be here, but evidence of who did it might be.'

'Everybody outside,' Adam Strachan barked.

'Ben, do the basics, while I get Scenes of Crime here. Mr. Strachan, you may stay, but touch nothing.'

When Naylor returned from shepherding everyone out, Ben was waiting. 'Two beds, Guv. Judging by the dip in the mattress, the woman was in the one she's lying beside. A double. The other one's in the box room, a single and unmade.'

'Did you know her, Mr. Strachan?'

'I only learned of her existence this morning.'

'The place has a bathroom,' Ben added—he had no need to say how unusual that was in such a place. 'There's a gas water heater and it's been used recently, leaving a bloody great pinkish tide mark round the top of the bath and water round the plughole.'

'According to her file she was a widow,' Adam added. 'Her late husband was a plumber.'

'So Mr. Strachan, unless our man, and I am guessing it's a man, wore gloves—'

'There will be fingerprints.'

'And if he's a known villain, we'll find out who he is.'

'And if he's a German spy?'

Naylor raised an eyebrow. 'Then there's nothing we can do for you.'

'How long will it take to find out?'

'The fingerprints boys will only move if someone puts a Spitfire up their backside. This morning one of those kids of yours threatened to phone the commissioner. I'd suggest if this is as serious as you say, it might be an idea for someone to do that now.'

Adam was already making for the door. 'I'll attend to it personally.'

CHAPTER FOURTEEN

Wednesday, July 24, 2:00 p.m.

The foreign secretary, Lord Halifax, a strong candidate to replace Churchill, was studying the opinion columns of the daily press, hoping to read words that would help sway the doubters in Parliament. Never loved by Labour and Liberal MPs, Halifax was seen, even by many of his Conservative colleagues, as badly tainted, along with Neville Chamberlain, by the disastrous Munich Agreement. Even his present position was causing concern: was he the right person to take the lead in any talks with the Germans?

The door was opened by his permanent secretary, to usher in the Duke of Alba, at present, a Very Important Person indeed. The message from the Imperial General Staff was unequivocal: Spain must be kept neutral at all costs! Gibraltar was untenable as a base next to an active enemy combatant backed by Germany.

Without the island access to the Mediterranean would be impossible. The Royal Navy would have to withdraw from the area, Malta could not be supplied and neither could Egypt, which meant the Suez Canal was at risk. With the short route to India gone, there was an increased threat to the Eastern Empire from Japanese aggression.

Spain had been given an indication of British naval power two and a half weeks past, in an act initiated by Churchill. The French battle fleet, based at Mers-el-Kébir in North Africa to keep it from the Germans, had been given the choice of sailing to the West Indies or suffering destruction. Admiral Gensoul, the man in command, was convinced Britannia was bluffing; he was soon proved wrong as his ships were destroyed and over a thousand of his sailors killed.

47

Alba was aware he could extract a price for his country's neutrality, but there were limits to what Britain would concede. The intelligence briefing paper Halifax had read, prior to the meeting, told him a great deal about the nature of the present Spanish administration. Regardless of his aspirations to be a dictator like Hitler, Franco did not have untrammelled power.

El Caudillo, as Franco liked to be called, was pressured by many conflicting polities: monarchists, Falangists even more nationalist than he. But crucially, he was dependant on the support of those generals who had helped him during the Civil War, men unwilling to accord him the honours he claimed as the sole victor.

According to MI6, they resented the way Franco had elevated his brother-in-law, Ramón Sūner, to power in military and diplomatic affairs. Sūner wished to join in Hitler's war, so the offended generals took the opposite view, as much for pride as policy. A number were willing to accept Albion's gold to press their objections, giving MI6 a conduit by which they could affect outcomes in Spain.

It was essential to let Franco know, discreetly, he wasn't free to act as he wished. It was also necessary to make known to him the men he saw as his rivals were not the only people who might receive subventions from the British Government. It was an offer to bribe, which the foreign secretary had to deliver with some subtlety.

'Let me tell you, Your Excellency,' Halifax added, 'we see you as an honest broker between our two nations. If there are any misunderstandings, it's our intention to work hard, with you, to eliminate them.'

Halifax could easily imagine similar conversations taking place in Berlin, where diplomats less friendly to Britain would be laying out their stall. Spain would be acting the harlot, seeking to attract from her suitors as much as she could, while giving away as little as possible. The British government had little to counter it. Bribery apart, the most significant asset was Force H, a powerful part of the Mediterranean Fleet.

If Gibraltar were put at risk, battleships would bombard every major Spanish port into rubble, cutting off trade and crippling an already ruined economy. The German navy was too puny to interfere, while the Italians would not dare send out their capital ships against the Royal Navy for fear of destruction. As for air power, the job would be done and the warships out of range by the time enemy aircraft arrived.

Halifax sought to look concerned as he continued. 'So, it gives me little pleasure to point out that, should confusions occur, my country has the means to make known its displeasure in a region of great importance to us both.'

In diplomacy, if it was incumbent to recognise a threat, it was equally essential never to allow it to be acknowledged or to proceed to detail. Alba was as aware as anyone of the risks his country faced in joining the other fascist powers, especially now, in the situation of a possible impending armistice. He was being told Great Britain would not take any precipitate steps and it would be wise if Spain adopted the same attitude.

The duke replied with an urbanity which was second nature. 'I see it as my duty to point out certain facts to Madrid, milord. That any actions they undertake which are distasteful to your nation, cannot be without consequences, just as I see it as necessary to work to maintain peace between our two countries.'

'It would be most unfortunate, following on from your recent travails, if Spain were once more thrown into political turmoil. It gives me no pleasure to tell you this is, according to sources I cannot divulge, seen to be a distinct possibility.'

A hint Franco could be toppled? Even if Alba had no idea how it could be engineered, he was fairly sure the possibility would not have been aired if the man suggesting it was uncertain.

'A tragedy indeed.'

Halifax was well aware the duke would not enjoy conveying such a message to a man as suspicious as General Franco. The mere suggestion of individuals working to undermine him might produce an effect opposite to the one intended.

'Of course,' he added, 'if support is required and is favourable to our interests, we would look very closely on that, even to a degree of financial provisions in specific areas.'

It was a case of reading what lay below such words and Halifax was pleased that Freddie Alba got to it quickly, acknowledgement coming with no more than a nod. Money could be funnelled to Franco if it would keep Spain neutral.

'I need to know we have the basis of an understanding, Your Grace?'

'Which I will make it my duty to establish.'

The foreign secretary stood, quickly followed by Alba and the permanent secretary. Courtesies were exchanged and the Spaniard departed, with those who had hosted him hoping he was both deeply troubled and partially encouraged.

'Do you think he got the drift?' Halifax asked.

The permanent secretary grimaced. 'He got it, but will both suggestions be understood where it matters?'

'As long as it unnerves Franco it's worthwhile, even if the threat turns out to be bluff. As to the other, let us hope he is as greedy as we have been led to believe.'

The look both men exchanged spoke volumes. Regardless of what was said by MI6, the Foreign Office lacked any certainty that the intelligence advice they were receiving was sound. Neither were happy to be relying on bribery, especially with foreign generals, doubly so since they would have to be fed British gold through a very questionable intermediary.

Juan March was an ex-cigarette smuggler and purveyor of illicit weapons, albeit a fabulously successful and wealthy one. A strong supporter of Franco in 1936, March had provided the aeroplane that had got the general from exile in the Canary Isles to Morocco. There he took command of what he needed to begin the revolt against the republic, the fighting troops of the Spanish Foreign Legion.

To make matters even more opaque, in terms of trusting their own intelligence, the de Havilland Dragon, sent to collect Franco, had taken off from Croydon Airport on that significant flight, the central act that precipitated the beginning of the Spanish Civil War. At the controls had been two British aviators, a pilot and a navigator, both serving members of MI6!

Wednesday, July 24, 2:47 p.m.

The day had been a furiously busy one in all the departments of Whitehall. The various people who would have a say in the formation of a government met to agree, disagree and bargain. The one area to command an unequivocal majority centred on the wisdom of talking to the Germans, rather than blindly rejecting their overtures, especially with so many British servicemen now in captivity.

At the level below, the top civil servants had a great deal of work thrust upon them. Cables flew back and forth to Berlin as arrangements were first mooted, then passed upstairs to be agreed. Eventually details were firmed up as to where and how talks would take place to cement an armistice and, if that proceeded well, to move on to peace talks. The suggestion of British soil was accepted, seen as a concession from a German leader in the full flush of victory.

Holding the talks on native soil, serving a government bound to be frail, eased collective responsibility. Negotiators could quickly communicate with London, if need be, in person. That brought up the question of security, given there were legions of people who might take exception to what was being proposed. The chosen location must not appear demeaning; it had to have both substance as well as security.

After much deliberation, the Isle of Wight was proposed, while the one-time royal residence of Osborne House presented an appropriate venue. Being on the northern part of the island, it was inside the naval defences set up to protect Portsmouth and Southampton. The suggestion was accepted, as long as the location and its surroundings could subject to a thorough inspection by the German government. A party would be despatched immediately aboard a warship for that purpose. The suggestion from Whitehall they should come by air was refused.

'Seems rather stuffy to send ships these days,' was the Halifax opinion.

A patient permanent secretary was obliged to explain to his master what should have been obvious.

'If they came by air, milord, they would be obliged to us for communication with Berlin. On the other hand, a warship will have a coding machine, which will allow them to talk to their people without our knowing what they are saying.'

'Immediately, they say?'

'I have been informed, as soon as we say we agree, we can expect said vessels within forty-eight hours.'

'A touch of unseemly haste, do you not think?'

'It's the German manner of doing things, milord.'

CHAPTER SIXTEEN

Wednesday, July 24, 3:59 p.m.

Billy Houston spent hours trawling the pubs and drinking dens surrounding Covent Garden, his first objective to seek out old acquain-
tances, people who shared his politics and who might provide a place
to hide. Most pretended not to see him; others were willing to talk, but
remained wary, knowing he was on the run. Having drawn a blank, he
decided to move on.

His chosen route, along Carlton House Terrace, took him past what
had been the German embassy, now shuttered and closed. Gone from the
flagstaff was the proud swastika, in its place a limp Swiss flag, insignia of
the protecting power, plus a policeman outside to stop people torching
the place. Moving down to the Mall, he passed a sandbagged Buckingham Palace, the gilded Victoria Memorial statue completely hidden.

He was aiming for Belgravia, one of the wealthiest residential neigh-
bourhoods of London, an area of wide streets, garden squares and huge
cream-painted town houses, some now embassies. The building where
Billy Houston hoped to find a contact was doubly dangerous, given
the Spanish embassy was bound to be under constant observation. He
ambled past it, only to reverse his steps and make for an afternoon drinking den called the Eaton Club.

The second Marquess of Westminster, who'd built this luxurious
residential enclave, was not one to sacrifice valuable land to build any
public houses. Yet he knew servants needed somewhere to take their ease,
so he had created his own hostelry, placed in the stable mews which ran
at the back of one of the main streets. It was a venue that served alcohol
with prices pegged to a non-profit making low, very necessary given the

affluent inhabitants were not inclined to pay very well those who saw to their needs. It also had the advantage of being a private members' club, so open all afternoon.

Good reasons existed for creating a dedicated watering hole; servants were as likely to over-indulge as anyone. In pubs there was the risk of loose tongues, of gossip to disturb the tranquillity of their masters' lives. Members of the gutter press might eavesdrop on conversations: criminals could be listening. Better those who knew too many intimate details of their life and locks should be encouraged to use a place that was relatively exclusive. If those manning the entrance didn't know your face, or if you could not produce a membership card, then, in theory you would not be able to get in.

For all this seeming philanthropy, the estate wouldn't subsidise any losses, which led to a loosening of the terms of entry. As the town houses became the legations of foreign countries, the club had been opened up to those who toiled below stairs in those establishments. Billy got membership because he'd worked in several of the hotels fringing Belgravia. This was the third group who qualified: people who toiled odd hours on tight wages, lower order chefs, waiters and porters.

Showing his membership card to the doorman got him an odd look. Was it just his changed appearance or had the law been down here looking for him? He couldn't ask, he just had to rely on the solidarity that existed between those on the lower rungs of the social ladder. You never shopped anyone because, one day, it might come back to bite you.

Besides, the Eaton Club was no haunt for Communists or even Labourites. Those who looked after the rich were the biggest snobs going, quite often a lot less liberal than the folk they served. The place was quiet these days: for every family who'd stayed in London, there were others who had decamped, to their estates or to the West Country, taking their servants with them. Some had even gone to Kenya.

The day war was declared, Billy had seen for himself the roads out of London, especially to the west country, jammed with traffic, as those with money ran for cover, not forgetting to spout loud patriotic slogans, telling the less fortunate to stand and fight to the bitter end.

Wednesday, July 24, 4:28 p.m.

'Afternoon, Bert.'

'Billy! How's tricks?'

The man who ran the Eaton was the polar opposite of Maltese Mary. With the purple nose of a heavy drinker, set in a long and lugubrious face, thinning hair neatly combed, Bert Reynolds was immaculate in bow tie and waistcoat, always polishing a glass when not serving a drink. There was an air of gentility about the place too, with its billiard table and dartboard, neat tables and chairs, as well as a small dance floor for when they held functions.

The clientele, even off duty, were usually dressed in the clothes they wore to work: butlers in black top coats and grey stripped trousers, footmen in tight waistcoats, the odd chauffeur's cap on the hooks inside the door. The cooks and serving girls knew their place: there was no loud giggling and a kitchen skivvy better be on her best behaviour if she didn't want to be shown the door.

'No busy then, Bert?'

'Who is, these days?'

'I'll have a pint and a double nip.'

'Singles only. Whisky's been scarce since they took it all for our wonderful Expeditionary Force. And you know what happened to that. Jerry's got it now, mate, so if you want a large one, you'd best *nip* over to Calais.'

Bert followed the pun with his familiar wheezy laugh, which forced from Billy a wan smile.

'Pity, Bert, I was looking tae stock up. You havin' one?'

'Don't mind if I do.' Billy's beer and chaser were produced, before Bert poured himself his usual gin and soda, then said 'Cheers.'

'Slange var.'

As soon as Billy knocked back the whisky, shaking the dregs into his beer, Bert's elbow was on the bar, head close enough for him to speak quietly out of the corner of his mouth. It was excessive caution given no one in the club was close by.

'What you lookin' for?'

'Anything that's goin'. I heard the Spanish were good right now.'

'News to me, mate, though the frog embassy's been flogging off brandy and fine wine left, right and centre just to eat. The Yanks are usually best, but they don't come in here often, do they? Bit too far off their embassy. One or two used to, but that's dried up.'

'It was only a whisper, the Spaniards. Any coming in?'

'They always turn up late, after they've had their nosh.'

Billy looked at the clock behind the bar, registering it was coming up five o'clock, only realising then something he had forgotten. Spaniards ate late and stayed up even later. Indeed, he had enjoyed one night in here, pre-war, that had gone on till near daylight, happy to be in the company of people who represented what he considered a properly governed country. When the Eaton shut the doors at night, it didn't shut the bar, which was when Bert got most of his drinks and tips.

'Best have another then,' Billy said, holding up his half empty beer mug.

Bert winked, lifting his own half empty glass. 'I'll see you another nip.'

'Champion,' Billy replied, 'an' don't forget yersel.'

Billy needed to find a contact quick and it was not just the risk to him that counted. For those maps to be of any use, the sooner they were in the hands of the German High Command the sooner they could make use of them to plan a successful invasion.

Like most barmen, Bert was a fount of information; he overheard a lot he was not supposed to, while being a repository of confidences went with the job. For some reason Billy had never understood, people told barmen things they wouldn't even tell their best friend and that was before they were drunk.

He tried to recall the conversations he'd had himself, not that he was inclined to confide anything. Yet Bert must know his views, given they had never been kept secret. Nor did he know what side of the divide Bert was on, if any; another barman's trait was being able to agree wholeheartedly with everyone. When Billy had made the odd remark about stinking communists or grasping Yids, the accord seemed to be unreserved, but was it genuine?

'You want me to run up a tab, Billy?'

Staring at the bar, lost in thought, he hadn't noticed the arrival of his drinks. 'You said one or two Yanks used tae come in, Bert?'

The barman's head bobbed left and right, as if he were crossing the Strand at rush hour. Then his elbow was back on the bar, the corners of his lips heading for his right ear, the voice a low growl. 'Had a bit of bother, didn't they?'

'What kind o' bother?'

'No idea, but we had some sods come in asking about them and who they talked to?'

'Coppers?'

'Naw, too lah-di-dah to be Old Bill. Snooty sods. Started asking about the Yanks using the place. They were interested in the Spanish embassy folk as well.'

'What did you tell them?'

'Bugger all, Billy. Old Bert hears a lot of stuff and he keeps it to himself. Showed me a photograph of one American fella who came in from time to time, but I made out I'd never seen him or couldn't recall doing so. Maybe he came in once or twice, I says, maybe not. Never grass anybody up, that's my motto.'

Billy reckoned Bert was a stupid git; blokes like those he mentioned tended to ask questions to which they already knew the answer. This might be a members-only club, but the use of borrowed cards was common. Someone with a bit of front would have little trouble getting in, provided they behaved themselves. The photograph they'd showed Bert had to be Tyler Kent, which meant they had probably tailed him to the Eaton. It also meant it was not Kent they were looking for, but his contact.

'They must have asked you more than that, Bert.'

'As I just said, they asked about what Dagos came in. Had to admit there was a few. Said I never really spoke to them outside serving their drinks, 'cause they struggled with the lingo.'

Had Bert made the connection between what he was talking about and Billy's earlier enquiry? If he had, he hid it well. 'But ye can tell me.'

'Why would I tell you what I wouldn't tell them?'

'I'm no MI5.'

'Who're they?' Bert responded with arched eyebrows. Like most folk, he had never heard of them.

Billy picked up his whisky and downed it, letting the dregs drip into his bitter once more. Then he lifted his eyes, trying to read Bert's expression. If Tyler Kent had used the Eaton to make contact with whoever passed on his secrets to the Germans, how had he known whom to approach?

'Truth is, Bert, I'm on ma way to making a few quid.'

'Best of luck. Never been sorry to see a customer enjoy a windfall.'

Kent would have come in here for the same purpose as Billy. Being a stranger, using a moody card, there were only two ways he could establish a contact. Either to spend half his life in the place and chat to every Spaniard he could find. Or, by talking to Bert, short-circuit that, especially if he spent a few quid and was liberal with the free drink favours. There was also downright bribery. Bert wouldn't be too well paid.

As a club bar steward, he would have his little fiddles, the odd bottle of spirits on the back counter be bought for himself, to sell and profit in place of club stock. Tips of course, as well as the paid for drinks he didn't consume. Come to think of it, did he have a special gin bottle full of water for his personal use? But if trade was down, Bert's income would be down too. If Billy was right, how much had Kent paid? Yanks were famously open-handed with money and right now Billy had the stolen cash burning a hole in his pocket.

'It's time I paid for my drinks.'

He hauled out a bundle of white fivers which, as intended, caught Bert's eye. Peeling one off, he slipped it over the bar under his hand.

'Keep the change, Bert.'

The barman's palm was over the note, his head shooting forward as he hissed. 'Bloke you want is called Leo. Comes in every night just before closing time.'

'And stays after hours?'

'Gotta live, Billy.'

'What's his job?'

'Driver, but he's a hard bugger, so he might be more'n that. Speaks a bit of English, enough to get by.'

Billy needed a piss. He nodded to Bert and headed for the gents to give himself time to think. The stream of urine was hitting the ceramic when he was joined in the act, a sideways glance revealing a fellow in a black butler's jacket.

'Better out than in,' the man quipped.

'Is that.'

'Haven't seen you in here before.'

'Ah dinna normally piss in company,' Billy replied, his eyes remaining firmly on the wall.

'I mean in the club.' The man buttoned up and went to the sink. 'Not what I'd call a regular.'

'Old member, but ah hav'na used the gaff for a while. You?'

'Drop in around this time for a livener.' Billy flashed his hands under the tap, the man shifting to make room for him. 'Maybe we'll have a drink some time, if I'm in.'

'I'll look oot fer you.'

'Old Bert's a card, isn't he?'

'Certainly is.'

'You seem to know him well.'

'Like ah say, old member.'

Billy headed back to the bar, the other bloke making for a table and an open newspaper. With more people drifting in, Bert was busy, so it was a while before he came close enough for Billy to question him further. He was also in a dilemma, given he could not stay there for hours. The club would close its door officially at nine thirty. Entry later on was hard, regardless of how loudly you knocked, in case it was the law. It required another roundabout conversation together with more gin and soda to get Bert in the right frame of mind to permit a late entry.

'Ah've got a few things tae do, Bert and a late meet up west, an' you'll be shut.'

The purple nose bobbed up and down. 'Best ring beforehand.'

'Will do. Had many applications for new members lately?'

'A few and we need them, what with all the blokes called up. Takings is well down.'

'That bloke reading the paper behind me?'

Bert was wise enough to make his glance look natural. 'Joined about six weeks back. Comes in most days, has a couple of light ales. Seems friendly enough.'

'If ah was you, ah would check out where he works.' Billy's voice hardened. 'And anyone else who joined recently. Might be they don't really qualify.'

Billy downed what remained of his pint. 'In fact, Bert, ah would say it's a racing certainty. See you later.'

Jamming his cap on his head, he made for the door.

Chapter Eighteen

Wednesday, July 24, 6:33 p.m.

Outside the sun was shining and, in midsummer, daylight would last for hours yet. As Billy made his way towards Piccadilly, he clocked a lot of coppers and military police. People were having their papers checked, probably a search for men dodging the call-up, rather than people like him. Still, it wasn't good because, right at the moment, he had no papers at all.

He kept his head and cap brim down till he got to Hyde Park Corner, entering Green Park to collect his thoughts, the obvious conclusion being he had to get out of sight till it was dark. Looking past the air raid trenches to the long row of buildings on the north side of Piccadilly a solution gradually materialised.

Once across the wide main road, he made for the alleyway behind the Berkeley hotel, where he had once or twice worked washing up in the kitchens. The back entrance was manned by a weary-looking one-legged Cockney, seated in a cramped booth, who'd been doing the same thing ever since he had been invalided out of the army.

He was another one of those boys who had gone off in 1914 fit and cheerful, only to return, having been gassed and badly wounded, to find his old job gone and few prepared to employ him at all. Accustomed to itinerant workers turning up seeking a day's employment, he glanced up from his paper and cast an eye over Billy, before thrusting his hand through the low opening of his window.

'Hav'na been to the agency,' Billy said, adopting a pleading look and whipping off the cap. 'But ah reckon they must be short in the kitchens wi' the war on.'

'Short,' the doorman snorted. 'It's the army that's short, mate. Half the sods comin' in here are dodging the bleeding call-up.'

'Too old now, massel,' Billy replied. 'Ah saw enough in the last lot, even if I wis'na.'

That was Billy's ace; the doorman was supposed to be strict on who got into the hotel. Getting up to the other floors, if not easy, was far from impossible and tempting for anyone intent on thieving. If you did not come from an agency which checked criminal records, then it was no go. But the camaraderie between old soldiers might trump it.

This applied especially to those, as Billy knew from a previous chat, who had fought in the same opening battles in 1914. Then, the so-called Old Contemptibles of the British regular army had frequently stopped the Germans with such concentrated rifle fire, the enemy thought they were facing massed machine guns.

'What was you in, mate?'

'Second Battalion, Highland Light Infantry.'

'West Kent's me.'

'Good regiment, had it hard like we did. Your lot were at Mons, were ye not?'

'Gave the Hun a right bloody nose. Cost us mind.'

'This new lot are no half as good as we were.'

'You can say that again, Jock, they're a load of bloody wasters.' The opaque eyes narrowed and the doorman peered more closely. 'You've done a bit here before, ain't ya?'

'Never did get back on my feet proper after the war.'

'Least you've got two to be goin' on wiv, mate.' The man's head swivelled right and left. 'Nip on through, but say nothin' to the kitchen manager if he comes round, got it?'

'Thanks, pal.'

'You can see me right on the way out. A sixpence won't go amiss, the bleedin' wages I get.'

Billy thanked him fulsomely, itching to curse the greedy bastard. A whole night's work was only worth a shilling plus a feed. The idea still rankled, even if he had a load of cash in his pocket and had no intention of doing any work.

He knew the layout of the basement and its mass of corridors well enough to find somewhere to sit out the time, so there would be no dishwashing or eating grub at a communal table. Certainly, he was hungry, but he had been hungry many times in his life.

CHAPTER NINETEEN

Wednesday, July 24, 6:42 p.m.

Billy was, at this very moment, the subject of discussion between Adam Strachan and Jasper Harker, though not by name.

'There's a good chance the killer of both victims is connected with right-wing zealots,' Adam observed.

The brigadier nodded, conceding the point.

'A friend of Bettina Wyvern at least,' Adam continued. 'I've given Naylor a copy of the Grey List, as well as the names of those we missed on the original roundup.'

'That still runs into a large number of possibilities.'

'The Metropolitan Police have everyone they can get hold of working on it. If that doesn't turn up a suspect, we'll have to move on to the records of anyone with a criminal past.'

Harker produced another of his severe looks. 'And, if the perpetrator has never been fingerprinted, what then?'

The answer to that was so obvious it didn't warrant a reply. They would be in the soup and no mistake, looking for a fellow who had bloodied the whole kitchen and dyed his hair black, judging by the bottle they had found. It was also assumed he'd changed into clean clothes. The wardrobe in Bettina Wyvern's bedroom contained empty hangers, while a drawer in the chest had been left open.

'I suppose we'll just have to wait,' Harker sighed, in a manner that suggested the whole world was out to thwart him. 'What are your plans for this evening?'

'Well, if nothing comes in soon, I'll go home and wait by the phone.'

Harker fumbled in a drawer, producing a card. 'I have been invited to a soiree in Mayfair tonight, by some lady from the US embassy, though only the Lord alone knows how she got my name. Might be an idea for you to go in my place and take your wife along.'

'What about the hunt for our man?'

'That's a police matter. Eleanor hasn't seen much of you these last weeks and you might soon be locked away on the Isle of Wight for God knows how long. It might be an opportunity to mend any broken fences.'

'Which do not exist, sir.'

'Just a suggestion, Strachan, no need to bristle.'

It was only politic to take the invitation, though Harker was poking his nose where it was not wanted. What his chief had implied could only have come to him through Eleanor's mother. Irritated though he was, Adam considered it might be a good idea, given things on the home front were undoubtedly a bit strained.

Not that Eleanor shared his thinking. She point-blank refused to go to a party to which she was not been personally invited. The phone going dead at her end, he was about to leave when it rang again, George Naylor speaking the minute he was put through.

'We've got our man through the dabs on the bread knife. Does the name Billy Houston mean anything to you?'

'He was on the original list of those to be deported to the Isle of Man, but we missed him. He was picked up and fingerprinted in Glasgow years ago. My sergeant is alerting the Scottish police to see if we can get a photograph.'

'Don't bother, we have him on file, an up-to-date full face and profile taken at Speakers Corner. I'll get them sent round to you within the hour. How long before you can get them printed and distributed?'

'I have the whole of the Met Police at my disposal, Mr. Strachan. It will be in the hands of every copper in London by morning.'

'Not sooner?'

'Miracles we can't do.'

With the time taken up in sending of the photographs to Scotland Yard, Adam wondered if he still wanted to go home. With the hunt clearly running hot, he might just bed down here, especially since he could imagine how Eleanor would react if the phone rang in the middle of the night. The invitation Harker had passed to him got another look, which showed it did not require a black tie, so he decided to give it an hour, unsure if his motives were prompted by a chance to unwind, or to spite his wife.

CHAPTER TWENTY

Wednesday, July 24, 9:00 p.m.

Having passed over sixpence to the hotel porter on the way out of the hotel, Billy made his way back to Piccadilly. The sun had just set but between the canyons of the buildings it was already gloomy. The only illumination came from angled personal torches or the slotted, tissue-covered lights of the cars and buses creeping slowly east and west.

Piccadilly Circus seemed unreal with no bright signs and the statue of Eros boarded up. The north side was still busy, full of bustle and quiet bargaining. It was on the edge of Soho, where the London whores, male and female, plied their trade to the sound of newspaper vendors crying out about the potential arrangements with the Germans.

Billy bought an *Evening Standard* and slunk into the Underground where he could read about it, all the time scouring the pages for news of the deaths of de Vries and Bettina. There was nothing and he realised the significance: it was being covered up, so what he had in his possession had to be genuine!

Discarding his paper, he moved on to note there were no banner lights in Leicester Square either, though long queues for the cinemas were as long as pre-war. The two biggest were showing *Gone with the Wind* and *Contraband*, those waiting being entertained by tap dancers, harmonica and banjo-playing buskers in front of a stall where he could get a cup of tea and a cheese sandwich.

It was ten minutes before closing time when he entered the smoke-filled snug, packed with a typical cross-section of West End clientele: actors of both sexes mixed with theatregoers enjoying a last drink before the journey home. There were also the layabouts and rogues, Wally

Burrell being a prime example. He was seated with a pair who looked like right scoundrels: thin moustaches, jackets too tight, lapels a shade too wide and their hats, over swarthy faces, at an excessive tilt.

'You mixing wi' pantomime villains, Wally?' Billy asked, when he was joined at the bar. 'They look as though they forgot to change their costumes.'

'Maltese, they are, Billy and good mates of mine, not to be messed with. Stripe you as soon as look at you.'

'Anythin' to do wi' ma papers?' Billy demanded. The Maltese had a finger in every illegal London pie, mostly prostitution.

'I hope you don't expect an answer. Anyway, I got what you want, so let's trade.'

'Last orders, gents,' the barman shouted.

'Not here,' Billy told him. 'Outside in the alley.'

'In your dreams, mate, I like to do my stuff where I'm safe.'

'How much for the cheque book?'

'I'm goin' to pass on that. There's too much on the market right now and the department stores are checkin' up to make sure they're not kites. I'll settle for the cuff links on top of what I've already got.'

'Pricey, them being gold. I was thinking the shirt studs would be enough.'

'Leave off. Anyway, strikes me you're in no position to trade.'

Wally glanced over his shoulder. The message was plain. The Maltese were there as muscle: *Pay up or my mates will sort you out and leave you to be found by a copper.*

Wally made a sucking sound. 'We got a deal?'

'A tough one.'

'Business is business.'

'And I always thought we was friends,' Billy replied sarcastically, as the exchange was made under the bar. As soon as the ID card and the ration book were tucked away, Billy downed his beer and made to leave, but not without a parting shot. 'One of these days, Wally, you'll push too hard and somebody might just put you up against a wall an' shoot you.'

'Me?' the spiv replied, pretending to look shocked. 'Can't see why, me bein' harmless.'

Outside in St. Martin's Court, the alleyway that ran between two theatres and now very gloomy, Billy made for a dimly lit telephone box. He was thinking that there were a lot of people who would suffer such a fate when he had power. Suppressing his mounting fury, he began to dial.

CHAPTER TWENTY-ONE

Wednesday, July 24, 9:32 p.m.

In the Eaton Club, Special Branch Constable Tom Finch was nursing the last of his beer. He'd heard Bert call last orders which he knew it meant nothing given those who were inclined to go on drinking were already in the club. Included were folk from the Spanish embassy but none who looked to be acting suspiciously. Apart from having no desire to do unpaid overtime, he needed to get home to his wife and six-month-old baby. So, standing, he waved his folded *Evening News* towards the bar and made for the exit, the ringing of the phone fading as the door shut behind him.

Outside, his shaded torch lighting his way, Finch made for the police telephone box in Pont Street to call in to the station. Using the code that got him through to Special Branch, he stated he had nothing to report.

'You might be hauled off that cushy job of yours tomorrow, Tom. There's a right to-do on.'

'Can't say I'll be sorry, Claude, this one is doing my innards no good at all. An' try going home at this time of night stinking of beer and telling the missus you've been working. So, what's happening?'

'Murder enquiry, though it must be more if the Branch is involved. Some fascist nutcase called Billy Houston is the bloke we're after. So best drop by the station regardless in the morning 'cause they're issuing a photograph.'

'Won't be the morning, Claude, I'm on a two-till-ten.'

'A lie-in, you jammy sod.'

'What, with a brand new kid? If I get through the night I'll be lucky.'

Chapter Twenty-Two

Wednesday, July 24, 10:05 p.m.

Now in possession of ID, Billy took the bus to Knightsbridge, this moving at a crawl because of the blackout. It was half an hour plus before he knocked on the club door, to be admitted after a swift examination.' He entered a bar now busy without being crowded, the Spaniards sat in a group on the far side of the dance floor. Billy crossed to the bar and ordered a drink, scanning the room as he went.

'Get a chance to check up on that bastard I pointed out earlier, Bert?'

'Asked about,' the barman murmured. 'Nobody knows where he works.'

'I'm goin' to need help, Bert. I want to talk to that Spanish bloke you told me about.'

'I don't much fancy trouble.'

Billy had known this was going to be tricky. Bert had been allowed time to think, which always brought on the shakes. He could slip him more money, but would it do the trick? It wasn't just an introduction; Billy needed the sod's silence after if anyone came asking questions. A man who felt he had masses of charm—nobody else did—it was not likely to work in this instance, so he resolved to fall back on a threat.

'If the bloke what followed me to the lavvy is who ah think it is, you're in the shit already. That's not goin' to get any better if ah have to keep coming in here day after day just so I can get a meet wi' your Leo.' Clocking the alarm on Bert's face, he added. 'Besides, one phone call and this place could be shut doon.'

The implication Bert had pointed Tyler Kent towards the Spaniard and had his palm well-greased for doing so—something Billy has sussed out—should be enough for Bert to open up. Even he didn't know how much Billy was wanted by the law; Bert knew him to be rabid in his politics and dangerous in his temper.

'Look, Bert,' Billy continued, softly. 'I would'na dob you in. All ah want is an intro, so ah can buy some drink to sell on in the black market.'

'There was no need to be so heavy.'

'Sorry, but ah'm sick of washing dishes and cleaning kitchens to earn a crust. This way, ah can make some good money and Christ knows, after what I've had to put up with, ah'm due.'

It took a moment for Bert to acknowledge he was being offered an excuse; one he could use if anyone asked questions. All he had to do was stick to a tale about black market booze.

'Wait here, I'll fetch him over.'

Leo was short and stocky, with wide shoulders and the loose hands of a fighter, held open, knuckles showing. Even in the gloom of the bar, with a face half covered by a thick moustache, Billy could see traces of scars, pale lines which stood out in stark contrast to his olive-skinned complexion. He had a broken nose, eyes black as his facial growth and bushy eyebrows. He looked like a man who needed to shave three times a day.

Billy, who sized up other men as a matter of course, noticed Leo seemed light on his toes: for all his square build there was nothing plodding about his movements. He was man to shoot from a distance rather than get close to and fight. Another thing Billy reasoned, and this was instinctive, Leo was in no way imposing. If he had no real idea of what anyone engaged in espionage should look like, in his gut, Billy knew it wasn't this.

'Drink?' he asked.

'Brandy's his tipple, Billy,' Bert said, in a tone of forced jollity. 'Ain't that right, Leo?'

A nod, the eyes never leaving Billy's face, who spoke slowly and clearly, taking care not to sound too Scottish.

'I asked Bert to introduce us because I am looking to do some business.' No change in the expression. 'Business that might make both of us a quid or two.'

'I think it's pesetas in Spain, mate,' Bert interjected, still artificially cheery.

Billy glared at him, so Bert retreated to get the brandy. It had to be from his own bottle, because he took it from under the counter and poured it right by them without using a measure.

Billy turned back to Leo. 'That interest you?'

It took several seconds before he got a reply. '*Si.*'

'Leave the bottle,' Billy said, as Bert made to move away. Another five-pound note was produced and laid on the bar. For the first time, Leo's eyes left Billy's face. Not for long, but reassuring, since they went to the money. 'That should cover it wi' change.'

There was a pause, Bert clearly considering if he should ask for more, but finally deciding against it.

Billy held up his glass. 'In my country we say *Slange.*'

'*Salud,*' Leo responded and both men drank.

Billy grabbed the bottle, noting it was Spanish brandy, not French, which told its own tale. 'What do you say we find a spot so we can talk?'

Leo nodded and Billy guided him towards the table so recently vacated by the man who had followed him into the toilet that afternoon.

'Ah need to know how good yer English is, pal.'

'I speak enough.'

'You been a soldier? Maybe fought in the Civil War?'

Another sharp nod. Billy had never doubted his man was on the right side. He wouldn't have been at the Spanish embassy if he'd been a Republican, but could he read a map and the signs? This was the thorny bit. There was no saying how he would react, but there was too much pressure to patiently rope him in. Billy kept the width of the table between them, with one hand close to the brandy bottle to serve as an emergency weapon. The label being in Spanish meant Bert had obviously made a few deals with this Leo.

'Look, Leo . . . do you mind if I call you Leo?' A shrug. 'I let Bert there think ah'm interested in buying some drink, like he does. Brandy and stuff to sell on the black market, but that's not what I'm about. A while ago you were introduced to an American called Tyler Kent.'

The twitch of the shoulders made Billy sit back. Although unable to see Leo's fists below the table top, he was certain they were clenched but there was one positive; this Leo's English was pretty good.

'The first thing yer goin' to think is I'm some kind of spy sent to catch you out, but I am, right now, on the run from the law.' Billy leaned forward again. 'My name's Billy Houston and I'm a member of an outfit called the Right Club. Everyone else is either in the jail or, like me, hiding out.'

There was no reaction to the name, and Leo made the first inching move to get up and leave, at which point Billy reached inside his jacket pocket. The Spaniard's reaction was alarm, which threw the Scotsman until he realised the man thought he was about to pull a weapon. What he actually produced stopped the man dead.

'All I want you to do is take a look at this.'

Leaning over, Billy began to unfold the map beneath the table. Once he had enough exposed, he slipped out his torch and shone it on a stretch of English coastline pointing out one very recognisable feature.

'That, near the bottom, is Dover Castle.' Getting no response, he asked with quiet desperation. 'Do you understand what ah'm saying?'

A grunt.

'To the north, beyond the cliffs, is beach running all the way to Ramsgate, wide open for miles and wi' flat ground to the rear.' His finger traced the line. 'See here. That, I think, is a heavy artillery position behind the Dover cliffs. There's more than one, wi' cannon able to hit the French coast and anything in between, like ships carrying suggers—sorry—soldiers.'

Billy had his attention alright; what he didn't have was a vocal response. He went on to point out what he thought might be minefields and the heavily protected RAF station at Manston. On another level, he was thinking about Tyler Kent, trying to imagine the man dealing with Leo, and it just didn't fit. The Yank fancied himself and would never have contracted any serious business with a mere driver.

'Ah'm going to take a guess you're not the main man in yer embassy when it comes to this. Maybe you only introduced Kent.'

No confirmation, just that steady look from unblinking black eyes.

'But if it's no' you, it means there's somebody in there who dealt wi' him and I reckon the law dis'na ken who he is.' Sensing confusion as pressure had him slip back into his own dialect, Billy translated his own words. 'Does not know.'

Slowly Leo gripped the edge of the map, pulling it closer, Billy continuing to shine the torch as the Spaniard's eyes were lowered. He too used a stubby finger to trace the various symbols in a way that showed he could make sense of what some of them meant.

'I have twelve of these, the whole coastal and inland defence of the country from north of the Thames Estuary to damn near Land's End. Do you understand what I am saying?'

'Yes.'

Thank Christ, some English at last.

'You must know the Germans are goin' to talk to the British Government?' An emphatic nod, followed by a heavy intake of breath. The importance of what he was looking at had hit home. 'So, ah don't have to tell you what these would mean in the hands of the Germans, do I?'

CHAPTER TWENTY-THREE

Wednesday, July 24, 10:22 p.m.

Leo let go of the map and sat back, then spun to look round the room, examining the faces, making sure those present were the same people he saw in here on other nights. Turning back, he lifted his brandy and downed it, before seeking a refill. Billy, breath held, was dying to ask him what he thought, yet he worried the slightest push would scare him off.

'I take map,' the Spaniard said finally.

'Who to?' Billy demanded, tugging at it to retain possession.

'Right person.'

'The same bloke who dealt with Tyler Kent?'

A long pause before a less than convincing nod. 'Tomorrow night, here, we meet. You bring rest of maps and I take to him.'

'Ah don't think so, pal,' Billy responded, leaning back, the half-folded map pulled back on to his lap. The Spaniard's brow furrowed, indicating a man ill-prepared to argue. Billy scowled back, dropping any friendliness in his voice.

'Listen, ah've spent half my life fighting communists and Jews. To get this map ah had to hurt a body or two, which I did'na do just to hand the whole lot over tae somebody else. Somebody who'll get the credit if the maps can be got into the right hands. Ah told you ah'm on the run, so it's only a matter of time before ah'm caught and shipped, like the rest of the real patriots of this country, to the Isle of Man.'

Billy paused. The only thing he was going to get if he was caught was a rope round his neck.

'Ah'm looking forward to the day when Adolf Hitler drives doon the Mall 'aw the way to Buckingham Palace in his bloody great Mercedes. I

want the road to be lined wi' the soldiers who have conquered this country and kicked out the soft bastards and stinking Yids who have ruined
it. If ye think I'm just goin' tae be one of the crowd cheering him, you've
got another think coming, cause if anybody is going to hand those maps
o'er to the Germans it's goin' to be me.'

He paused to let the words sink in.

'I want to meet the main man. I want to be sure them that matters
know who to thank, and it would be good to be alive when it happens.
So, what I need from him is a way to get the maps and me to where I can
hand them o'er and get the reward ah deserve. Now tell me you understood what ah've just telt ye and we might do business. If no, ah will leave
here and look for another way tae go.'

He had to hope that Leo did not see this for the bluff it was.

'I need map,' Leo insisted. 'To get belief you say what is true.'

Which made sense. Yet Billy was reluctant to part with any of what
he had, the whole being so valuable. Would it be diminished by the loss
of one map? Trust he was not much given to, yet there was really no
choice but to have faith in Leo. But even about to agree, he made it look
as if he was thinking long and hard.

'Right, but get this. If ah feel that I am bein' messed about, ah'll make
a phone call. Before you know what's hit ye, your embassy will be crawling with policemen, prepared to tear the place apart to find that map.
And me? Well, you'll no see me for dust.'

The map was passed back to be stuffed inside Leo's jacket, from
which he next produced a small diary and a pen. Unscrewing the cap, he
scribbled a number on one of the pages, added a name then ripped it out
and passed it over to Billy.

'This you call tomorrow night before come here.'

'It needs to be sooner. Every minute I'm out on the streets ah'm in
danger.'

Leo considered. 'Ring morning, nine on clock.'

'This you?' Billy asked, looking at the name Aviles. Leo nodded.

'If good to meet, I talk about Spanish food, if not I talk about Spanish wine.'

'What's your real job at the embassy?' Billy asked.

77

'Job not important. Use my name, not yours.'

'Don't worry,' Billy tapped his breast pocket. 'Ah've got a false one, so when I call, I'll be Mr. Harris.'

'Real name?'

'I told you, Billy Houston.'

The little book was passed over then the pen. 'Write for me.'

Billy twigged he was going to check, without the slightest clue as to how he might do so. Did the Spaniards have a list of fascist sympathisers in the embassy and did Leo have access to it? Maybe Leo was a bit more than Billy thought; maybe he *was* the main man. There being no point in asking, Billy did as he was bid, stood up, gave a farewell nod and, having fetched his cap, left, ignoring the enquiring look from Bert.

Outside it had clouded over, hiding both the moon and the stars. The night was pitch black and warm. Billy switched on his torch and shone it on the pavement.

'Evening, sir.' The voice had a very recognisable tone and another torch was shining on his face, with a black gloved hand over the top to prevent upward spill. It had to be a copper. 'You're out late.'

Time to lay on the Glaswegian with a trowel. 'Am a wee bit lost, tae tell the truth.'

'And where would you be trying to get to, sir?'

'Euston Station. Ah've been telt ah can get a doss doon near there.'

'You're not local then?'

'Naw.'

'I can tell you that you're well lost. Mind if I look at your ID, sir?'

Billy fetched it out and handed it over, immediately asked for the address, which he rattled off. Thank God he had not asked Wally Burrell for a made-up one.

'Long way from home?' the copper enquired.

'Aye. Ah came doon tae see if ah could get news of ma wee brother. He's gone missing in France and we dinna ken if he's deid or captured. His Ma is going roond the bend wi' worry.'

'Any luck.'

'Naw. The buggers' dinna ken nothin'. Typical suggers, eh? Euston Station. Is it a long way awf then?'

'Miles away! You'd be better at Victoria.' The copper handed back the ID card. 'You can take the Tube to Euston in the morning. End of the road, turn right and straight on, can't miss it. There's a WVS stall set up for servicemen selling tea and buns. Ask them about a place to stay and they'll put you right.'

'Thanks, constable.'

'No trouble. Let's hope your brother is safe and well.'

The same tale worked at the stall set up outside by the Women's Voluntary Service, busy as the last trains from the south coast arrived. Billy was directed to a place nearby to lay his head. With a pocket full of money, he had the means, as well as the need for release. This was easy to satisfy, given the streets around the back of the station were a haunt for prostitutes. What he got lacked conversation, with a grunting, single shilling knee-trembler in an alleyway, so swift it would have barely registered on a clock.

That done he went to the so-called hotel, a dump with a single unshaded light bulb in a box-room with frayed blackout drapes. The place smelled of the unwashed and the mattress was lumpy, but it was only when he sat down Billy realised how exhausted he was. Still dressed, he lay back to think through the events of an anxious day and fell into a deep, untroubled sleep.

Wednesday, July 24, 10:50 p.m.

Within ten minutes of parting company, Leo Aviles tried to phone the man he knew as Rodolfo de Bázan, but got no reply, which came as no surprise, as the cultural attaché had a reputation as a man about town. Nor did he live in the embassy, renting an expensive apartment in a modern block above an underground garage in Cadogan Place, to where Leo now made his way. There was a concierge during the day, with a porter at night, in a building blacked-out from top to bottom, with only a glimpse of faint blue light under the entrance canopy.

Leo had to wait outside, obliged to walk past the entrance each time a chauffeur-driven car or taxi disgorged its passengers. This happened fairly regularly in a block of flats for the wealthy, people who could avoid the restrictions on petrol rationing. When another gas-powered taxi pulled up and de Bázan finally appeared, it came as little surprise to find he was not alone.

Clearly in high spirits as he emerged from the rear, he handed out a slim woman with high-stacked hair, wearing under her shawl a long shimmering evening dress and a good deal of jewellery. De Bázan overpaid the taxi driver with a half crown, loudly imparting he required no change. As he bent to whisper something in the woman's ear, Leo came into his line of vision.

Reverting to Spanish, the cultural attaché angrily demanded what he was doing there at this hour.

'A matter of grave importance, Señor.'

'Has the embassy sent you?' carried a note of concern.

'No.'

'Who is this bally chap, Rodolfo?' the woman enquired in a voice, by its very nature, imperious; it also indicated she was slightly the worse for drink. 'A beggar, is he?'

The reply was in English. 'Not a beggar, Clarissa, but one of the embassy minions who plague my life.'

She pouted. 'Then I hope you are going to send him away with a flea in his ear.'

'Alas, my dear——.'

'You must,' she pleaded, adding a slight one-handed shove. 'I've waited weeks to get you all to myself.'

The exchange had given her escort a few seconds to think. He, too, had been drinking but his mind was sharp. It didn't take a genius to work out Aviles would only be here if his need was vital and, given his real role at the embassy, it might presage danger. Careful to keep his identity a secret, he had recruited the driver shortly after taking up his post.

Observation had quickly alerted him to the man selling embassy property. The process of letting him know, without scaring him off, had taken time, but it had turned out to be fruitful. Aviles was a fellow who could go to places and talk with people barred to man of diplomatic rank, as well as carry messages to those who were sympathetic to the politics of Germany.

Canaris might insist he remain passive, but that was an instruction his London agent, as a committed National Socialist and German patriot, had been reluctant to accept. He saw it as part of his duties to encourage English fascists so they felt their efforts had value. He had to admit, objectively examined, the people he came across were a poor lot when it came to doing anything beyond talking. If the Kent business had ended up as trouble, it had made his existence feel worthwhile for a short spell.

An ex-soldier, Aviles knew how to take and execute orders while never posing awkward questions. If he guessed what had happened to Tyler Kent, with whom he'd acted as a go-between, he never said a word. Likewise, if he guessed de Bázan was something other than what he claimed, it never surfaced in his manner. The man had a large family to support, a factor his pay did not begin to meet, hence the selling of alcohol. The stipend now sent directly to his nagging wife and endlessly pleading mother-in-law saw to their needs, ensuring his four children were kept healthy. It was an arrangement which provided a reason to be loyal as well as, if required, active.

Aviles had picked up, without any deep explanation, the nature of what his paymaster was looking for, even if he would have no real idea of the use to which it would be put. Not just Tyler Kent, he had been tasked to carry and take communications to and from people with whom it would have been impolitic for the cultural attaché to be seen. And, since he could not read English, he was a secure emissary.

Throughout the exchange the cab driver, busy rolling a cigarette which, given the source of power sitting on his roof, seemed risky, was still parked by the pavement. He lit up and engaged a gear, forcing his recent fare to decide. Shouting for the cab to wait, he turned to his unhappy paramour.

'My darling, I must send you on your way.'

'Rodolfo, no.'

'Tomorrow I will call and we can have dinner.'

This earned Leo a look of pure hate, but the words were aimed at her putative lover. 'That's no good at all. Jack will be back from his beastly tour of inspection tomorrow night.'

Opening the cab door got her a peck on the cheek. 'Then we must wait until his duties take him away again.'

'It's not fair.'

'*C'est la guerre, Cherie.*'

The pressure on her arm forced her, still complaining, into the cab. Door shut, he gave the driver her address, proffering another half-crown. As the cab pulled away de Bázan turned to Leo and barked in Spanish.

'Given what I've just been obliged to sacrifice, Aviles, this had better be important.'

If the light had been stronger, de Bázan might have seen the right fist clench, might have sensed in the man's features the desire to use it on him. Leo liked the money that came through his association with this Hidalgo bastard, but he didn't care for the man or the way he had been pressured into working for him.

Quite apart from his manner, he was officer class and Aviles had hated them all his soldiering life. The mainland Spanish ones he had served under as a young recruit were utter shits, stuck-up bastards who would sell the unit rations and see their men employed as labourers, pocketing what pay came from the people making use of them. This was before they got their men into a position which, through their stupidity or indifference, could get them killed.

Necessity and better pay had Leo move to Morocco and the Spanish Foreign Legion. There the officers had been superior soldiers but harder taskmasters, too fond of petty punishments in the name of maintaining iron discipline. Stifling his anger, Leo edged under the canopy, obliging his employer to follow.

'I have something I must show you, Señor.'

'Show me!'

'A map.' The blue light overhead seemed to magnify de Bázan's expression, precursor to the kind of rebuke Aviles was unwilling to take, so he added forcefully. 'Possibly a very important map, one it would be wise of you to examine. I would humbly suggest it cannot be done standing in the street.'

The glare this got, followed by a look at the door, spoke volumes. It said that an embassy driver was not of the social class to cross the threshold. It was rapidly replaced by an expression of disbelief, then a stiffening as it was concluded there was no alternative.

'Very well, follow me.'

The door was opened by the night porter before they got to the taped-over glass, this being the kind of place where it was considered a want of service if a resident was obliged to do anything for themselves. The tips that bumped up the pay came from the ability to grovel to those you despised.

Without acknowledgement, his toffee-nosed tenant swept across the marble floor of the hallway, the other man, clearly not of the right sort, on his heels. Past the desk took them to the lift, where a pressed button was followed by entry. The night porter waited until the doors closed before he forcibly stuck up two fingers.

CHAPTER TWENTY-FIVE

Wednesday, July 24, 11:05 p.m.

Using a magnifying glass, Rudolf Graebner examined the map on his coffee table, with Aviles, who had told him what he knew about its origin, as well as who had supplied it, sat opposite. To a naval officer who had studied and played war games in the Baltic, involving amphibious landings, both in assault and defence, the symbols were no mystery. They were like a language Graebner knew as well as the four he spoke.

Minefields were obvious but he could go beyond identifying trench systems, reading the signs for heavy artillery, machine guns, pill boxes, concrete and tank traps. Most vital of all, it showed potential troop concentrations designed to thwart any landings. Two critical questions arose: was the map genuine and, if it was, what was he going to do with it? Then there was the fellow who had possession of the rest.

'I call him, he brings the rest of the maps to embassy.'

'No!'

If the response was graceless, the reasons were obvious. Anything that compromised the embassy had to be avoided. There was only one place where Graebner could examine the maps this fellow was supposed to possess and it was here, where no one would ask what a stranger was doing on the premises.

'I will call the embassy first thing in the morning and request a car for a short journey. You will drive it.'

'I have to be in the embassy garage at nine, Señor de Bázan, to take the call.'

The expression this engendered was typical to an ex-sergeant of how an officer reacted to being questioned by a soldier of lower rank, irritation brief but obvious. Then, in order to preserve dignity, it was followed by a look away, as if a superior mind was being applied to the problem.

'When Houston calls, get him to come to you. Call me and say the car is ready. Bring him to the underground garage from where you can phone.'

A swift glance towards the door was all that was needed to tell the driver he was no longer required, but Rudi was not through. Leo was on his way when he produced a key before issuing a last imperious command.

'There's pistol in my right-hand lower desk drawer, as well as a full magazine. Go to my office and collect them for me.'

Once Aviles had left, Rudi went back to studying the map, but not to learn more. He was thinking, as he bent over the coffee table, here was the coup for which he had always prayed, one that would free him from a cross he had never quite been able to shake—his Iberian birth, a burden he endured with silent resentment.

Any hint of a Spanish lisp, in what was marginally imperfect German, had been mercilessly played upon by his fellow cadets, who thought themselves racially superior to Latins of any kind. To deflect this Rudolf had struggled to be the best in his class. He had also joined the Nazi Party in 1932, when it had been forbidden to those serving in the armed forces, so those inclined to condescend to him would have no misgivings as to where his allegiance lay.

He could not avoid his thoughts from the previous night. If this map and the others Aviles had talked of were genuine, there would be no need to beg Wilhelm Canaris for anything, he could name his own price. Equally troubling was the recurring suspicion it was a trap set by MI5, a worry to keep him awake for some time, until he reasoned if it were, then they already had enough to arrest him.

Chapter Twenty-Six

Thursday, July 25, 7:18 a.m.

When Billy Houston woke up, it was to the realisation of how vulnerable he was. It hadn't occurred to him success would put him in the hands of total strangers, yet he could think of no other route which would work. He rose, feeling stiff and, following a quick visit to the stinking lavatory and a splash of water over his face, went down to be presented with a breakfast of porridge more lumpy than the mattress on which he had slept.

Being the kind of 'hotel' where you paid in advance, he was free to leave and make his way to a nearby worker's café where, using his false ration card, he procured a plate of something edible.

The newspaper billboards carried headlines about the British government having accepted the invitation to talks, together with the location. Even with restrictions on ink and paper, the *Daily Mail* had splashed out on a photograph of Osborne House, adding a map to show where it lay on the island. Again, the papers made no mention of either de Vries or Bettina Wyvern, which cheered him.

Arriving at Victoria Station, Billy found it packed with travellers plus members of all three services. It was also well provided with coppers in their easily identifiable 'Bobby hats'. Suitcase retrieved, cap low and weaving left and right; he was on his way to the gents for a wash and shave until the thought struck. There could be no better place to look for those on the run. Spinning round he made for the middle of the concourse, to stand, suitcase at his feet, seemingly waiting for his train. Watching the station clock as the minute hand crept round, he knew his only protection was the sheer number of people jostling their way to and from the platforms.

At ten minutes to nine he moved, only to find there was a queue for the bank of telephones. Every wooden booth was full, with people queuing, which had him cursing under his breath. Desperately he forced himself ahead of a middle-aged woman as one came free. She called out angrily, her complaint muffled as he slid shut the folding door, Billy ignoring the angry tapping on the glass. The smell from an overflowing ashtray was acrid, the heavy black handset still warm. He slotted in several pennies then dialled Leo's number, pushing the Button A as it connected.

The voice, in Spanish, threw him completely. He muttered, 'Aviles', which got him a stream of incomprehensible gibberish.

'Do..you..speak..English?'

'*Si, señor.*'

'Ah need to talk with Leo Aviles.'

A series of clicks followed and a voice said, '*Garaje.*'

Aware of the heat in the booth and the sweat running down his spine, Billy repeated the name. A shout produced the kind of echo you get in an empty building, then he heard footsteps before a gruff voice came on.

'Señor Harris?'

'Aye.'

'You like Spanish food?'

'Ah love it.'

'Come to little road behind embassy, you call mews, to *garaje*. Name same as street. I wait you. How long you be?'

'Fifteen minutes, maybe.'

'Good.' The phone went dead.

Exiting the booth, Billy came face-to-face with the still irate female, who berated him roundly for his 'appalling lack of manners'. Billy glanced around anxiously to see if there were any coppers close by. With not a single one in sight, he stuck his nose close to the woman and hissed.

'Shut yer bloody face, ya silly old cow.'

'I say!'

The exclamation was directed at Billy's back, his glare enough to put off anyone feeling chivalrous but he never did realise how lucky he had been. The policemen on duty had been called into the station office and handed the photograph and name of a suspected double murderer. By the time they had studied it and re-emerged, Billy was heading out of the station to join the queue for taxis.

Rico Caruana, a Royal Signals operator, noted the time of the call and wrote down the exchange with the embassy switchboard, the garage and the short conversation. He consulted the list pinned to the wall, holding the name of everyone of importance at the Spanish Embassy, searching in vain for Leo Aviles or anyone called Harris. Not that he had much time to look. There was an outgoing call to monitor and this time it was in Spanish, no problem for a man who had spent the first ten years of his life in Gibraltar.

'Señor de Bázan, your car will be with you within the hour.'

'Excellent, Aviles.'

De Bázan was on the list, so the transcript of his conversation was placed in the despatch box, which would go to MI5 headquarters at the end of the shift. It was something of an afterthought that made Caruana, in adding the previous slip of paper, connect it with the exchange between Aviles and the Scotsman.

Part of a fast disappearing queue, Billy was soon poking his head through a front window to give the cabbie his destination, conscious of the look he got in return. Unshaven, and his jacket bearing the creases of having been slept in, Billy knew he must be some sight. The case he was carrying was so battered it looked ready to fall apart.

'You look a bit rough, me old mate,' the driver said.

Billy pulled open the rear door. 'There's a war on, pal, or haven't you noticed?'

'Call this a bleedin' war? More like a pasting. Bloody Nazi swine.'

Billy had to bite his tongue as the meter flag was turned down and the cab set off. He wanted to tell this bastard he might be getting a proper personal pasting shortly, not that he got the chance. The driver was a talker and, even if the journey was short, it gave him time to put the world to rights. Billy, when he alighted, paid the sod, mostly in pennies and without a tip.

'Typical bloody Scotsman,' greeted his ears as the cab pulled away.

Leo, dressed in a charcoal grey chauffeur's uniform and gleaming boots, was waiting beside a large black limousine, all polish and sparkling silver metal. He opened a door, beckoning Billy into the back, before shutting it then going to occupy the driver's seat.

Billy sank back, taking in the luxurious interior; the jump seats with the walnut veneer cabinet in the middle, no doubt containing drinks, the silver box for cigarettes by the spotless ashtrays, the thick rugs on the rear shelf and the deep pile carpet beneath his feet. They were exiting the mews when he picked up the little speaking tube by his side, an object he knew the purpose of from watching films.

'Where we going, Leo?'

All he got was a dismissive wave from a black-gloved hand.

CHAPTER TWENTY-SEVEN

Thursday, July 25, 9:11 a.m.

DCI George Naylor was reading the report of the questioning of Roger Sheridan, sent up from the Torquay police, concluding there was nothing in it that would be useful. De Vries he hardly knew, the RAF officer becoming his tenant through an acquaintance, whom Sheridan declined to name.

Naylor put down the report with a sigh and turned his attention to the image of Billy Houston, glowering up at him from his desk. Beside the photograph were two files, the top one listing the things MI5 had on the sod, below his criminal record. This was wholly violent, him having been arrested several times for affray. Yet, the man was no murderer, or at least had never been done for such an offence.

It had taken a few hours longer than predicted, but the mimeographed photograph was all over London now, sent out to every station in the hope of catching those coming on duty for the morning shift. Later it would be passed to every force in the country. The phone rang and, not a man to leave it, Naylor picked up the receiver immediately, to find Adam Strachan on the end, enquiring if the photo had been sent out and when.

'First thing this morning, Mr. Strachan,' Naylor replied. 'Nothing back as yet, but our man will find it difficult to move without being spotted.'

'I had a call from Special Branch to say they've only just got it.'

'They were last on our list,' the DCI replied, winking at a bemused sergeant sat at another desk. 'Thought it best to get it to the beat coppers first.'

The pause was minimal. 'Special Branch will know how to get hold of me if anything comes up.'

'Fine.'

Adam put down the phone, sure he had just been on the receiving end of a fib. Not, to be sure, a very important one, but a lie, nonetheless, this as a yawn engulfed him. Hardly surprising; the hour of distraction he had allowed himself, using Harker's invitation to the Mayfair party, had turned into a very pleasant night indeed. He had indulged in a mild flirtation with a very attractive American woman, first at her crowded apartment, then subsequently in a night club with her and a naval captain friend.

The knowledge it could go nowhere didn't diminish the sense of enjoyment. And, given she was a press attaché at the American embassy, it could even be said to work, though not the kind he wished to share in detail with Jasper Harker.

CHAPTER TWENTY-EIGHT
Thursday, July 25, 9:17 a.m.

The journey to the underground garage was over in minutes. Leo drove down the ramp and parked the vehicle, emerging from the front seat carrying a brown paper package. He made a quick call on an internal phone before directing his charge to a lift which took them up to a carpeted corridor. Billy was ushered through an open door and a short hallway into a room. It was all glass and modern furniture, with a fine view of the green space fronting the block, as well as the busy road beyond, this lined with five-storey redbrick houses. Open on the coffee table he could see the map he had given Leo.

Before him stood a tall, good-looking man, wearing a rather forced smile, but there was nothing about him to suggest he was Spanish. With blond hair, a light grey summer suit, a white shirt and a plain Windsor knotted silk tie, he could have stepped straight out of the German magazines Billy had been fond of reading. Even if he hadn't understood the words, he'd liked the pictures.

What his 'host' observed was a square-faced peasant, not young, at least in his forties, the skin reddish, unshaven, with a mop of dark hair and a moustache which did not match his complexion. The hair was in need of a cut and he had on crumpled clothes of indifferent quality, which sent out a faint odour of mothballs. His blue eyes flicked towards the battered suitcase and back again as he suppressed a yawn, which Billy suspected was for effect.

'What do I call you, Houston or Harris?'

The English was near to flawless, if anything, a bit too precise.

'Up tae you.'

'Aviles, wait outside.' This being in Spanish. Leo raised the packet he was carrying. 'Ah yes, leave it on the hall table.'

He waited till his chauffer had disappeared before indicating the case in Billy's hand and reverting to English. 'Aviles tells me you have more of these maps.'

'Aye.'

'Would I be allowed to look at them?'

'Don't ye think it would be an idea tae tell me who ye are first?'

This got a slight nod. The man walked past Billy and opened the door, disappearing into the corridor, which made the Scotsman jittery. When he came back, he carefully shut the door and turned to face his visitor.

'I think you must tell me who *you* are first.'

'Leo has'na told ye?'

'I prefer to hear it from, as you English say, the horse's mouth.'

'Ah'm no English.'

A slight, indifferent lift of the eyebrows. 'He told me you claim to be a member of the Right Club, several of whose supporters I have met. Perhaps you would like to name some of them.'

Billy smiled, exposing uneven teeth. He had seen the main list often and, if many of those on it had been stuck-ups, the man who had started the Right Club was not. A proper toff, he had the easy manner of one who had spent too much time with common soldiers in a fighting trench.

Being Scottish himself, he had treated Billy with a degree of indulgence, but most important of all, he'd trusted him to go recruiting among his own class. If only he hadn't got involved with Tyler Kent, he might still be walking the streets.

'It was set up and run by Captain Archibald Henry Maule Ramsey MP.'

'Go on.'

The names poured out, the dukes and duchesses, earls and viscounts, two minor members of the royal family, as well as a list of businessmen, bankers and a couple of High Court judges, this before he started on the politicians. He then began to name sympathisers who'd not actually joined and who, if they subscribed, did so in cash. When Billy stopped talking, the owner produced a pistol and aimed it at his visitor.

'All of this you could have learned by examining files.'

'Right enough.'

'Just as that map, as well as the others you claim to be carrying, could be false.'

'I don't know if they are real or not and I cannae make head nor tail o' most of the symbols. But I took them off a high-up RAF feller and he did'na want tae give them up. When I left him, he was deid, but you'll no see anything in the papers. I had tae see to another body, as well, an' that's not been reported either.'

'It might be safer for me to kill you than tell you my name.'

'I did'na come up the Clyde in a banana boat.' The man struggled to make sense of the response, which gave Billy time to think as he forced out a pitying smile. 'Yer done for if you do. I'd be a right ejit if I'd no taken steps to cover my back. There's two letters out there, sealed and they will stay that way as long as I let the people that have them know ah'm all right. If not, they will read about me meeting wi' Leo, where, how and why.'

The gun was lowered and placed on a coffee table, at a distance between them which wasn't great. Was it enough to get to it and neutralise the threat? His 'host' took out a silver cigarette case, extracted one and lit it, his gaze remaining steady. Having exhaled a cloud of smoke, he picked up the gun again, to click on the safety catch. Now it was Billy's turn to exhale: what he let out was anxiety.

'Be assured, if I feel you are a threat to me, I will kill you, prior to alerting British Intelligence. Now get out the other maps and put them on the table.'

The commanding tone was irritating, but that was nothing compared to Billy's curiosity. 'So, who are you?'

'Aviles knows me as Rodolfo de Bázan.'

'Is that yer real name?'

'It is not, but you must never, in front of him, refer to me by anything else. All you need to know is this. If those maps are genuine, you have brought them to the right place. My real name is Rudolf Graebner and I am a serving officer of the Kriegsmarine and also an agent of the Abwehr, German military intelligence.'

Billy's heart leapt but so did his arm, which shot out and up.

'*Sieg heil, Mein Herr.*'

CHAPTER TWENTY-NINE
Thursday, July 25, 10:07 a.m.

Temporary Special Branch Constable Tom Finch left home early. If he and his wife had longed for a baby, the reality had proved less starry-eyed. Their tiny flat, when not smelling of dirty nappies, was full of freshly washed ones. With nowhere to hang them out, it made the whole living room damp, even with a window open. The bedroom they shared was small anyway; the advent of a cot made it even more cramped, so there was nowhere really for Tom to sit in comfort and neither was he now top of the list when it came to attention.

Thus the station canteen beckoned, a place where he could get a cooked breakfast, a cup of tea and a chance to sit and read the papers. Or even engage in conversation which was not baby talk or related to the needs of his little girl. Despite his qualms, the aroma of her from the last cuddle, of talcum powder and fresh washed skin so smooth and soft, stayed with him till he got on the bus. It was rapidly displaced by clouds of cigarette smoke.

The grey-haired desk sergeant, glancing at the clock, was surprised to see Finch come through the double doors. Even if he was merely uniform, he knew what Special Branch were up to and when they came and went.

'You're early, Tom.'

'New baby, mate. Thought I'd get a bit of peace.'

'You'll be the only one, son. The whole Met is running around like blue-arsed flies and them being up half the bloody night already.'

'I got a mention last night when I came off shift.'

'A murderer they say, but it has to be more. You don't put the whole force on chasing a killer unless he's done for one of us.' The sergeant leaned over his desk conspiratorially. 'And especially one that hasn't been reported in the papers.'

'Who is it?'

'Fella called Billy Houston.'

'Never heard of him.'

'Got a photo here.' He pulled a mimeographed black and white copy out from the pile under his desk. 'One's been issued to every beat copper as well as your mob.'

'Jesus Christ!'

'No,' the desk sergeant replied, with mordant wit. 'Billy Houston.'

But Tom Finch had gone. Within a minute the hallway was full of rushing men, Finch included, as the staff of Special Branch headed for their cars. The bells were ringing within seconds, followed by the sound of screeching tyres as they swept out of the station parking bay.

'What was all that about?' asked the duty inspector, poking his head round an open door.

'Buggered if I know, sir. Prima donnas showing off as usual, I expect.'

Jammed in the back with the bulbous Alf Ward, Tom Finch was suffering a barrage of questions from DCI Eddie Banks, who wanted to know why this young constable had not seen something he, with his vast experience, would have reckoned obvious.

'You had the bastard bang to rights, for Christ's sake.'

Tom would have liked to tell his boss to get stuffed. How could he have known the man everyone was looking for had shared the same lavvy? Remembering the extra Special Branch pay, he uttered a meek, 'Sorry sir.'

'I can tell you, son,' Banks responded, as he picked up the radio, 'if I get it in the neck, so will you.'

Banks began to report what had been discovered and where they were headed.

The door to the Eaton Club was open and the sight of so many burly individuals piling in had the lady mopping the floors screaming. She had no answers to the questions fired at her. Bert, who lived above the place, came down to see what the fuss was about, only to find himself pinned to the bar as the intruders demanded to know what he knew about the man in the photo shoved under his nose.

'Billy Houston.'

'A known enemy of the state,' barked Banks.

'Never,' Bert replied in a half gasp, 'a bit of a fiery sod yes, but—'

'Who did he come to see?'

'He came in for a drink.'

Being a well-practiced liar came to Bert's aid. There was no way he was going to tell these sods Billy had even come back to the club, never mind that he had introduced him to Leo. He had to own up to knowing him, since the man who had triggered doubts with Billy, about his being a genuine member, was now clearly a policeman.

'And what else?'

'Said he was looking to buy some drink, embassy stuff to flog under the counter.'

Fat Alf spoke up, jowls wobbling portentously, his voice grave. 'I don't think this geezer knows how much trouble he's in, Guv.'

'End of a rope, I reckon, Alf.'

'What, for serving a bloke a couple of whiskies!'

'It's more'n that, sunshine, and you know it.'

'Do you mind if I take over now?'

The Special Branch officers turned to see Adam Strachan in the doorway, holding up an ID card, at his back the same pair of young thrusters Banks and Alf had come across the previous morning.

'Might I suggest you take your hand off the man's throat?'

Tom Finch, being closest to the speaker, could read his card. He glanced at his boss and nodded vigorously. Before he could say who and what it said, Adam cut him off.

'No one needs to use my name, young man.' He murmured, before putting a couple of questions to Eddie Banks, whom he'd met before. Then he turned. 'Yours is?' he asked amicably.

'Albert Reynolds, Bert to most.'

Several equally gentle enquiries established his age, how long he had worked at the Eaton, as well as much of his background. Then Adam asked him to join him at a table out of hearing distance from the others.

'We should search the premises, sir,' called Banks.

'In a moment,' was the reply as he smiled at Bert. 'I am assuming the person we're looking for isn't here?'

'No.'

'Mr. Reynolds, I suspect you're as patriotic as any man in this room.' That got a nervous nod. 'So, if I were to tell you this is a matter of vital national importance, you would be only too willing to tell us everything you know.'

Bert nodded once more but, eyes averted, he was busy calculating. These coppers he was sure he could lie to and maybe get away with it. But this feller, with his well-cut suit, air of authority, fine manners and lah-di-dah voice, was a different kettle of fish altogether.

'The person we're after has committed two murders, which means anyone aiding and abetting him faces prison. But I wish to impress on you it's much more than that. Therefore, anything withheld comes under the heading of high treason.' Bert Reynolds stared at him in alarm, silently mouthing the last two words, as Adam added. 'I doubt I have to spell out to you the penalty for such an offence in wartime.'

'I didn't know he was up to anything like that.'

'How could you? But in the desire to not incriminate yourself, a perfectly natural way to behave, you may aid the enemies of your country, which I'm sure you would not wish to do. We'd find it hard to believe what you told the Detective Chief Inspector, that the man came in here just on the off- chance of a drink, or to purchase some stuff for the black market.'

'I don't know much.'

'Best to tell us everything and let us decide the value, don't you think? Perhaps you could start with how you gave assistance to a fellow called Tyler Kent, an American citizen who is, at present, a guest of His Majesty and may well hang for selling secrets to the enemy.'

Outside his purple drinker's nose Bert Reynolds didn't possess much colour, but what he had drained from his face. 'Blimey.'

'Time to talk I think, don't you?'

Which he did non-stop, until Adam, who had only set out to bluff him, was given confirmation on Kent and the fact Bert had been well paid to point him in the right direction. This also got him the name of Aviles and what he did at the embassy. The barman had no idea what he and Billy had talked about, or any arrangements they'd made, even when pressed. So Adam called a halt, stood up and turned to Eddie Banks.

'You may take Mr. Reynolds into custody.'

'What for, I ain't done nothing?'

Adam's calm demeanour evaporated and his voice was icy. 'I think you'll find, Mr. Reynolds, you have aided and abetted the enemy, enough to spend the rest of the war breaking rocks, and it may well be worse.'

He then went to the telephone.

CHAPTER THIRTY

Thursday, July 25, 10:50 a.m.

The maps in their entirety told Rudi Graebner an enormous amount. It was obvious the British saw the long open stretch of the east coast of Kent, with the coast of France so close, as the most vulnerable. It also had two ports with crane loading facilities, Dover and Ramsgate, which any invader would need. They had planned accordingly, with what had to be, after their various defeats, limited forces and a massive shortage of equipment.

An attempt would obviously be made to stop any invasion on the beaches. If that failed, it appeared the aim was to draw any advance by the Wehrmacht northwest. This would pit them against a prepared defensive position between the high ground of Maidstone and the Thames Estuary. There they would be met by what trained formations still existed.

The number of anti-aircraft batteries placed on the Isles of Sheppey and Grain were an object of curiosity. This could indicate the defence line could be supported by naval gunfire from battleships and cruisers. These, having fought and survived the opening sea battles in the Channel, would retire to the mouth of the River Medway. There the warships would also be protected by flak from the heavily defended naval base at Chatham, added to what air cover still existed.

Other contingencies had been set out and were marked. The high cliffs behind Folkestone Harbour presented the possibility of surprise assault, so had artillery units, which in an emergency could be supported by infantry. These could also cover and bombard the beaches fronting Romney Marshes and the flat ground to the west, to gain time for better equipped army units to deploy to the south.

Further along the coast, past Hastings, the defence began to thin out, this being where some of the troops lost in France might have been positioned. Rudi had gleaned, from some overheard and indiscreet remarks, the rumour there were something less than two fully equipped and battle-ready divisions in Britain. The maps told him they were based in mid-Hampshire, ready to move to whatever front required support, including which routes and by what methods they would take. The available air power was marked out in designated vectors of attack.

Exciting as it was to be in possession of such plans, he knew the only place they could be of use was on the other side of the Channel where, despite the talk of an armistice, an invasion force would surely be assembling. Yet, having studied the problem of a sea-borne assault on England in war games and taking into consideration the situation since the conquest of France, the major problem had not massively changed. The German navy could never match the British for firepower in a fight to the death in their home waters.

And where was the Kriegsmarine to get the kind of boats to convey a major invasion force? Even if they could be found, it would have to be flat calm in a waterway notorious for heavy seas. Also learned from loose gossip, he reckoned the Royal Air Force had substantial squadrons of fighter planes as well as the pilots to fly them. They would be bound to go after whatever transports were carrying troops and supplies. The problems would be difficult to surmount.

Had the whole notion of an Armistice come about because of these difficulties? It was frustrating not to know. Adolf Hitler had proved to be a genius, so was he now formulating a plan to reduce the capacity of the British to fight a proper war, by demanding, in negotiations, restrictions to their armed forces, the navy especially? This would pave the way for a future assault, when the conditions were more propitious and the right kind of shipping was available.

With these maps, could such an approach be completely overturned? Never mind the Kriegsmarine and the Wehrmacht. Such documents, for the Luftwaffe, would be priceless, enabling them to pinpoint and destroy any defensive efforts made by the British, as well as cripple both reinforcement and resupply. Similarly, paratroopers dropped in precisely the right place could wreak havoc in the rear of the invasion beaches. This might then make a sudden landing by regular troops feasible.

Rudi had no doubt these plans were important enough for him to abandon his post, yet that posed another dilemma. Could he get them out of the country? His luggage was immune to search, but could such diplomatic privilege be trusted, given the suspicion caused by the Tyler Kent affair? What he had hold of now was ten times more precious and he had no doubt, in their present parlous situation, the British would risk an upset with the Spanish government to recover them.

Even if he could get through unhindered, what was he to do about the fellow who had brought them to him? According to Aviles, Houston had been adamant; wherever the maps went, he went, too. The British must know they were missing and would be tearing London apart trying to find both them and probably him too. He needed time to think, yet having a fellow who was likely the subject of a manhunt here, with him, was more than a hindrance. He was a liability.

'You have the means to shave in your case, I trust?'

'I do.'

'Then I will permit you the use of my cloakroom, where you can do something to make yourself presentable?'

'Presentable fer what?'

'As yet I do not know. I have to consider how we are to make proper use of what you have brought to me. I doubt I have to explain such a thing is not without difficulty.'

'We've got to get them to Germany.'

'Precisely! And unless you have already formulated some fool proof plan, which you have declined to share with me, I suspect that is a problem I am going to have to solve.'

The observation got a flash of irritation, one which could mean many things to the person on the receiving end. A lack of trust, resentment at the assumption just made, which was demeaning, or perhaps annoyance at the tone of voice. None of this bothered Rudi: Houston's appearance did.

'You look dishevelled and that, should we need to show ourselves in public, attracts attention.'

Billy Houston's eyes went to the pile of maps and there was no doubting the train of his thoughts; while he was shaving, they and the German could just disappear. Rudi noted this and gave a wry smile, intended to reassure.

'I have not forgotten your warning. Added to which I am not stupid enough to risk my position here just for a bit of extra glory. There is enough on my table for us both and, if it troubles you, you may leave the cloakroom door open.'

The sound of the doorbell dispelled the mutual glares and turned it into one of alarm, though the German did his best to keep his concern hidden.

'Who's that?' Billy demanded.

'I have no idea, but it is best you are out of sight.'

Billy snatched up his case as Rudi, who had picked up his pistol, gestured for the Scot to precede him. Leo was out in the hallway, sitting by the telephone. He leapt up when his superior appeared and the buzzer went a second time.

'Were you followed?' Aviles was asked in Spanish.

'No, Señor.'

'Look through the eyehole and see who it is.'

Billy was ushered into the cloakroom with no time to ask what was going on.

'He is dressed like the man from the desk in the hallway,' Leo reported, his face pressed to the woodwork.

This provided little reassurance: if anything, it increased suspicion, it being a typical ploy to put someone innocent ahead in a raid. If it was British Intelligence he was done for. With those maps on his table—there was no point in trying to hide them—he would be shot as a spy for certain. He flicked off the safety catch and slipped the pistol down his trouser leg, just enough to be hidden.

'Open the door, Aviles and stay behind it.'

'What's happening?' hissed Billy through a crack in the cloakroom door.

'I do not know, Mr. Houston, but if it is trouble—'

He shrugged then gave Leo a nod. The door sprang open, surprising the man who liked to call himself the concierge. In his hand he had a pile of newspapers, the editions on permanent order.

'You didn't collect these this morning, sir.'

The breath the tenant had been holding left his body. 'Pass them to my driver and thank you.'

Leo, appearing from behind the door, did nothing to dent the porter's confusion as he did as he was asked. He remained rock still, waiting for a tip, as the door was closed in his face.

'Shave, Mr. Houston,' Rudi said, before reverting to Spanish. 'Aviles, come with me.'

'No closed doors, if ye don't mind.' Billy opened the cloakroom door to its full extent.

It made no difference; the Scotsman knew no Spanish, so could not understand what the man went on to ask Leo. How much petrol he had in the embassy car, also if he had any qualms about the need to dispose of the man he had fetched here, which would, of course, qualify for a substantial cash bonus. Since Leo, after a moment's thought, merely nodded, Billy would be none the wiser.

The idea, then outlined, was to get Houston out of Central London and find some spot where the deed could be carried out quietly. All they needed was a reason to adopt such a course. Rudi Graebner, who said nothing of this to Aviles, could then return to the embassy and make preparations to leave, which would require the assistance of the ambassador. For a diplomat to depart a country at war on board a busy plane heading for Lisbon required very special permissions, which had to come from the Foreign Office.

Finished shaving, Billy emerged from the cloakroom to find Leo had been banished to the hallway again, though he indicated he should pass on into the sitting room. The German was sat in a chair reading a newspaper, the headline of which was stark. In bold black type, it trumpeted the news that Britain had agreed to armistice negotiations.

A cough told Rudi the Scotsman was back in the room, so he lowered the newspaper and smiled at him. If it was intended to encourage, it had the opposite effect. Billy had been on the receiving end of the same kind of false beam from any number of snobs in the Right Club. It usually preceded the carrying out of a task they found distasteful to themselves, but quite fitting for the likes of him.

Thursday, July 25, 11:11 p.m.

'Please close the door, Mr. Houston, I think we have a solution to our problem.' That done Rudi spoke again, his voice low as he indicated the headline. 'The British have suggested as a venue for talks, the Isle of Wight and my government has provisionally accepted.'

Billy shrugged as the German suppressed another yawn.

'Do you not see? There is no need to get those maps to Germany. The very people who need them most are coming to us. Within days the cream of the German general, air and naval staffs could be on their way to England.' He made a point of examining the paper again and spoke from behind its pages. 'The chosen venue is Osborne House. Do you know it?'

'Naw.'

The paper came down again, Billy exposed to another condescending smile. 'I have visited when I crewed at Cowes Week. It has fine gardens and a very famous painting by Winterhalter of the family of Prince Albert, who was of course German, though I am told it is only a copy. There is also rather a grotesque room decorated in the fashion of India, much loved, I was told, by your Queen Victoria.'

'She's no my queen.'

The mention of Cowes Week said a great deal to Billy. The annual sailing regatta was a place for right stuck-up bastards, not that he'd ever been there. But it was the kind of gathering the people he'd been involved with went to in summer; Henley, Wimbledon, Ascot as well, then brayed to each other about the experience.

Head buried again, Rudi was reading more and clearly excited. 'The Führer has immediately ordered a flotilla to sail and bring an advance party from Wilhelmshaven to inspect the location and the arrangements before the delegates can travel. Wilhelmshaven to Portsmouth? If they set off at once and sail at reasonable speed, they could be there in less than forty-eight hours.'

'Bloody hell, that's quick.'

'It is at the express command of the Führer,' was barked. 'When he directs, men obey. He has always realised the less time his opponents have to prepare, the better. This will be no exception.'

The man spoke with the kind of pride Billy wished he could express regarding his own country, one he had spent years hoping to see created. The speed of the German action invited an inevitable comparison with what would have happened if it had been the other way round. The British government would take a week just to pack the tea and biscuits.

'Let us assume the advance party will be ashore within a couple of days. The question then becomes, how we can get those maps to where they will set up their base of operations.'

'And me?'

The irksome smile reappeared. 'Once we get to the island, Mr. Houston, our next task will be to transfer you to a place of safety. Fear not, there will be a way.'

Sensing Houston's reservation, the German threw aside the newspaper and stood up, whereupon he launched into a soft but insistent lecture, pacing back and forth before the windows. The maps, for all their worth, should his superiors wish to invade, were just as valuable as a tool of negotiation. If the British delegation was made aware of their newly established defensive weakness, the men entrusted by the Führer to act on his behalf would be able to press for many extra concessions.

'I'd prefer tae see them marching up Whitehall.' An armistice and peace were not much good to Billy.

'Which means you struggle to understand the brilliance of the Führer. Do you really think he will make peace and just leave England to go on its merry way?'

The sharp featured face took on a look of devotion and the voice hardened. Rudi punched his fist into his hand as he marked each point.

'It will be of the same kind of peace he made with those Czech scum. Our panzers entered Prague within months of making an agreement at Munich and it will be the same here. Britain will be conquered when the time is ripe and, when the time comes to march up Whitehall, perhaps you, in the appropriate uniform of a newly formed National Socialist British elite, will be well to the fore, as the man who helped to make it possible.'

By sheer chance Rudolf Graebner had stumbled on the very dream in which Billy sometimes indulged. Not that the German stopped to register the effect of his words; he was off on his pacing and punching again.

'We must plan how we are to get to a place already remote and will become much more so in the coming days. If we can find a boat, which I admit will be difficult, then I can sail it to wherever we need to effect a rendezvous.'

'We've got to get to the coast first.'

'Aviles will drive us in the embassy car. Until we reach any restricted zone, the diplomatic number plates should protect us from any interference.'

'Then?'

'We must use our wits, Mr. Houston. And also, we must succeed. Now, ask Aviles to re-join us. But I must once more admonish you to be careful as to how you address me.'

'A wee bit o' background on Leo would help.'

The request clearly annoyed the German. Billy could not know that the circumstances of an embassy driver's life were of no account to a man like him. But to keep the Scotsman content, he composed his features and gave him a potted version of what he knew.

'Ah thought he'd been a soldier. Foreign Legion, eh? Are they as tough as the French lot?'

'I have no idea.'

Billy went to the door and called in Aviles, who glowered at him, until an admonition in Spanish altered his expression. Reverting to English, Graebner turned back to face the Scotsman.

'The bulkiness of the maps, as well as their obvious appearance, present a problem. They are just too recognisable, so I require your permission to transcribe the contents to something more portable. To do so, I need peace and privacy.'

Billy looked at him as if he had just filched his wallet, which produced another smile.

'I know what you are thinking but never fear, the maps go where we go and will only be discarded if they represent to us a danger. It is not the fact of their existence which matters, but the information they contain.' Seeing the Scotsman remained unconvinced, he added. 'And just so you are free from concern, it is to you I will give what I have written.'

The apartment had a separate dining room, a place where Rudi could spread the maps on the table, leaving the other pair behind a closed door to twiddle their thumbs. Outside Billy stared at the door, fighting off the desire to kick it open. Uncomfortable as it was, he had to trust this man because, without him, he could get nowhere.

Graebner had quietly pushed a chair under the handle since locking the door would be audible. He had been provided with a Minox miniature camera for photographing documents, usually one page at a time, but reasoned it was useless with maps of the size before him. He had no choice but to produce a written copy so, sat down with a fair-sized notebook, rubbing his tired eyes, he began to list map references alongside the symbols and numerals.

These denoted locations, heavy weaponry, obstacles, the source and routes of supplies of men and ammunition needed to maintain a defence, the nature of the defences themselves, troop numbers, as well as the bases from which fighter support would come for the various sectors.

This he did not once, but twice—one for him and another to keep the Scotsman docile. All the while part of his mind rehashing how he was going to get this information into the right hands, along with all the additional problems before he could do so. He had to get the details out of the country without being discovered. Loose sheets of paper and possibly one map he could secrete about his body, in the hope he remained immune to a personal search.

The rest were too bulky; they would have to be put in a diplomatic bag, and he had no certainty it would remain secure. It was this which had led to his previous conclusion they should not be taken. Given his position in the Abwehr, with these notes, plus a single original document, he would have everything necessary to convince his superiors of their value.

He was no more immune than Billy Houston to what it would mean, possibly be the greatest intelligence coup of all time. If he saw himself as being of a superior intellect, Rudolf Graebner was not beyond speculating on the rewards which would accrue for being the person to deliver. A *Ritterkreuz* was certain, but it could even qualify for the personal thanks of Adolf Hitler.

Thinking of those who had dared to condescend to him, he knew such a chance to end it would never occur again. For all his professed love of his adoptive homeland, he had always been made to feel like an outsider. Succeed at this and he would never again have cause to suspect, behind his back, his contemporaries were mocking him. Instead, they would grovel for his approval.

If time was a factor, he calculated it was not massively pressing. Even if an invasion was in the planning stage, nothing would happen while talks were mooted, even more if they went ahead. He had, at the very least, several days to arrange matters in a situation where any sign of haste might raise suspicions among his Spanish colleagues.

There was the tiresome problem of Houston, of course; he would have to be dealt with before anything. At least he seemed to have fallen for the farcical notion of getting those maps to the Isle of Wight. As if crossing Southern England at present was as easy as it had been in peacetime.

The maps showed the real truth; the whole coastal region was a restricted military enclave, with the beaches mined and wired. That was only the start of a series of difficulties which rendered the idea utterly ridiculous. Still, the notion of proceeding with such a plan would serve to get Houston out of London to a spot where he could be disposed of and that should be today.

What about the threat Houston claimed he had left behind? On examination the notion of a contact having information which could be passed to the police didn't hold much credence. Houston had only met Aviles the night before and had possessed no knowledge regarding himself until this morning, which made the driver the sole one at risk. If he had to be sacrificed, so be it.

Under such circumstances, Aviles would be questioned, perhaps unpleasantly interrogated? In the absence of a true identity, would he betray Señor de Bázan to the British if, in doing so, he must incriminate himself? Given he was small fry, the ambassador would have no hesitation in offering him up to placate his hosts, which would probably mean him swinging from the end of a rope. It was a thought which momentarily stopped the flow of the pen.

He, too, would suffer that fate should he be apprehended. This took the matter of timing on to a different plane. Every agency in the British State would be working flat out to find their maps, so he was really sitting on a time bomb. Were they looking for Houston, worrying, since he had no knowledge what point they had reached in either endeavour?

The pause was brief, the pen soon busy again. There were potential pitfalls and dangers, it was true. But a competent officer could only deal with the matter before him, which had to be taken care of as a priority. Everything else would follow in due course.

CHAPTER THIRTY-TWO

Thursday, July 25, 12:44 p.m.

Adam Strachan knew, even in wartime, he could not just go barging into a foreign embassy and effect an arrest; everyone inside had diplomatic immunity. The only person who could waive such a safeguard was the ambassador, who would need to be shown definite proof of transgression before he could be persuaded to act. This required the direct intervention of the Foreign Office and they had already been alerted to the need.

While the wheels were put in motion and, by stretching a scarce resource, he had managed to place a watcher on every approach to the Spanish embassy. He had, as well, covered the mews running along the rear, with a description of Leo Aviles to add to their photograph of Billy Houston. He'd put a call through to George Naylor to say the same description of the Spaniard would be sent over. It was to be circulated with the caveat of his immunity, added to the fact he had no idea if their man was inside embassy property or somewhere out on the city streets.

Seated in a car with his two younger operatives, Adam had tipped his hat over his eyes to facilitate a much-needed snooze. He'd sent Fat Alf to walk along the mews, using the old loose shoelace trick, to crouch down and get a look into the garage where Aviles was thought to work, his bulk and interfering belly making the time it took seem normal. Not that it told him much; there were a couple cars in the gloomy interior but if the man they were after was inside, he wasn't in sight.

A tap on the roof of the car brought Adam out of his slumbers, the information he had sent for passed through the rear window, a thick file on the occupants of the Spanish embassy. This comprised documents applied to all diplomatic personnel, so they could be assessed prior to taking up their post. Each member of staff from the ambassador down-wards had a profile, photograph included.

'Anything leap out, sir?' asked Jocelyn Devereux from the driver's seat, leaning over to study the face of Leo Aviles. Sefton Avery occupied the front passenger seat and Adam passed Leo's details over to him.

'Have a look and tell me what you think.'

Both, heads together, the two young men took an age to study what was a small amount of information; Leo's name and birth details, his home in La Linea on the border with Gibraltar, which had no doubt given him a knowledge of English. His family in generational order, as well as his record of military service. Clearly, they were worried about making an error and blotting their copybook.

'Just tell me what you think, it's not an exam.'

It was Avery who replied. 'Seems a rather lowly chap to be engaged in espionage, sir.'

'Which leads you to conclude what?'

'He's no more than a conduit for someone else.'

'And how do we find out who that someone is?'

'Aviles will have to tell us.' Devereux replied.

'And if he declines to do so, Jocelyn?'

'He must be coerced!'

It wasn't the solution because it didn't reach the nub of the prob-lem—to get back those maps. Not that he shared the thought. Even if this pair knew they were involved in something big, they had no idea of the real extent.

'Looks to be quite a tough bird to me,' Adam said, passing over the photograph. 'Might take some time to break him.'

Before either could respond the radio crackled into life, asking for Adam. In a brief exchange, he was informed his presence was required by Sir John Simon. He had taken over from Lord Halifax at the Foreign Office, the previous holder having been elevated to 10 Downing Street. The whole file was passed over to the younger men.

'Get round our watchers and show them the Aviles photograph, the one of Rodriguez as well, just in case. Once that's done, get the file back to HQ, so the driver's photo and details can be copied and sent to

Scotland Yard. Tell DCI Banks where I've gone and, in my absence, he's in charge.'

As the pair clambered out of the car, Adam took over the driver's seat, having repeated his previous instructions to ensure everything was covered. If any of the watchers saw Aviles and Billy Houston together, they were to collar them both and leave him to deal with any fall out.

Houston on his own, they could arrest without question. But if the Spaniard Rodriguez was alone, he was to be tailed, either walking or driving.

CHAPTER THIRTY-THREE

Thursday, July 25, 12:56 p.m.

Leo was in a chair opposite Billy. With nothing in common the two men sat in silence beside their drained coffee cups, but that didn't preclude thinking and worrying. The Spaniard was wondering if he should have gotten involved in this, given he realised the ante had been upped on the services he was going to be asked to provide.

When de Bázan said this Britisher had to be got rid of, there was little doubt what it involved. It wasn't the act that troubled him; in the Civil War he'd done plenty of killing, including lining up and shooting dozens of captured Republicans. But the Hidalgo bastard had been vague about what was to happen next.

Billy was wondering if he could trust the German and his talk of shared glory. It all sounded too pat, only for the lack of alternatives to keep surfacing. He'd tried to read the newspapers and the manoeuvres regarding the forming of a government, but struggled to concentrate. His mind was a tumult of thoughts, many of them the same kind of fantasies about his future he'd envisaged in Bettina's bath, mingled and made opaque by the rest of his imaginings. Not least getting to the Isle of Wight was going to be hard if not impossible. That was until a conceivable way suddenly presented itself.

Aviles was jolted out of his concerns as the Scotsman suddenly shot out of his chair, pounced on his suitcase and pulled out a notebook. This he began to leaf through, turning pages, carefully folding the outside top corner of some before hurrying on. The activity was only halted when the dining room door opened and their host appeared, a sheaf of lined papers in his hand. His own copy Rudi had put in an envelope, now in his safe.

'Here you are, Mr. Houston.'

Billy examined the papers as if they were diseased, forcing a smirk from Graebner. 'Do not worry if you cannot understand the symbols and numbers.'

'Double Dutch tae me, most of it.'

This expression again confused the German, which pleased Billy. He was finding the man's air of authority a pain.

'Before we plan for our departure, I must make certain arrangements at the embassy which will cover our tracks.'

He glanced at Leo, as if to impart such a precaution applied to them both, though it was Billy who responded.

'Ah've had an idea of how we might get to the south coast, though getting tae the island will still be a problem.'

'Really?' asked Graebner absent-mindedly.

Rudi knew he'd got the tone wrong by the flash of impatience in the Scotsman's eyes. It had seemed to imply someone of Billy's station could not possibly come up with solution, when what it truly signified was his utter lack of interest. He had no intention of going anywhere near the south coast, but the game had to be played; he dredged up an expression of curiosity, in response to which Billy held up his notebook.

'In here, ah've got the names of folk who might help us, the ones I took donations from for the Right Club.'

'Who will surely have been picked up by now?'

'Not these, *Mein Herr*.'

'You mean *Señor!*'

'Aye, sorry an' aw that.' Billy waved his book once more as Leo shifted uncomfortably. 'Not this lot. They never made the membership books taken by MI5, 'cause they were penny and shilling contributors.'

'This you will need to explain.'

Which Billy did: the money collected from most of the people he had recruited on his travels had never been banked. Being in coin, with the very occasional pound or ten bob note, the club had used it as petty cash, added to which their names had never been listed as full members. It didn't need to be said why; they were simply not considered important enough. Some of them, being too vocal, might have been picked up, it was true. But he was sure the majority would have had the sense to keep their heads down.

Explaining took Billy back to those smoke-filled rooms, in which he had relayed his vision, mainly upstairs in pubs belonging to landlords of the correct persuasion. Publicans tended to be right-wingers by nature, people who knew their customers well enough to gather like-minded souls to hear Billy's message.

A new dispensation was imminent in Britain, and people of the correct political persuasion would have to be prepared to take up the positions to impose and maintain order. Folk who would not scruple to be as hard as would be necessary.

What he was holding represented over a year of travel on Green Line buses and provincial trains. They had taken him all over Southern England as well as the Home Counties surrounding London, and it had been fertile soil. He had talked to people who rightly saw Bolshevism as a threat, not only to their livelihoods, but their very existence. They would support any system of governance which ensured the lower orders did not rise to rule the country. It was also a world in which anti-Semitism was rife.

As the German listened, he had to acknowledge it was a partial solution to a theoretical problem. Yet enthusiasm was necessary and had to be contrived; at all costs this dolt had to think the plan was one he shared.

'Mr. Houston, you have hit upon a sound idea. While I am away, I urge you to use the time to work on it.'

Still nodding he turned to Leo and spoke in Spanish. 'Aviles, come with me.'

In the hallway, out of sight, Graebner passed the driver his pistol, adding a look which required no words. It would ensure the Scotsman gave no trouble. Then, with his gas mask container in his hand, he was gone, to walk the short distance to the embassy.

Thursday, July 25, 1:37 p.m

Whatever the hobgoblins were up to, this was an occasion for the Metropolitan Police to lean on anyone who might know anything, to visit every low life dive and villain on their patch in search of information. Never to be admitted, there was rivalry, too; Naylor wanted to get to the killer before Special Branch.

When the two detectives from Bow Street entered the Barracuda Club, everyone present suddenly became busy with a fingernail, a newspaper or the contents of a glass: these were people who could smell a copper. Maltese Mary was suddenly occupied cleaning and polishing behind the tiny bar, too busy to catch their eye.

It took the slap of a warrant card on the surface to get her to turn round. The smile she produced, through heavily rouged lips in her pancaked face, under dyed ginger hair, to the pair examining her, would have done service as a shocker in a fairground Ghost Ride.

'You want sometink?' Billy's face was on the bar now, the glare of the two coppers obliging her to look at it, which was followed by a shrug.

'We heard he uses this place.'

'This maybe news to Mary.'

The senior of the two nodded slowly, his face immobile. 'How long is it since we paid you a proper visit Mary, say checked your cellar for gear that's been nicked? Or maybe we could get the licencing lot round to test your beer and spirits are the proper strength.'

'What his name?' she asked, stalling.

'All you need to know Mary is that Billy here's in trouble, real trouble, the kind to see anyone who helps him, or does not help us, locked up with the key chucked away.'

Threatened too many times in her life, Mary seemed unimpressed. But she did glance past the pair, as if she was thinking. In truth it was to throw a glance at Wally Burrell, a signal for him to get out quick. The senior of the two, a Detective Sergeant, who had seen every trick in the book, chuckled before spinning round to see the back of the unmistakable covert coat.

'Well, well, well, if it isn't my old friend Wally.'

'Billy Houston, I tink his name,' Mary said, tapping the photo.

'What a memory, Vic,' the sergeant said to his younger sidekick in mock amazement. 'Should be on the boards, Mary here. She'd put the Memory Man out of business in no time. Nip upstairs and make sure our boys don't rough Wally up.'

Having survived in the West End of London for three decades, both working the streets and the bars, Maltese Mary had a good nose for not only trouble but also how deep it could be and this was not ordinary. Men outside as well as this pair meant it was serious. Wally might be a regular but, when it came to survival, it was not a contest.

'He and Wally were talking yesterday, heads close.'

'Thank you, Mary,' came the reply, full of irony, 'and don't bother to offer us a drink, we're on duty.'

'What he done?' she asked.

'Enough to get you closed down just for talking to him. So, if he comes back, pour him a free one, then get on the blower to us.'

'Sure, sure,' she called as they made for the stairs.

Outside the two detectives came across their man, pressed against a shop front by a pair from uniform branch, already sweating profusely.

'Afternoon, Wally. That coat of yours making you a bit warm.'

'What's going on, Sarge?'

'Name Billy Houston ring a bell?'

'That sod.'

'No way to talk about a mate of yours now, is it? And you all hugger mugger yesterday.'

'Who told you I was his mate?' The fact he already knew it had come from Maltese Mary shone from his worried eyes.

'Strikes me, if he was talking to you, Wally, it would be to do a bit of business.'

'I talk to all sorts, din I?'

'Then you'd best talk to me. In case you're reluctant, let me tell you what your mate has done.'

'Jesus Christ,' Wally gasped, when he heard about the murders. 'I knew that bastard was trouble.'

As George Naylor took the call, Ben Foulkes knew from the 'well dones', the scribbling and positive nods, someone had got a result. The conversation concluded by an instruction to 'send them over.'

'Not that it helps us much, Ben,' Naylor remarked. 'They've recovered some of de Vries' possessions.' He handed Foulkes a slip of paper. 'Bugger is still out of sight somewhere but we have a new name.'

'Strachan?' Ben asked.

'Best tell him, show we are cooperating fully.'

CHAPTER THIRTY-FIVE

Thursday, July 25, 2:08 p.m.

Adam was ushered straight into the presence of Sir John Simon and Jasper Harker, to find Sir Stewart Menzies, head of MI6 also waiting. Menzies immediately demanded to be told precisely what had happened and what actions had so far been taken. Adam looked hard at Harker, who'd been kept well enough informed to supply those facts before his arrival. If he hadn't done so, there was a reason.

The only one Adam could think of was silence lessened the possibility of later censure if things turned out badly. Harker had been reluctant to take over when Vernon Kell was booted out after the Tyler Kent affair and had only accepted under pressure. If it was a job he was prepared to relinquish, this made him a less than wholly reliable man in whom to place both one's faith and one's own career. All Adam could do now was respond to the request and tell what he knew.

'So,' Sir John said, summing up sententiously like the barrister he was. 'We have no idea of the whereabouts of the National Defence Plan, or of the person or persons who purloined them?'

'We can guess what he is trying to achieve,' Adam replied, again filling the silence left by his superior, 'which is to use the conduit of the Spanish embassy to get them out of the country.'

'Which must be prevented at all costs,' put in Menzies, stating the bloody obvious.

Adam struggled to avoid giving him a scowl and asking what he thought he was doing, muscling in on an operation that had nothing to do with him or his department. MI6 worked outside the country; anything internal was MI5, which did little to lessen their rivalry or mutual ability to tread on each other's toes. Menzies would have picked up the rumours, of course, poking his nose in where it was neither wanted nor needed. Anything to imply his sister service wasn't up to the job. Given Harker's so recent elevation, he would be lording it where he could.

'Mr. Strachan,' the foreign secretary remarked, 'I cannot but agree with Sir Stewart. Whoever is to undertake negotiations with the Germans, and it may well be myself, will find it near to impossible to extract any concessions from them, if they are in possession of the entire extent of our defences.'

'Which surely requires that we act?'

'With circumspection. As I've already explained to your colleagues, any matters to do with the Spaniards are, at this moment, extremely delicate.'

Menzies spoke up again. 'We cannot afford to have them join with Hitler. As of now, and this I must remind you is strictly confidential, we have good reason to suppose they are inclined to maintain their neutrality.'

'The whys and wherefores of that are outside my area, while I am, of course, obliged to obey any instruction issued by the government.'

Sir John Simon, who had an aesthete's countenance, fashioned a thin-lipped smile. 'However, you'd like to raid the Spanish Embassy?'

'If they were all under arrest, the possibility of Houston getting to the contact he needs would be diminished.'

'What about this Aviles fellow?' Menzies demanded. Clearly, he had been briefed about that.

'He's an embassy driver,' Adam snapped, 'an ex-sergeant in the Spanish Foreign Legion. Do you really believe he has the status required to deal with someone like Tyler Kent, plus the means to get the cables Kent stole into German hands?'

'A fair point,' Harker intoned, giving his deputy a look, which hinted he should contain his irritation. 'I think you'll agree, Stewart, if it is the Spaniards, and it now seems little doubt of their transgressions, there has to be someone higher up in the embassy staff?'

'May I posit a reminder it was our service that first indicated the existence of the Kent leak?'

'For which we are grateful,' Harker acknowledged, before turning to Simon. 'Sir John, I think taking Mr. Strachan into your entire confidence would be wise. In short, to tell him everything, given a solution must be found.'

The silence lasted for half a minute, the foreign secretary weighing the pros and cons, no doubt wondering why he had been landed with such a hot potato, when his feet were barely under the table. But it was an office he had held previously, so he knew what he was about and, in reality, the dangers were manifest.

He sighed deeply before he spoke, listing the perils of the German advance, the loss of France and the enmity of Italy, as well as the risks to Gibraltar and in the Mediterranean. He finally admitted that HMG was hoping to bribe certain Spaniards to keep their country out of the war.

'And we have sound intelligence,' he concluded, with a look at Menzies, the man who would have provided the information, 'they are very willing to accept our offer.'

'They are, in fact,' Menzies insisted, 'desperate for it.'

'Bearing in mind the reaction they can expect if they do come out on the German side,' Simon continued. 'Be assured we'll not be passive in the face of such a threat, any more than we were with the French fleet.'

'The solution seems to me to be obvious,' Adam said, to suddenly raised eyebrows. 'I presume the ambassador would be the man to send through your warnings to Madrid?'

The minister nodded, but so did Menzies. MI6 would have intercepted the messages in both directions which brought Adam to the crux of the matter. 'And his attitude?'

'I believe he is inclined to aid us,' Simon responded. 'The Duke of Alba is related to our own royal family and has many friends in this country. Though I would emphasise, his reasons for advising neutrality are likely to be more practical than personal.'

'Then, Adam maintained, 'he must be persuaded to give us the person who passed on Kent's cables, who must be the man to whom Aviles reports. With any luck it will get us Houston and the NDP maps as well.'

The door opened, occasioning a frown as the permanent secretary entered. As a career civil servant of high seniority, the man could afford to ignore it and, besides, he knew what was being discussed.

'There is an urgent call come in for Mr. Strachan from his HQ. Given the gravity of the matter, I felt it my duty to disturb you. Also, I've been given a name by the Metropolitan Police they are sure will be helpful.'

The slip of paper was passed to Adam. It told him that the name William Harris was the one now being used by Houston. With a nod to the others, he went out to take the call. If the information he received was invaluable, he had to wonder, as he re-entered the meeting, at the juggernaut of bureaucracy, which had taken so many hours to get it to someone who knew it should be acted upon.

'We think Houston called Aviles this morning. He has a pronounced Scottish accent and he used a name for which he has recently acquired identity papers. Having talked to Houston, the chauffeur immediately called a fellow called de Bázan, both conversations being extremely short.'

There was no need to elaborate on this, implying, as it did, codes being used. The post de Bázan occupied only took a moment to establish and, if the conclusion could not be certain, it was enough to point to him as someone well enough placed to have dealt with Tyler Kent.

If he was willing to pass low-level intelligence to the Germans, what would he do with the gold dust being carried by Houston? There was only one person who could confirm they were on the right track, but the foreign secretary insisted diplomatic necessities dictated that the Duke of Alba be consulted. Simon picked what had to be an internal phone and said.

'Please telephone the Spanish embassy, I wish to see the ambassador at his earliest convenience'. That was diplomatic speech for, 'Immediately and NO excuses.'

At the same time, Adam demanded any intercepts from the embassy should be brought to him immediately they were transcribed, wherever he happened to be. A message should also be sent to DCI Banks to keep a lookout for de Bázan, whose photograph and details were in the file Adam had left with his two young tyros.

Chapter Thirty-Six

Thursday, July 25, 2:12 p.m.

Conscious he might be the subject of surveillance, Rudi Graebner kept an eye out for a tail. Yet as he walked a circuitous route, he realised that, for all his apparent sangfroid, he was behaving anxiously. He had to force himself to walk slowly, nodding to people he passed while, in his heightened imagination, he seemed to see all around him potential enemies; men in buttoned-up suits and wide hats on a day warm enough for open jackets or shirtsleeves.

Should he take the ambassador into his confidence? Alba would surely put the needs of Spain ahead of those of the Reich, so best he be told nothing. Would he make difficulties and refuse to permit him to accompany the next diplomatic bag out of the country? Rudi thought not; the man had always been unhappy with his presence and would be glad to see the back of him.

The Rolls Royce, Alba's personal property, was outside the entrance to the embassy, the red and gold pennant fluttering on the wing and the engine running, signifying the ambassador was on his way out. This made Rudi quicken his pace, so he met his superior on the top step of the entrance, to be greeted, as he lifted his hat, by an unfriendly stare.

'Having visited there yesterday afternoon, I have just been summoned to the Foreign Office, Rodolfo and in the same manner as I was over the affair of that American cypher clerk.'

'I cannot imagine why, sir.'

'You're saying it has nothing to do with any action of yours?'

'None at all. I gave you my assurances, did I not?'

'I have to tell you we are, at this very moment, in very delicate negotiations with the British government.'

'Regarding what, sir?' Graebner asked.

'You don't need to know. What you do need to be aware of is this. If you have again overstepped the bounds of your mission, I will not act to protect you. Please make yourself available to see me upon my return, so I can appraise you of what it is that has so upset the new foreign secretary, he has summoned me as if I were his butler!'

Graebner was left standing on the steps as the Rolls purred off and, if his thoughts had been concerned before, he was doubly so now. He had to allow, of course, there might be no connection between the maps and the summoning of the ambassador, but to do so was risky. He went inside the building and made his way to his office to sit down and think. If trouble was brewing, how long had he to react and what were the ramifications?

Houston had met Aviles, and the driver had brought him to his apartment. Assuming the worst, and that was the only safe thing to do, he reasoned MI5 had possibly made the connection between the driver and the Scotsman. Aviles might hold out for a while against MI5, but would he do so against his own people when questioned, especially Rodriguez?

The likelihood was slim. Rudi would then become embroiled in any investigation, while the ambassador had just told him, in no uncertain terms, he wouldn't be protected. Even if his true identity wasn't divulged—the Spaniards would not do that for fear of the consequences to themselves—he'd still become persona non grata and be obliged to return to Spain.

A diplomat being thrown out of Britain would not be travelling with sacrosanct baggage for he would have lost his immunity. This would leave him subject to search and, if he was even thought to be connected to Aviles in any way this would be thorough. Could he bluff it out? Was it worth the possible outcome?

A German officer was trained to think clearly in any situation, to assess the risks then set them against the likely consequences, taking into account the needs of the position in which he found himself. With the maps in his possession, he could not take any chances at all. Even the most cursory question regarding Aviles would put the man and his car at his apartment. He had filled out the requisition himself, and his apartment would have been logged as the destination before the car left the garage.

Which meant neither his home nor the vehicle was safe, the former doubly so as Houston and Aviles were still there along with the maps. Rudi shook his head as the obvious conclusion surfaced: he must act as if he was in danger until he could be sure he was not.

For all its seeming absurdity, the notion of getting to the Isle of Wight, or even the south coast, might be the only one that presented any chance of success. If he stayed still and did nothing, every avenue would be slowly but surely choked off until his inevitable arrest. It also seemed likely he would be tied to the theft and the murders Houston admitted carrying out. His only way out was to leave London immediately.

He couldn't use the embassy Hispano-Suiza, a very unusual marque which would stand out. Could Aviles steal another car? Was that even the right choice, driving something bound to be reported stolen? His mind spun with self-questioning, but one thing was clear: he needed to make himself scarce until he could assess if there was any real threat.

After a few minutes of contemplation, Graebner picked up the phone and asked for an outside line. On hearing the tone, he began to dial, then stopped, slowly putting down the receiver. The means by which the connection could have been made between the Scotsman and Aviles presented itself. The phones must be tapped and that would have included the driver's call to him.

Thursday, July 25, 2:34 p.m.

The watchers who'd seen the man in the light summer suit talk to the ambassador, then enter the building, now observed him leaving with a much more urgent tempo, of little concern since he was not on their list to watch for. He was quickly out of sight round a corner, so they didn't see him stop and, after a quick look around, slip into a phone box.

His call was to Clarissa, the woman he'd been obliged to disappoint the previous evening. If she was surprised to be called from a phone box, she hid it well. No, husband Jack was not going to be back till much later in the day and yes, she would love to have Rodolfo to luncheon.

The instructions to the concierge, given as soon as Graebner entered the lobby of his block, were brusque. 'A taxi as soon as you can!'

The man picked up the phone. 'Might be a while, sir, what with the shortages.'

'Which will be fine. Come up to my door in ten minutes and I will give you a parcel for the fellow to take.'

'Going to, sir?'

'Hampstead.'

In the lift, Rudi was gnawing on another possibility, sacrificing Aviles by sending him and the car back to the embassy. He could no longer contemplate disposing of Houston who, improbably, might yet hold the key to an escape. On balance the driver had to be more of an asset than a liability, especially since he knew so little of the Scotsman. Houston came across as impulsive, perhaps too much so for him to handle on his own.

Aviles he found where he'd left him, sitting in the same chair, his face expressionless. The man had the patience which went with his job, one which often left him sitting waiting in a limousine for hours at a time. Billy was in the dining room poring over the maps and it was there that Graebner went first.

'Mr. Houston, put the maps back into your suitcase.'

Billy bristled, his face reddening, plainly not pleased at the tone. 'What for?'

'We are leaving.'

The driver had followed Graebner into the room.

'Where are we going, Señor?' He asked in Spanish.

'Wherever I say, Aviles.'

'Señor?' the driver responded, with a troubled expression.

'You must do as I tell you. Things have gone too far to do otherwise.'

Billy watched the exchange keenly, confused not only by the language. 'Can somebody tell me what the bloody hell's goin' on?'

'There is no time for that. We must leave.'

'Are ye telling me we've been rumbled?'

'*Rumbled* is not a word I know. But if it means what I think, then the answer may well be yes. My ambassador has been called to the foreign office and I have no idea why. It may be nothing but it may be we are at risk. Therefore, as a precaution, we must move from here and swiftly. That Aviles, includes you.'

There was a moment of immobility as Leo unravelled the English, then contemplated the ramifications, there being no doubt he had understood. Graebner closed with him and said softly.

'I have a duty to take care of you, as much as I have a need to act and I will pursue both. Now I think it best if you return to me my pistol.'

The gun came out so slowly, neither Billy nor Graebner had any assurance he wasn't about to use it. Another couple of seconds passed before the driver slipped on the safety catch, then turned it so he was holding the barrel. As the German took it Billy spoke, his tone bitter.

'I won't ask why ye left Leo wi' the gun?'

Graebner, on his way to the safe in the bedroom, replied just before he shut the door. 'You can guess why, Mr. Houston. Now get packed, maps included. I am assuming you have about your person the papers I gave you?'

From a drawer Rudi took the package intended for the concierge, a standard ploy to put any immediate pursuit off the scent. It contained nothing but tightly folded newspapers in brown paper and string, to which he added an address, one decided upon not long after he had been sent here. It was a real street in North London and so was the number, but the place was shuttered and empty.

Next, he went to the safe, buried in the wall, which contained not only his copy of the map details but everything he needed to escape—money and false documents. Not that he had hitherto seen them as anything other than mere window dressing to make him feel his handlers cared for his survival.

The same applied to the tube of Pervitin tablets, methamphetamine pills he had been told would help to keep him awake and sharp in a situation where sleep or feelings of despondency would increase the risk of capture. They would be of use now, given he was suffering from too little sleep over the last two nights. If they were going to get away, he needed to be alert, so he quickly downed a couple.

There was a British passport with the other requisite papers, as well as an Identity Card, a compass and ration book, identifying him as a Pole. This might serve him better than those who supplied it had realised, given the number of nationals who had fled to Britain after their country's defeat. He decided to hang on to his diplomatic passport but reckoned the money, two hundred pounds in sovereigns and the same in five-pound notes would be more effective. The latter went into his wallet. The coins in a chamois pouch, being both too heavy and bulky, would have to be put in his bag.

Standing in front of his open wardrobe, he had to work out which clothes to take, eventually deciding the garments suited for country pursuits would serve best. So, in they went, along with the envelope containing the duplicate notes, the brogue shoes, the lightweight plus-fours and woollen socks, as well as the fisherman's canvas waistcoat, several shirts, to which he would add his trench coat from cupboard in the hall.

The bathroom shelf was cleared into a travelling bag: razor, shaving soap, tooth powder and brushes for teeth and hair, as well as the smaller items needed to keep at bay hair that now grew too fast in the wrong places. The last items he recovered from the bedroom cupboard: his fishing rod, binoculars and a pair of Armas-Garbi side-by-side shotguns, these in a polished wooden case, including the necessary shot.

He emerged, parcel in hand, to find his two 'companions' standing in silence, not looking at each other or him. Had they spoken in his absence and, if so, what might they have been said? How might it affect him, given he doubted it would have been flattering?

Aviles could have told Houston of the original plan to dispose of him, which would complicate matters. He subjected his driver to a piercing stare to which he barely responded. But surely it would be the Scotsman who would let on? Could that be relied upon? Best to assume the worst, which did nothing to change the present situation.

'Aviles, my luggage is on the bed, please be so good as to take it down to the car.'

This brought another pause, not defiance, more confusion, forcing Rudi Graebner to tell the man how much difficulty he was in. Billy might not understand the Spanish words, but Leo's crestfallen expression was enough to give him the gist. In the last part, the man for whom he worked promised he would take care of the driver and his family would still be provided for. These also went over Billy's head, there being no change of expression. Leo looked less the hardened soldier now, more like man about to face a firing squad.

'Mr. Houston, it may be we will require a place not too far from London, a location where it will be possible to stay out of sight for a time. I suggest you consult the list you have and find us somewhere suitable.'

A sudden ring of the doorbell had Billy jerk in shock, rendering Leo pale enough to highlight his scars. Graebner answered the door himself, giving the concierge instructions regarding the delivery of his parcel, together with a five-pound note—much more than a day's earnings even for the busiest cabbie—to underline it must be handed over regardless of how long it took. If there was no one at home, he was to wait.

'The fellow must get written acknowledgement, and when I have it—.'

He didn't finish the sentence, merely flinging the man a knowing look, enough to imply he would be in receipt of an equally valuable gratuity once the task had been completed.

'It'll be seen to, sir, take my word on it.'

'I know you will not let me down.'

'So, my luggage?' he said as, having grabbed his trench coat, he reentered the drawing room.

Leo, having had time to think, must have seen there was no alternative and he moved. The German in turn indicated to Billy, who had his subscription notebook open in his hand, he should gather up his case and follow him to the lift.

'And on the way to the basement garage you may tell me where it is we have to go.'

'There's a place called Wisley in Surrey, home tae the Royal Horticultural Society where there's a sympathiser. A retired old fella I recruited to the cause and went to tea with a couple of times. He lives in an isolated cottage at the end of a quiet country lane.'

A pen was produced. 'Copy out the address for me in case we become separated.'

Billy unscrewed the fountain pen and scribbled the address, tearing out the empty back page from his notebook and handing it over, before following the German out of the front door.

More details were demanded as the lift descended: the location of Wisely and the nature of what went on there. Plant research, cross breeding and cultivation, the name of the contact and where his cottage stood in relation to the grounds.

All of which made Billy doubly curious when, once by the embassy car and sure there was no one waiting to arrest them, he told Leo to take them to Carlyle Square.

Thursday, July 25, 2:54 p.m.

The Duke of Alba was on edge. Not only was Sir John Simon more formal than his predecessor, Lord Halifax, the questions being posing were troubling. Even if he was prefacing them by such anodyne equivocations as '*we have reason to believe*' or '*our enquires tell us*', there was no doubt about the aim. It left room for him to admit he could, unknowingly, be harbouring in his embassy a man working on behalf of the enemy. Alba managed to deflect this by diplomatic obfuscation until Adam Strachan was brought in.

Introduced, he was subjected to close scrutiny, the ambassador taking in the Cary Grant type good looks and the well-cut clothing, but it was the steady grey eyes which proved the most compelling. When he smiled it had no warmth, but certainty the truth of what he went on to say was crisply delivered. Given this less elliptical approach, the ambassador immediately sensed the game was up, not that he contemplated surrender.

'Mr. Strachan, you must accept that if anyone under my tutelage has inappropriate associations they will, of necessity, be matters of which I would be unaware.'

'So, you know of no overt aid to our enemies?'

'None.'

'The driver Aviles?'

'I cannot say he is known to me at all. I never use the embassy drivers. I have my own car and personal chauffeur, who is a long serving family retainer.'

'You are, I'm sure, aware that some of your people use the facilities of the Eaton Club?'

'What, pray, is that?'

Examining the older man, of whose background he had certain knowledge, Adam couldn't help but be impressed by his demeanour. It was one of blue-blooded assurance, allied to natural noblesse. Elderly now, you could still discern traces of the handsome young man who had once been a staple in decades of high society photographs. Now his features had a chiselled aristocratic cast, while his hooded eyes seemed to suggest a hint of indolence. A grandee of Spain, descended from half the royal houses of Europe, including the last Stuart King of England, Freddie Alba spoke English with the facility of a well-born native, down to a laconic clubland drawl.

The holder of over forty titles, including the Dukedom of Berwick, he had moved in the highest political and patrician circles all his life, and it was obvious he was never going to be rattled into indiscretions. Yet it was necessary to edge him into a position in which, even if it was not visible, he would feel acute discomfort.

'We have a witness who assures us Aviles dealt with the American traitor, Tyler Kent.'

'Dealt with?'

'They met in the Eaton Club.'

A shrug of frustration obliged Adam Strachan to explain what it was and the service it provided, as well as who used it.

'Given Aviles station, we have every reason to believe he acted as a conduit to someone of higher standing within your embassy, the person who passed Kent's information on to the Germans.'

Alba swung his gaze to the government minister. 'These matters were aired before and I denied all knowledge of the business. Indeed, as I pointed out at the time, and I had reason to think I had been believed, the culprits came from the Italian Embassy.'

'We have more up-to-date information which renders that incorrect,' Simon replied.

'How sound is this information?'

'Irrefutable,' Adam assured him in response to a nod from Sir John to respond.

His certainty tested Alba's diplomatic skill to the core, for he dropped his head to break eye contact. '*Irrefutable*, young man, is a very strong word.'

'It's the only one that will suffice,' Simon said, before pausing for a second. 'I really must ask you to respond, Your Grace.'

Alba glanced at the foreign secretary again, then shrugged. Was it to accede, or to imply such matters were of no account? 'If what you imply took place at all, which I continue to strenuously deny, they were at no time officially sanctioned.'

Adam interjected forcefully. 'Which doesn't absolve you of responsibility,'

'Mr. Strachan,' Sir John intervened, 'while I appreciate your need to find out what has been going on, you must recall you're addressing the ambassador of a friendly nation.'

The word "friendly" stuck in the younger man's craw, but he'd been told why kid gloves were necessary with a potentially belligerent Spain.

'If I have spoken out of turn, please forgive me.' Alba inclined his head. 'But there's no doubt in this case about Spanish embassy involvement. What we now need is some assistance from you to pin down a person who will have already caused your embassy some embarrassment and is, probably at this very moment, actively engaged in causing a great deal more.'

'More?'

'We have reason to believe he's made contact with another person whose activities are inimical to the security of Great Britain and they are of a far more serious nature.'

Alba looked at Simon again, to be gifted with a very emphatic nod. 'What is this assistance you require?' he asked.

Again, Simon indicated it was for Adam to respond. 'That you waive immunity for any individuals we name, so we may question them as well as carrying out any searches deemed necessary, including within the embassy building.'

For a second the haughty demeanour cracked. It was only a tiny fissure, but it was significant. Adam hoped, by asking for such permissions, he would drive home to Alba the seriousness of the situation. How much easier it would have been to just tell him but that had been ruled out by Harker. Information on the loss of the National Defence Plan was not to be vouchsafed to a foreign ambassador.

'Do you have anyone in mind?'

'Two men in particular, apart from Aviles. Señor Rodriguez, your passport officer and the cultural attaché, Rodolfo de Bázan, though of course our enquiries might lead to others.'

Those hooded eyes flickered towards the ceiling. 'Why de Bázan?'

Alba wasn't going to pose any whys when it came to Rodriguez, his true function being no real secret, hence his desire to avoid eye contact.

'We suspect it was to de Bázan's home Aviles went this morning. He may have taken with him a man we're sure has committed two murders and has in his possession information which would be of great assistance to our enemies.'

'This man is?'

It was mere prevarication, so Adam stood his ground. 'His name would not be known to you, Your Grace, any more than that of Leo Aviles.'

'Sir John, prior to granting such a request, I wonder if I may be allowed to return to the embassy and institute my own enquiries?'

'We are not gifted with time,' was the reply.

'An hour?'

The foreign secretary, having checked with Adam, nodded as the ambassador stood up to leave. 'Let me accompany you to your car.'

This gesture got him a sharp look from Alba. There could only be one reason for such an offer from a man who was no more than an acquaintance: words to be spoken without record or witnesses. Both men departed, leaving behind a very frustrated Deputy Director of MI5. Right now, an hour could mean the difference between success and failure. When the Foreign Secretary came back, he addressed himself to Adam.

'I told him that if he doesn't help us, the matter is so serious we will, if forced, take over his embassy building and arrest every member of his staff, including himself.'

'And how did he respond, sir?'

'Like a diplomat, how else? For all his blue blood the man is as slippery as an eel.'

'Sir John,' Adam asked. 'We have a decent file on Carlos Rodriguez, but this de Bázan fellow is less well covered. I wonder if a signal could be sent to our embassy in Madrid, to fill out any information that might be relevant.'

The minister failed to respond immediately and Adam knew why. He was being asked to use the FO communications network for a task far from its remit. The proper avenue for such a request was through MI6. As a way of pointing up the competition which existed between the domestic and foreign intelligence agencies, it could hardly have been bettered. Adam was hinting if MI6 found out anything, they might try to act on it before sharing it with him or Harker.

'It would have to, of course, be flagged as most urgent.'

'Obviously,' Simon replied, but still, he didn't agree. He threw a glance at his permanent secretary, who had ben silent in the preceding conversations and was now equally unforthcoming.

'Sir, this is not just an intelligence matter. Our file indicates de Bázan is not a career diplomat, yet he has been given what has to be a top-level posting. This suggests he is very well connected to the Franco regime. One would imagine the social circles in which he must move, might bring him into contact with some of our embassy personnel. I merely wish some background that will shortcut what may well get bogged down by the notion of our sister service seeing it as a different kind of issue.'

'I'll do as you ask, Mr. Strachan, as long as you're aware there may be consequences.'

Meaning Sir Stewart Menzies would go through the roof. Given what Adam had so recently seen of the two together, he was far from sure Harker would protect him.

'For which I am ready to accept responsibility.'

'Any specific question?'

'General background, sir, anything that might help.'

The message regarding de Bázan had taken time to reach DCI Banks. He in turn had sought to find the file on the Spanish embassy personnel, to be told it was in the possession of Jocelyn Devereux, currently on his way back to MI5 HQ. A radio message was sent to turn the man round but, even with ringing bells, it took time before the Special Branch detective had the file in his hands. The fact de Bázan lived in a block of expensive flats not far from the embassy leapt out, and the only spare bodies were the MI5 pups.

'Right, you two, get round there and keep the place under observation. And don't get spotted.'

'We've been trained in what to do,' Sefton Avery replied, miffed at such basic advice. 'Thoroughly so.'

'Orders are clear from Mr. Strachan. Nobody to be touched until it is authorised by the FO.'

The pair rushed into position, one at each end of the street. Even so, they managed to miss the embassy car and its trio of occupants, albeit by less than a minute.

Thursday, July 25, 3:16 p.m.

Carlyle Square turned out to be a cul-de-sac in Chelsea, there being only one way in and out for motor vehicles. It consisted of three terraces of five-storey semi-detached town houses, overlooking a central garden, with lawns and ordered greenery. Evidence of affluence was apparent and not just from the buildings. It was also in the quality of the few cars sat in the square. Leo was ordered to pull up and park on the garden-side pavement.

'What's goin' on?' Billy demanded through the voice pipe, this from his seat alongside Leo. He'd not been allowed to share the rear compartment, which Graebner had made plain in the time it took Aviles to walk to the exit and search for surveillance. The fact it rankled with Billy Houston was obvious; that the German didn't care was equally so.

'We need to get out of London and I think it unwise to do so in daylight. This vehicle is foreign, luxurious and thus could be noticed, not least by the very obvious number plates. I decided to find a place where, if it cannot be hidden until it is dark, then at least it will not be too obvious. You will have observed it has only one way in and out and is home to residents who can still afford to run quality cars. The only other people coming and going are tradesmen. It also enjoys the advantage of two foot exits in an emergency.'

'Easy to block off, that tells me?'

'Only if there is reason to do so.'

'So we just sit here aw' day?'

'For you, I am afraid it may be the case, the same for Aviles. In a location such as this, a waiting chauffeur is not remarkable.'

'So where are you goin'?'

'To a house over the road where I have a friend.'

Billy followed Graebner's languid finger. 'Who's this friend?'

'None of your concern!'

'Why can we no come too?'

The German shook his head and clambered out, rattling something in Spanish to Leo through his open window, before talking across him to Billy. 'I have told Aviles to use the horn if there is trouble.'

'Then what?'

'Get away and make for Wisley, Mr. Houston, where we will meet up at the home of this Mr. Pyeworthy, you mentioned. I leave in your care for the maps and Aviles, too, who will need your aid, given his imperfect English.'

Graebner passed over a couple of five-pound notes. 'Do not use a main terminal. I suggest a taxi to a suburban station, then some kind of public transport.'

Then he was gone, crossing in front of the car to the house and practically skipping up the steps. Whoever opened the front door must have been waiting, given the rapid response to the knocker. Even straining forward, Billy couldn't see who it was. The German was inside and the door shut in a blink of an eye.

'Have you got any papers, Leo, aside from what ye get from the embassy?'

Billy's question got a shake of the Spaniard's head, accentuating his heavy, jet-black moustache, as well as the need he had already for a second shave. This took no account of the chauffeur's uniform: high buttoned jacket and shiny black boots, which would stick out a mile.

'Terrific. Well ah'll tell ye, if we're on a train or a bus pal, don't sit right by me.'

Leo produced a cigarette and lit up with the car's silver lighter, filling the compartment with the pungent smell of his rough foreign tobacco. Billy, a rare non-smoker, waved his arms furiously, then wound down his passenger window. In truth he was frustrated: to a man on the run, movement was reassuring. Sitting here was just the opposite.

'I cannae just park ma arse here 'aw day,' he coughed, 'especially if you're goin' tae puff away on that muck. I might go for a wander roond yon garden.'

Leo shrugged, which made Billy wonder if, left alone in the car, he might just take off. You didn't need to be a mind reader to sense he was miserable with his predicament. In the short time Graebner had taken to pack, Billy had asked Leo some very pointed questions but established almost nothing. The chauffeur wasn't going to open up to him, yet Billy had picked up his attitude to his boss was far from friendly. If Graebner couldn't see the looks aimed at his back, Billy did, which left him wondering about their relationship.

Was Leo a man to rely on? He was certainly someone you wouldn't want to be seen with in public: his features screamed foreign before he opened his mouth. Which led to the conclusion a man too dangerous to abandon might have to be disposed of. When Billy considered how it might be achieved, he was sure it would be far from easy. Leo would be no pushover.

But that applied to the whole situation. Trust not being a feeling to which Billy was much given, nothing Graebner had done so far made him someone with whom Billy felt secure. He wasn't going to rely on Leo either, leaving him with a sinking feeling, no matter which way he squirmed, he could not avoid descending even further into what looked like a quagmire. The notion of going for a walk would mean taking his suitcase, not a good idea in a square overlooked by hundreds of windows.

'Maybe best a stay put, eh! Just in case yer man wants us.'

Leo Aviles grunted, then exhaled a blast of smoke, thick enough to bring forth a protesting Scottish cough.

CHAPTER FORTY

Thursday, July 25, 3:18 p.m.

Rudi Graebner was wondering if the wild rutting in which he was engaged could be classed as comical. Clarissa Strathallan had always been an impatient paramour; not for her, slow foreplay followed by languid lovemaking. She had grabbed his crotch with one hand as soon as they clinched against the closed front door, her other hand dragging his down onto her breast, at the same time as her tongue investigated the inside of his mouth.

Now they were on the staircase, she with the loose dress she'd been wearing up around her waist—there had been no underwear—him humping, knees stuck on a tread of carpet, with his trousers round his ankles. Clarissa was gasping and pleading in what could not be a coupling of long duration, her panting breath turning into a series of rising moans, which became a long groan as she climaxed, shortly followed by him.

'Oh Rodolfo, I so needed that,' she purred, 'I was so angry with you last night.'

'I take it we are alone?' he gasped; his voice muffled by her shoulder.

Clarissa emitted a throaty laugh and, since he was still inside her, he could feel her muscles contracting. 'I was so desperate for a good rogering, I don't think I'd have cared.'

'No sign of Jack then?' he asked, pulling away and hauling up his underwear and trousers.

'On his way back in his silly little car,' Clarissa replied, lying in an indolent stupor, her eyes fixed on some point overhead. 'He telephoned to say he wouldn't be home for dinner, my sweet, which means I have time for more of you.'

She looked at him with seductive eyes and ran the tip of her tongue across her lips, letting him know what pleasures she had in mind. He held out his hand and hauled her to her feet, the dress falling to cover her legs.

'No maid either?'

'I gave her the rest of the day off after you called,' Clarissa turned away, leading him by the hand. 'Can't trust a servant not to gossip. She's gone to stay the night with her mother in some ghastly South London hovel. Now let's have lunch my sweet, and then——.'

It was a cold collation of meat and cheese, washed down with Hock and Seltzer. During the meal, Rudi was treated to an account of the Strathallan marriage more comprehensive than any to which he had been exposed before. He had guessed it was not one that could be described as fulfilled, which proved the case. She certainly had no great respect for her husband's fellow generals, being a source of gossip about their foibles and military prowess, of the kind he had been sent to London to gather.

Clarissa was an occasional indulgence; their couplings dependent on the movements, or rather absences, of husband Jack, so little time had been available for intimate conversation. Night clubs and noisy parties were not designed for talk of that nature, while she had never lingered in his apartment long enough for deep tête-à-têtes. He had mined her for information, of course, but when it came to the tactics which might have been employed by the British Expeditionary Force, she was useless, utterly indifferent to the whole subject.

'To tell you the truth, Rodolfo, I think Jack prefers to be away on his dratted tours of inspection just so he can be with his driver, who seems a nice boy.'

Graebner's expression was enough to make her laugh. 'He's not really that way, but he's so bally shy and not at all interested in sex, so it wouldn't shock me to find he is tempted by a possible bum boy at the wheel. Jack has never recovered from being at school, all that fagging, whipping and avoiding buggery if, indeed, he managed to do so. I knew he was like that when we married.'

'Then why do it?'

'He's damned handsome, well-connected and rich. I admit security played a large part in the arrangement. My family were in the City and our money went west after the Wall Street Crash, so I needed a roof over my head and a decent allowance. He needed a wife to advance his career on the social side and one who'd make few demands.'

'How dull.'

'As for my boudoir, he shies away from anything exotic. It's all thankfully brief. Once it's over, he scuttles back to his own bedroom clutching his pyjamas bottoms.'

Swallowing a piece of cheese, Clarissa continued in a more serious vein. 'Odd how jealous he becomes though, bloody furious if he thinks I am eyeing another man. It's damned annoying when he invites some of his junior officers to dine, every one a bachelor, some of them seriously dishy and very, very willing.'

'Have you--?'

'Good God, no! Handsome they might be and randy as hell, but they're also inclined to be serious, which would never do.' The horrified look she was giving him turned to one of enquiry. 'Had enough?'

'Of this, yes.'

She picked up her glass and drained it, murmuring huskily, eyes aimed at the ceiling. 'My bedchamber awaits.'

'Are you sure we have time?'

'Certain. Jack driver won't drop him off for hours yet and that's only if he avoids any hold ups.'

'And where might they occur?'

'Anywhere along the south coast, where he's doing his tour. You're not scared, are you?'

Deliberately taking the wrong connotation, he replied. 'I might ask to borrow a pair of Jack's pyjamas.'

That brought forth a peal of laughter, as she led him out of the dining room. 'Don't you bally well dare, Rodolfo. I want a rampart Spanish bull, not some nervous English schoolboy.'

The bedroom was feminine; flouncy drapes, pale, deep pile carpet and rather garish floral wallpaper. He was left alone as Clarissa disappeared, declaring she needed a pee. Another partly open door led to what looked like a dressing room and curious, Rudi looked in to see a second door at the far end, which he assumed led to the bedroom occupied by Jack.

On one side there hung a row of dresses and coats, with the shelving above bearing hat boxes and the floor below racked for shoes. The other side was full of men's clothing, tweeds and suits, including a bright red mess jacket, dress blues alongside several khaki uniforms and a British Officer's pale beige Warm. That was topped with hats of various kinds and bottomed by shoes and a pair of highly polished riding boots.

He had been aware since leaving his apartment the weariness he had felt earlier had gone, while neither the rutting nor the wine had diminished his newfound energy. Could it be down to the Pervitin pills? He was wide awake, alert and had a feeling of invincibility, his mind whirring as he contemplated what he saw before him. The flushing toilet sounded a warning, so, when Clarissa appeared, stark naked, he was already back in the middle of the room.

'Still fully clothed Rudi? Perhaps you're not a rampant bull after all.'

In two strides she was upon him, his hands going round her bare buttocks to pull her closer. Slowly she slid down his body until, on her knees, she began to unbutton his flies. Rudi's cock swung out to strike Clarissa on the cheek, bringing forth a gurgling hoot. This was muffled as she took him in her mouth, head rocking slowly to and fro, hand ringed around the base of his penis.

His mind was a confused melange of thoughts. It was impossible to think straight and, given Clarissa's skill, it seemed no time at all until he felt the stirrings in his groin of an approaching ejaculation. Clarissa sensed it, too, and stopped, wriggling her way up and planting her mouth on his. She broke away, intending to lead him to the bed so, when he slipped his arm around her neck, it occasioned no alarm. It was only as he drew her tightly into his own body and began to squeeze that Clarissa Strathallan got some inkling all was not as it should be.

Fixing her head with one arm just above the back of her neck, he applied all the pressure he could muster with the other, hooked under her jaw. The sudden jerk that broke it would have delighted his trainers in unarmed combat but what he found odd was the way it felt slightly euphoric. Slowly he lowered her body to the floor and checked she was dead. With another quick look at the contents of the joint dressing room, he turned and went downstairs.

CHAPTER FORTY-ONE

Thursday, July 25, 3:20 p.m.

The Duke of Alba found the drive back to the embassy exasperating. He knew there was no alternative but to offer up de Bázan—Aviles was of no account. The problem was how to do so while mitigating the effect on his mission and ensuring his personal view prevailed. For Spain to join the Germany and Italy would be a disaster both immediately and in the long term. Peace with Great Britain must be maintained, with the addition of financial aid for the broken Spanish economy.

He now regretted having dodged the consequences of the Tyler Kent affair, providing cover for a man for whom he personally had no regard. Yet furious though he was, he was also aware he'd been presented with little choice, any admission of culpability being out of the question.

Sending de Bázan away after the affair had died down was not, and he'd failed to act decisively. On arrival, the command that Carlos Rodriguez attend upon him at once was delivered in a brusque tone, which did not subside when the order was obeyed. The ambassador relayed what he'd just been through and his conclusion was blunt.

'Given you're going to have to answer for this to the British, I hope you have ready what you people call a cover story?'

'Answer to?'

'Can you not see what will happen? To merely remove the immunity of de Bázan is tantamount to admitting we know of his role here? And please do not pretend your true occupation in the embassy is any kind of secret. You have one task only now, Carlos, to convince the British de Bázan is truly Spanish and not just by birth. Also, if he has stepped beyond the bounds of his position, it is without your knowledge or mine. If they find out he's a serving German officer then—'

The duke threw up his hands, an indication it did not bear thinking about.

'You must cooperate with MI5 and convince them you will do anything in your power to help them. I last saw de Bázan coming into the embassy. If he's still here, he's not to be allowed to leave, this Aviles fellow likewise.'

'If they question him, he may tell them his true identity and of the arrangement with Admiral Canaris.'

'He will keep such information secret if he can, though our hosts are not beyond the use of questionable methods to find out what they need to know. It only matters if he tells them we knew. So, stick to his being of Spanish birth and deny any knowledge of how his appointment came about. I will do the same. In a very short time, I must phone Sir John Simon and inform him both you and de Bázan are available to be questioned.'

It was quickly established neither de Bázan nor Aviles were on embassy property, while a call to the attaché's apartment produced no response. In the time it had taken the ambassador to get back to the embassy, Adam Strachan had radioed ahead to redeploy his men. There was no need for subterfuge now, both ends of the mews were openly covered and so was the front entrance. The surplus officers had been moved to join the pair watching the apartment block, with orders to wait for permission to enter.

When the call came from Alba to say access had been granted, Adam was on his way to the embassy to interrogate Rodriguez. A radio message had him change his destination to find Eddie Banks outside the apartment building with a trembling concierge, who quickly established their man had obviously left in a hurry.

'Who searched?'

'Two of us, Mr. Strachan' Banks said. 'We were careful.'

He went on to describe the interior of the apartment and the open drawers and wardrobe. Given there were two dirty cups in the kitchen sink, there had been more than one person present at some time, presumably Aviles. No mention was made of any maps, so Adam had to assume they were not there, but he asked about papers just in case.

'I'd say anything which might be of value is gone with our bird.'

'Not to Hampstead,' Adam responded.

'It's such an old trick, the taxi thing,' Banks grunted. 'You'd think the Abwehr would have given up on it by now.'

'But what does it tell us?'

'Our man has very likely been trained by the Germans.'

'Prints?'

'Met bods are on their way.'

'Car?'

'Looked in the underground garage and the nearby streets. No sign.'

'We need the make and number.'

'Got it,' Banks replied pulling out a notebook. 'Hispano Suiza J12 plated with ESP4. I've been on to the Yard for an all points search.'

'If we find the car, we'll find our targets. We need the search to be in every part of the Home Counties within fifty miles of London and it will have to include the Military Police.' Seeing the response on the face of the detective, Adam was quick to add. 'Believe me, it's that important. I'm going back to the embassy to question their intelligence bod, not that I expect to get much out of him.'

'Any word on the Houston bloke?'

'Not yet.'

CHAPTER FORTY-TWO

Thursday, July 25, 4:05 p.m.

He was inside Clarissa Strathallan's house along with Leo Aviles and the luggage. The pair had been treated to a brief explanation of what Graebner had done, but with no clue as to why he had decided on murder as a solution to their difficulties. Billy hid any bewilderment he felt, able to persuade himself, given their ultimate goal, it was as necessary an act as the killing of Bettina Wyvern.

How easy it was to become immune to it, something of which he had never before been guilty, if you excluded the Great War trenches. There death and mutilation, at first horrifying, became commonplace and unremarkable, a place where you had to close your heart and head to pity.

Leo, quizzed, admitted to being even less troubled by the woman's death. A one-time mass executioner, he related to Billy how, as well as their menfolk, he had shot Republican women during the civil war. But and this was added with what passed for glee from such a taciturn creature, only after they had been repeatedly raped.

'Is that right,' was Billy's guarded response.

'Women spoiled break soldier's heart and babies not their own soon born.'

'Where ah was, we never got the chance, pal.'

The first task, according to Rudi Graebner, was to get rid of the embassy car, now too dangerous to have parked outside. Enquiries from Billy as to how he was planning to hide something so obvious induced a flash of irritation. The German was thinking on the hoof, just as he had been when he broke his mistress's neck. In his mind he was behaving like an officer faced with the need to react rapidly in combat, which would have been the case if he'd had had a proper plan in the first place.

It was Leo who finally provided a solution. The embassy sent what was a French-built car to the cavernous and iconic Michelin Tyre building in the Fulham Road, to have the tyres checked or changed. It could therefore be a perfect hiding place. He would have liked to send Aviles, but he could not risk him vanishing, nor did he relish the notion of leaving Billy Houston on his own. Thus, he was obliged to leave them both and to drive the car himself.

'What happens if anybody comes tae the door?'

'Don't answer it! I will be back as soon as I can.'

The drive, even with a couple of security diversions, was not much over a kilometre, while the large open-fronted building was easy to access. Driving straight it and making sure he parked out of sight of the street, he hurried to the desk, asking for all four wheels to be checked and any worn rubber replaced. At the very same moment a policeman was making a call to the station from a police box on the corner of Sloane Avenue and Fulham Road. This, and it applied to every one of his uniformed colleagues, was done at regular intervals while walking his beat.

If he struggled, with his stub of a pencil, to spell Hispano Suiza, he had no trouble with such a simple plate number as ESP4 and his orders were straightforward. If he spotted the car, he was to stay clear and call in with its whereabouts. Emerging from the stifling interior of the box, he observed a blond fellow in a pale linen suit outside the Michelin building, furiously hailing a passing taxi, to clamber aboard as it came to a halt.

'Cadogan Arms on the King's Road.'

'Pub's shut now, Guv,' the driver replied.

'I know,' Rudi growled, before he realised such a tone was inappropriate for a passenger who was reluctant to be remembered. 'But I thank you for pointing it out.'

The journey took less than ten minutes and, having got out and paid, he crossed the King's Road to head down Old Church Street until he was sure the taxi had gone, before spinning round to retrace his steps. It had become imperative to know what risks he faced, if indeed there were any. A telephone box at the junction allowed him to ring the embassy, to be answered by the switchboard girl who, once he had identified himself, put him straight through, without being asked, to Carlos Rodriguez.

'Rodolfo.' The voice sounded pleasant and relaxed. 'Are you coming back to the embassy today?'

The temptation to probe, to play the espionage chief's game, had to be resisted, even if Rudi thought him an idiot, an opinion just proven by his utter lack of subtlety. Without replying, he slammed down the phone and left the box. He forced himself to walk at a normal pace as he assessed what had just occurred, heading for one of the two pedestrian footpaths at the bottom of Carlyle Square.

There was no other conclusion to reach: he was now a fugitive and so were his companions. What had been a safety measure in coming to Clarissa's house, now looked like a very narrow escape.

Thinking on how to proceed only had one result; the emergence of an endless series of obstacles, the major one being where to go from a place in which they could not securely stay and how to get there. That, right now, rested on a hope not a certainty?

After a full circuit of the central garden to ensure he was not being followed, he crossed the road and approached the door. Rapping on the knocker and getting no response, he realised he was bound by his own injunction not to answer and, annoyingly, this obliged him to shout both names through the letter box. The door was opened by Billy, Leo being by the staircase, holding one of Rudi's shotguns, which he assumed was loaded.

'A wise precaution,' was all he said as he passed Aviles, who had failed to lower a barrel aimed squarely at his chest. 'The embassy car, you will both be glad to know, is out of sight.'

'What happens now?'

'We wait, Mr. Houston.'

'Fur what?'

'Circumstances which may work out in our favour. In the meantime, there is food in the house, so I suggest if you have not done so already, you eat.'

'There's drink an' aw', the cellar's full o' stuff.'

A questioning look got the information from the Scotsman how he knew; the naked body of his lover had been placed there.

'Drinking is best avoided.'

'I saw the half empty bottle on the table, so I can guess you had a right good slurp.'

'I did so, but in the cause of duty.'

Later, sat at the same table, eating some bread and cheese washed down with water, he set himself to studying Billy's book of contacts, concentrating on the pages the corners of which Houston had turned down. He began to cross-reference them with the requisite maps to mark out anything that looked promising from what seemed to be numerous possibilities. In truth, the options were limited, given whatever he scrutinised had to have certain features, not least it being within reasonable striking distance of the south coast.

Ranging between Worthing and Bognor Regis seemed to provide several candidates, Houston having acquired many followers in the area. Quite a few, to varying degrees, were not far short of the Channel waters, but increased study had Graebner discard them. Too many lived in sizeable urban communities which were inherently dangerous. With others, the coast they occupied showed a series of enclosed beaches, often backed by heights and isolated by headlands.

Even less appealing, such beaches had to be accessed by a single-track road, while the symbols on the map indicated the presence of pill boxes and anti-tank defences, this in area the British thought as suitable for a landing. He doubted the pill boxes were fully manned, they might not even be built, but such features made it perilous.

Moving further west he examined the coastal area south of Chichester and immediately saw it as more suitable: a mass of small bays and inlets, numerous little harbours and beach-fronted marshland. It was useless for any kind of mechanised warfare, while also being unsuitable ground for a beach landing and infantry assault. The lack of symbols showed the British agreed, it being short on the things needed to mount a stout defence.

The rest was tedious and time consuming. The residence of each of Houston's old contacts in the area had to be located and examined for suitability and many, if they looked promising, also came with difficulties.

Too far from the sea, too close to decent sized habitation, on the road and not an isolated dwelling like farmhouse, difficult to access. Elimination brought him to the most promising, several others being listed in order of potential. When he called for Houston to join him, it did not occur to Graebner to explain his thinking; he merely stabbed at the map and posed an abrupt question.

'Your book tells me you recruited a contact, Mr. Houston, in a place called East Lavant. A Mrs. Jean Milburn?'

Billy followed the finger, but paused and drew breath before replying in the affirmative. Graebner wasn't looking at the Scotsman, nor was he interested in his tone of voice. He thus missed the slightly reticent note in acknowledgement of the name.

'Tell me about it and her?'

'Small village. Farming country, a kirk and two pubs, old coaching inns and some folk who take the bus to work in Chichester.'

'And the lady?'

Jeannie was the proprietor of one of those inns, running it on her own and tough-minded enough to do so. Married, she had been rendered a widow by a husband so bent on drinking away the profits of his inherited pub, so he'd gone to an early grave.

'She sounds to be a person of competence.'

'She ran a good group of supporters. Strong in the cause, she was.'

'Do you think she might be willing to help us?'

The response was cautious. 'Ah'm no absolutely sure she will still willing to aid the cause.' He meant him.

'Do you have a better suggestion, someone who would be amenable and is as well situated?'

'Is she well situated?'

It was a barely patient German who explained why he'd come to his conclusion, as usual irritating Billy, so the admission of the truth was even slower in coming: for what they needed, the village of East Lavant looked perfect, though he did wonder how they were going to get there.

'Good, then that is the basis on which we will plan.'

'And if it fails?'

Graebner waved Billy's book. 'Then we will seek an alternative, of which I have marked several.'

Thursday, July 25, 4:58 p.m.

Adam Strachan was kept waiting for nearly an hour before he could question Carlos Rodriguez.

During this time, he was told of the aborted phone call from a West London phone box, picked up by a Signals Corp listener, untraceable due to the brevity of the exchange, but passed straight on as instructed. Even with so very few words spoken, it told the recipient a great deal, which made the waiting even harder.

He also got a message regarding the American woman he had been with the night before. She had called MI5 HQ, saying she wanted to talk to him, leaving her number and mentioning knowledge of a threat national security. Supposed to be a secret number, he had to wonder how she'd got it. At the HQ switchboard, the same question was aired, as was the gossip and giggling about what the Deputy Director might be up to.

Right now, he had too much on his plate, but he would have to follow it up. That said, he resolved he must, if the reason for her message was a blind for some kind of second night out, be stand-offish. He was, after all, a married man.

The interview with Rodriguez finally took place in the Spaniard's office, the plaque on the door saying *Pasaporte Oficial*, which got a jaundiced look from Adam. Rodriguez chose to sit behind his desk and, since it was now late-afternoon, Adam had the sinking sun right in his eyes, shining through the large southwest facing window behind the man he was about to question.

Rodriguez was as thin as a rake, with a suit jacket which seemed to hang off his shoulders, his face likewise gaunt, the cheeks hollow and the nose as sharp as the widow's peak above it. But the eyes, under pencil thin brows, on a high forehead, were steady and unblinking. As each question was posed, there was an extended pause before an answer, usually a negative, came in heavily accented English.

Adam knew it to be a fabrication, even if he had no idea what parts were true and what was invention, all a bit too pat and obviously rehearsed. Rodriguez was also adept at avoiding any of the little traps being set and it would not do. The matter was too important, yet the man doing the interrogating was at a loss as to how to change matters.

The knock at the door was unwelcome and when opened revealed Sefton Avery holding a piece of paper, which had written on it a transcribed message. There was no need to say the matter was urgent, the youngster would never have dared interrupt otherwise. Rodriguez responded to Adam's apology with a shrug as he crossed to the door and read the message.

From the Foreign Office, the information it contained was quite categorical in the way it underlined a thought at which Adam had already arrived. Rodriguez was lying, but short of thumb screws and electrodes attached to his private parts, nothing would get him to admit it. Simon and his PS might lecture him about respecting Spanish sensitivities, but they weren't the people who would be pilloried for failure to get back the National Defence Plan. Desperate times required extreme measures.

'Señor Rodriguez, I wonder if I might speak with you bluntly.' The thin eyebrows arched slightly. 'I can assure you it would be in the interests of both yourself and your embassy, given what I'm required to deal with is likewise unusual. The German army holds the French, Belgian and Dutch channel ports and my country is under the threat of invasion. Can I add, while it's possible to continue this interrogation here, given your immunity has been waived, I could insist on it taking place somewhere less comfortable?'

There was no immediate reply, but Adam was sure the Spaniard got the drift. If the British claimed to be pure in regard to torture, anyone in the community these two men shared knew this to be pie in the sky.

Rodriguez had to be curious as to what was contained in the message just delivered, for it had changed the whole tone of the questioning.

Adam sat down once more, shifting his chair to avoid the glare of the sun, as well as the heat generated by the glass. He then fixed his man with a direct look.

'Who is Rodrigo de Bázan?'

'I have told you—'

'Nothing, Señor Rodriguez, which I do not resent as it's your function.' Adam waved the note. 'This is from our embassy in Madrid. It seems no one there has heard of anyone of that name.'

'Which proves little.'

'Except the ambassador had his senior aides rung round the other legations. No one amongst their counterparts in other embassies has heard of him either. So, who is he really, this man, who seems to have fled from his apartment in a great hurry?'

'*Fled?*'

'De Bázan is on the run, for which there can only be one explanation. I must tell you, since you are known to be responsible for spying, it is you who will bear the consequences. I will arrest you and take you to a place where, when one of my people asks a question, it is generally answered truthfully.'

'The Duke of Alba . . .'

'Will be rendered persona non grata and sent back to Madrid. Furthermore, I wouldn't be surprised if what has taken place is seen as an act of war.'

The silence lasted several seconds before Rodriguez responded, having mulled over the alternatives. 'I must consult with my superior.'

'Please do.'

'And then I think he may contact the Foreign Office.'

Given it sounded like the promise of an honest answer on de Bázan, Adam concurred. Anything imparted to them would come to him at HQ, which applied to all sources of information. This was quickly proved, even before he could sit down in his office, by the Metropolitan Police.

'Mr. Naylor?' Adam replied, when the policeman was once more came on the line.

'There is something I wanted you to hear from my lips.'

'Which is?'

'Given this is a murder enquiry, any information related to Billy Houston, in any way, would naturally be passed to my office. Such facts have just reached my desk a half hour past.'

'Go on.'

There was a short pause before Naylor said. 'The search of that apartment in Cadogan Place.'

'Yes.'

'Billy Houston's dabs were all over it, dirty cups and more in the hallway cloakroom.'

'Thank you, Mr. Naylor.'

'Just cooperation, which is what you asked for.'

'Has this been passed to Special Branch?'

'I thought it best to contact you for approval first. Do you wish me to do it?'

'No, leave it to me.'

CHAPTER FORTY-FOUR

Thursday, July 25, 6:45 p.m.

Having decided on East Lavant, Graebner quizzed Billy regarding the best route. The Scotsman ticked off, on his fingers, the towns he had so many times passed through. This had the German referencing them on the map and working out distances, the other two left to watch until boredom had them sit down.

As the afternoon had worn on, Billy begun to feel the same frustrations indoors as he had waiting in the car, this not helped by the chiming hall clock and the softly playing wireless. Both marked the passage of several wasted hours, to which was added the frustration of not knowing what was supposed to come next.

Graebner had seated himself close to a net-curtained window overlooking the street. The map of the coastal parts of East Sussex and Hampshire, as well as the Isle of Wight, lay open on his lap. The ashtray by his side was filling with half-finished cigarettes, while his pistol was within reach on the table beside his chair.

He emitted an occasional yawn but, if he appeared relaxed, Billy guessed he was far from being so. Seated apart and contemplating their own uncertainties, did nothing to induce confidence, quite the reverse, it allowed for fertile imaginations to do their work.

An occasional glance at the German provided no clues but had he been mind reader, Billy would have been seriously troubled for, unbeknown to him, Graebner was not even seeking a way to get to the Isle of Wight. Just getting to the south coast would be perilous enough and, once there, the difficulties of such a proposed course only multiplied a thousandfold.

Much better to think of finding a way to make for the recently occupied Channel Islands and this he probably must do alone.

Left for future solution was how this was to be achieved and there was no simple answer. The first task would be to detach himself from his two unwelcome companions. He hoped it could achieved without violence, but it was easy to imagine elimination as the solution. If it came to that, would it be too much to hope one would cancel out the other, leaving him with either Houston or Aviles. His preference was for the embassy driver, who would be easier to deal with.

All he could reasonably hope for was a sudden opportunity to effect a quiet separation. But first he must get to where he needed to be, then find one of the small engine-driven boats of the kind he needed, those used for off-shore fishing. These would have been drawn up on the strand in peacetime, but would no longer be there. The beaches were laid with tank obstacles and barbed wire, many stretches also heavily mined and had been barred to civilian use since the outbreak of war.

This raft of difficulties accepted, Graebner was determined to find a way to succeed, given the prize on offer. If he saw the possibility of dying in the attempt to get the maps into the hands of his fellow-countrymen, he could also see the certainty in merely giving way to despair and a meek surrender. The end of hangman's rope or a dozen bullets from a firing squad.

Leo Aviles was in an equally reflective mood, which grew increasingly gloomy at each ding of the chimes, sinking ever lower in an armchair as he gnawed on his thoughts. The death of the owner of the house meant totally burnt boats, while the man who had set them alight and had dragged him into this situation was now sat in silence.

Despite any assurance and, just like most officers he had met, he knew this one would care little about his survival. Occasionally Leo's hand would reach out for the loaded shotgun leaning by the chair, fingering the elaborate engraving on the jointing between the stock and the barrel. Billy noticed each time he did this and so did the German, who stiffened and moved his own hand closer to his pistol.

The shadows of evening had covered the garden square before Graebner finally moved. He stood up, stepping back from the window, before slipping a sliver of net aside and peering out for a couple of seconds and saying softly, 'Danke Gott'. He then crossed to Billy, handing him the map.

'Put this back in your case, Mr. Huston. Aviles, take your shotgun into the hallway. Stay well back under the staircase, out of sight of the front door. Come out when I call, but do not shoot unless you have to. We do not want the noise.'

Then he turned back to Billy again. 'I suggest you stay where you are, Mr. Houston.'

'You could give me the other shotgun.'

'Too late now,' Graebner said as Leo moved to obey, albeit with little enthusiasm.

CHAPTER FORTY-FIVE

Thursday, July 25, 7:13 p.m.

Rudi took station behind the slightly open door to the drawing room, as the muffled sound of slamming car doors came in from the street, soon followed by the rasp of the front door key, then an echoing shout.

'Clarissa, my dear, I'm home.'

The next voice was respectful. 'Shall I take your kit upstairs, sir?'

The reply was clipped. 'No Walters, just leave it there for now, most of it is destined for the laundry room.'

'Permission to use the facilities, sir.'

The repeated shouts for Clarissa were louder before the driver got a reply. 'You know where they are.'

The ranker's boots echoed on the polished wooden floor as he made his way towards the door leading to the basement. This brought him abreast of Leo and his shotgun, where he stopped dead. At the same moment Rudi stepped out to find Major General Jack Strathallan, briefcase and swagger stick laid down, removing his service webbing. This included his pistol, secure in its canvas holster, while the driver's rifle stood behind the door and out of reach.

'What the ...'

'Please continue, General Strathallan.' Leo had stepped out to cover the driver, who now had his hands raised. 'And order your man to remain still.'

'Who the hell are you?'

'Shall we say a family friend,' Graebner responded. 'Mr. Houston, you may join us and clear away the weapons.'

Billy emerged into the hallway, to see a tall, patrician looking soldier, dressed in tailored battledress, hatless, with his hands raised. His cap was hanging on a hook and right away Billy recognised the bright red band of a staff officer. At the foot of the rack lay a battered briefcase. Closer to, before he bent to take up the webbing, he observed the penetrating blue eyes and silver hair, aquiline nose and high cheekbones. The face, added to the look of pure disdain, brought to mind some of the members of the Right Club. To an ex-WW1 sergeant, the bastard had Brigade of Guards written all over him.

'Where's my wife?'

'Safe, and so will you be as long as you do as I say,' Graebner replied.

Billy had the pistol, webbing and rifle now, a .303 Lee Enfield, the weight and feel bringing back memories of fighting a war. Graebner stood to one side and waved his Walther at the drawing room, indicating the general should enter, before issuing orders in Spanish to Leo, followed by a word to the baby-faced young driver.

'You may use what you call the facilities, my man. We would not want you to disgrace yourself. The fellow with the shotgun will escort you and please, be warned, not to try anything.'

He followed Strathallan into the drawing room with Billy, bringing up the rear. The Scotsman laid aside the rifle and extracted the Webley to check the safety, all the time watched by the owner of the house.

'I don't know what it is you want . . .'

'Please let us not go through what you English call a rigmarole. Perhaps if I tell you I am a German officer it will still your tongue.' The shock was palpable; what was a fairly bloodless face to begin with was rendered the colour of parchment 'You are attached to the War Office and have just returned from a tour of inspection of the defences on the South Coast.'

If the general wasn't going to ask how he knew, Graebner had no intention of leaving him to wonder. 'Your wife was most obliging in telling me the nature of your travels.'

'I know you. I've seen you before.'

'I believe Clarissa introduced us once, at the Café Royal.'

'De Bázan, Spanish embassy,' came after a short pause.

'Sadly, for you, a masquerade.' He aimed a quick glance at the basement door, where there was no sign yet of Aviles, the next words said in a quiet, even voice. 'I am Oberleutnant zur See, Rudolph Graebner of the Kreigsmarine, at present serving with the Abwehr.'

'A damned spy!' Graebner shrugged as Strathallan warned, his voice firm and threatening. 'When you are caught, and you will be, you'll be shot.'

Leo then appeared, giving a quick nod to a questioning look from the German. Billy understood it and so, it seemed, did the general.

'Where's Walters?'

'Somewhere where he cannot help you. Now you have been carrying out certain duties.'

'I want to see my wife.'

'You will be allowed to join her in due course. But first oblige me by telling me of the places you have visited and what you observed.'

'Like hell I will.'

Graebner turned to Billy. 'The maps. Get them out and let us see what our Major General makes of them.'

Billy's suitcase had been set down by the fireplace and he passed, unarmed now, within a few feet of Strathallan to retrieve it. The general lashed out with his boot, catching him on the shin, which provoked an anguished yelp, off-balancing him completely. Shooting out of his chair, Strathallan had his fists balled to strike. Too much of a street fighter to hang about, Billy dropped and rolled out of the way as Graebner stepped in to swipe his attacker with his pistol butt.

Strathallan took the blow and recoiled, blood spurting from the wound. Undeterred, he ducked his head and charged, hitting the German in the midriff and driving him backwards as he tried to strike him again. The armchair behind Graebner took the back of his knees and he collapsed with Strathallan raining blows on top of him. Leo leapt forward and smashed the shotgun down on the man's head with a sickening thud. He slumped on to Graebner, so Leo grabbed the general's collar and pulled him clear, to drop him on to the floor beside Billy.

'Check if he's still alive, Mr. Houston.'

Billy, staring into those blue eyes, was back in the hallway with Group Captain de Vries. How many murders was he becoming involved in?

His voice cracked. 'If he's no dead he's no long for this world.'

'Then I require one of you to make sure.'

'What about the maps?' Billy asked as Leo, sensing Scottish reluctance, leant down to squeeze any remaining life out of Strathallan.

'That is a pity, it would have been good to have them acknowledged as accurate.'

Graebner, dabbing at the blood on his suit with a handkerchief, wore the slight smile which rankled so with Billy. The man was such an arrogant bastard.

'Search his pockets, Mr. Houston, while I examine his briefcase.'

'A please wouldn'a go amiss.'

'I have no time for such things,' Graebner snorted, as he left the room.

He was out in the hallway for a while, rifling through papers, returning to inform his companions they were Strathallan's reports. These listed the state of preparedness of the defences from Hythe to the exposed beaches fronting Dungeness. Troop dispositions were seriously under strength, while the artillery lacked the number of shells and the experienced troops required to man them. Anti-aircraft batteries were being taken over by women to release men for the field guns, but they, being untrained, could hardly be said to be effective.

'All a very useful addition to your maps, Mr. Houston.'

'Ah've found his pay and ration books. Fancy a general carrying the same as a private soldier, eh?'

'Do I see you also have his watch?'

The tone was disapproving. Billy ignored it. 'He dis'na need it. So, what now?'

'Thanks to my ability to see ahead, we have, out in the street, what I had anticipated and waited for. A general's official car and uniforms into which we can perhaps change.' Graebner was feeling smug and it showed in both his expression and his voice. He held up another bit of paper with an air of triumph, before ramming it into his pocket. 'Added to which, we have a document that will get us through any roadblocks.'

Then he turned and spoke to Leo in Spanish and the driver left the room, this as Graebner observed the doubts on Billy's face.

'I asked Aviles to take the driver's body to the wine cellar. If there is any blood, he is to ensure there are no traces left. So now you and I must take the general's body there also, but not before we bind the wound on his head with something from the kitchen.'

A tea towel found and applied, dragging one arm each. They were halfway across the drawing room when Graebner asked Billy if he could drive. The recipient's first reaction being the question, like the truth of his rank and position, had both been posed out of earshot of Leo. Were such absences deliberate? They exchanged looks and several seconds of silence until Billy finally said.

'Had a few goes once or twice in a pal's wee motor,'

'Would you say you're capable of driving a car?'

'I wound'na want to swear tae it without having a go.'

'The driver's uniform is about your size; it would provide for you a good disguise.'

'Ah had a wee look upstairs when you were out, Mein Herr. Must say ah fancied getting myself dolled up as a general.'

Graebner entirely missed the irony and reacted acerbically. 'It would serve our cause better if you were to be serious. Having the general's car and a uniform is only half of what we need. Before we even think of moving, your hair must be cut. Also, both you and Aviles will have to forgo the moustache.'

'That'll cheer him up. Christ, is he no miserable enough already?'

'Am I required to explain it is necessary none of us attract unwanted attention?'

'Course not.'

'Good! As soon as it begins to get dark, we will be on our way.'

'Do I get to have a say in this?' Billy barked.

'What purpose would it serve?' was the indifferent reply.

Dragging the body was somewhat easier on a polished floor and Leo was on hand to help Billy get it down the basement stairs. This left Rudi Graebner to allow the relief he felt and had kept hidden to surface. But quickly he had to wonder about a whole set of fresh problems, not the least the pass he had found in the general's briefcase would serve as he had implied. Leo was sent out to check the petrol in the tank, able to report it was nearly full, allowing the German to put bones on what had been, up till now, no more than a possibility.

'Time to put on our disguises,' he said, with an officer-like look at Billy and Leo. 'Aviles will cut your hair Mr. Houston and we all must shave to look like soldiers. I suggest you use the cloakroom and maid's facilities in the basement. I will use the bathroom upstairs.'

'Hear that, Leo? We're Other bloody ranks, the lowest of the low. We don't get to piss in the officer's lavvy.'

With Leo looking confused, Graebner glared at Billy, picked up his grip, left the room and began to ascend the stairs. This took him back to Clarissa's boudoir where a glance in the mirror convinced him he looked as weary as he now felt. The effects of the added dose of Pervitin had worn off and, with it, the sense ensuing problems could be overcome. He needed a feeling of resilience, both to proceed and carry with him the burden of Houston and Aviles. Another couple of pills were a necessity.

Once washed and shaved, he had the pick of what he required from the male side of the dressing room.

Thursday, July 25, 9:03 p.m.

Messing about with a swagger stick, his mood restored, Rudi did not look quite as elegant in the tailored khaki uniform as the man to whom it had belonged. Two inches in height made a difference, while the red-banded hat, with his less fulsome locks, was slightly too large. Billy, with his hair cut in the prescribed military fashion, showing his ginger roots and facial hair removed, looked every inch the squaddie cum Royal Army Service Corps driver Walters had been.

Leo, shorn of a moustache he had sported most of his life, was positively ugly, like some villain out of a B-film. It was made more gruesome because, where the growth had been was now a pale strip over his upper lip, skin that had not seen the sun since his balls had dropped. His disguise was no more than the standard issue waterproof cape, the only thing which fitted his shoulders, plus a forage cap. It was hoped would look suitably military in the dark.

Graebner, while shaving, had wondered about the Strathallan maid and decided not to mention her existence. He recalled what Clarissa had said about her staying the night with her mother, but one fact was clear. She was bound to return in the morning and waiting to silence her was too dangerous to contemplate. The bodies of all three victims were now laid out on the floor of the wine cellar, the door locked, any evidence of how they had died having been cleaned up. Strathallan's blood had stained the fireplace as well as the armchair in a way impossible to fully eradicate.

Leo had raided the pantry and, as soon as twilight provided decent shadow, the food was placed in the boot of the general's car, where he had also found two sets of standard issue British Army rations and the driver's kitbag, along with his full webbing including front and backpack. The quality of the car, a Hillman, was an object of derision, until Graebner reasoned more suitable vehicles for high-ranking officers had been abandoned in France and would now be transporting his fellow-countrymen. Billy's battered suitcase went into the boot, along with the German's grip, trench coat, shotgun case and fishing rod. Graebner would keep the general's briefcase with him. The driver's rifle fitted into a spring clamp fitted to the dashboard.

After a last look round, and sure it was now near enough dark, Graebner pronounced himself satisfied with the state of the light and, noiselessly shutting the front door, they set off. The Hillman Deluxe 16 was painted in dun khaki and fronted, just above the white painted bumpers, by the general's rank insignia, with the crossed swords and crowned lion of the British Army. Leo took the wheel, Billy beside him in the passenger seat.

If Aviles looked odd, and he did in a too small forage cap, this had to be accepted, given it would look even more so for a general staff officer to drive himself. Carlyle Square was no place to test the skill of Billy Houston behind the wheel either.

'Drive carefully, Aviles, we cannot have any attention drawn to us.' Reverting from Spanish to English. 'Mr. Houston, please direct Aviles to this place you call Wisley.'

'Do we need tae go there now?'

'We do.'

No explanation for this being provided, Graebner registered the grunt from the frustrated Scotsman, one he again ignored. They required somewhere discreet to test Billy's driving ability and this clearly couldn't take place on a public road. Wisley, as described, sounded eminently suitable, being off the main road and quiet during the hours of darkness. South of Guilford there could be checkpoints and when these were approached, it must be the Scotsman at the wheel.

How long might it take? Too lengthy and the idea of getting inside the restricted coastal zone in one night shrank, and it was an area where they were bound to encounter Military Police on high alert. The only way to approach was in darkness, with weapons at the ready to blast a way though if it couldn't be done by subterfuge.

'Has this goin' tae Wisley got anything to do wi' what you said about me driving the car?'

'A clever deduction, Mr. Houston.'

An unhappy grumble came from behind the wheel and, aware that the Spaniard couldn't pose the question himself, Billy did so for him.

'And what does Leo do?'

'He lies on the floor, covered by a travelling rug and hopes to remain unseen.'

'And if he is?'

'Then he will have to use the shotgun. Now, please, enough of these questions. It is time to go.'

A sharp order had Aviles move, with an occasional grinding gear as the Spaniard adjusted to the car, not least the gear lever being on the wrong side. His speed had to be slow, constrained as it was by the fading light: they had nothing more than the two slits in the regulation headlight covers to illuminate both the road ahead and other vehicles, mostly buses. He proceeded at a slow pace, keeping a sharp eye on the new white lines, which marked the centre of the carriageway and any road junctions.

There were no road signs for what had been the A3, these removed to frustrate an invader, but at least they were on the west side of London and a main trunk road out of the capital. It was blessedly free from the kind of roadblocks set up by over-enthusiastic members of the newly formed Local Defence Volunteers. These, too many by far, were heartily condemned by the newspapers as making life miserable for the average citizen.

'It's no far from here,' Billy advised, as they ran out of the Kingston suburbs in a line of sluggish-moving vehicles, a certain amount of moonlight illumination their outlines. 'Who knows, they might have left their sign up on the roadside. The Wehrmacht is no likely to be interested in plants and flowers.'

Sat in the back, Rudi Graebner was ruminating once more on a whole host of possible dangers. He was relying on the boards on the front of the Hillman, really a major general's crossed swords and pip, to get him through on nothing but military deference, with the pass Strathallan had as a back up. If the Scotsman could manage the task of driving, it would give them a chance. But then Aviles would become not only surplus to requirements, but possibly a dangerous liability. God help them if he was ever forced to open his mouth in the presence of a policeman, military or civilian. Reflecting of previous thoughts, this was not the time to do anything about it.

If they made it through to end up close the coast and in a position to put his own personal aim into effect, would a point arise at which Houston also became more of a danger than an asset. In such a case having Aviles along would be helpful? He was aware he might not be alone in such musings, not being fool enough to think the Scotsman was the trusting sort. He was also damn certain Aviles was wondering what was to become of him.

He, at least, had to do as he was told. Rudi had to hope Houston would see he had little possibility of getting anywhere near any German Armistice delegation, maps or no maps, without his assistance. He would thus stay obedient as long as he believed that was the plan. The problem would arise, and this would apply to both of them, the moment they realised the true intention. Looking at the back of their heads, he patted the webbing holster at his side, his own automatic nestling in one of the deeper side pockets in his trousers.

Wondering how and if they might come into play, he found himself thinking about a book he had read called the *Der Schatz de Sierra Madre*. That too was about a trio of desperate men in search of a secret goal, in their case, a source of gold, with all its shifting alliances and deceits. A lack of trust had led to eventual killing, which revived the concern he had harboured in his apartment.

Had Aviles alerted Houston to his possible disposal? His driver was so phlegmatic, it was hard to tell what he was thinking, but not the Scotsman. From the little he had seen of Houston he would not have been able to avoid reference to such knowledge. The devil in Rudi, as well as a way of issuing a warning, had him asking Billy if he had read the book, for it had been published in both English and German.

171

'*Treasure of the Sierra Madre?*'

'Written by a B. Traven, not his actual name. No one ever found out his true identity. It was suspected he was German and famous, but wished to remain incognito.'

'No ma sort o' thing. Facts are what I like, stories like yon are for bairns.'

Bairns had to be explained to a German. 'I am curious to know what your taste is, when it comes to reading.'

'*Mein Kampf* and the like. What else?' He leant forward to peer through the windscreen as the moonlit road. 'Steady Leo, the road we want is on the right and we must be getting close.'

Thursday, July 25, 9:52 p.m.

With a moon not yet fully risen, Leo nearly missed the turn, forced to make a sharp right as Billy yelled to warn him. The car behind braked with its horn blaring, and they narrowly avoided a collision with an army lorry trundling north. The lane which led to Wisley was shrouded by a canopy of trees, cutting out much of the overhead light, with barely enough glow to pick out the painted white rings on the tree trunks lining the unmade road. It was a rackety ride to their destination, a small cottage in a moonlit clearing, lying close to the gates leading to the research laboratory.

'Huge it is and a proper palace,' Billy informed them. 'A right nob's set-up.'

'I speak, as you will have observed, Mr. Houston, good English. It would help me if you would do the same.'

'Ah'll do my best.' Billy, pleased to have upset the sod, replied as the car slowed to a halt. 'Stay here, we dinna want to make our man jumpy.'

His torch lit his way to the low doorway, illuminating his face when the door opened to reveal Cecil Pyeworthy, an elderly and thin wispy-haired fellow in a plaid dressing gown. There was no way for him to follow what was being said, but Graebner sensed it was taking too much time to be proceeding smoothly. He reached for his pistol, prepared to use it should any difficulty arise.

'Nervous as a wee tabby,' Billy reported when he came back, talking through the open window, his words received with a sigh of incomprehension. 'He din'sa want us tae go in and certainly not to hang aboot either. There's a whole load of folk come by in the morning to go tae work. Christ knows what for, unless they're planning to chuck roses at the Wehrmacht.'

'Does your man have a telephone?'

'How the hell would I know?'

'Can I suggest you find out?' Rudi snapped angrily, opening the rear door.

Billy returned to the cottage, pushing open the door. In the dim hallway light, he found his onetime National Socialist recruit at the far end, hunched over a wall-mounted telephone receiver. The blow from the torch felled the old man, who slumped to the floor, dropping the mouthpiece, leaving it swinging by his head.

'Did ye no think tae shut the bloody door?'

Billy pressed the bracket to break the connection. Intending to hit his victim again, he stopped, the torch mid-air, as Graebner's voice cut through.

'I think you will need to be more positive. Or do I have to call Aviles to do what you find so difficult?'

'Does he have to—?' Billy got no chance to finish.

'You know the answer.'

Spinning an old man, of wiry build and weak muscles, on to his back, was easy, as was putting his hands on the neck and his thumbs either side of the windpipe, this as Pyeworthy clawed feebly at his head and neck. The hard part was the cold-blooded killing, not one carried out in anger or desperation.

He was looking into the rheumy, terrified eyes of a fellow who had talked of the need to weed out Jews and Communists, likening them to plants, which had to be pulled out by the roots to ensure they did not spread. If that couldn't be achieved, then the selective breeding of strains of flowers showed a way, albeit a slow one, to eradicate them from British life. Billy found it easier, as he increased the pressure, to close his own eyes.

'Do you think he spoke to anyone of importance?' Graebner asked, when the drum of the heels, rendered soft by the pair of worn slippers, had ceased.

'He did'na have much time to tell anybody anything.'

'Not an auspicious start, Mr. Houston.'

'Do you ken what a smart arse is?'

If he'd hoped to rile the German he failed; the response was delivered in a frustratingly even tone. 'I dare say I can guess.'

'Best we dinna stay, in case.'

'I had no notion to do so.' Graebner stood over the old man, his mouth and eyes now open, the former toothless, the latter lifeless. 'How well did you know this fellow?'

'What's that got to do wi' anything?'

'I recall you told me he is retired.'

'Aye. He worked at the plant gaff nearby until a few years back. Got this place for a cheap rent when he packed in.'

'It is therefore reasonable to assume no one will expect to see him there in the morning?'

'Suppose so.'

'So, we leave him where he is and merely close his front door.' Sensing acceptance, Graebner added. 'You must practice driving the car, in a way that will pass scrutiny at the checkpoints through which we will be obliged to pass.'

'How do you think Leo is goin' tae take tae that?'

'Aviles will see the need to do as I tell him. Understand, Mr. Houston, as a German officer, I have a responsibility to take care of those under my command and I will do so.'

'Which dis'na include me, pal! I'm no under anyone's command.'

'True, but I would prefer it if you did not question my right to make decisions.'

'Try asking instead of just giving out bloody orders.'

'I have already told you, there is no time for such niceties. So let us get you behind the wheel, which you can take as an order or a request, whichever you wish.'

'And if trouble comes?'

'Then it will have to be dealt with. We have no alternative.'

The trio endured the frustration of several jerky and shuddering starts before Billy even got the car moving. Next came crunching gears as he tried to change up, a noise that sounded as though he would wreck the gearbox before he got close to mastering the way to drive it. Turning it round in the confined space took forever.

Leo was at Billy's side whispering instructions to try and match up the use of the clutch and the accelerator, the German silent in the back. At the wheel, Billy could feel his frustration, which more than matched his own. Graebner was impatient, but he was also pondering what might lie ahead.

The gap before dawn was rapidly diminishing. There were less than seven full hours of real darkness at this time of year and they had used too much already. Billy's driving did become smoother as he got used to the car, the jerky starting reduced and the change of gear less noisy, until the German eventually barked.

'Enough! It is time for us to proceed.'

'Ah dinna ken about Leo here, but ah'm getting a wee bit sick o' being ordered about like some kind of dogsbody.'

'What does that mean?'

'Work it out, which is no hard.'

'*Please* Mr. Houston, do as I ask?'

'That's not asking, mister.'

'I promise I will be polite when we are where we need to be. Now, can we move? We are running out of time.'

'Bloody cheek,' Billy hissed, as, still lacking finesse, he let out the clutch.

They stuttered back down the lane, easing on to a quieter A3 and, once Billy got through the gears, it became about steering, with Leo taking care of any excessive pressure on the wheel. They swept through a pitch black, sleepy Guildford, meeting their first obstacle at the top of the hill, where the road split between the A3 and the turning to Farnham.

The actual roadblock was, of course, in darkness, the only sign to stop, a waving torch, until the moonlight revealed the shape of the man holding it, a fellow in a light-coloured, belted raincoat wearing a Local Defence Volunteer armband, his sole military piece of kit a steel helmet with *LDV* painted in large white letters.

He snapped to attention and saluted, as the gleam of his torch revealed the rank of the passenger, Billy bringing the car to a smooth halt at the crest, aided by the upslope. Behind the torch bearer, illuminated by the sliver of headlights, was a barrier across the road and a limp Union Flag above a makeshift hut.

A shout brought half a platoon of men in suit jackets and blazers spilling out to line up on parade, each carrying some form of weapon. As he came to the side of the car, they could see the man issuing the orders wore an armband with two stripes. In his mirror, Billy saw Graebner begin to put his hand to his cap, which had him snap.

'You're a general, use the swagger stick. Just put the tip to your hat and smile.'

Billy opened his window, to identify his passenger, the Scotsman confirming they were headed for a conference and time was pressing. The rear window was wound down as the corporal addressed Rudi with something of a tremor in his voice.

'I am required to see your pass and papers, sir.'

'Of course,' Rudi replied, leaning forward to hand over the pass which, dated until midnight, gave him permission to enter the restricted zone, before posing a question designed to distract the man. 'Who is the officer in charge?'

'No officer on duty, sir. It's Captain Fernhill, our local doctor. I can fetch him if you think it necessary.'

'Asleep?' That got a crisp affirmative. Rudi responded, aiming to sound as languid as many of the folk he had met in London's café society. 'Let's leave the poor blighter to his slumbers.'

He looked past the corporal at the line-up standing rock still in the moonlight, a motley crew of varying sizes, shapes and ages, two carrying what looked like shotguns, the rest having wooden pickax handles, though one carried a golf club.

'Fine body of men, corporal.'

That got a second snap to attention, the pass returned, followed by a crisp salute. Rudi responded languidly with the swagger stick, before issuing the command to drive on. He held his breath as Billy engaged first gear and slightly over revved the engine. Graebner's eyes were fixed on the now rigidly saluting LDV corporal, his Walther, safety off, sweaty in his hand. Thankfully the clutch came out reasonably smoothly and, barrier raised, the Hillman passed through to steer between the offset concrete-filled oil drums set up as obstacles.

They were immediately on a downslope, which favoured Billy's driving. Behind them the volunteers went back to their hut to smoke their fags and talk of the excitement of being so close to a real general. And how no doubt, should the Hun come, they would put the kibosh on them.

'That went aw'right,' Billy said, as Leo Aviles huffed his way back on to the seat.

'They were not Military Police, which we will be bound to encounter further on. I doubt they will be so easily fooled.' The flash of the torch told Billy Graebner was consulting his watch and map again, his hands tightening on the wheel at the man's next remark. 'Now concentrate on the road and look for somewhere to pull over. I need to relieve myself and I daresay you do, too.'

Billy, for once, suppressed his irritation, pulling into a farm track about a mile further on. Once they'd all made use of a roadside tree, they set off once more on what was the main road to Portsmouth, which was too risky to continue to use. Closer to the coast and on such a thoroughfare, roadblocks would, unlike their first encounter, be manned by professional soldiers. These would be overseen by officers who would be bound, within the rules of soldierly convention, to engage Rudi in conversation. It was time to turn off.

Chapter Forty-Eight

Thursday, July 25, 10:50 p.m.

It seemed that every LDV group in Surrey and Sussex had decided to erect an obstruction in their own area, the first of these being outside Haslemere. This time, as Billy came to a bumpy halt, Rudi leapt from the Hillman and strode up to the two men on duty, shoving his papers brusquely into their hands and demanding that they lift their barrier at speed. The trick worked, flustering men not accustomed to dealing with high military authority and he was hurriedly waved through.

That gambit was repeated twice, but Graebner suspected the next obstacle would be different. He explained, when they got to Easebourne, they'd be obliged to briefly join the A272, which in this area marked the northern extremity of the coastal exclusion zone.

It would take them through at Midhurst, before the turn-off they needed for Chichester. Being a major east-west trunk road, which carried traffic from the southern parts of London to the west country, it was an obvious choke point. It was thus likely to be manned by MPs controlling any traffic passing through, including vehicles headed south.

'Mr. Houston, you have the rifle to hand?'

'Am no daft, ye ken.'

The question was posed at the right turn taking them on to the main road. Any inspection point could not be far off. Graebner addressed Aviles in Spanish, telling him to get back to the floor and cover his body with his cape.

'You have the shotgun, make sure you are ready to use it.'

'Queue ahead,' Billy hissed nervously.

Within a minute, they were in it and stationary, the engine idling as the tension rose. Rudi Graebner had never been in real action before, and he felt a lack of breath in his lungs, his mouth suddenly dry. Dare he just sit still and let people come to him? Could he bluff a professionally trained enemy and, if not, could they shoot their way through? Billy was winding himself up to fight, feeling a stirring in his bowels, a sensation he'd not experienced since he had taken part in those deadly attacks on German trenches twenty-two years previously.

Creeping forward as vehicles were let through, he swallowed hard as a torch-bearing soldier in a peaked cap peered at the front of the car, before executing a swift salute and running off. Movement, which had been slow, suddenly quickened and Billy found himself looking at the entrance to a pub right next to his nearside door. The space overhead was cut down by an overreaching building, narrowing to less than the width of the street beyond. Across that, there appeared an area lit by blue lamps under a heavy canvas canopy.

A soldier with a shaded torch appeared out of the gloom: was it the same one? Billy slowed even more, as he had to when the man waved, aware before him lay a clear road, so he prepared to put his foot to the floor. If what happened next took a matter of seconds, it seemed a lifetime. In the pale blue glim, there appeared a whole party of running, uniformed men armed with rifles. Billy felt for the Lee Enfield, upright in its dashboard bracket, sensing the German sitting forward behind him, also tensed and armed, ready to go down fighting.

The soldiers began to dress right for parade and, as the Hillman drew abreast, they were in line, properly spaced. There followed a sharp, shouted command and the torch holder stepped aside to execute a neat salute, this as the boots of the soldiers coming to attention crashed on to cobbles. The platoon rifles were raised simultaneously in two sharp moves, followed by audible slaps as arms were presented, the barrier ahead lifting.

'Swagger stick,' Billy croaked as they slid slowly past, an instruction Rudi Graebner had to force himself to obey. He caught a brief glimpse of the saluting officer, who was so rigid in deference he wasn't even looking him in the eye. In the clear, Graebner would have liked to let out a whoop of joy, but this was suppressed: his dignity as an officer did not allow for such display and soon, he was slumped back in the seat, wondering at the stroke of luck which had got them this far.

Not long after they made the right turn which would lead them to East Lavant, Graebner calling off the distances in miles so they could use the odometer. They pulled off the road on the edge of the village, reversing deep into a forest track, so Billy could approach The Black Jug, to check out the lay of the land. It was time for Billy and the German to change back into their normal clothes, while Aviles ripped off the boards on the Hillman's bumper and hid them in the boot.

The food taken from Carlyle Square was quickly consumed, washed down with tap water from a wine bottle. There was no time to wait, they needed to know before daylight if they would need to seek help elsewhere.

'Jeannie's gonna love being knocked up this early.'

'There is no choice.'

'You dinna ken how much it hurts tae admit yer right.'

The others were hacking at the undergrowth with the dead driver's bayonet as Billy left, cutting bushes with which to camouflage the car. Inside his jacket, he carried a map of this stretch of the West Sussex coast. If Jeannie was to be of any use, she would need to be told exactly what was at stake, while he reckoned it would be the only thing to convince her, given he was unsure of what kind of reception he was going to get.

The last time he had been here, he'd found not only comfort but an audience of listeners eager to hear his words, as well as a landlady willing to act as the local organiser. How many would still subscribe now and would one of them be her? Billy Houston had discovered a woman with a temper fiery enough to match her russet hair. It couldn't be easy for a woman alone to run a pub. Jeannie managed it, not to mention any customers who broke her rules.

He thought about the way the name of Jeannie Milburn had come up, Graebner naming her as being recruited. That was how they had begun a relationship, which over time had blossomed into a bit of a fling, but he hadn't been near the place or made contact since the German attack on Norway. Jeannie was no soft touch: turning up unannounced, she might send him packing with a flea in his ear.

A single oak tree stood in the garden at the front of the old timber framed building, looking ghostly in the moonlight, along with a couple of wooden benches outside, a temptation for folk motoring out for a day at the seaside, to stop for refreshment on the way. It was also a space for the locals to park their kids while they drank indoors.

Friday, July 26, 2:12 a.m.

The dog began barking as soon as Billy's foot touched the gravel path. He stopped halfway and looked up at the windows, softly dragging a sole to keep up the canine interest. The one above the door swung open eventually, the moonlight showing Jeannie just a few feet above him, her long russet hair disordered. Her face registered shock as, by his voice, she finally recognised him.

'Morning, Jeannie.'

'It's the middle of the bloody night. What in the name of Christ are you doing here, and at this bloody time of day?'

'Just passing.'

The Ulster accent had not mellowed and nor, he soon discovered, had the coarseness of her language. 'My arse, you're passing.'

'Right now, I ah'm not too popular wi' certain people and I can use a bit o' help.'

She looked up the road and down. There were houses nearby, but not so close as to overhear and anyway, they would still be slumbering behind their blackout curtains. The pause had Billy's heart in his mouth.

'I should tell you to bugger off. Not a word in months.'

All he could do was open his hands in a gesture of futility. 'Be fair, Jeannie. It did'na seem wise to have meetings wi' a war goin' on. Anyway, it's not much more than three in all.'

'You counted, did you?'

'Every day, hen.'

'Liar!'

'Good one though. You always told me I was.'

A rueful shake of the head. 'Talk about a bad penny turning up.'

'There's no that many places this bad penny can go. If you've been reading the papers, you'll ken that.'

'To be sure, I read them all right. Only the saints know how they missed you.'

'You still safe?' A shrug. 'So do I move on?'

For comfort, the reply was too long in coming. 'I'll be right down.'

The window closed and Billy heard, muffled by the glass, Jeannie yelling at her dog to shut up. The studded oak door of The Black Jug had more locks and bolts than the Tower of London, setting off a cacophony of metallic creaks and thuds before it swung open. At Jeannie's side stood her black Labrador, a bit overweight, a lolling tongue and waving tail reminding Billy, outside barking, it was no great guard dog.

'In quick, for Christ's sake.'

The light was only switched on once the door was closed, locked and bolted. Billy found himself exchanging stares with a woman dressed in a long linen nightgown, showing a full figure underneath, one he recalled with approval. The face, another good feature, was far from friendly.

'You best tell me why you're here.'

'Is it no obvious?'

'I read the papers, so I suppose you're on the run?'

'That and a wee bit more.'

Her expression became even less welcoming; if anyone knew he was not passive, it was Jeannie. She reckoned Billy, and had told him so, as a man to take on the whole British Army if the mood came upon him.

'I don't fancy trouble, Billy. Life's hard enough without you adding to it.'

'Ah could murder a cup o' tea?'

A second moment of truth. The silence told him she was thinking of sending him packing. Something else struck him, a kind of reserve which contrasted with the way she'd connected with him previously, but it could hardly be otherwise.

'Kitchen, you know where it is,' broke the tension.

The pub had one of those ovens heated by coal that stay hot forever, there being no more talk until the kettle had begun to boil. Billy reckoned Jeannie was thinking hard about their previous encounters, as well as what it had led to. He needed to find out what her attitude was now.

'So, Jeannie, what do you reckon on this armistice bollocks?'

'Same as you, Billy, judging by the way you talk of it. Won't give me what I want, for there'll be nobody calling for it.'

He watched as she warmed the teapot, then spooned in the leaves, waiting till it was on the table before speaking, deciding any mention of their previous intimacy was probably unwise.

'We had braw meetings here Jeannie, some good folk, who saw what was right and all down to your efforts.'

They had been ten in all listed in his book, their addresses, bar one and for security, the Black Jug. The exception was a well-off solicitor called Borden who had been one of the most generous contributors. He was a bit of a pain, and too full of himself, but he had good local and well-heeled contacts, the kind of members who, if recruited, might write decent cheques. There had been a couple of farmers able to subscribe a monthly half crown and a trio of tradesmen more in the shilling line, taken gratefully, because every penny helped. More importantly, such recruits would be in the vanguard of the new dispensation.

Three women, a varied bunch in big hats, attended with their three-penny subscriptions. Each had their own axe to grind in a whole slew of sentiments, from eugenics through racial purity to a hatred of Jews, foreigners and even the Pope. Billy had suspected the presence of the local bobby, even if nothing had been said to identify him and he had kept his views to himself; the man's thick soled and polished boots gave him away.

With his own prejudices, Billy had found it easy to tap into those of his listeners, whatever the well spring of their frustration. One emotion was common, the feeling of righteous concerns not addressed, of a nation being failed by feeble politicians. It needed to be replaced by a strong central authority, one that was far from being met by the likes of Mosely. He had looked like salvation only two years ago but had seemed washed out after Czechoslovakia was overrun.

'Bit thinner on the ground now,' was her response when he listed the attendees.

'Aye, same everywhere.' The pause was long enough to let Jeannie know what was coming next. She turned to look at him, to find her dog sat by his chair having its ears tickled. 'But what about you?'

'Sure, if you're looking for somewhere to hide, I can put you up for tonight. More'n that's a problem. This is a small place and anything not regular sticks out, you know that. You got looks enough the times you stayed over here.'

'Do we still have any support?'

'Everyone is careful now, but those who are still strong meet every month.'

'That has to be a risk.'

'Ever heard of a Pig Club?'

Billy nodded. It was one of those suggestions from on high that folk, to beat rationing, gather in groups to raise a pig or two. 'Are there real porkers?'

'We're not complete ejits,' Jeannie bristled. 'The sty is behind my barn and we meet on Sunday afternoons, when round here is like the grave.'

'Some must smell more than swill.'

'If they do, they're not inclined to poke their nose in it.'

'The local law?'

'It's not as if we're shouting our mouths off, but he stays clear, too busy, he says. I wouldn't be having him as one to rely on, but he won't hand you in unless he has to.'

'Feart fer his pension, most like? You?'

Her eyes flashed. 'I'm not one to waver!'

The cups were out and the tea was poured through the strainer, with Jeannie sniffing the milk jug, which had been left overnight in cold water, to make sure it hadn't gone sour.

'I hope you don't want sugar, Billy.'

'Sweet enough as it is, hen, which you know.'

For the first time she laughed; it was not much of one, a soft cackle but it put Billy at ease. Once he had sipped his tea, he went to pull the map from his jacket but stopped. Would it make sense to her; would the uses for which it was intended make her uneasy? Instead, he just mentioned where he wanted to go.

Friday, July 26, 2:29 a.m.

'The Isle of Wight, are you joshing with me?'

'We'll be safe there. Have you no heard, the Germans are coming tae talk about peace?'

'Sure, you'd best be after sprouting wings,' came the emphatic response, before the brow furrowed once more. 'How in the name of Christ do you think you'll get on a ferry?'

'They're still running then?'

'For workers and, would you believe it, there are a few souls, war or no war, going over for bloody holidays?'

'We might be able to get aboard then.'

'Never. Holidays are bound to be stopped with this armistice business and even now every passenger has to show ID to travel. Wouldn't surprise me if they might be searched from now on.' Her expression changed. 'Anyway, who is "we"?'

'Ah'm not on my own.' That made her sit back, rigid, with a sort of growl that made the Labrador nervous enough to slink away. 'Ah've got a couple of bodies along with me.'

'On the run like you?'

'Ah'll no lie to you, hen. One's a German and the other, well he dis'na matter as much, but it's what they're facing that's the bugger.'

'Jesus, you telling me they're spies?'

'They're folk fighting for the cause, but if they're caught? Well do I need tae a say what'll happen? If we can get them to the island, they've a chance of making contact with their own and getting out of the country.

Wi' my background, ah'm hoping they'll take me too. If no, it's the Isle of Man.'

'You're fooling yourself Billy. If you help them and you're caught—?'

'Ah don't like to think on it, girl.'

In a split second, about to pull out that map, Billy had decided against an appeal to her femininity instead of her hatred of the British. This was a fact she kept well hidden from most of her customers—her Northern Irish background helped—to whom any grievances aimed at the government was taken as a comment rather than a reality. Besides, most propping up the bar, chucking darts or clicking their dominoes, had no time for politicians of whatever hue.

Jeannie never made a point of her opinions at the meetings, outside the general agreement the country needed radical change and strong government. A degree of flattery cum banter from a fellow Celt, added to one who had a bit of metropolitan gloss, had led to her bedroom and intimate pillow talk. It was there he'd learned of her background in Irish Republicanism and her hopes for a united Ireland.

Born Jean Connery into a Catholic family, she and her parents had been obliged to quit Belfast when Ireland was partitioned. Her father, prior to Home Rule, had been an active unit quartermaster in the Irish Volunteers. Yet he was on the wrong side of the line south of the border too, caught between the men led by Michael Collins and those, like himself, who opposed the partition settlement. This had led to what she called her exile, forced on the family after her beloved Da had been assassinated by the IRA.

Jeannie blamed all her own troubles and that of her blighted nation on Perfidious Albion, even the way her mother had died in agony from cancer, not long after their flight, unable to afford the doctor's bills. All this she divulged in quiet whispers and, once she started talking, it was like an opening of floodgates. Out poured a story full of curses, swearing and tears: how she had lost her father and why, of the family flight and struggles, through to an unhappy marriage to Frank Milburn, who'd drank himself into impotence and an early grave. It was a background never before fully revealed to anyone, including him.

'Why me?' Billy had asked.

'Only God knows, but just hold me, will you?'

And he had, as she sobbed into his shoulder. If Billy was indifferent to the reunification of Ireland, from that night on he hid it behind false enthusiasm and, right now, that gave him a button he could press.

'You're right, hen, it will be me in front o' the firing squad as well for helping them, as your Da would've been. That or a rope.'

The mention of her father set her thinking, sipping tea until the cup was empty. When she spoke again it was not about Ireland.

'How did you get here, Billy? If you're being hunted, I can't see you sat on a Green Line bus.'

'Car.' Billy explained the Hillman, the uniforms and the insignia boards, but as just stolen.

'And these others, what about them?'

'They're hiding in a track along the road.'

'Do you really think you can get clear?' she asked, he doubts obvious.

'We can,' he insisted, 'we have to?'

Another long pause followed. Jeannie stared deep into her empty cup, as if she was reading the leaves and seeking guidance; maybe that was the case, her being Irish and superstitious.

'Best go and fetch them and bring the car as well. There's a barn at the back of the pub with its own track to it, stick it in there.'

'And then?'

'Inside and upstairs. Stay out of sight until I close this afternoon.'

'We need tae crack on.'

'Jesus, not in daylight. Now get a move on and fetch your friends, before the whole bloody village wakes up.'

As Billy ran back to the car, the first hint of grey was edging the horizon, with the dawn bird chorus under way. The farm workers would be heading for their fields, so when Graebner protested the car should stay hidden, Billy lost his rag.

'Will you put a sock in it and just do as ah tell ye for once? If ye leave it here it'll be found by some dog walker and then what? They'll call the police and they'll start to search for us? Leo, you drive.' The Spaniard looked at Graebner until he got a nod, before beginning to remove the camouflage, Billy revelling in the ability to issue more orders. 'Ye can keep yer pistol on you, but leave everything else, an' don't even think of arguing.'

The distance was no more than a few hundred yards. The barn into which Leo was directed had the usual detritus of a country pub; empty beer barrels, broken furniture and a dilapidated dog cart, but there was enough room to accommodate the Hillman with the double doors shut. Graebner grabbed his grip and followed Billy carrying his case, Leo bringing up the rear.

Jeannie was at her back door, now dressed, hair tidied, overweight dog by her side, urging them to hurry. As soon as the door was shut, locked and barred, they were hustled upstairs and into a back bedroom containing a saggy double bed and two armchairs. There they found bread and cheese on the table, as well as glasses and a pitcher of beer, instructions issued quietly to Billy.

'Stay here and keep clear of the windows now it's light, don't talk except in whispers and, in God's name, don't walk about when the bar is in use. The floorboards creak awful. Billy, you can't use the lavvies out the back, so there's a couple of chamber pots under the bed and some old newspapers you can read or—.'

The secondary use left hanging, she was gone, leaving Graebner, for once, looking at Billy for an explanation, the food ignored as they'd not long eaten, the beer welcome in a room warm from a day of sunshine. Billy obliged with an outline of what he'd said and the things he'd held back on, like the map.

'You seem to know the lady well, Mr. Houston, better than you led me to believe.'

The slightly hurt tone, Billy ignored. 'Well enough to reckon I've got tae take it easy with her. Jeannie's no one tae push too hard, but you've got to admit we've landed on our feet here.'

The acknowledgement from the German was no more than a nod, as Billy pressed home he was now in charge.

'Sleep, ah reckon, two at a time wi' one keeping lookout in the chair.' Aviles got a look. 'You first Leo.'

The Spaniard moved the chair so, once sat down, he could just see over the rim. Graebner, looking at the bed, was obviously reluctant to lie on it with Billy, his distaste barely disguised.

'Dinna worry, Herr Sailor Boy, ah'm no like that, even if you are.' The title had Graebner jerking his head towards Aviles, which amused the Scotsman. 'Ah reckon who you really are is no a mystery to Leo now. And what does it bloody well matter anyhow?'

Billy lay down and was soon asleep. Graebner, lying on his side, back to him, was exhausted, but right now he had too many concerns, one being he no longer felt in control, which made a man used to command uncomfortable. He must stay awake in case of unforeseen eventualities, so he got up and took the other armchair, fumbling for a couple more Pervitin.

If anything, the pills heightened Graebner's concerns rather than easing them. What had happened in the last twenty-four hours amounted to an amazing run of luck, but that, as a commodity, couldn't last. It seemed odd to see matters, for him, as approaching a crisis, given they'd been in that state since he left the embassy. But it was true and he was wondering if he'd be best slipping out of the place now, only to see it as impossible to do so silently.

The fat tail-wagging dog seemed friendly, but one bark would be enough to wake his owner and then what? He had no real idea of the layout of the place, but he did know the way they had come meant a locked and barred door. Was the key still in the lock? If not, he had no idea where to find it and blundering around in, at best, pale morning light, was a bad idea.

The need to get clear of Houston and Aviles, along with finding a suitable boat, was still paramount. Perhaps the Scotsman, in telling him to keep his pistol had made a cardinal error, all the other weapons being left in the boot of the car. At the thought, Rudi Graebner allowed himself the ghost of a smile, because it gave him the means to reassert control.

Best wait to see what the next day would bring, which made him regret taking the pills. He wanted to sleep but, try as he did, it would not come.

CHAPTER FIFTY-ONE

Friday, July 26, 6:07 a.m.

Living in a tree-lined and canal-side street in Maida Vale conferred many benefits, but it also had its disadvantages, one the number of cooing pigeons that, in summer, had an absolute need to call to their mate from first light onwards. It was hot again, with a July temperature which, overnight, hadn't dipped very much.

Uncomfortably sweaty, sick of listening to the birds and again with too many disturbing thoughts, Adam got up to make himself a cup of tea, running over in his mind the known facts, like the Spanish diplomat was almost certainly spying for the Germans. Was he a one-off or were there more? If there were, how were they to be exposed? The lack of an overnight phone call made clear no information had come in on de Bázan or Houston.

Not long after Adam's kettle boiled, Betty Leyland put her key into the basement door of the Strathallan house. Thankfully, being summer, there were no ash-filled grates to clean out, but she fully expected a sink full of dishes, as well as dirty pots and pans. Her employer might have had to master the art of occasional cooking now they were down to one servant, but she never washed up.

Seeing nothing, Betty assumed, with her husband due back, they had eaten out, so was annoyed to find a dining room table marked with glasses and teacups. This brought forth a litany of mumbled complaints about the better-off in general and her employers in particular, though she was obliged to temper it in the case of General Strathallan.

He had the kindly manners and attitude to servants which went with his upbringing. Madam was different, mutton dressed as lamb to Betty, and no better than she ought to be. She concluded she might have been up to no good the previous night given a look in the hallway, produced no evidence of her husband being home.

'Poor man, if he only knew what she gets up to.'

Clarissa Strathallan might think herself discreet, but she forgot the woman who changed her bed sheets. Not that Betty Leyland would ever say anything; it was not her place and it was one she would lose on disclosure. When it came to cleaning, she was fastidious, angry that the downstairs cloakroom had been used and left with hair in the sink and some on the floor too.

She spotted the faint new mark on the drawing room chair, tutting at what looked like a failed attempt to remove it, which she determined to come back to later, after her usual chores. Polish was applied liberally around the reception rooms, the clock kept in view, so she would know when to take her mistress a cup of morning tea.

Back in the basement, she was passing the wine cellar, on the way to the scullery with the dirty dishes, when she saw reflected in the over-head light a gleam of something shiny. It lay in the crack between the flagstones. When she bent down, it smelt like pee but was coloured pink.

The key to the cellar was missing and this too seemed strange, the general being a trusting soul and besides, Betty was teetotal. Nor, after a search could she find it, yet the feeling something was wrong didn't translate into immediate action.

The likes of Betty Leyland was never going to raise the alarm, though she did go upstairs to check the bedrooms, which were empty, beds still made. Sitting on the main stairs, she nearly jumped out of her skin when the telephone jangled. It rang several times before she dashed down, to gingerly pick up the receiver, speaking in her poshest tone.

'The Strathallan residence.'

'Captain Dawkins here, can I speak with General Strathallan?'

'He's not here, sir.'

'Sorry?'

'Neither is his wife.'

'The whereabouts of Mrs. Strathallan don't concern me, but I am due to meet her husband this morning and I need to change the time.'

'But I told you, sir, he's not here.'

'When he dropped me off last evening, he was on his way home.'

'There's something not right here, sir.'

'What's not right?'

'I don't know.'

CHAPTER FIFTY-TWO

Friday, July 26, 9:11 a.m.

'Blimey, if Jerry does invade, he'll find the only people left are laid out in the morgue.'

DCI George Naylor was looking at the back of the pathologist's head as he made this remark. The reply he got was a professional one.

'Female's been dead some hours longer than the men. A broken neck, with the kind of bruising on her throat that suggests foul play. No doubts about the other two, blows with blunt instruments and possible asphyxiation.'

'How's the maid, Ben?'

'In shock, Guv,' his sergeant replied. Every time I ask her anything she just bursts into tears. All I've got is there were some dirty things on the dining room table and the cloakroom was a disgrace. She went about her normal cleaning before she discovered her lady was not in her bed.'

'What about this captain?'

'Very correct and anxious to get back to his duties, defence of the realm etcetera.'

'Well one of his duties is to tell us about the next of kin, and he might have to identify the bodies if there are none. There's no point in asking Miss Leyland.'

'Best you tell him, Guv, with your rank.'

Given the look of Captain Dawkins, all spit and polish, added to a good dose of condescension, he had a very great opinion of himself, bound to come it all high and mighty with a mere Detective Sergeant. Come to think of it, he might do the same to Naylor himself, a point he made to Ben.

'And?'

Naylor grinned. 'Stand by to arrest him.'

Naylor found Dawkins pacing back and forth in the drawing room. As the detective entered, he made a point of examining his watch, with an accompanying sigh and was about to speak when he was cut off.

'We will let you go as soon as we can, sir, but this is a murder enquiry, which takes precedence over everything.'

'I don't think you quite understand your situation, man. My work is important. I can leave when I like and, if necessary, I will do so. The taxi that brought me here is waiting to take me to the War Office.'

'Do shut up, sir, and cooperate. If you do, you'll be out of here in no time. Maintain your present attitude and I'll be obliged to interview you down at Scotland Yard.'

'You wouldn't dare.'

'I would and I will. Answer my questions or leave in handcuffs.'

This got another look at the watch, but it was accompanied by a huffed act of surrender. Naylor took him through the phone call and his subsequent arrival at the house, where he smashed open what was quite a sturdy door, to reveal the trio of dead bodies.

'Did you touch anything?'

'Checked for signs of life, then called you chaps. Got Miss L sat down and calmed her till you arrived.'

'You were on the staff of General Strathallan?' A nod. 'And what of Mrs. Strathallan? We are assuming the killer or killers are one and the same, but it seems she was their first victim.'

A slight blush. 'Knew her, of course.'

'And?'

'Well, let us say the lady was a bit flighty.'

Experience told George Naylor to stay silent. Dawkins was a handsome cove, slick dark hair and dashing eyes to go with his tailored uniform, as well as being physically fit. When he said 'flighty', it could mean with him. When Dawkins resumed, it was to tell the detective about a woman who liked to party the night away and gave the impression of being somewhat free with her favours.

'One doesn't like to speak ill of her, but I think she led the general a merry dance.'

'Which might lead us to suspect she knew the person who killed both her and her husband, the driver just being in the wrong place.'

'I don't know.'

Sensing he was about to clam up, Naylor hurried on.

'Look, I know this will be hard for you, but out there is one person or more, who's killed your senior officer, his driver and his wife, while I can't say to you other people might not be at risk.'

'Mind if I smoke?'

'Please do.'

The taking out of the cigarette, the tapping on the silver case was deliberate, and Naylor knew it to be a ploy. Dawkins was working out what to say, perhaps feeling he had been too open already and the detective could guess why. If Clarissa Strathallan had a chequered history, it might come out and the damage to the general's reputation would be appalling. Then there was the army, already under a heavy cloud after the debacle in France. The last thing they needed was a sex scandal. Dawkins walked to the window, lighting his cigarette and drawing deeply, using a finger to pull aside the net curtain.

'I know you need time to think, captain.'

He wasn't listening, leaning forward and examining the street in both directions. 'Have you moved the general's car?'

'No.'

'Then where the devil is it? If Walters is here, it should be too.'

'Describe it to me,' Naylor demanded.

The feeling in Naylor's stomach, far from good to begin with, didn't improve as Dawkins described the Hillman, its colour and, more importantly, what it had on the front fenders. Today he had a dead Major General, yesterday a mutilated Group Captain, with the obvious fact something valuable was missing. Then Dawkins mentioned the general's briefcase, which contained documents relating to the south coast defences.

'Ben, when will Scenes of Crime get here?'

A head came round the door; he had been listening.

'They should be on their way, Guv, not that it'll do them much good as far as I can see, with what the maid has been up to.'

'There might be something left to pick up. Phone the Yard and check, will you? Hurry them along if they're still there. And while you're on, get me the number of Mr. Strachan at the Ministry of Information.'

His sergeant looked curious; all he got was a gloomy shake of the head.

Friday, July 26, 9:42 a.m.

Adam Strachan, once in receipt of the subsequent phone call, as well as an outline of the detectives thinking, had to report to a less than enamoured Jasper Harker.

'If DCI Naylor's supposition is correct, our trio will have used the Major General's car to make a getaway. We've put out an alert to the military to see if they have any reports of it passing through their areas, but nothing has come back yet.'

'No forensic proof then?' Harker enquired.

'It's hoped the bodies might yield something.'

This was said more in hope than truth. According to Naylor the Strathallan maid had done such a good job of destroying evidence, the police had no hard facts: she'd even been busy with the brass polish on the front door handle, letterbox and bell. It was so shiny you could comb your hair by it.

'Still no sign of the embassy car?' Harker asked which had Adam shake his head. 'We cannot exclude the possibility of them using it until we're certain.'

'Of course not,' came the required response.

'So I suppose we must just wait and see, what?' The tone of the voice, after a false cough, changed. 'One other thing, Strachan. I had a call from Sir Stewart Menzies.'

'And?' Adam had a fair idea of what was coming.

'The proper procedure, if you want information from anywhere out of country is, as you well know, you apply to me and I ask MI6 to investigate.'

'In my defence sir, the NDP maps have been missing for coming up forty-eight hours.'

'That may be so,' Harker said waving his pipe, 'but we depend upon our sister service as much as they depend on us.'

Adam's face remained a blank. The so-called sister service was, to his mind, staffed by a bunch of fruitcakes to whom cooperation was anathema. On foreign stations, the Germans usually ran rings round them, while they were very adept at ignoring the notion internal matters were none of their concern. Some of the MI6 lunatics he had encountered were so wedded to secrecy, they kept information from each other and were certainly disinclined to share anything with MI5.

'I have managed to mollify Sir Stewart, but only because he understands I'm new to my responsibilities.'

'I daresay he demanded my head, sir?'

The bitterness with which this was said surprised Harker, whose lack of an immediate denial indicated to Adam he had the right of it. Not that he was going to get confirmation.

'In future, go through the correct channels, Strachan. It is, after all, only a couple of phone calls. You will be delighted to know Sir Stewart acted promptly when he heard what we required. His man in Madrid is on the case.'

Adam wanted to say he already had what he needed, but silence there was best.

'I think we can say,' Harker continued, 'regardless of which vehicle has been used, our quarry in no longer in London, so neither need you be. All the alerts are out and I cannot see what more can be usefully achieved from here. There's a mass of vetting to do, of course.'

A conference of the nature being proposed would involve a great number of bodies, many with prior clearance, but also those requiring to be interviewed and assessed as security risks. It was one of the tasks Adam would be glad to avoid.

'Already packed I believe?'

'Suitcase is in my office, sir.'

'Said a proper farewell to Eleanor, I hope?'

'Of course.' It had been frosty, but that was none of his boss's concern. 'I'm taking with me Sefton Avery and Jocelyn Devereaux. Avery speaks German, which will save us asking MI6 or the FO for an interpreter.'

'Fair enough, I suppose.'

'What have we got in the way of military assistance?' Adam asked.

'Ah soldiers?'

Harker responded to the enquiry as if such creatures were aliens, even though the requirements had been previously laid out. Enough men had been requested to ensure the grounds of Osborne House could be sealed off and regularly patrolled day and night. A large body of Military Police would be required to set up the roadblocks needed to form a cordon sanitiare for several miles around.

A hint those troops presently defending the south of the island could be redeployed from their forts and pill boxes had been met with a blank refusal. The nearest soldiers were a single company of the Black Watch, stationed south of Wooton Creek, too far away to provide security for Osborne House and hardly enough for what was required.

A request had been put forward that a battalion of Foot Guards, presently protecting London, as well as the required MPs, should be despatched to the island, though it had to be accepted withdrawing such units, as well as all their equipment took time. Given there was still uncertainty about enemy intentions, Harker had been told bluntly "not yet".

'The shortages are acute in all branches,' he explained,' 'while I've been told, in no uncertain terms, how dangerous it is to move soldiers from their present prepared positions when an invasion is still possible. They will be despatched when everything is clear but, as a temporary measure, there's a body of Territorials based in Chichester Barracks.'

'Territorials,' Adam asked, before adding, 'in barracks, at a time like this?'

'Not a full-strength battalion, badly cut up in France, it seems, and reforming.'

'Which translated means unfit for front line duty?'

'Bodies will do for now,' Harker responded, pipe aimed at his deputy's head. 'The chaps the Hun are sending ahead hardly warrant the same treatment as Hitler's satraps. They'll be hunkering down aboard their ship, so it's not as if they will be wandering around. I'm assured, when the top fellers indicate they are preparing to come, anything we need will be in place.'

The pipe bowl was then tapped on the desk, Adam's boss producing a mischievous look.

'That said, we trust them at our peril. Our military will, no doubt, act at their usual fashion when called upon to do so. Backward movement is the only manoeuvre which they seem to be able to master with any haste.'

Harker smiled at his little dig, unconscious of the fact it was somewhat laboured. A former senior officer in the Indian Police Service he had, vocally, been no fan of the abilities of the nation's armed forces prior to Dunkirk, an opinion hardly raised by that catastrophe.

'There is a risk from them being ashore at Osborne,' Adam pointed out.

A threat could come from those opposed to the notion of talks, which took no account of someone who had been hurt by the actions of Hitler and was now resident in the country. Britain was awash with Norwegians, Czechs, Poles, Danes, Dutchmen, Belgians and Frenchmen, though no danger would come from communists since the Nazi-Soviet Pact. Certainly, members of the Jewish population would be a hazard and, if they were British citizens, it rendered them doubly dangerous. None of this washed with Harker.

'It's the main lot of the Hun who matter, Adam, and they'll not arrive for several days if at all, maybe even a week or more, so we have time to get our skittles lined up.'

The "we" was as much nonsense as the mention of skittles; it had fallen to Adam, at the same time as he was chasing Billy Houston, to oversee what security arrangements were necessary, to study the layout and assess the risks. This led him to conclude they would be internal, someone already on the island or travelling there seeking private vengeance.

'I'm sure, Strachan, you can manage whatever is required.'

The mouthing of the Harker pipe, to be firmly clamped between his teeth, was a sign the meeting was over.

CHAPTER FIFTY-FOUR

Friday, July 26, 10:00 a.m.

Cooped up in a room under the eaves in midsummer, the heat was stifling. When Billy awoke, covered in sweat, it was to find Leo still by the open window and still asleep. Graebner was sitting in his chair staring at him, his face a sheen of perspiration, his expression definitely not inviting conversation, which pleased Billy because their relationship had definitely altered. The Scotsman was on a more equal footing now; it was more him calling the shots. So he felt free to rib the snotty git as he fetched out a chamber pot and retreated behind an armchair to hide himself from view.

'Christ, you'd no last two seconds in a trench.'

Graebner replied, obviously irritated 'We are not in a trench.'

'Try having a shite while your lot were shelling the line to buggery. You should'na have scoffed so much nosh when you were with that tart of yours.'

'These words! I can see, when we take over the country, there is going to be a requirement for some kind of phrasebook.'

'You'll no need one, mister, ye'll have the likes of me to interpret.'

It was not possible to tell if the strained look had to do with what Graebner was engaged in, or the notion of Billy translating. All of it had been whispered, but it did little to curtail the inbuilt vehemence: the German got on Billy's nerves and he didn't care if it was a two-way street. Graebner was far from happy to be depending on anyone, but he had more of a hold on his emotions. Leo, once brought awake, was silent, only his gloomy expression giving any indication of what he was thinking.

'Christ,' Billy hissed, waving one of the old newspapers Jeannie had left and glaring at Graebner's head. 'What a bloody stink.'

Below them and for a couple of hours, Jeannie Milburn had been about her morning tasks, cleaning the bar and scrubbing the wooden tabletops, dogged by her pet. She had tapped a new barrel of beer and restocked the bottle shelves, with a set of pipes in need of cleaning in between, stopping only for a cup of tea and a read when the *Daily Mail* was delivered, telling her the crisis in Whitehall was over.

The advance party from Germany was said to be already on its way and was expected to arrive the following day, with a photograph of a big warship, as if proof were required. An old airport at Bembridge was being brought back into use as a place for the Germans to land the leading delegates like Ribbentrop. The name brought a smile to her lips. He had been the ambassador to Britain a few years back, reckoned to be such a dolt the papers had nicknamed him Brickendrop. They'd have to change their tune and suck up to him now, which served them right.

Tea finished, she went back to her tasks, her mind on Billy and the dangers he was facing. If she had told him things not divulged to anyone else, she had never quite gone as far as sharing the whole truth about her father and his republican allegiances. This had meant involvement for Jeannie herself. With an Ulster police force of entirely the wrong religion, a sweet and innocent looking girl child provided her Da with a secure means of moving pistols and money from where they were hidden to where they could be employed.

Young Jeannie became a dependable messenger, passing on communications, which sometimes led to beatings for those suspected of being unreliable. She conveyed, as well, a choice of targets—human, motorised and brick-built for republican action. Likewise, she had visited the places where bombs could be put together in safety.

On a couple of occasions, the instructions she carried came from on high, to send a message that one of their own needed to either disappear or be publicly executed. Worse, she had seen men betrayed or caught and the price they had paid was the one Billy and his friends were facing:

death at the hands of the British state. This was not something she could let happen without trying to help.

Polishing her beer glasses, Jeannie was conscious of the near two decades of frustration, secretly sending money to a faltering Fenian cause, these musings curtailed by the noise of movement above her head. Hauling off another jug of beer, she went through the kitchen to pick up the boiled eggs she'd made earlier, these taken upstairs to enter, after a knock, a room with a strong odour of human occupation. With all eyes on her and in anticipation, she abrupt in saying nothing could happen until the departure of the lunchtime trade.

'Then, Billy, you and I must talk.'

'Perhaps better all of us,' Graebner suggested.

'Billy first,' was a sharp rejoinder and one which brooked no argument. 'And I say again, bloody keep still. I heard you minutes past moving about.'

'It's no easy, Jeannie,' Billy responded.

'What is?'

This was said as she shut the door behind her.

As the clock struck eleven, immediately followed by a knock on the outer door, Jeannie thrust a jug under one of the taps and went to unlock it, to allow entry to the bane of the publican's existence. The early morning bores who trickled in between now and noon, some to sit in morose silence over a solitary pint and these she could abide. Others came to tell the same stories over and over, which she could not.

'Jesus, come to think of it, it's just as bad of a night.' Door open and back to pouring drink, she murmured, 'Morning Arthur, your usual tipple?'

'Aye, a pint of your very best mild, Jeannie, to clear the cobwebs.'

One of these days, she thought, you'll say something original and I'll bloody well faint. Arthur Craddock didn't know it, but this repetition of his morning mantra made up Jeannie's mind; she would help Billy if only to get at sods such as the man before her, who had come to represent his nation.

A slight creak of the floorboards made Arthur look up at the ceiling, his curiosity obvious.

'Bloody building,' Jeannie said. 'It's been creaking like it for two hundred years or more, has it not?'

'Blistering weather we've had these last weeks,' Arthur opined, his rheumy eyes exuding the confidence of the never, ever wrong. 'Beams drying out, I do expect.'

'Sure, the auld place will fall about our ears one day and with us sat beneath it.'

'Don't care, I say,' Arthur cawed. 'Long as ah don't get no plaster in my beer.'

Friday, July 26, 11:44 a.m.

The manager of the Michelin Tyre Company had run out of space. His head fitter had assured him there was nothing wrong with the tyres on the Hispano-Suiza, so he had it moved out to park by the kerb. He reckoned such a smart and unusual car, even more expensive than a Rolls Royce, was a good advertisement for a business suffering from the wartime privations on rubber. To aid the presentational value, he sent out an apprentice to wash it, then polish the already gleaming paintwork.

The lad was in the middle of his chores when a trio of wailing police cars pulled up, to disgorge a group of pistol waving coppers in tin helmets. Cloth in hand, the youngster found himself bowled over and flung to the ground, while half the policeman rushed past to secure the garage and pin the suited manager to the wall of his office.

'Well, at least we know where the embassy car went,' George Naylor murmured when he put the phone down, 'Get a message out to our lot and all the Home Counties forces will you, Ben, to stop looking. I'll do the hobgoblins.'

This formed one of the two messages waiting for Adam Strachan when he arrived at Osborne House. The second was from his own HQ, which established MI6 had for once been diligent and cooperative. The only Rodolfo de Bázan the Madrid intelligence chief could rake up had moved from Spain, following his mother's remarriage to a German naval officer named Graebner. As far as the MI6 man could tell, his home was now in Germany.

'Anything significant, sir?' asked Avery.

'Too soon to say.' Adam replied.

The two tyros were sent to the cubbyhole dorm allotted to them while Adam retreated to his top floor room to unpack. Reflecting on the report soon led him downstairs to the tiny communications centre, which had been set up in the basement. He asked that Madrid be contacted for further information on de Bázan, added to which he had a hunch.

'And ask that someone at HQ looks for both names on the German Officers List, all branches Wehrmacht, Luftwaffe, Kriegsmarine and SS.'

CHAPTER FIFTY-SIX

Friday, July 26, 2:20 p.m.

Jeannie Milburn was not one to dither once her mind was made up, but one conclusion she had come to was firm. Having these three men in her pub, given the penalties for aiding spies, was too dangerous to contemplate. East Lavant was small and as nosy as any village of its size, a place where little changed, war or no war so anything out of the ordinary stuck out a mile.

The whole lunchtime session had been, between pulling pints and chattering to her customers, an examination of how to proceed in a way to help Billy and his companions. She was not one to just chuck them to the wolves. When she had said they would need wings to get to the Isle of Wight, it had been far from a joke. Every beach nearby was barred to the public, with not a boat left on or above the tide line.

The harbours of Chichester and Bosham, home to many a yachtsman, were not open for use to anything other than officially registered fishing boats and they went out under scrutiny. If such restrictions had been lifted for the Dunkirk evacuation, they were fully back in force now. Just getting to a wired-off beach was a problem, too; the route dotted with a line of concrete pill boxes, which were said to house men and machine guns. She had found out on her frequent walks this was far from the case. Nearly all were empty.

The land immediately behind the beaches were patrolled but, owing to troop shortages the duty had recently, with much fanfare, been handed over to the Local Defence Volunteers. If they were a bunch of amateurs and few of them had weapons, they were still a nuisance. Oddly, it was a problem of her own, barely related to Billy's conundrum, which presented a possible solution.

She had the help of a fifty-year-old widower willing to run the bar on weekends, as well as when she needed a night off. Ted Walker had a grandson, also Edward, who often helped out as a pot boy, bringing in the empties from the outside tables at a weekend for a few pennies of reward. That afternoon, knowing the school holidays were on, Jeannie wrote a carefully worded note, told the trio upstairs she was going out, put the dog on its lead and went to find the boy and his bicycle.

'Mr. Borden's office is in Pallants,' she told him, adding precise directions to the large, red brick Georgian building occupied by his firm of solicitors. 'Drop this into him for me and there's a tuppence for your trouble.'

'I'm saving for a Spitfire, Mrs. Milburn,' squeaked the keen twelve-year-old.

'Then you'll be knocking the Germans out of the sky in no time, Edward.'

'It's only a model one, miss.'

'Sure, it might be enough if you chuck it hard enough. Now get on, or Mr. Borden's office will be shut.'

Major Alaric Borden was the man Billy had thought too full of himself and not shy of letting folk know. He saw himself as the quintessential Englishman and he had a raft of opinions to support the pose. Jews were rodents, not humans, gypsies the dregs of humanity and Bolsheviks he would feed to the pigs for they were unworthy of burial, though there was a concern they would taint the meat. Homosexuals, of whom there were many more than people realised, should be bound together in their unholy congress and dropped from a boat into several fathoms of water.

Given he was a sailing man in possession of a sizeable boat, he was more than happy to provide the means. Indeed, he was quick to offer himself as a willing executioner for anyone he despised. His prejudices formed a never-ending list and extended to petty thieving and poaching.

As a student of eugenics, he was firm in his belief the mentally ill and the physically disabled would be better off dead, and there should be an official body set up to supervise the disposal. This would bring with it the added bonus of saving the tax such blighted misfits imposed on the state and himself.

The country of which he was so proud to be a citizen could look back into the mists of time, to King Arthur and beyond, as a beacon of what a realm should be and of which it was now a pale shadow: Britain was no longer the nation of Boudicca, Drake and Nelson. He had, pre-war, prayed for the day when proper order, lost by the political classes to the likes of the labour unions and the suffragettes, would be restored.

Borden saw a solution in the way the German nation had been brought back to greatness as a template for his homeland. Britain to his mind had, after the Great War, been bankrupted by rapacious American capitalism. He was vocal on the voracious costs that Johnny-come-lately nation had imposed on a country bleeding its own treasure over three years to make the world safe for democracy.

A fellow of furious activity, Major Borden was a local and noisy member of the County Council, as well as a leading fellow of the Chichester Freemason's Lodge. He was also a less secret philanderer than he supposed, but for all that he was a man very welcome, as were his views, in places like the Yacht and Golf Club.

With the pub now shut till evening and back from her outing, it was possible for Jeannie to call Billy down. As she ironed his crumpled clothes, she had time to explain the thoughts she had formed throughout the morning. Most particularly, why Borden presented an avenue of escape. This took place out of earshot of Graebner, left upstairs and far from happy at the exclusion. But at least he had been able to use the toilet and wash himself in the hot water basin provided, Aviles as well.

He'd also been told, as long as he stayed out of sight, he could open the rear window of the bedroom, breathe fresh air, smoke several cigarettes and, after Billy had looked it over, read Jeannie's paper. He concentrated especially on the conjecture on what Adolf Hitler might demand as the price of peace. Then there was the state of British politics, a report the German advance party had sailed and the timing of its anticipated arrival. Aviles, having emptied the chamber pots and shaving water in the outside lavvy, had returned and lit up too. But he was soon back on the bed, snoring.

'Would that be the Borden I met?' Billy asked, as he climbed into his freshly pressed trousers, over a clean shirt once owned by Bettina's husband, pocketing his change and ill-gotten fivers, an act to draw Jeannie's attention.

'You seem well found Billy?'

'Been lucky, hen,' he replied. 'If you need some—.'

'I'm doin' as well as I require.'

'Borden?'

'He's the secretary of the local Lifeboat Committee.'

'You've lost me.'

She spoke with enough of a smile to extract any sting from her response. 'Jesus, are you sayin' it was ever hard? The local one is in an elevated boathouse, with the shoreline being so flat.'

'So?'

'The launching ramp runs over the beach defences, with a channel through the mines to allow it to get to sea.'

'How d'ye know?'

'Christ, everyone who lives hereabouts knows. It's you that live in the likes of London who'd be ignorant. They can put to sea in bad weather if a call comes. All the coxswain has to do is send up a flare to alert the crew to come running, get permission from the Navy to launch, and they're away.'

'How do they get permission?'

'By bloody carrier pigeon, how else?' she snapped, her frustration overflowing. 'They pick up the bloody phone.'

Billy raised a hand to acknowledge his stupidity. 'This coxswain—?'

'You'd get no help from him. He took his own boat to Dunkirk and, from what I hear, has been boasting of it ever since. He hates Borden, too, the pair are at each other all the time.'

Jeannie went on to explain how each lifeboat station operated independently under its own local committee. The chairman of West Wittering was a doddery old Colonel Blimp, well past it. The task of overseeing the work of the lifeboat was carried out by Alaric Borden, the man who raised most of the money to keep the thing afloat. He bullied the female treasurer and made life difficult for the fellow who actually had to take it out in emergencies by the way he controlled the funds.

'The coxswain stood for Labour in the Council Elections and you can imagine how that went down. Borden wants him out and a man of his choosing and the right opinions in place. So there's a bit of argy-bargy going on, especially since yer man is a sailor himself and sure he could do the job better.'

'Are you saying we can steal a lifeboat?' came with a look of incredulity from Billy.

'They always have a man on guard to stop their fuel being stolen, as it was as soon as rationing came in. He'll be locked inside and there's the phone.'

'Will ye stop going roond the houses Jeannie, and tell me what yer thinking.'

'As secretary, Borden has keys to the boathouse. I'm hoping tonight the man guarding it will be him.'

'Are ye saying he'll take us to the island?'

'No, I'm saying when you knock, he'll open the door and not pick up the phone.'

'Why will he open the door, girl?'

'I've asked him to meet me there.'

'And why would he agree to do that?'

'If you can't guess that Billy, then it's you that's the ejit. Did you never see the way he was always at me after our meetings?'

Billy shrugged, unwilling to say he had and not cared, reckoning himself more than a match. The man he remembered was no portrait. Borden was as bald a coot with an Adam's apple nearly as big as his nose, added to a loud voice and a braying laugh. Was he now being told he was wrong?

'Have I been sharing your favours with this feller?'

'No, you have not, for you were never here. Though it won't be for his lack of trying, with his nudges and hints we might, you know. Only now it's at meetings of our Pig Club.'

'With you playing along?'

'Never.'

'But not giving him the elbow.'

'Borden is on every committee that matters, Billy. He's not a man to cross if you make your living selling drink and you need a licence. I've kept him dangling, without giving him what he's after. The note I sent him today, well, you can guess what it suggested.'

'I had you as more choosy, Jeannie.'

'Would that be you flattering yourself or me?'

'Why the boathouse and not here?'

'He's a married man, a big noise to the locals and ugly enough to be easy to spot. This place is too public, especially now when it gets light so early.'

'It's been thought through then?'

'By him, not me,' Jeannie snapped. 'And why would I not if I was minded? You don't own me.'

Maybe it was spite, or just to level things up for the sake of his own pride, that Billy responded the way he did. 'Likewise, hen. Ah've had ma own wee fling or two on the old travels.'

He saw the anger flare in Jeannie's eyes and had his hands up to ward off the coming blow, accompanied by spittle-filled accusations he was a right bastard. Billy seized hold of her wrists to restrain her, the noise of which brought Rudi Graebner far enough down the stairs to observe their tussle, his pistol in his hand. It was the sound of screeching brakes on a bike that stopped the tussle, but there was no comfort in her glare as she told both men to get out of sight.

'What is going on, Mr. Houston?' Graebner demanded as Billy ran up the stairs, furiously gesturing him to retreat.

'Nothing for you tae worry about and put that bloody gun away.'

This reply came from a man wondering if he had blown what sounded like a possible way off the mainland. Jeannie was at the open door, chatting in a calm voice, to whoever was on the other side. When the door shut, Billy went a few steps down to see her holding an open note in one hand and a torn envelope in the other. She looked up at him.

'He'll be there from ten o'clock. That's when the shift changes.'

'Will we?'

It was a question imparted with some anxiety. Nothing would work without her help and the answer was a long time in coming. She was still not mollified.

'Might be time to properly introduce me to your friends, Billy. We've got to make a plan before I open up this evening, and you'll have to be out of the place before then, whatever you decide. You can't stay here another night.'

'Jeannie?' Billy replied, in a pleading tone.

'No,' was emphatic and final to a man who knew her well.

CHAPTER FIFTY-SEVEN

Friday, July 26, 3:33 p.m.

Upon introduction, Graebner kissed Jeannie's hand, clicking his heels, which surprised and oddly delighted her. Leo Aviles was brought forward, his greeting just a slow and silent nod. She sat them at a table with some food, shooed away the dog, then repeated to the German what she had told Billy about the means by which they might get to the Isle Wight.

It was a measure of Rudi Graebner's intelligence, the rapidity with which took on board what she was saying. Upstairs, he'd reasoned the only way to stay in the Black Jug was by the use of threats, something to which Houston would be unlikely to agree. Nor was he sure a woman like Mrs. Milburn could be intimidated and the idea was unenforceable in any case. It would require the pub to be shut—how else could things be controlled—so he might as well fly a swastika out of the window for the locals to react to.

Set against his own prospects of finding the right kind of boat, here was a better alternative. Scoff as he had about the notion of the Isle of Wight, he was now being presented with what sounded like a workable plan. It was also one in which the need to get clear of Houston and Aviles would not be required. Instead, he would need their help.

Possessed of a precise military mind, he required more before he could reach a conclusion. Graebner insisted on a full description of the location of the station, the terrain surrounding it and how it was manned at all times of the day. He demanded to know what kind of boat was housed there and by what fuel it was driven, the size of the engines, their range, none of which Jeannie could help him with. Slightly thrown by the interrogation, she stuck to her part, which was to get them there.

'We go on foot and use a route to miss the town centre and make for the railway line to get to the south of the city.'

'Car would be quicker,' Billy suggested, with glance at the silent Leo Aviles, who was, no doubt, struggling to keep up.

'Jesus, you'd never get there,' Jeannie insisted. 'The level crossing on South Street is the only one for miles and it acts as a checkpoint, barriers both sides and they're manned by MPs. There's the barracks of the Royal Sussex on the road into Chichester a well, though the only poor sods there now are the dregs from Dunkirk.'

'How then?' Graebner asked.

'Footpaths. There's a gate on the Portsmouth side. Once over the tracks I can take you down a route close to the Fishbourne Channel.'

'Are there no people living there we should worry about?' asked Billy.

'There's the odd house and a couple of hamlets.'

'Folk might see us?'

'From behind blackout curtains?' came with a rueful laugh. 'Round here they expect to be jumped on by German paratroopers every time they poke their nose out the door and that's in daylight. The only bodies about after dark should be the LDV.'

'Useless buggers they are,' Billy opined, a view quickly countered by Graebner.

'It would only take one to be alert to raise the alarm, Mr. Houston. If it requires we gamble, it must be with a proper appreciation of the obstacles.'

'I thought about it all morning,' Jeannie intervened. 'What other chance do you have?'

Graebner let that pass and stuck to his questioning. 'So, we get to the boathouse and . . . ?'

'The door will be opened when you knock.'

Graebner raised an eyebrow, so Billy spoke quickly. 'It will be, take my word for it. Jeannie's arranged it.'

'By whom?'

'Someone I know,' Jeannie replied, eyes downcast.

No one spoke, yet it was obvious the German had arrived at the correct conclusion. 'Mrs. Milburn, do you understand we are armed and will use our weapons if we have to? Does that not concern you?'

Jeannie looked at Billy again. 'Not enough to make me pull back.'

'And this man you have made an arrangement to meet, I assume it is a man?' A nod. 'What of him?'

She didn't reply right away. Her mind had drifted back to pre-partition Belfast, to her father and his actions as a senior man in the Republican Volunteers, to killings that took place of both Irishmen and Brits she had heard about. Sometimes these came from her Da, sometimes by a bit of eavesdropping.

'There's an old saying you might have heard of, about making omelettes.'

Graebner threw his hands up, obviously he had not, but Billy got the drift. Even if she tried to hide it, the loathing was in her eyes. 'What she's saying, is not to worry about it.'

'You are sure?'

'Certain!' She snapped. 'Now if you're up for what I say, I think you should get yourselves into the barn and wait there so we can leave without drawing attention. If not, get ready to go your own way.'

Graebner sat in silence for a good minute, no one else speaking. All were waiting for him to do so, which pleased him: clearly and for obvious reasons, the decision fell to him. It was a proposition full of risk, but set against possibly more dangerous alternatives, was it any worse?

'The car we came in?' he asked.

'I have a place for that.'

'It seems you have thought of everything Mrs. Milburn.'

'I have,' she said emphatically. 'Like running out of time to make your bloody mind up.'

Graebner nodded, stood up and looked at Aviles, which was enough to have the driver on his feet. The need to state the decision had been made was unnecessary and they went upstairs to get the things they'd brought into the house. Billy hung back to apologise for his blundering, but there was another thing bothering him. Jeannie was feisty enough and a very determined lady, but could she really countenance the fact the man she had sent the note to might pay with his life, just for seeking a bit on the side?

'If I'd ever agreed to it, I'd have been doing it to see to the bugger myself, except I don't have the means. Major Alaric Borden didn't leave the army when the war finished, Billy. The bastard went to Ireland.'

'Not a Black and Tan?'

The laugh from Jeannie was hollow and humourless, as befitted any mention of the men who'd come under that moniker. Ex-Western Front soldiers in the main, money and bloodthirsty murderers, recruited as auxiliaries to the constabulary, tasked to put down the Irish uprising. The brutality employed was never going to be forgotten in the folk memory of Ireland.

'Aye, he was one of them filthy swine right enough. And to think he boasted of it to me at the last meeting of the Pig Club. Never pegged I was Catholic born and a republican, coz I never go to mass. Why would I, when the priests are as crooked as the government? Had me down as a Belfast Prod, he did. So, if you do for him, it will be a favour to me and my kind.'

'Revenge for your Da.'

'That, too.' There was a moment when the grief creased her face, but it soon cleared. 'Get yourself and the other pair in the barn now, Billy. I've got work to do.'

Chapter Fifty-Eight

Friday, July 26, 5:14 p.m.

Graebner was sat by a cracked, dirty window on the opposite side of the barn to the pub, not far from the pig sty, the south-western sun penetrating the filth-encrusted glass. Besides his own thoughts and ruminations, he had been examining once more the fact he might be deceiving himself in the hunt for recognition.

Occasionally his brow furrowed and his head lifted to gaze in deep thought as he contemplated what the stealing of a lifeboat entailed. In terms of fuel and sailing ability, getting to the Channel Islands would be easy, but such a craft in the water would be singular and easy to spot. Once stolen, the loss could not be hidden for long, while the time taken to get to where he wanted to go meant risking a search by air. So, once aboard, if they could manage such a thing, it was the Isle of Wight or nothing, which did not come as a solution to all their problems.

At a rough calculation, and it could be no more, there were some seven thousand troops stationed on the island, concentrated on the southern shores, headquartered in Shanklin and deployed behind formidable defences. On the island itself he would need a place to beach, and they were either guarded or were laid with minefields, quite possibly both.

Any waterway they came across would have bridges, providing natural checkpoints, which had to be avoided, but how? The top third of the island presented the only viable approach, but landing there was not without a different set of problems, perhaps even harder to overcome.

This moody contemplation had lasted for what seemed like an age, the map Billy had fetched along that morning and declined to show

Jeannie often examined with many a frown. But the German never spoke about what seemed to be worrying him, if indeed anything was. Such expressions and the accompanying silences were driving Billy mad and he said so.

'You told me you were a soldier once, Mr. Houston.'

'A fightin' one, mister.'

'You do not have to have been in a battle to know time spent in preparation and an appreciation of potential difficulties is never wasted.'

'That ah'll grant ye, but is there any chance you might tell us what it is ye've got in mind?'

The German made no attempt to make his reply sound other than evasive.

'First, Mrs. Milburn must get us to the coast and the lifeboat station. Only then can we examine the possibilities of progressing further. Now please leave me to my studies'

Graebner's head was lowered over the map once more, as Billy responded bitterly. 'Suit yersel.'

CHAPTER FIFTY-NINE

Friday, July 26, 7:05 p.m.

Jeannie saw to the early evening trade until Ted Walker came in at seven to take over from her; he would stay till closing and lock up. To his enquiry if she was going somewhere nice, he was told it was a meeting of the National Savings Committee, to organise a week of events to support the war effort. The lie he swallowed without a murmur, given it had been well advertised.

Once Ted was engaged in chatting, with her dog circling the bar in search of affection, she went upstairs and changed into dark clothing. Looping her handbag over her shoulder, she picked up the sack of food and bottles of beer she had assembled, before sneaking out of the rear to knock on the barn door. It opened immediately.

The first task, it still being light, was to get the Hillman off her premises, which meant pushing it silently out on to the road, the risk they might be seen from the pub's outdoor lavatories being deemed unavoidable. Jeannie then went ahead on her bike to ensure the road was free of pedestrians, cars coming through being rare now and likely to be strangers. As she cycled ahead, the Hillman, engine near to idling, followed slowly.

The journey was short, no more than five minutes, to a lane and then a dirt driveway leading to a derelict house, fallen into disrepair after the Great War. Jeannie explained the two sons of the family had died on the Western Front, their despairing mother, victim to the Spanish Influenza epidemic just after the peace. No one knew what had happened to the father, so the place had been left empty. A substantial dwelling, it had one asset known to their guide, a workshop into which the car could be driven and concealed.

'Kiddies come here sometimes, but not if their mothers know of it. Some reckon it's haunted.'

Rudi Graebner opened the boot, distributing coats and Leo's cape—warm night or not, outer garments had to be taken. The Spaniard collected the food Jeannie had given them, along with the army rations. Next came the German's grip, the fishing rod, with Billy reaching for his suitcase.

'Is that necessary?' demanded Graebner.

'We'll need what's in it.'

Leaning into the boot, Graebner opened the shotgun case, a beautiful, highly polished piece of woodwork in walnut with brass fittings, as befitted a pair of finely crafted guns. Strapped within the lid lay two shoulder carrying cases, the German extracting both.

'I would suggest, rolled tight, they would be better off in these. They are easier to carry than a suitcase and leave the hands free.'

'And when did ye work out that one?'

'Some hours past, so you will observe time spent in thinking ahead has not been wasted.'

'Clever bloody clogs, eh? There nothing else in that bloody case I want.'

'Can I also suggest we take with us the private soldier's uniform?'

'I don't get to be a general this time, either?' Billy griped.

'A uniform better abandoned. It would be well to ensure you have the means to wash and shave.'

'He's a right bossy git, don't you reckon?'

Billy called this out to Jeannie who, although in earshot, had no idea what they were talking about. The maps were extracted, rolled up tight and inserted into the waterproof cases, the one pertaining to the Isle of Wight and the mainland coast, which Graebner had been studying, kept out for reference.

Billy hauled out the kitbag, rolled in the squaddie uniform and looped the strap over his shoulder. Aviles took one of the shotguns, Graebner the other, while the Enfield rifle and its bayonet were handed over to the

Scotsman. Last came the general's revolver and, when she spotted Graebner had his own automatic, Jeannie demanded a weapon too.

'This is not a gun for a woman,' the German replied condescendingly, weighing the Webley in his hand: the Walther was not an option.

'Sure, it's one for an Irishwoman, so give it here.'

It was handed over with a smirk, which evaporated when Graebner saw her break the chamber open and check the number of bullets, expertly spinning the magazine.

'You have found us a remarkable woman, Mr. Houston.'

'Why don't you call him Billy?' Jeannie asked.

'There are sound reasons.'

'What he means is he's an officer an' am' no. Christ, 'am lucky tae get the "mister".'

'As of this moment, rank is meaningless. The person to whom we must defer is you, Mrs. Milburn. You may command us, but can I please suggest we move. It will be dark in less than two hours.'

'Hear that, do you now, Billy? That's the way to talk to a lady.'

'Which I will do, hen, when I find one.'

Ridiculous as it was, at such a time and in such a situation, she stuck out her tongue.

'Some bloody lady,' muttered Billy.

CHAPTER SIXTY

Friday, July 26, 7:42 p.m.

Over the years, since coming to live in East Lavant, Jeannie Milburn had traversed every footpath and bridleway for miles around. Walking was her solace, a time to contemplate what she had ended up with and why, just as often, to hark back to more comforting or sadness filled memories. The West Sussex countryside was crisscrossed with paths and lanes, each one leading from one parish and its church to another, employed since time immemorial by the locals.

She chose the less trodden routes where, at this time of year, she had often gathered wild flowers to scent her bar-room with something other than pipe smoke and cigarettes. The likelihood of them being used in late evening was small, but Jeannie went ahead, pushing her bike to block the way for a while if the others needed to get out of sight; easy, given most paths were hemmed in by overgrown hedges.

The evening was warm and muggy, even now the wind had got up. Coming from the south-west, it did nothing to cool the air, making the men sweat in their coats and capes. They had to try and get across the railway line to the west of the city in twilight, because the gate might have an LDV guard detail invisible in full darkness. It seemed these volunteers were expected to be everywhere, but the truth was obvious; the men who came forward were enthusiastic but few.

It was a relief to find the gates on either side of the tracks clear. Once across, Jeannie parked her bike behind a hedgerow, looped her handbag round the bars, then set off down another lane which skirted round any dwellings as the last of the light began to fade. Crossing a couple of single-track roads, everything had an eerie quality, while the sky was clear. It mutated to something quite different when the canopy of cloud shut it out, plunging them into darkness. This necessitated a torch, the risks accepted so they could keep moving.

Close together now, Billy and Jeannie had a fractured conversation, the fear being it could all go terribly wrong. She tried to garland her words with confidence, but her apprehension was evident. Where would this escapade leave her? Borden would know she had put them on to his where-abouts, and he would be quick to tell the law if he ever got the chance.

'I don't think that's likely,' was Billy's response, playing the innocent when it came to killing. 'You don't know the German like I do.'

'I've seen folk wriggle out of worse, and don't go thinking Borden's an ejit or a coward, because he's not.'

'He's in your Pig Club, so he's at risk himself.'

'And slippery as he is, the bastard will be after telling the authorities that he only joined it to spy on us.' There was a long pause before Jeannie added. 'I've no mind to go to the gallows any more than you.'

'The gun Graebner gave you. Best hang on to it.'

She suppressed a snort. 'And save the last bullet for myself, is that it?'

'I cannae offer you more.'

'I know,' she sighed.

They came close to trouble once, only the naivety of an LDV patrol saving them from walking straight into the spot where they had set up a post. The faint smell of cigarette smoke, blown inland on the breeze, alerted Billy to the possible danger. Cautiously approaching, they heard conversation and, at one point, what must have been a joke, given the burst of laughter.

'We'll have to go back and round.' Jeannie whispered. 'There's another path we can use which will take us a bit inland.'

'Time,' was the German response after a glance at his torch lit watch. 'It is nearly ten o'clock now.'

'He'll not be there till then.'

'And if you are not, Mrs. Milburn?'

'Never fear, yer man will wait,' Billy assured him.

It took an hour more of catching brambles and once pushing through hedges, until finally before them lay clear marshland and beyond, the sea.

The elevated Lifeboat Station was bathed in moonlight, a round-topped hut on pillars overlooking the flat seashore. At its front lay the steep ramp down which the craft could be launched, at the rear the walkway which took access clear of highest tide, the landward end accessed by a ladder.

'There you are, Billy,' Jeannie said softly.

'Borden's goin tae get a shock, seeing what he thought he was in for.'

'He'll be getting less than he deserves.' There was a small pause before she added. 'If it all works out, you know where to come back to.'

'I do and ah will. It'll be a different Billy to the one you ken now, important like. So stay safe, girl, and maybe you can share in ma good fortune.'

'You always were a dreamer.'

'Is that bad?'

'Never. Only Christ knows how a body can live without wanting something better.'

Then she was gone, heading back to where she had parked the bike, leaving her charges to cover the last two hundred yards of marshland to the base of the rear staircase. This creaked ominously as they climbed, even more as they crept along the ramp towards the boathouse, Leo passing what he been tasked to carry to the others and getting his weapon ready.

A grinning Borden opened the door at the knock, to find a shotgun muzzle jammed into his face, which cut his lip and sent him reeling back. He fell against the blackout screen, his weight dragging it down forcing the to be quick to get inside with everything they were carrying and shut the outer door.

It was quick but not so much so before one of the LDV patrol, a young shop assistant at Gieves and Hawkes in Chichester, had spotted the faint flash of light. By the time he told his sergeant, a slightly deaf ex-navy gunner, what he had seen, the evidence was gone. Given his age, the lad found himself disbelieved and ridiculed.

'Lightning, young 'un, that's what it were, an' far off. Take it from an old salt, who can sniff the wind and spot the clouds thickening up. There's a proper storm on the way.'

CHAPTER SIXTY-ONE

Friday, July 26, 10:33 p.m.

Adam Strachan, having fully absorbed the problems of protecting Osborne House, had also discovered just how poor was his military support, not due to arrive until the following day. The remnants of the Sixth Battalion, Royal Sussex, had been sent to France in early April to be trained there and brought up to standard. In reality to do rear echelon work like digging trenches and tank traps. They had never been intended for front line service.

The subsequent German attack had caught them even less prepared than the fighting forces, so they had suffered accordingly. Abandoning their position and any kit the unit possessed, the battalion joined the rest of the British Expeditionary Force running for the coast, many failing to make it. The unit was now seriously understrength, which implied low skills and probably even worse morale.

As night fell, the anchorage between the island and Portsmouth, visible in daylight from the terrace of the house, had been thrown into darkness. The blackout was still in full force on British soil, as if to send a message to say, despite all the warm words from Berlin, peace was far from being assured. Adam had listed all the internal security arrangements which would be required and checked the positioning of hidden microphones, hopefully well enough disguised to fool the Germans. The listening post was set up in the communication's room behind a steel door, which also acted as the link to the outside world.

'Our technical chaps have done a good job, sir,' was the opinion of Sefton Avery.

'For which we are now wholly responsible. Anything goes wrong, we will carry the can. Have we got the means for a nightcap?'

'Came down ahead of us with the wiring party, sir.'

'A very rare example of departmental efficiency,' was the biting response from Adam.

After a long and tiring day, they were sitting enjoying their second gin and tonic, when a message came up from the basement, a communication from Special Branch, one read with incredulity. It had taken a whole day to find out from an LDV group in Guilford, who had, in the morning, returned to their civilian occupations, that a staff car bearing General Strathallan had passed through their checkpoint, heading south at around eleven PM.

The Branch had contacted a radiating number of the same kind of volunteers, the route being confirmed as continuing, until they could only be heading for Midhurst in West Sussex. Then came the final nail; some dolt of an MP, a newly promoted from the ranks subaltern, had just waved the car through on the strength of the major-general's fender badge, without checking the occupants.

No great leap was required to place de Bázan and Billy Houston as the pair seen in the car, while no map was required to tell Adam Strachan their destination had to be the coast. He was immediately on the phone to Major Gilbert, Adjutant of the Royal Sussex, demanding every available man be sent out on patrol around Chichester.

'Take a while to get them up and out. Three possible fugitives you say?'

Adam needed to be cagey then; mention of the National Defence Plan was forbidden to the army, just as it had never been vouchsafed to anyone outside a tight circle, which did not include the police or Special Branch. It even failed to embrace the two youngsters he had brought along with him, now listening in to his side of the conversation. Yet he had to gee this man up.

'Dangerous ones, I can assure you, armed and possibly acting on behalf of our enemies. There's a possibility they're trying to find a boat and get across the Channel. Whoever comes across them has my authority to shoot on sight, if they can be possibly identified and seek to evade capture. But this is vital Major, anything they might have is not to be touched until my people turn up.'

He meant himself, but the words had Sefton and Jocelyn exchanging looks.

'Please contact me immediately if there's anything to report.'

Phone down, Adam found the two young men staring at him. Having been part of this from the beginning, they were more than curious. They knew the names of the men being hunted, that the Spanish Embassy connection was possibly a spy, while the other was at least a double murderer, but not what they had in their possession. But they were a bright pair and Sefton deduced much the same as his boss.

'They'd need a proper boat to cross the Channel, sir,' Avery said. 'Be suicide to try in anything else.'

'It's best we take every precaution.'

'Am I allowed to ask why, sir?'

'Sorry, Sefton, I'm not at liberty to tell you.'

'Sounds unlikely to me that they'll get anywhere at all.'

That got a sharp response from his superior, who carried and felt the responsibility.

'They got out of London, down and past one of the main roads from east to west. If you want to underestimate them, laddie, be my guest. And, maybe for your trouble you'll end up in clink like that dolt of a Midhurst MP.'

'Sorry, sir.'

'We need to take turns guarding the house. Also, get a message to DCI Naylor at Scotland Yard. Tell him what's happened and ask if he will put a rocket under the local Bobbies. And make sure they've got the photographs distributed in London and he'll need a description of the car they used.'

'Do we need to go through Naylor, sir?' Devereaux asked.

Adam recalled the earlier conversion with the man these two had upset, which made him wonder if the best route was through Special Branch. But Naylor was plainly not fond of them either and, besides, it would be a good idea to show the detective that cooperation was indeed a two-way street.

'Mr. Naylor has the excuse of a murder enquiry, something the local police will comprehend. Anything to do with us will only muddy the waters, so it's best any request for action comes from him.'

Sefton and Jocelyn spent a good ten minutes outside in the corridor trying to pass the buck to each other. Neither wished to once more be on the receiving end of Naylor's sarcasm, now seen as justified given the had failed to acknowledge his rank. Sefton alluded to the time; it was doubtful the man was at the Yard, so it would be impossible to speak to him personally. In the end they decided to leave a message.

Friday, July 26, 10:35 p.m.

With the vessel housed there was little room in the boathouse. In the dim light it was some time before Borden, holding his split lip, got a clear sight of Billy Houston, at which point his eyes came out like organ stops.

'*You!*' he gasped.

'It's just like in the films,' the Scotsman responded, his tone cheerful and chatty. 'Here's you getting all worked up for a quick shag—.'

'Silence!'

Graebner cut right across Billy, pressing the pistol hard into Borden's belly, making him gasp. If it hurt him physically, it also caused serious offence to the Scotsman.

'Will you fuck off talking tae me like that?'

'I do so for all our sakes.'

The fact the German was right didn't pacify Billy. He had to breathe hard and long to get his temper under control. Graebner and Aviles dragged Borden to the bottom of the staircase leading up to the office and, no doubt, a bed. The light coming from it made it easier to see.

'Sit down on the staircase and don't move.' Graebner turned to Aviles, instructing him to cover Borden with the shotgun. He looked around, taking in what he could see of the structure. 'Is the boathouse secured for blackout?'

Borden had to let go of his lip to reply. 'Who the hell are you?'

'Just answer the question.'

'Get stuffed.'

The German hit him again, a hard belly blow with his pistol point, which threw Borden back against the corrugated iron wall.

'I need to know where to turn on the lights and, when I do, I must be sure no one will see anything. Know this, I am prepared to kill you. You have a chance to stay alive, but only if you cooperate.'

'Talk about asking daft bloody questions,' Billy hissed, his anger far from abated. 'You're no as smart as ye liked tae think, are ye? Blackout has to be tight. They'd get shot by the wardens if it leaked and they must be in here doing stuff at night when the boat is no going out.'

Graebner, back in charge since the decision had been made at the table of the Black Jug and determined to show it, took some time before he nodded, to then follow the trunking and locate the main light switch. The boathouse properly illuminated, he made for the short ladder up on to the boat deck. The dimensions were negligible, really only a small area at the stern with two narrow walkways along the upper housing. The sunken wheelhouse and its glass screen provided cover from the elements.

A square hatch low down at the front gave access to the main chamber, above that a brass plaque to tell anyone who came aboard that this was a Watson Class RNLI Lifeboat, built by T. White of Cowes and paid for by someone called Dame Lucy Brett. Space in the centre part of the hull was for those rescued, the rear being taken up by the twin engines in separate compartments that could be sealed off.

Everything needed for the boat's function was neatly lashed off to the inner hull: first aid kits and stretchers, as well the kind of tools and equipment needed to save men trapped in wood and metal vessels, added to foul weather. Powerful flashlights, coiled ropes, axes, saws, crowbars, hammers and, most vital of all to the man who was still seeking to formulate a workable plan, a strong set of bolt cutters. There was also a rack holding two rifles, which confused him until he worked out they would be for wartime defence.

Back on deck he inspected the masts, the main stepped and well forward with a second smaller gaff on the stern bearing lights and a radio aerial. Both were lying flat, being too high to fit under the station house roof. The main mast, as well as the canvas sail lashed to it, would act as a mainsail for emergencies in which the engines failed. The boat was on a slight tilt, to ease the exit on to the much steeper slipway. Affixed to the sides were chains with quick release couplings which required only a mallet to remove the pins.

Troubled ever since he had left his own apartment, Rudi Graebner and still marginally so before setting out from East Lavant, felt a palpable surge of exhilaration, absolutely sure now this was a far better solution than anything he could have conjured up for himself. He might have never sailed a lifeboat, but they were essentially no different, when it came to handling, than the kind of motorised training boats used by the Kriegsmarine.

It was, however, not without problems, which included a shortage of muscle power. This boat, in an emergency, would be sent to sea with much more assistance than he could muster. The next difficulty was the engines. Once they were started, the noise would be deafening and not confined within the boathouse walls: it would be audible for miles along a flat, guarded coast.

Both of his companions would be needed to carry out tasks for which they had no experience. As soon as the boat was in the water, it would be necessary to raise the masts and much more, all before trying to land on a coast possibly more comprehensively patrolled than the one they were about to leave.

The questioning looks he got as he ascended the stairs were ignored. The blanket-covered cot was worth a glance but no more, unlike the large chart of the surrounding waters on one wall beside a graph listing the tide tables, both of which he examined in detail. He then turned to the thick manuals on the shelf above a desk covered in papers. Laying aside his pistol, he took the books down and began to study them.

They told him the lifeboat was double hulled, driven by twin diesels, had a top speed of eight and a half knots and a maximum range of one hundred and fifty nautical miles. Such speed made it vulnerable to fast patrol boats so, even flat out, the lifeboat could not avoid being inter-cepted. This put any idea of making for somewhere other than the Isle of Wight even further out of the question.

Yet he was beginning to see the outline of a possible plan and the time factors it might involve, while being equally aware he needed all the help he could get. There was a moment of hesitation. Was it wise to keep taking things which might have unknown side effects? He dismissed the thought. The mission demanded total concentration, nothing else mattered, so once more he resorted to the methamphetamines.

'Mr. Houston could you bring up the map of the Isle of Wight, please?'

His smile was wiped off as the cropped, carrot top head appeared and with it a scowl. He paid it no attention, merely clearing the desk and opening out the map, a document which might make conceivable something which should have been impossible. Pacing between the desk and the wallchart detailing the depth of offshore waters, he finally ran a finger down the tide tables. Having watched Graebner for what seemed an age, Billy was unable to keep the frustration out of his voice.

'What in the name of Christ is happening?'

'I think I may have found a way to get us to the island and, quite possibly a place in which to land.'

'Any chance ye might tell me where?'

'To do so would make no difference. If we are to succeed, it will be by my efforts and my skill. All that is necessary is that you do as I tell you.'

'Ah've dealt wi' some right stuck-up bastards in ma time but you take the biscuit.'

'Again, you confuse me.'

'For aw yer nose in the air shite, you wouldn'a be here in this boat-house without me.'

'This I grant you.'

'Then the next thing you can grant is tae tell me what you're planning, so I can say if I want to go along with it. And before you tell me there's no alternative, poke it. Ah've risked my neck enough to get this far and I want to be the one tae decide if what you have worked out is a good idea or just bloody suicide. And am no taking part in some daft plan that gets me killed and you left standing.'

'I intend we should all survive.'

'But you first and me and Leo last, eh, or have I got that bit the wrong way roond?'

'What do you know of the Spithead Boom?'

It took a second for a slightly thrown Billy to respond. 'Bugger all.'

235

Rudi Graebner was in a state of recall, as he had been in the barn behind the pub, with the long silences which had so irritated the Scotsman. He was remembering his time at the Flensburg Naval Academy, specifically the long and exhausting night he and his comrade cadets had spent studying the problem of how to overcome the very obstacle named, in order to mount an attack on Portsmouth Harbour.

With the freedom to think the unthinkable and no regard to cost or casualties, they had designed a large flat-bottomed boat nicknamed, if translated into English, the Pregnant Sow. The Sow, perhaps dozens of them, would be equipped with a square drop bow and would act as nothing more than a container for a fast torpedo boat inside its hull.

Called Piglets, these would sit on a wheeled launching trolley, the notion being by ramming the upright and barely submerged steel rails of the Spithead Boom with the Sow, it would become fixed. Dropping the bow, the Piglets could then be rolled out into safe water, to launch an attack with torpedoes on the inner anchorage, destroying whatever warships were anchored there.

The group attended class the next morning, full of hubris at this superb and stunningly original plan, which had held for a moment of congratulations. Then their instructors punctured their egos with the information every class for the last forty years had come up with something similar as a solution.

'What's so bloody funny?'

Memory of deflation had made Graebner chuckle, but he merely shook his head in response. Leading Billy over to the chart on the wall, he pointed out the various standing obstacles protecting Portsmouth from attack. As he did so, the names he had studied resurfaced, along with the dimensions and materials used to create the defensive construct, which had protected the main fleet anchorage for nearly seventy years.

The Spithead Boom stretched from Lumps Fort, Southsea, through a series of mid-channel bastions, to Nettlestone Point on the Isle of Wight. There were also anti-submarine nets supported on large mooring buoys, those equipped with great spikes to snare and hole any surface vessel coming close. The net had thick steel cables at head and base, the latter loaded with iron and moored to buoys to which over a thousand tons of chain had been attached.

Nearly two hundred heavy anchors held it on the seabed so not even the smallest vessel could slip underneath. At a point on both boom and net was a chain gate, operated by hydraulic winches on a pair of guard ships, which could be opened to allow incoming and outgoing vessels to pass. On either shore of the approaches lay a whole series of gun emplacements, housing weapons of a calibre sufficient to sink a battleship. In addition, there were the old gun batteries strung across the Portsmouth approaches, known as Palmerstone Forts, which now served as emplacements for anti-aircraft guns.

'There is another boom on the western side of the island, but that is of no concern to us.'

'You seem to ken a lot about it,' Billy responded, with an air of grudging respect.

'I do,' Graebner replied proudly before explaining the reason.

'Have things no been changed since the sinking of the *Royal Oak*.'

That had been a great coup for the Kriegsmarine, getting a U-Boat through the defences of the main Royal Navy fleet anchorage at Scapa Flow last year. It had sunk a battleship, albeit an old one and not of the first rank.

'I have no information anything has changed and, if it has, I cannot allow it to enter my calculations. I just have to hope not. It appears we are presented with an insurmountable obstacle, one only a madman would attempt to cross. When we get to sea, the last place our enemies will look for us is north of the boom.'

'They'll look. You cannae pinch a lifeboat and not have it noticed.'

'They will, I think, suspect we have gone elsewhere.'

The question was in Billy's eye, so Graebner explained about sailing distances and what would be within range, like the Channel Islands. Having had that idea in the bath, Billy was quick to rate it as sensible, only to have it dismissed.

'We would be at sea in daylight and for many hours. I suspect aircraft sent to search for us would do so with an order to sink on sight. Your maps would be of little use at the bottom of the English Channel.'

'Are you the madman, then?'

'We are in a position where this is less likely to happen, given we have a singular craft and are about to experience a spring tide.'

'Ah've no idea what that is, but I ken it's no spring.'

'It is an especially high tide, caused when the planets are in alignment, which happens twice a lunar month. The sea level will be high and I think it is possible to anticipate a decent swell. Did you not hear the waters breaking on the shore when we arrived?'

Billy shook his head. A distant rumble of thunder seemed to underline the point. 'So we can get across this boom?'

'Possibly not without damage. But the lifeboat has a double hull and this means we might be able to remain afloat for a time.'

'Enough to get us to the island?'

Billy was led back to the map, with Graebner's finger running along the waters and the coastline north of the eastern boom, before showing the comprehensive defences and troop dispositions on the southern part of the island to demonstrate a stark difference.

'What you will not see, Mr. Houston, are minefields, pillboxes or forts on the northern shoreline, nor are there soldiers according to your maps. Mrs. Milburn told us there is still a regular link by ferry carrying passengers between the island and the mainland. It will be for traders, workers and those holidaying, though I suspect the last has been curtailed since Dunkirk. It is impossible to lay mines in those waters, especially since they can break their moorings and float free.'

The finger ranged round past Cowes to the Western arm of the Solent, where there was another boom. 'Those who have responsibility for the defences are relying on both booms to protect the waters around the north of the island, added to which, there are thick woods there but few beaches of any size on which large bodies of troops can land. They have thus provided for us a chance to get ashore.'

'Ah'm wonderin' how much of a chance?'

'Can you swim, Mr. Houston?' Billy shook his head. 'Then it is just as well there are lifejackets. My plan is to take the lifeboat as close to the shore as is prudent, then try to get over the boom with the outer hull possibly damaged, but not enough to prevent progress. If we can do that,

I will head for shore, the precise point depending on how long we can stay afloat.'

'And if ye can't, we end up swimming, or in ma case flopping. That's one helluva choice.'

'We cannot hide forever and those searching for us have only one fate in mind.'

'Could be the same either way, then?'

'Do you believe in providence, Mr. Houston?'

'I might if ah knew what it meant.'

Graebner had been surprised, the first time he took the Pervitin tablets, at how quickly they changed his gloomy mood. He was now experiencing the same sensation, a surge of confidence reflected in his voice.

'Years ago, I studied the obstacle to be crossed, as if I was fated to one day overcome it. Is this not the object for which you too were intended, after so many years seeking to effect change in your country?'

Billy would have preferred not to nod, but he couldn't avoid it.

'Think of the surprising good fortune of acquiring those maps, which tells us there are safe stretches of the shore where we can land. You led us to Mrs. Milburn, a singular woman, who contrived a way to get us to the island when I must admit to you now, I saw it as impossible.'

'Jammy, right enough?'

'I am assuming jammy refers to luck.'

'What else?'

'The power of the will. I know you to be an admirer of the Führer, yet I wonder if you truly understand his brilliance?'

For once the German's smile was not designed to condescend or annoy. As he spoke Graebner's eyes took on a preachy look, while his index finger jabbed away like that of a politician on the stump.

'Many of my fellow countrymen do not. They thought it unwise of the Führer to re-occupy the Rhineland, cautioned against Anschluss with Austria, even more so to risk war over the Sudetenland. He ignored these doubters to occupy the whole of Czechoslovakia and challenged Britain and France to react.'

'I never doubted him, mister, ah was cheering him on.'

'Now Poland is smashed, France defeated, the Low Counties occupied and two-thirds of Scandinavia too. Who would have predicted such a thing seven years ago, when Adolf Hitler became Chancellor? All this was brought about by the power of his will.'

Graebner's face was close to Billy's own now, his voice low and husky.

'I have come to believe, Mr. Houston, he is not only a genius, but has some direct line to a higher power. How else could he have taken Germany from a dependent nation to the greatness we now enjoy in less than eight years? Believe me when I say this. I think the Gods are with him and they are going to be with us.'

The thunder was a clap now, distant yes, but presaging something greater; the look in the German's eyes seemed to imply even the weather was part of Adolf Hitler's genius.

'Time to load our possessions Mr. Houston.'

CHAPTER SIXTY-THREE

Friday, July 26, 10:43 p.m.

Jeannie Milburn made her way back to the southern end of the rail line to retrieve her bag and bike. No longer needing to detour, she elected to go back by the main road. It was late to be out, even in peacetime, and this applied in spades to a single woman. Knowing she might be stopped, she put the revolver in the bike's pannier.

The journey allowed plenty of time to think on the events of the night and what might come from them in the future, musings still chasing each other round as she approached the South Street level crossing. This railway track split the old part of Chichester from its lower suburbs and the coastal villages. From out as sea came a flash of lightning, followed after several seconds by the rumble of distant thunder, but the sky overhead was clear, the bright moon revealing a crowd of men around the crossing.

The normal number of MPs, backed up by a few LDV volunteers, had been augmented by a large body of troops, men carrying wooden staves, who had to be from the nearby barracks. Given they lined the approach on both sides, it made sense to dismount and walk. Even in the far from perfect light, she sensed they were nervous, eyeing her suspiciously.

With the barriers down, there was no option but to stop. As she closed with the striped pole, an officer stepped forward, hand in the air. A shaded torch was lifted to illuminate her face, which, as it moved, flicked across the brass MP badge on the front of his cap.

'Good evening, madam.'

'Sure, it's past evening, is it not?'

'Which makes me wonder what a lone woman is doing out at this time of night?' Getting no answer, a gloved hand appeared. 'May I see you ID, please?'

'Of course.'

The fumbling in her bag hid the initial shaking. She had expected to have to show her card, but not to the crowd now assembled. It took no great leap of the imagination to sense it might have something to do with Billy Houston and his compatriots. Jeannie's thoughts harked back to Belfast, seeking to get past a Prod copper with messages from her Da safely tucked in her knickers.

The recollection strengthened her so, by the time she passed the card over, her hand was steady. The torch moved to the card, flicking over it before returning to her face. Another rumble of thunder, closer than the last, added to the drama of the moment.

'Mrs. Milburn, can I ask you where you've been?'

'I'm not sure it's any of your business.'

'You will be aware there's a war on, madam.'

'Jesus knows, I could hardly forget it, with what you've got out here, could I?'

She couldn't see the man's expression, but the intake of breath gave her a good indication of his likely response. He was an officer and people did not speak to him in such a manner. Long ago she had learnt that appearing nervous in front of authority could be fatal. This bloody MP had to be convinced if she was out, even if up to no good, there were limits to what he could ask.

'I am going to require you to tell me where you have been, where you are going and what you have being doing. In order that you fully understand, I have to tell you, should you fail to comply, I will have you escorted to the police station. There you will be locked up until you can be questioned by the civil power in the morning.'

'What's going on with all this?'

The question was intended to give her time to think. In normal circumstances she would have told this officious bastard where to go, but these were not normal. The country was on invasion alert and seeing spies everywhere, while she had a pistol in her pannier.

'I'm no more obliged to answer your questions, madam, than you seem to be willing to respond to mine.'

The voice that emerged then was very different in tone, almost girlish and slightly giggly. 'Sure, can you not guess?'

'I have no time for guessing games. So, I repeat, where have you been and where are you going?'

'I'm headed for East Lavant, where I live. I'm the landlady of the Black Jug.'

'A public house?'

'It is.'

'And you have come from?'

To lie or tell the truth? Did this shit of an MP know Borden? It was possible, given a unit of the corps were billeted in the local barracks. She knew he mixed socially with the officers of the Royal Sussex, played golf with the colonel and some of them were honorary members of the yacht club. Chichester might be a city, but only because it had a cathedral: it lacked the population that normally went with such a designation.

In what was socially a tight set-up, men of Borden's stamp would meet blokes like this MP at social gatherings all the time. He had certainly boasted of having had dinner in the officers' mess more than once and might have even sat with this sod. Given what she was about to say, he might even cover for Borden.

'I was on my way to visit a friend.' Jeannie paused. 'A male friend, but decided against it at the last moment. I'm on my way home.'

His tone changed; there was nothing like the notion of illicit sex to divert attention. From being gruff, he began to sound seriously curious. 'Indeed? And who is this friend?'

'Major Alaric Borden. You might know of him?'

'I have met the major, madam, on many occasions and I happen to know he lives within the city, north of this level crossing.'

'Which is why I wasn't going to meet him there. He does duty guarding at the lifeboat station.'

With the obvious in the air, the MP took a deep and audible breath, which could mean he reckoned Borden was a dirty bugger or a lucky one, maybe both.

'And would the major be willing to corroborate that?'

'I'm sure he would, if it was put to him with discretion. It wouldn't do to be calling round his house and asking. And just so you know, sir, I'm a widow and mistress of my own affairs.'

Jeannie Milburn had been an attractive young lady and was still a good-looking woman. She had rarely met a man who did not eye her up on first acquaintance, which had been true before and after she was married. Men thought women couldn't see the gleam in their eye, the immediate calculation as to their chances. Right now, she was hoping this MP would be thinking like most of his peers—a widow, a bit loose—not afraid to say so.

'The Black Jug, you say?'

'Drop in some time and have a drink.'

'Perhaps I will, madam.'

Her card was passed back, a hand went to his cap, while a shout got the pole raised on both sides of the railway line. She set off up South Street until she got to the sandbagged Market Cross. The reaction only came after she had passed the monument, the trembling shaking her body. Her thoughts turned to how to deal with what might happen as the consequences of being honest hit home. The lie about backing out had come easily, but would it hold? It might if she stuck to it.

The sky to the far out to sea showed another streak of lightning, high in the sky, illuminating a line of thick clouds, the rumbling of thunder seconds closer now. Jeannie felt a draft of colder air on her skin. Rain was on its way so it was time to pedal faster, to get away from her thoughts as well as the approaching storm.

Friday, July 26, 11:50 p.m.

Dressed in oilskins and life jackets rendered them anonymous, all except Alaric Borden. Tied up below, he had been given nothing to wear to save him if the boat sank. The storm they had heard in the distance was over them now, rain falling onto the arched metal roof, setting up a deafening tattoo, forcing Rudi Graebner to shout his instructions. With everything they had brought fetched aboard, it was time to kill the interior lights.

They used torches to open the outer doors, revealing a torrential downpour, as flash after flash of lightning illuminated the seascape. The launching mechanism was simple; a cable held the lifeboat in place, with a knock-out pin which, struck off, would put it in motion, slowly but with increasing speed as it tipped on to the steep ramp.

The chances of being observed were lessened by the downpour, but the roar of the twin Gardner engines, when the German fired them up in the confines of the shed, sounded loud enough to be heard in Portsmouth. It was a risk which had to be taken: the boat required power as well as the ramp's momentum to clear the shore.

As soon as this was achieved, Billy and Leo Aviles had the task of raising both the masts, which they had to do after only one dry run, a partial attempt within the boathouse. If they were not yet necessary, the equipment they carried might soon become so. With two men who were not sailors and in the dark, Graebner would probably have to try and get the canvas aloft on his own.

Rain driving into their faces, the pair were exposed to a sudden rush of air as the lifeboat accelerated, followed by the body thudding check as it hit the sea. The deck lifted alarmingly, prior to the twin-recessed propellers getting the grip needed to drive the boat forward. Protected by the glass screen fronting the tiny wheelhouse, Rudi's attention, as they hit the water, was fixed on the binnacle and the compass within. The wheel quickly spun to get on to the course already plotted, which would take him through the minefields and due south. He needed to get well away from the shore until it was safe to change course for the Spithead approaches.

The raising of the masts took time. What had been partial and awkward on a steady dry deck became treacherous on one not only wet, but rising and falling several feet, while swaying from side to side. At one point Aviles lost his footing, Billy grabbing the collar of his oilskin to stop him slipping overboard. Much cursing ensued, but finally the masts were raised and locked in place.

The storm moved over and, once the lashing rain began to ease, it did so rapidly till it was no more than spots, the lightning flashes and claps of thunder heading in over the mainland. This soaked the patrols of soldiers in their tin helmets and capes, traversing the lanes, to look for a trio of dangerous fugitives. If any of them saw the lifeboat launched, why would they question it? When else would such a vessel put to sea except in a storm?

Alaric Borden was fetched up from below and put near the prow, Aviles set to guard him. Sat with his back to the forward hatch, the motion of the vessel caused the Spaniard's stomach, already affected, to churn. It was difficult to hold the shotgun steady and finally the waves caused him to spray vomit, much of which failed to go over the side.

He might not be the most pleasant person in existence or the best looking, but Borden was, as Jeannie had said, no fool, no coward and he, too, had been a soldier. Still in some pain, his mind had never ceased to seek out some means of escape. Tied up below, he had been afforded time to consider other things, like how did these men know he would open the door?

Billy Houston had let it slip. Information about what had been anticipated for the night could only have come from one source. His first thought was of some inadvertent mistake by Jeannie Milburn, but that didn't hold for long, even if his vanity fought what was an obvious conclusion.

She had sent the note, when months had gone by in which she had many times fobbed off his suggestions. He would have needed to be blind not to have observed, in the past, she had a soft spot for Houston. The coincidence was just too great to ignore and, as angry as that made him, he knew he had to put it aside.

A man who had survived the Western Front, then later and more murderously as a Black and Tan military auxiliary in Ireland, he sensed his captors were the kind who would not hesitate to kill. In fact, he was struggling to figure out why he was still alive and why he had been brought up from below, with no attempt to re-tie his bonds.

Billy Houston, who felt fine and was pleased about it, having had a look below, had gone to sit behind Graebner on the wheel and he posed the very same question, albeit with a near shout over the roar of the engines. The equally loud reply was delivered with a wolfish grin.

'We need to be able to throw him overboard, a trick the natives play in South America. They travel by dugout canoe and have to pass through stretches of river teeming with crocodiles. Every family has a dog and, if they are attacked, they throw the animal into the water in order to save themselves. We will do likewise with this Borden fellow. I can assure you, anyone pursuing us will try to save his life, even when trying to catch us.'

A flash shot across the clouded upper sky to the southeast, another burst of lightning presaging what might be a second squall heading their way. Rudi, pointing, shouted to Billy it might be in their favour. They would benefit from a troubled sea, the crest of a wave which might take them over the boom in a boat that drew very little water under its keel, necessarily so for inshore rescue. The defences had been designed to rupture the bottom of deep-hulled warships.

'How long?'

'High tide is at zero two forty, Mr. Houston,' Rudi replied, his watch illuminated by the binnacle. 'Less than an hour and a half from now.'

Rudi Graebner was aware his precise position was far from certain. There were navigational tools aboard which would help him by using the stars—a sextant and charts. But he lacked the time to make the necessary observations cum calculations. Besides, the sky was not always clear, alternating with thick, scudding clouds. They had been heading west for some time now, the point at which he had to turn north down to guess-work, a mental appreciation of the time used up, set against the speed of the lifeboat. The pills ensured his mind was still razor-sharp and he suffered no feelings of fatigue.

They needed to approach the boom between the island and No Man's Land Fort, now home to one of those anti-aircraft batteries. The men operating them would have weapons enough to protect themselves from being raided by boat. If he got too close, they might be turned on him as an unknown vessel at a time when tensions were high. Even if they decided not to fire, they would surely put out a searchlight, then contact the mainland for instructions.

Given he would not reply to any radio appeal, at best it could mean the sending of a patrol craft to intercept a vessel at sea without per-mission. At worst it would culminate in an order to those in the fort to sink him! It was pointless to curse the sky, briefly clear now, star-filled and showing a crescent of moonlight. As long as they could keep their distance, shorn of lights, with a dark blue hull and a superstructure painted with wartime camouflage, to be spotted would take a measure of luck.

But his major worry was the sound of the engines. Would someone hearing them likewise seek an identity by searchlight? The possibility had to be mere calculation; there had been so many things in the last two days about which nothing could be done and this was just one more.

'Have faith in the Führer,' he said to reassure himself and, in his present state, the words made him feel immortal.

Billy, still seated behind him, heard only the sound. He shouted to ask for clarification, getting a shake of the head as the German spun the wheel to get on to a northerly heading. Fearful of the Palmerston Forts, he reduced speed and with it the engine noise, which served to make conversation possible.

'How are we doing?'

'Assuming we can get across the boom, we need to stay afloat long enough to get past an estuary called Wooton Creek. There is an inlet a kilometre or so to the north, the outlet for a stream called Palmer's Brook, surrounded by woods, which the charts in the lifeboat house told me is exposed mudflats at low tide. Should getting to there be impossible, I will make for shore immediately I think we can make no more progress and beach us.'

The thought they might just go under hung in the air, unspoken. 'An' then what?'

'South of Wooton Creek presents us with an obstacle, a long detour to the nearest crossing. Unless we come across an unguarded ford, we will be forced to go far inland to find a way round. You will know as I do every bridge will have a checkpoint. There is a warship on the way so those we need to contact will be anchored offshore. They will come and go by to the island by launch, so we will need to be on the shoreline to make contact and to hopefully get taken off.'

'That's bound tae be well patrolled, especially now.'

'It is a hazard we must overcome, just as we have everything else. Now, since I suspect we are close to the boom, I think it wise to alert Aviles of what might happen very soon.'

'Which is?'

'We must approach at full speed and hope to cross on a cresting wave. Clear it and we will feel nothing. If we strike in any way the boat will either be checked and keep going or brought to a standstill, stuck on one of the steel uprights, It is to be hoped the former. Then it is down to the level of damage to the hull.'

'Have ye heard the expression, about bein' stuck up a creek without a paddle?'

'I fear it is something else you must explain to me.'

'Christ, I hope ah' get the chance.'

'Aviles,' Graebner repeated. Billy got to his feet, then staggered, ending up seated again.

'One hand for the boat, Mr. Houston, always keep one hand for the boat if you want to be safe.'

'Are you sure you dinna want me falling overboard?'

'Please do not. There will be no stopping to rescue you.'

There was an immediate increase in engine noise as Graebner put on speed, making the effect of the swell more telling. Lifeboats being extremely buoyant vessels, designed for use by men with much sea-going experience, there was a limited amount on which to get a grip as far as Billy could see.

At the very moment he moved, a cloud began to obscure the moon. Soon the only light he had to guide him was the silver lining on the edge, and it was fast diminishing. He took time and care to cover the distance from the wheelhouse to the tiny foredeck, traversing the narrow walkway between the side and the upper works. He had to stop frequently to prevent himself from falling, cursing the fact the only thing between him and water was a series of metal uprights through which ran sets of canvas-covered chains.

Alaric Borden was up ahead, wondering how to get his hands on the shotgun with which he'd been hit. He would have acted immediately if he had known the ugly brute guarding him with that very weapon was under a strict orders to threaten, but not to shoot. The sound of a gun going off, added to a flash which might be seen a mile away, could be fatal to their mission.

Leo was really suffering, turning away more than once to retch, every heave followed by a deep groan, the muzzle of the shotgun barrel dropping to the deck. As a sailing man, always willing to take lubbers out for a cruise, Borden knew about seasickness. The longer it lasted, the weaker the sufferer became and this presented him with a ghost of a chance.

The sudden increase in cloud came as a godsend, producing precious darkness and blinding them both. When Borden next heard retching, he closed in, hoping his opponent would be slow to react. Leo heard the scrabbling shoes and tried to poke forward with the barrel, but he was hampered by his oilskins and life jacket. Leo was thus still seated while the man attacking him was now upright so, lacking an alternative, he swept the gun barrel across what he hoped were Borden's legs. This took away the man's feet and, slipping on the Aviles vomit, sent him crashing to the deck.

Billy heard a shout of warning. As he moved the sea caused the lifeboat to lift and yaw sideways, making him stagger backwards, his hands scrabbling to get a grip on something, anything. Leo Aviles was struggling to get to his feet, not aided by the same motion, or indeed his calf-length rubber soled boots.

A touch of silver cloud edge showed him on his hands and knees, shotgun on the deck, also Borden aiming a boot at his head. No more balanced than his opponent, the kick missed and Leo, rising underneath the swinging leg, he had time to grab hold of his attacker's upper leg. Having got a grip, he hauled him in until his stubble raked the Englishman's cheek.

Being upright on a moving deck nearly proved fatal for Billy Houston, who had tumbled dangerously. Hanging on for dear life to a linking chain he saw, as the cloud cover eased, the two silhouettes locked in a swaying embrace. Not that he could do anything about it except shout to Graebner and hope he could hear.

It was a contest Leo Aviles would have won with ease on dry land. Borden could fight, but he lacked the muscle of the Spaniard, who had finally got an arm round his throat. Having bent him double, he pinned Borden in a lock destined to choke the life out of him. Gasping, Borden did the only thing he could. Grabbing Aviles's knee, he tugged viciously, trying to unbalance him till one foot spun off the deck, forcing the Spaniard back a little.

At that same moment the lifeboat came into contact with one of the steel uprights on the Spithead Boom, which caused a judder, followed by a grinding sound, as the boat scraped over. A following wave lifted the stern and carried it forward, but the deck canted so violently neither man could hold his ground. Borden, the weaker, slipping on more vomit, staggered against the chains, which struck him in the lower back. He was still clinging on for dear life to Leo's knee as he hurtled backwards.

On his belly, one hand locked round the chain, Billy saw the two silhouettes tumble over the side. A cry of panic came from Leo, followed by the sickening splash as they hit the water. Billy hauled himself forward, yelling out to Graebner to leave go of the wheel and come to his rescue, this as a hint of phosphorescence revealed the two men in the water.

They were no longer in an embrace but separate, with Borden beginning to strike out and swim. Leo floundered around splashing, kept afloat by his life jacket until, screaming in panic, he drifted out of sight of the speeding boat. A hand grabbed Billy's collar and hoisted him half upright as he wheezed out what had happened.

'Make your way to the wheelhouse, there's nothing we can do,' bellowed Graebner.

'We can save Leo.'

'How, when we cannot even see him? Which side of the boom is he on? We have got across it once, to attempt to do so twice would be foolish.'

'You're no even goin' tae try?'

Graebner didn't bother to reply; he returned to unlash the wheel on a boat still making headway. Billy joined him, observing in the faint light off the binnacle, a grim-faced man, eyes straining straight ahead, which was as good a way as any of saying the matter was closed. Billy wondered if doing nothing was a convenience, reviving a feeling which had never lain dormant. Would he now become expendable, too?

'Mr. Houston, please take the wheel and hold it steady on the course I have set. The boat is taking in water. I need to go below and get some idea of how fast this is happening.'

The mutually unfriendly stare which followed spoke volumes; the German looked as if he knew exactly what Billy Houston was thinking.

CHAPTER SIXTY-FIVE

Saturday, July 27, 4:05 a.m.

Down below, water was already seeping into the inner hull. The crunch had told Rudi Graebner the lifeboat had struck something, but there was no actual sign he could see of the damage caused. Holding the flashlight steady, he watched the level as it crept up to surround the soles of his boots, trying to calculate how long it would be before a boat built for buoyancy became unseaworthy. It would be a race between what water was being shipped, against what the pumps could discharge.

At least they had got past the No Man's Land Fort without any reaction; if the men manning the anti-aircraft guns had heard his engines, they had failed to respond. On the wheel, Billy was holding a steady course, still thinking it could just as easily have been him who'd gone over the side. The notion of floating off into nothingness, in total darkness, was terrifying and he could not avoid putting himself in the Spaniard's place.

Borden's plight surfaced too, but he had to assume the sod would drown. Leo was wearing a lifejacket, so there remained a chance he could stay afloat till daylight and a possible rescue, which led him to wonder if this was really something to hope for. Naturally it mutated into an assessment of what harm the embassy driver could do. If he had been angered by the way he'd been kept in the dark, Leo had been told even less. Reluctantly, he was forced to admit the German's way of keeping things to himself made some kind of sense, albeit he reckoned the habit came from the bastard's arrogance.

'I will take the wheel now.' Graebner shouted, as he activated the bilge pumps.

'What's the damage like?'

'Enough to be of concern, not enough to deflect us from our course.'

'So she's no gonna sink under our feet?'

'It is to be hoped not.'

'I was kind of eager for a wee bit of certainty.'

'Not possible. I suggest you get assembled on the foredeck what we must take with us, because if we do make the shore, we will have little time to act.'

'I'd be happier steering.'

'Which I would allow, if you had the knowledge to make the necessary calculations to keep us alive, but you do not.'

The German shone a flashlight through the open hatch, revealing the sea water slopping around, sight enough to persuade Billy the man was right. Careful not to take risks, he made several trips. Each time he returned he looked to the German for some kind of reassurance, only to receive nothing but a growing list of items they might need if they could get ashore.

It wasn't arrogance that made Rudi Graebner ignore his concerns, but concentration. He knew exactly the distance he wanted to travel, while being acutely aware of the lifeboat's diminishing speed. The vessel was becoming increasingly sluggish, which meant the pumps were fighting a losing battle. It was only a matter of time before the water rose to a level which would shut down the engines. If he delayed too long and that happened, there would be no salvation.

Even if he could close the shore where he hoped, the keel could ground too far out to make a landing feasible until the tide fell. In his calculations there had been a hope the first hint of dawn would coincide with the attempt and at least allow him to steer for a promising spot. Thankfully, the sky was clear once more, the cloud cover broken, the moon and starlight providing some visibility.

The shore off the port side was a line of featureless black, until it flattened out to bands of silver, which told Rudi they were passing the estuary at Wooton Creek. The stolen map indicated the shoreline to the north was covered with woods, which came right down to the uninhabited beach. So, once he was past the creek, the course was changed to get inshore. He needed to be able to land quickly in an emergency, on a coastline the charts told him was free from underwater obstacles, even as he prayed he would not be forced to do so.

There is a long period in the upper latitudes of northern hemisphere, hours during which the sky begins to grey before the sun actually rises. The first tinges of this edged the horizon to the east and it increased until, as his watch hand crept past four, a limited degree of visibility became possible, enough to turn the black shoreline into the discernible shapes of treetops.

More importantly, it illuminated the water between there and the wallowing lifeboat. Rudi felt sure he was still south of Palmer's Brook, but another examination with the flashlight made him doubt he would still be afloat when he got there. He spun the wheel to head for what would be nothing more than a strand of pebbles a few metres deep, suspecting the hull was going to ground long before he could get ashore without hours of delay.

Peering ahead, the sight of the fallen tree trunk, half in the water and stretching several metres out from the shore, raised a faint hope. Whatever storm had caused it to tumble, and by the lack of any foliage it would have happened some time past, it had fallen outwards, its torn roots still amongst the other trees. He was rocking back and forth now, hands gripped tight on the wheel, as if by his body motion he could coax an extra half a knot, as he shouted to Houston to get ready to jump.

Billy could see what Graebner was driving at, but he was far from happy at the prospect. The trunk looked, in the grey light, round and smooth, glistening as though covered with ice. The upper branches, even where they had been worn away, still constituted barbs which could do serious damage to a human body.

He was still hesitating as Rudi eased the lifeboat close, reducing power so it was close to zero but still making headway. He then left the wheel lashed again and came forward, having secured a length of coiled rope on the way. Swiftly he lashed the boat to an upper branch, before racing to the wheelhouse to put the engines in neutral. Seconds later he was back with Billy.

'If you get on to the trunk, I will pass to you the things we need.'

'What about we do that the other way round?'

The man he was speaking to was in a highly strung, drug-fuelled state and for the first time Rudi Graebner really lost his temper. A stream of German invective gushed from his lips. Bunching his fists, he looked as if he was about to strike the Scotsman. Billy balled his own ready to retaliate, giving as good as he got in the 'dirty looks' stakes. Finally, Graebner got control of himself, but he was panting for breath as he spoke.

'We have no time for this nonsense.'

'An' I have no time for being treated like a bit of shite on your shoe.'

Graebner could not work out the words, but the sentiment was obvious. 'Please, Mr. Houston?'

'That's bloody better.'

He climbed over the chains and perched on the gunwale, reaching out for a branch. As he put his weight on the wood, weakened by age and weather, it snapped. He arched forward then leapt in panic, his hand scrabbling for something to get hold of. Seizing another jutting branch, he scrambled to a safer spot, jamming himself in place with both his body and feet.

The first objects passed over were the waterproof shotgun cases, the straps used to loop them around another branch. Next came the German's grip, the soldier's kitbag, followed by the food and ration packs, then a whole heap of things, the difficulty being where to put them which was secure. Cutters, flashlights, a hacksaw and wood saw, a spade, several levers and a pair of heavy canvas gloves followed. Then Graebner passed over his fishing rod.

'What in the name of Christ do you want that for when you left two bloody rifles down below?'

If you excluded the look of near despair, the question was ignored. Billy was then obliged, once Graebner had ensured the safety catch was on, to take the stock of Walter the driver's Lee Enfield and the remaining shotgun—Leo's was assumed to have gone overboard. Finally, he held out a hand to the German.

All he saw was Graebner's back. He was on his way to the wheel-house to re-engage the engines, this time gently in reverse, obvious from the way the prow strained on the rope. Once he had returned and got on to the tree trunk the line was untied. As soon as it was free the lifeboat moved very slowly backwards out to sea. Graebner watched it go, his mood recovered enough to sound even more superior than he'd managed previously.

'Two things you should seek to learn, Mr. Houston, as taught in training to every German officer. The first is to plan ahead, the second to be open to sudden opportunities. Both of these, plus the will to implement them, are the reason the forces of the Reich have enjoyed such success. I would suggest this applies to us as well'

'You're no goin' tae tell me you planned this, pal?'

'No, but I saw the chance to say goodbye to the boat. If those engines can take her far enough out to sea, she will sink in water so deep no one will know where she has gone, or where we have landed. The luck and will of the Führer has come to our aid once more. Now I suggest it is time to get ourselves and this equipment in amongst those trees.'

Wearing heavy gloves, they had to cut the strands of barbed wire looped over the landward end of the tree trunk. By the time they were through, disguising the break by careful plaiting, it was close to full daylight.

CHAPTER SIXTY-SIX

Saturday, July 27, 4:13 a.m.

Alaric Borden was a strong swimmer and, when he had a clear sky, the North Star gave him a course to follow. But it soon clouded over and the still blacked-out shore gave him no help. So it was hope over knowledge that kept him going, he being unaware it was often in a circle. The noise of the Gardner engines had long faded, leaving him in an eerie silence, broken by faint and diminishing calls for *ajuda* from his equally distressed opponent, until both ceased completely.

The water was cold and he knew, unless he was very lucky, eventually it would kill him, not that he ever contemplated giving up. He had survived the Great War trenches for three whole years, from subaltern to his majority which, if not unique, was unusual when the average life expectancy of a new lieutenant was two weeks.

Ireland had been just as deadly, with an enemy full of guile, in a population which would never let you know who was a danger and who was not. Comrades had been ambushed and assassinated, others shot in their beds or blown up in their cars. He had come through that too and, as he swam, he tried to concentrate on the memory of the Irish rebels he had killed, happy to look them in the eye as he blew their brains out.

Desperate thoughts led to desperate hopes: when the lifeboat was seen to be missing, so would he be, which would happen as soon as the next man on duty arrived. These were soon overtaken by reflections on the treachery which had caused him to end up in this predicament, one he was obviously not meant to survive.

'Jeannie Milburn. I'll see you hang for what you've done, you scheming bitch.'

No one was close enough to hear his shouted curse, but issuing it made him feel better. Mentally, he ran through all the other people he hated, those he would happily string up or burn alive, until the cold of the Solent finally penetrated his being to the point where he could keep going no longer. Exhausted, he was unable to keep his breathing above the waves. What stopped him yelling at his fate, as well as his hatred of so many of his fellow humans, was his lungs filling with seawater.

CHAPTER SIXTY-SEVEN

Saturday, July 27, 5:06 a.m.

Stripped of their foul-weather gear left Billy, lit by the low, early morning sun, in a suit even more crumpled than before. Graebner, stripped to the waist, took a towel and his wash bag from his grip, then walked down to the shoreline within the strung barbed wire. Using salt water and with the aid of a small mirror, having got a thin layer of lather going, he very carefully began to shave, calling over his shoulder as he slowly stroked his chin.

'I would suggest you follow my example, Mr. Houston. It never does to look unkempt. Also, you will be less obvious in the driver's uniform than a civilian suit which has seen better days. Who is going to ask someone so dressed what they are doing at such a time as this?'

'Is it part of the master plan?' Graebner flung him a crabbed look as he towelled his face, prior to going to his grip and pulling out the clothes he required. 'I'm no goin' to argue what you've done up till now has'na worked, but I want to know what's next.'

'The inlet to the north will be mudflats when the tide recedes. We must cross them to get into the woods which run up the coast to Osborne House.' The Scotsman's reservations were obvious. 'We can do little until my comrades arrive. Once they do and begin to go about their tasks, we look for opportunity. In between, we must assess what danger we will face in making contact. Does this tell you what you want to know?'

'It could be days.'

'Let us hope not.'

Graebner, now dressed in garments suitable for country pursuits, which seemed not to suffer from appearing a bit crumpled, reached into his grip for a tweed hat festooned with fly-fishing hooks and placed it on his head.

'Goes wi' the fishing rod right enough,' Billy remarked.

CHAPTER SIXTY-EIGHT

Saturday, July 27, 5:25 a.m.

Adam Strachan had taken the middle duty of the night, two till four, watching the grounds, pistol on his lap, for any hint of movement. With the advent of daylight, he had been able to reflect on the potential threat, leaving him with the feeling he might have over-reacted. His youngsters had been right: if the men they were after had been favoured by a run of astonishing luck, it surely could not extend to finding a boat.

Even if it had, it would be, at best, something propelled by oars and easy to intercept, unlikely to get them anywhere significant without their being spotted. When Jocelyn relieved him, he removed his jacket and shoes, loosened his tie and lay down. He was tired enough to fall rapidly asleep in what were, if you excluded the bird song, fairly quiet surroundings. But he wasn't left in peace for too long, being shaken awake by his replacement.

'It's Jerry, sir.'

Adam was up and at the window in seconds, peering through binoculars to pick out the distant outlines of a clutch of warships. They were backlit by the sun, their foaming bow waves and black smoke streaming from the funnels. The trio in the centre, one capital ship and two destroyers, flew huge swastika pennants on their mastheads.

Along with them, on either beam, came their British escorts: an aircraft carrier, as well as a couple of cruisers. Watching these vessels eventually became tedious so, leaving the task to his juniors, Adam lay down once more and was soon fast asleep again. When he did come round, it was to the information he was no longer in pursuit of a man called de Bázan but an officer in the Kriegsmarine called Graebner.

CHAPTER SIXTY-NINE

Saturday, July 27, 6:35 a.m.

Cecil Hendy was seriously hungover. A fifty-year-old member of the life-boat crew, openly acknowledged as not the brightest, he was the next on duty. Thirty-five minutes late in turning up, and assuming his predecessor to be asleep, he employed his key with great care. Coming from shore side, he had failed to see the slipway doors were open, so he received a shock on entering. The first thought to enter his befuddled brain was, with the heavy squalls of the previous night, there had been an emergency and he had missed the alerting flare.

Hendy had downed too many pints the night before, following a successful darts match, then gone on to drink more home-made beer with a mate until well past midnight and this led to a deep sleep. Indeed, if his elderly mother had not dragged him out of his bed, he would still be there. Now there was a worry about the consequences.

He had no choice but to wait for the boat to return, nor did he have any doubt he would be in line for a proper roasting. All he could do was lock the landward door and wait. The ramp doors he left open; the boat would be coming back sometime and no one could get onto the beach below without coming through the boathouse.

Tottering up to the office, the sight of the unused cot was too tempting. Hendy took off his boots, lay down fully dressed and began to reminisce about the good arrows he thrown the night before. He soon fell asleep, sure the roar of engines on the returning boat would be sufficient to wake him up.

CHAPTER SEVENTY

Saturday, July 27, 7:14 a.m.

From an elevated position at Osborne House, it had been possible to see the warships from a distance. But it was almost an hour before they became fully visible to Rudi Graebner, standing just inside the treeline. He used his binoculars to range over a vessel, one he soon recognised as *Prinz Eugen*, and the pair of accompanying destroyers.

As the British escorts dropped back, his heart lifted at the outline of the heavy cruiser, as sleek and as handsome a vessel as any navy could possess, as well as a triumph of German shipbuilding. Approaching the access point, the guard ships winched open the boom over the deep channel running along the Southsea shore, waiting till *Prinz Eugen* was passing slowly abreast of where he stood, with no need for magnification, before calling Billy to join him.

'There you are, Mr. Houston. There is our route to safety and success. All we have to do is get those maps aboard.'

'Us, too.'

'Obviously. Now please, it is time for you to change into uniform.'

'Another please, is it?' was the sarcastic response. 'Yer goin' soft, Mein Herr.'

Another irritated sigh came from a man beginning to feel weariness creeping over him once more.

'It is necessary we move up the coast to Palmer's Brook. The tide is falling now and I wish to cross it as soon as it as possible to do so. I suggest it would be unwise to move improperly attired, since we have no idea who or what we may encounter. Should it be troublesome, the bayonet you carry will provide the best means to keep our presence secret.'

Once Billy was in khaki, it was essential to tidy the site and hide evidence of their presence. The only visible sign left was a patch of disturbed earth behind a tree, which lay right on a sliver of still wet beach, just by the barbed wire. This is where the German had buried the lifeboat gear knowing the next high tide would cover any evidence of digging. It still left a lot to carry and, if spotted, they would be bound to raise eyebrows, so they moved with great caution through the trees until they could observe the fast-receding waters of their destination.

At the entrance, where it met the sea, Palmer's Brook was blocked off with thick, driven-in stakes, connected and covered with a mass of coiled barbed wire. They examined the ground between the treeline and the water's edge carefully, especially a partially overgrown pathway, which disappeared into the brook.

'Now we must wait,' Graebner said.

'Time tae tuck in then,' was the Scottish response. 'Ah'm bloody starving.'

Billy and Graebner ate and drank in silence—they would now have to exist on the British Army ration packs—before the German returned to the tree line to observe the slowly falling waters. This left his companion to think and, having come this far, Billy yearned more than ever for his dream to become reality. He felt he was in touching distance of fame and power, so tantalisingly close it was like an itch.

Yet it all still depended on the German: if he had a plan to get them both aboard those warships, he was, as usual, keeping it to himself. There was an equal chance he was hoping for a solution, not plotting one. It was an attitude which had got them this far, but at any time their luck could run out, and if it did, what then?

'Providence and the Führer's will have tae do the business, he probably reckons.' This was spoken softly to himself, and it was almost with fascist blasphemy he added. 'Well, ah'm no buying such bollocks.'

So little time had passed since the fight in the Group Captain's hall, which had him going over what had happened since, not least Graebner's attitude. Leaving Leo with his pistol was bad enough, but the bastard hadn't even tried to disguise the reason. He might as well have said outright, now he had the maps, the man who had brought them to him was expendable. What was he thinking right now? Maybe the time had come when going it alone would present a greater chance of success than as a pair.

In considering the possibility, as well as his previous actions, the conclusion Billy arrived at was inevitable; he wasn't safe now and never had been, so what followed was natural. Those maps represented the only chance he had of living, never mind prospering, so if only one person was going to survive to deliver them, it would be him.

He had a loaded rifle and knew how to use it. Graebner might strut and boast, but Billy was sure he had never been in real combat. Talk all you like and act big, but there was nothing to compare with the real thing. Billy had lain under continuous machine gun fire, knifed, bludgeoned and shot people trying just as hard to kill him.

Sat against a tree trunk, with the kitbag supporting his lower back and recalling the fights he'd been in, he couldn't help his drooping eyes. What he had been through since leaving the Black Jug had been exhausting. After several jerks into wakefulness, his chin dropped onto the rough soldier's battledress and stayed there, a faint snore alerting Graebner.

The equally exhausted German felt a deep sense of resentment because the methamphetamines had worn off again. He was drained and with it came a gloomy feeling the final act might be insurmountable. His comrades were so close, but how was he going to get to them and, could it be done before those bound to be pursuing them caught up?

As soon as that lifeboat was missed, it would take no great leap of imagination to work out who had been the thief. When would his newly arrived comrades make the first foray ashore? How long would the window of opportunity stay open? He looked at his watch, thinking the Scotsman could have another half hour, then it would be his turn.

But could he sleep soundly with Houston awake? Was he at risk in doing so? The man was impetuous, which was bad enough, but he was also ambitious. Rudi was sure he wanted to be the one to deliver those maps, but he could never fashion a way to proceed. No German, an inability to swim and probably useless when it came to a boat. There was not too much reassurance in such a conclusion; Houston was fool enough to try. The tube came out and two more tablets were slipped into his mouth.

At all costs he needed to stay awake and remain alert; if what he was taking carried dangers, these must be ignored. He dragged the map out again to study the locality—lanes, roads, the extent of the woods and local landmarks.

CHAPTER SEVENTY-ONE

Saturday, July 27, 9:00 a.m.

Graebner woke Billy when the crossing was in sight, the water having fallen, revealing a muddy path leading to a slightly elevated section, poking out from the northern shore, with a flat bridge where the water was deepest. Once they left the tree line, they would be clearly visible, but it had to be accepted, albeit they needed to move swiftly.

'After you, Mein Herr,' Billy said at the water's edge. 'Ye want to be the leader, so you get the honour of getting wet first. If the water's deeper than you think,' Billy cawed cheerily, 'you'll get yer arse soaked.'

'You think it a time to be making jokes, when we are in imminent danger?'

'Danger ye call it? You'd no say that if ye'd ever been in real fighting. Wait till you've got bullets cracking past yer heid and shells chewing up the ground around ye. Without jokes tae keep up yer spirits, you'd go doolally.'

Graebner waved the strange word aside and bent to undo his brogues, removing his long socks and unbuttoning the plus-fours. Billy took off his boots, socks and gaiters, rolling up the khaki trousers, which proved barely necessary. The water was halfway to their knees at the middle and ankle height on the mudflats, and they were soon on the north bank, splashing the silt off their feet and calves.

The strip of forest was narrow and not far inland from the northern edge lay a group of dilapidated farm buildings. They looked deserted but no chances could be taken, so they were forced back into cover. The German found a climbable tree in which they could hide the things they dare not be seen carrying. Billy was far from happy when he realised this included the shotgun cases, until Graebner held up his fishing rod, also encased in canvas.

'I hope to be taken for a person in search of a spot to fish. I would not be seen as such if I was carrying all these other articles, which would apply even more to a soldier. Therefore, we must hide our equipment as well as the maps. We can recover them when we attempt to get off the island. A tree in full leaf is better a far less obvious than digging up the ground.'

Graebner did not wait for agreement. He began to climb, reaching out for the things to be passed up and lodged where the leafier branches joined the trunk, the gun cases once more looped by the handles. A check was made, once he re-joined Billy, to ensure none of this is visible from the ground.

'We must split up and reconnoitre.'

'I'd prefer we stay together.'

Graebner's hands shot up in the air again, the eyes, too, unnaturally wide, eyebrows high on his forehead. Putting this down to the man's temper and officer bullshit, Billy failed to register the tension in his jaw, brought on by his fast thumping heart.

'Then you had best come up with a reason for a man out fishing, to be walking around in the company of a lone private soldier.'

'Wi' some of the dirty buggers ah've known, ah could think of a few.'

'We need to know what we face, both around Osborne House, as well as between there and the shore. Can I—we—find a spot from which we can attract the attention of a boat coming to and from *Prinz Eugen* or one of the two destroyers? You can examine the area around the house, while I explore our surroundings before we meet back here.'

Billy had no choice but to agree and, at the German's bidding, they synchronised their watches.

'I will aim to return by six o'clock, Mr. Houston, though it cannot be precise. So let us get busy, or half of the day will be gone and we will have no idea what we need to do.'

CHAPTER SEVENTY-TWO

Saturday, July 27, 10:43 a.m.

Fred Shillingford, coxswain for the West Wittering lifeboat, had paper-work to complete. This brought him to the station mid-morning, glad to find the door double locked, given Cecil Hendy was inclined to be forgetful. He had been through no end of trouble the year before when petrol rationing had been first introduced and half his fuel had been nicked within days.

The mood only lasted until he stepped inside. There was an empty ramp and the sea beyond the open doors, blue in the sunlight. He rushed up to the office to find Hendy snoring his head off, incurring a blasphe-mous awakening which didn't abate, for all his insistence the boat had been gone when he arrived, and there was no sign of the man he was supposed to replace either.

'Just your luck Cecil, it was Borden.'

'He's not on the roster, Fred.'

'Mister high and bloody mighty does what he likes.'

Shillingford had received a phone call the day before, to say that whoever was due to take the night's guard shift should be bumped off in favour of the committee secretary, no explanation given and none required. But if Borden thought what he got up to in the lifeboat station was a secret, he was wrong.

Had the sod taken the boat out without alerting him? How could he without a crew. Hendy had been adamant he had been at home the previous night and heard nothing. As a precaution, Shillingford called the solicitor's office, to be told rather archly by the receptionist Mr. Borden was not yet in. He then dialled the number of the Naval HQ, to be greeted by a duty officer, who thought he had a sense of humour, or maybe even an idiot on the line.

'Have you looked in the cupboards? Down the back of the couch usually yields a few surprises.'

'This is no joke, mate.'

'No? How am I supposed to take it? Someone's mislaid a bloody lifeboat?'

'Was there a request to take it out last night?'

'Hold the line.' A muffled conversation ensued, followed by. 'No.'

'Well, the boat's not here.'

'Try lost property?'

'You want to give me your name?'

'Why?

'So I can find you and stick my boot up your arse.'

'You and who's army?' The line went dead.

The next call was to the police station, to talk to an equally incredulous desk sergeant, though one who knew Fred from the bowls club, so was less inclined to take the mickey. He sent for the duty inspector, on his way to the canteen. When the inspector spoke, it was with no courtesy at all. A friend of Alaric Borden and a fellow freemason, he knew of the relationship between them, so saw the caller as just out to cause trouble.

'We are short of staff, overloaded with work and I do not appreciate being called upon to search for a lifeboat. It must be obvious to you that the vessel has been taken out and will return in due course. Now I suggest you contact Mr. Borden and ask him.'

'He was here on duty last night,' Shillingford protested.

'Then there you have it. Major Borden has obviously responded to some emergency. Even you must be aware of the nature of last night's weather.'

The duty inspector had only just finished his tea and scone when he was summoned to the telephone a second time, to talk to a DCI Naylor from London. He was obliged to listen to a repeat of the unwelcome news, which he had been told when he came on duty at eight. A trio of murder suspects, the subject of an all-points national alert the day before, had almost certainly come into his area. He was quick to say it would be dealt with, pointing out the shortage of staff he was labouring under. This did not go down well with a fellow copper also under strain.

'We are all in the same boat.'

'Really, sir,' responded the inspector sniffily.

Scotland Yard detectives were not much loved in the provinces, being seen as a load of publicity-seeking prima donnas and, with this inspector being from a different regional force, Naylor's seniority meant nothing.

'We are on the front line of national defence at the same time as being required to keep the King's Peace. And, speaking of boats, when was the last time someone rang you to report a missing lifeboat?'

'Can't say I've had that one before.'

'Nonsense, of course. Who, in God's name, would want to pinch a blasted lifeboat?'

Naylor was back in the Wyvern flat, curious about Adam Strachan's question regarding German spies. The killers were now apparently in a coastal part of the country, so he could easily think of someone who would want to steal a lifeboat. It was necessary, however, to be careful with an officer from whom he wanted cooperation, so his voice was conciliatory.

'It might be an idea to take that seriously.'

'We will keep a look out for your suspects, sir. Perhaps, if you have the time, you can look for a missing lifeboat, because I have not!'

Naylor put the now dead phone down slowly. In every move since the de Vries murder, time had been a factor and this was no exception. They had missed Billy Houston at the Wyvern flat, who knew by how long? Another failure occurred at Cadogan Place, though that was down to the hobgoblins. And then there was Carlyle Square.

The inspector in Chichester needed a rocket up his arse, but Naylor lacked the means to fire it. Luckily there was a commander on duty who was a good mate, so he went to find him. Nor could he issue orders to an officer of another force, but he could get in touch with Sussex police HQ and ask the most senior man there to give his inferior a quiet hint. Given the case involved the intelligence agencies, it might involve unwelcome repercussions.

'Sorted, George,' he said as he put the phone down. 'You owe me a pint.'

Naylor waited for a bit, then phoned Chichester again, finding a much less irascible fellow on the line, willing to talk about the missing lifeboat but, more importantly, how and where it was housed. A phone call to MI5 was unavoidable, just as Naylor knew he would be required to motor down to Sussex and take charge of the investigation. It was still, to him, about murder.

A gentle rap on Adam's door was the prelude to an abashed Jocelyn, coming in to relay a message from Scotland Yard.

'Got that copper on the blower, sir, Mr. Naylor. Says he needs to talk to you urgently.'

Saturday, July 27, 11:50 a.m.

Patient explanation of the lifeboat station's position was required for Jasper Harker. A prior call by Adam to the Royal Navy HQ had brought an assurance it was outside the Solent defences. His concerns aired, he was unequivocally told entry to the inner anchorage was impossible, which left the southern part of the island as a possible landfall. More worryingly, the boat had enough fuel, it went slowly, to get all the way to Normandy.

'Naylor is engaged in a homicide enquiry, sir and, even if he reckons it's more, he doesn't know the facts. But the man is sharp and he's wondering if his suspects might have tried to escape to France.'

'Does no harm to trust a copper, Adam, I have always said so.'

'We need the boat found and either brought in or sunk, I don't care which. It could have set out any time after ten last night and it can do eight knots, so it will still be at sea. That means naval and air patrols, which are well above my level to organise.'

'Meaning it has to come from me?'

'Yes, sir, and time is clearly of the essence. The coast of France is a lot less than a full day's sailing away, so are the Channel Islands and, as the reports will have already told you, our enquiries have identified one of our suspects as a naval officer. Also, given I have no assurance where they're headed, I have to be sure both the Barton Manor and Osborne estates are sealed off.'

'You have those chaps in Chichester, Strachan,' Harker reminded him.

'Not one of whom is yet to set foot on the island.'

'Very well,' Harker sighed. 'I'll see what I can do with the Navy and the RAF. But I must leave it to you to sort out the soldiers.'

'Thank you, sir,' said Adam, thinking Jasper Harker was turning out to be man only too keen to avoid responsibility.

In Cowes, an antiquated paddle steamer was disembarking a file of weary and disgruntled Tommies, men who had been up all night getting soaked while chasing shadows. Finally, they had been ordered to move to the station in Chichester for onward passage to Southampton and the ferry. Once landed, they had to march to the proposed camp site at the Osborne Golf Club, north of the house and closed for the duration, it being, on the fairways, packed with obstacles designed to thwart German paratroopers.

As soon as he heard they had arrived, Adam went to meet with their officer, a fresh-faced second lieutenant called Trenton, who looked to be similar in age to Avery and Deveraux. The subaltern was quick to call the men on parade.

'B Company, eighty strong, Mr. Strachan.'

'I was hoping for the whole battalion.'

'The rest will follow in a day or two. Our task is to get the camp ready, sir. Latrines dug and tents up. May I introduce my Company Sergeant Major, Mr. Grout, on secondment from the Hampshires?'

An enquiry from Adam established most of the previous Royal Sussex NCOs were either dead, casualties or possibly German POWs. Grout, at least, looked every inch a soldier, he had the kind of attitude which would spot an undone blouse button or a scruffy boot at a hundred yards. Adam guessed it was he who was really running the company. He had also registered something extremely worrying. The soldiers were parading with pickax handles, not rifles.

'Not been issued yet, sir,' Trenton admitted. 'Only myself and the NCOs are armed.'

'Permission to speak, sir?' asked Grout. He had a pistol holder on his webbing.

'Of course.'

275

'What rifles the company had were lost in France, sir. Even then, I'm told the regiment didn't have its full quota.'

'And I'm afraid we're sucking the hind tit here at home, too,' his subaltern added.

Adam was tempted to mention Harker scrapping the military barrel. He also wanted to say, should they encounter the men he was after, they would be facing bullets. He held his tongue on the grounds of what it would do to what was already poor morale. It would mean another call to Jasper Harker, followed by a written request for properly armed and disciplined units, couched in no uncertain terms. The chance of something going badly wrong was high and he was damned if he was going to carry the can.

'I need them patrolling round Osborne House with whatever they possess, so I must ask you to forget latrines and tents.' Trenton looked set to protest, but Adam cut him off. 'And should you be thinking of demurring, I won't be calling Chichester. I'll telephone GHQ.'

This was a very serious threat, but Trenton knew instinctively, like Harker, how to dodge responsibility. 'An opinion, Mr. Grout?'

'Best oblige the gentleman, sir.'

This reply came without any hint of what the CSM actually felt, though Adam could guess.

CHAPTER SEVENTY-FOUR

Saturday, July 27, 12:45 p.m.

Graebner left first, fishing rod case over his shoulder, pistol rammed into his plus-fours. His route took him through the woods skirting Palmer's Brook, to where they ceased to provide cover. Examining the open ground ahead, Rudi nearly jumped out of his skin, mistaking a pair of pigeons with flapping wings, frightened out of the full leaf tree under which he was standing, for a human presence.

He had to follow a narrow lane going south towards Wooton Bridge, the only town within walking distance. His aim, which he had been mulling over since landing, but kept from Billy Houston, was simple in theory, less so in practice. It would be foolish and risky to rely on getting aboard any craft going to and fro from *Prinz Eugen*. The solution was as it had been before the Black Jug, to secure a boat and nothing fancy. They might be barred from the coastal waters, but the owners would house them inland for the duration. Could he find one and steal it?

It was an area with few roads, lined with hedges and the odd gate, but no houses that he could see, thinking they must be hidden by acres of woodland. A sudden bleating made his heart jump for a second time, which had him chastising himself. What could he possibly have to fear from a flock of sheep coming into view, supervised by a lad who looked about twelve, assisted by a sheepdog? Breathing deeply, he stood aside, smiling artificially till flock, boy and dog had passed.

Further on, the track opened on to a wide playing field, with youngsters kicking a football about. He skirted round them, turning west along a wider lane bordered by open farmland to the south, until it became bounded on either side by large dwellings within substantial grounds. In some of the drives he saw motor launches and yachts on trailers—not much use without a slipway to launch them.

He needed something like a small dinghy, aware that the further he got from the coastline, even if he could find one, the harder the task would become. It would have to be carried by he and Houston along the very lanes he had just tramped, the risks of such an undertaking painfully obvious.

In time he came to a proper road and the crest of a long hill dropping down to Wooton Bridge itself, the houses lining it becoming smaller and more numerous. He passed a post office-cum general store, advertising tea, soap, cigarettes and various well-known confectioneries and, being a Saturday, locals were stood outside gossiping until his passing drew their eyes.

Rudi waved cheerily, engendering smiles in response. Further down the hill he stopped at a fountain erected, it declared, to celebrate the jubilee year of Queen Victoria. There he bent his head to drink, enabling him to glance back up the road and see if he had excited undue attention but there was an even greater worry. He knew he was far from composed and had to be approaching the point where to continue taking Pervitin must become dangerous.

His heartbeat was too fast, his head burning so much he desperately wanted to lay it against the cool stone of the fountain. Instead, he cupped a handful of water and mopped his brow, breathing deeply until he felt his heartbeat slow.

At a set of crossroads, he came to a garage, used to repair and store cars, vehicles taken off the road because of the war. In front of a drum fitted with a pump handle, a sign declared no petrol would be dispensed without official ration stamps. But it was the yard at the rear which made him stop. The kind of boats he sought were dotted amongst larger craft, the type it might be possible to carry away. But he lingered too long, allowing a fellow in oil-stained overalls to emerge from inside, rubbing his hands on a dirty cloth, to stare at the newcomer inquisitively.

'Splendid weather,' Rudi called, his chest thumping again.

'Ain't it just,' replied the mechanic, 'Lookin' to fish, is you?' Rudi wasn't, but there was no way to deny it, given what was hanging from his shoulder. 'Best of a morning' with the tide at full. Be back in enough by twoish. I'll be down there myself with this lot closed up. Got a spot in mind?'

'I have indeed,' was an over the shoulder reply from the German; the last thing he could handle in his state was a discussion with another angler. 'Let us hope they're taking the bait today.'

Steadying his pace, he carried on, passing a number of shops closing for the day, confining himself to a smile and nod to anyone he passed, until he came in sight of the weathered stone bridge, which gave the town its name. The arched structure was dominated on the far side by what looked like a mill, while in the roadway, oblong concrete blocks formed a chicane, designed to allow cars through but which would stop tanks.

A natural checkpoint, it was manned by a platoon of Scottish soldiers in their distinctive hats, a troubling presence, given they were not marked on the stolen map. Could there be other troops unknown to him on the island? Were they here because of him and Houston? Would his papers stand up to scrutiny if they were? Could he pass for a Pole with just the ration book?

Standing still in a busy area might draw attention so, turning away, he strolled on, past an inn called The Sloop. A policeman stood outside, chatting to people enjoying a drink in the sunshine. Graebner moved on, making his way along the north of the river until the shoreline houses and cottages petered out into woodland and sloping meadows.

What he had seen in the garage provided his best chance so far, and Rudi tried to calculate what he needed to do. First, he must get Houston and himself into a position where they could steal without attracting attention, something small and portable enough to be carried the distance. A certain amount of daylight would be required.

How he could reconnoitre the yard and pick one out without being spotted and arousing suspicion? The mechanic had intimated he would be fishing himself in the afternoon. Best give time for the man to leave—an hour or two, which he could pass by doing the same. Then he could return the way he came and see what possibilities existed.

In search of a suitable spot from which to fish, he passed a small field, occupied by a dilapidated old caravan, but it was another object which had Rudolf Graebner stop dead in disbelief. In front of him, leaning on the caravan, its base stuck in long, uncut grass, lay an object to set his already fast heartbeat pumping furiously. In his heightened state, it was like a miracle, nothing less than another manifestation of the near divine protection being afforded to him by Adolf Hitler.

Surely only a superhuman presence, like that of his Führer, could have guided him to this very spot, at this time and the presence of a Klepper folding *Flatboot?* A German invention, a craft which had won gold in the Berlin Olympics, the *Flatboot* was a special type of kit-formed kayak. When dismantled, it could be carried by one person in a backpack, to be assembled where it was required. As a cadet he had taken them out on the Baltic, so he knew them well.

This one bore traces of moss; it was, like the caravan nearby, neglected, but poking out from the seating area was one end of the double paddle. Was the frame sound, the pliable covering watertight? Was there anyone in the caravan and what about the backpack into which, broken up, it would fit? His mind was racing faster than his heart. If he could get it to Palmer's Brook, it would provide a perfect way to get him and the maps to *Prinz Eugen.* A second thought should have been troubling to him but was not: a kayak was a one-person vessel.

Rudi knew he must take possession, but should he do so now or later? There was no one else in sight, which could not be guaranteed to last. Others, like that mechanic, might come down to fish. Immediate action was the only course, so he flung his rod into the long grass and eased himself over a rickety fence, pulling out his pistol as he approached the caravan, to gently knock on the door.

Getting no reply, he turned the handle and the door creaked open. The interior was empty, a mess of used bedding and old clothes. Climbing in, then rifling through the detritus, he searched desperately and fruitlessly for the backpack. Downcast, he realised he would have to carry the boat built, but not at this time of day. He would have to stay out of sight till the light faded and the only place to hide was in this filthy mobile hovel.

Going outside, he dragged the Klepper behind the caravan to inspect it, encouraged to see the outer skin seemed intact. Then, pistol in his hand, nerves still jumping, he went back inside to sit and wait, knowing if the owner returned, he would probably be required to kill again.

CHAPTER SEVENTY-FIVE

Saturday, July 27, 12:20 p.m.

Billy had watched Graebner depart with mixed feelings, to then focus his binoculars on the warships, particularly *Prinz Eugen*. What the Germans called a 'pocket battleship' was a hive of activity, nets being strung along its sides, a gap left for a stepped gangway down to water level. Armed German marines stood at intervals along the deck, while a motorised launch circled the hull, shadowed by a Royal Navy patrol vessel. The two other German ships, much smaller, had anchored further out which made the bigger boat the one to aim for.

'But how in the name of Christ are we to get aboard?' he asked himself out loud. 'Smart arse better come up wi' a bloody hot air balloon.'

Tempted to linger, he knew it was time to investigate Osborne House. Climbing a tree at the woodland edge, he examined first the dilapidated farm buildings, until he was sure they were derelict in terms of use. Next it was the rest of the surroundings, small fields criss-crossed with hedgerows, trying to come up with some kind of route which would avoid contact.

He would be a strange sight, clad in a full set of infantry webbing, a solitary rifle-bearing Tommy wandering around in the middle of nowhere. So, back on the ground and walking, he audibly began to rehearse the responses he would use if he met anyone.

'Bloody officers, eh? Here ah am, all on my tod looking out for Germans, as if I could do anything if ah found any.'

'It's plain daft. Ah'm telt the buggers have arrived in their ships, but there's no any roond here.'

The voice altered to mock posh. 'Make yourself useful, Walters,' says the general. Aye, a bloody general it is ah'm driving. Come doon to look the place over afore Jerry comes ashore.'

'Peace? Ah bloody well hope so, pal, cause if we get that, I can go back tae Civvy Street and get on wi' earning some real lolly instead o' shite army pay. Cannae come quick enough.'

Again and again, he went over the phrases, with minor variations, wasted because no one came near him. Eventually he stumbled on a single-lane metalled road, leading to what the maps told him was Barton Manor. Osborne being less than a quarter of a mile away, he set off.

On a hot day Billy was seriously thirsty. In imperfectly fitting boots, he also had sore feet, which promised blisters while army battledress was not designed for summer sunshine. The thick khaki sucked in and retained the heat, so he was sweating heavily as well, which led to a deal of hissed cursing. Feeling sticky, he cursed silently but roundly as he trudged along. Sore feet or not, it was safer to step out, boots cracking on the road, because he needed to look military as well as purposeful.

Turning a tree-lined corner, he came across a trio of men, erecting what looked to be a pill box. Knowing he had been spotted, he had no choice but to keep going, past the pile of bricks, sand and bags of cement. By the side of the road ahead stood a small water bowser, which he eyed greedily.

'Aye, aye,' one of the workers called out, lifting his hat and exposing his sweat-soaked hair. 'Here comes the flippin' army.'

Billy's response was more cheerful than his feelings. 'Make sure that's solid, pal, ma life could depend on it.'

'Where's all your mates?' asked another worker.

The oldest of the trio, probably the gaffer, answered for him, pulling at his braces, a fat-faced creature with a big belly, so deeply tanned he looked as though he had spent his life outdoors.

'On their way to prison camps, Dennis. This poor sod is the last one we've got left after Dunkirk.'

'Yer safe then, fellas. Ah can see to Adolf on ma own, nae bother.'

Amused, the first man indicated a kettle boiling on the brazier. 'Just about to brew up, Jock, if you fancy a cuppa?'

'Can't pal. Got tae report to my officer at the jetty. It's where the Jerries' will come ashore, he telt me.'

'Bloody Germans comin' here?' was Big Belly's scoffing response. 'Wouldn't have happened in my day. Soft, you young buggers are. My lot fought Fritz to a standstill.'

A hoot came from his youngest workmate, the one called Dennis. 'Here we go again. How old Ted won the Great War.'

'Got an officer, have you?' asked the one who'd spoken first.

'Course ah have.'

'Blimey, they've sent some proper soldiers at last,' responded old Ted. 'Typical of Jerry to get here first, mind.'

'Is the place no swarmin' wi Tommies?' Billy asked

'Is it buggery?' came from the youngster. 'Not a squaddie in sight.'

'What aboot officers?'

'Same.'

Billy digested the information, quickly scanning the road. 'Ah might take a chance on that cuppa then, lads.'

'Come and park your arse,' said Ted.

It was risky. He could easily say the wrong thing, yet they had been surprised to see him, which was more than odd. The seat was a couple of planks on bricks, Billy handed a metal mug and tea sweetened with condensed milk, names exchanged. There was Ted, the gaffer, Dennis his nephew and Percy, who was their labourer.

Talk was of Dunkirk and its aftermath, the wisdom of speaking to the Germans, with none sure if it was good idea or a bad one. Billy enquired what was happening at the house, to be told 'hardly anything', except the folk who'd been using it had been moved out. The trio peppered Billy with questions, particularly Ted, who reckoned Billy looked a bit long in the tooth to be in uniform. This he managed to deflect this by claiming to be an ex-regular, a reservist called back to the colours a year before the outbreak. To other questions, he fell back on his rehearsed answers.

Billy posed his own queries, to learn his tea drinking companions were locals and had been working round the area for near six months. He also found out some bods from London had arrived at Osborne House a couple days past but, as yet, no soldiers, which led to another stream of gentle, ribbing jokes. The last of his tea drained, Billy stood, stretched and reached for his rifle.

'Best get goin'. Ma officer'll be wonderin' where ah've got tae.' He pulled his water bottle off his webbing. 'D'ye mind if I top up from yer bowser?'

'Help yerself, mate,' said Ted.

As he marched away, Billy realised he had no need to take risks by getting close to the big house. According to these brickies, there were no soldiers there and none they knew of between him and the coastline either. The way was clear.

'So, bite on that, Herr bloody German bastard,' he muttered to himself. 'It's me, Mr. bloody Houston, who is'na as clever as you, ye reckon, who's found the solution to getting us off the island.'

Heading back the way he had come, Billy had no idea his information was out of date. The Royal Sussex were, at that very moment, coming in from the golf course to take up positions protecting the house and grounds. A wiser head would have checked on what the bricklayers had told him, but he was too eager to get back. He was desperate to take off his boots and have a paddle to ease the blisters.

Khaki blouse off and feet in the shallows allowed Billy to check on the German warships, just in time to see a series of flashing lamps from the big one, obviously a signal. Within minutes a clutch of people, two in uniform, descended the gangway, boarding a motor launch. It pulled away, heading for the shore, quickly hidden by the curve of the land.

Billy's hopes soared: according to the map and Graebner, the Osborne House jetty was the only place to land for miles around, so it must be headed there. This provided a chance which might never come again but, how long would it be before it returned and, more to the point, where was the fisherman?

'Don't you be gone too long, sailor boy. If we're goin' to move, it has to be quick.'

Saturday, July 27, 3:35 p.m.

Adam Strachan was far from relaxed. Osborne House might have some kind of guard at last, but it was, he considered, in numbers and fighting ability, too poor to be effective. How could it be otherwise with no rifles? He had at least been assured by Gilbert, the Adjutant, the rest of the troops requested, were soon to be despatched to the island, a promise yet to be confirmed.

The missing lifeboat troubled him, there being no sign of it or his trio of fugitives on the mainland. DCI Naylor was driving down from London, promising to keep him informed, while aerial reconnaissance had reported no sightings of such a craft out at sea. When he aired his other concerns to a now very cooperative navy, he was offered a flying boat to circle the island and survey the coastal waters.

'How long before they can report back?'

'Need time to get it crewed and airborne, Mr. Strachan, and it would be wise do more than one sweep. I reckon we can get back to you within three or four hours if they find nothing, sooner if they do.'

Adam might want a quicker result, but there was no point in saying so. He was in the hands of the flyboys. His burden was immediately increased when Sefton knocked and entered.

'Jerry has signalled they're sending a party ashore and they've already set off. Didn't even wait for us to acknowledge.'

'Hoping to catch us off-guard, I suppose.'

'We could refuse them permission to land.'

'No,' Adam sighed. 'Let them come. How are they going to get from the jetty to the house?'

'A hay cart is all we have.' Seeing Adam's expression he added. 'It empty. No hay.'

'Don't tell me Sefton, it's pulled by a shire horse.'

'No sir, we do have a tractor.'

Adam swore under his breath, having, along with everything else, failed to secure the proper kind of wheeled transport.

'A tractor should make them think twice about invading.'

The sarcasm went right over Avery's head. 'I suppose we owe then some kind of formal greeting.'

'I give you permission,' Adam replied, hauling himself out of his chair and straightening his tie, 'to shoot the first one that gives us a fascist salute.'

'I say, sir, steady on.'

'Just joking.'

CHAPTER SEVENTY-SEVEN

Saturday, July 27, 4:40 p.m.

'You say this Mr. Borden's decision to man the station overnight was not planned.'

Fred Shillingford didn't immediately respond to DCI Naylor, and he kept a wary eye on the sergeant, too, standing to one side taking notes. He was looking for any traps that might do for him, so what came out was the minimum.

'It was not.'

'Do you want to help us with our enquiries?' Naylor demanded.

'Course I do.'

'Then could we try being a little more forthcoming. If I'm going to have to drag everything out of you, it'll be done down at the Chichester nick.'

The coxswain opened up slowly, trying to manoeuvre round the personal animosity between him and Borden. He did this while detailing some of his less pleasant attributes, not least his skirt chasing, all noted down by Ben Foulkes.

'A bit of a lad, then?'

'You might call him that. I wouldn't.'

'And what would you call him, Mr. Shillingford?'

'A bloody fascist.'

'A common term of abuse and often misapplied.'

'He was the real thing, all right, worse than Mosley's lot by a mile. Had me down for a concentration camp, I reckon, and maybe something worse.' Shillingford paused. 'Any sign of the boat.'

'No.'

Naylor asked the local sergeant, who had accompanied them here, to direct him to Borden's office in Chichester, the building was red brick Georgian, reeking of age and expensive legal advice. The receptionist, a middle-aged woman in glasses, wore a permanent frown under tight grey curls and she was never going to be cowed by a senior detective's warrant card.

'If Mr. Borden is not in, can you tell me where I can find him?'

'Certainly not. The movements of Mr. Borden are his affairs and not to be disclosed to all and sundry.'

'Sundry is it. So, you have detectives from Scotland Yard, engaged in a murder enquiry, coming in here every day?' The irony went right over her head. 'I noticed he has several partners, so I'd like to talk to one of them and it's not a request, it's an instruction, which you block at your peril. I have a police sergeant outside and a car ready to transport you to a cell if you obstruct us.'

A loud sniff followed. 'Has anyone ever told you that you sound just like the Gestapo?'

'I try not to respond to compliments. Now, get on that phone and ask whoever is next in the pecking order to see us.'

A junior partner called Elphick was selected and he, at least, was quick to admit Borden had missed several appointments.

'Unusual?' Naylor asked.

'He does take days off, to go sailing or play golf and the like, but not without informing us in advance.'

'I'm told he has quite a wide range of interests other than sport.'

It was obvious Elphick picked up the drift, because he coloured slightly. 'Major Borden is a very active man.'

'Would it be possible to look inside his office?'

'You should really have a warrant, Detective Chief Inspector.'

'I have four murders to investigate, sir, and, even if I'm not sure what connection your senior partner has to them, there seems to be one. You, as a solicitor, will know I'd have no trouble procuring a warrant to rip your offices apart. I'm sure you wouldn't want that.'

'If I can accompany you.'

'Of course.'

'Wait here Ben,' Naylor said quietly. 'Who knows, he might show up?'

On the first floor, it was very much the senior man's bailiwick, plush and spacious, polished and wide old floorboards, the furniture and paintings expensive as well as a wall lined with a glass-fronted bookcase full of legal tomes. Naylor went to the substantial desk, looking at the dairy which lay in the centre.

'Could you open this for me, please? I don't want to touch anything at this point.' Dated the day before, a short note lay between the pages, to which Naylor pointed. 'And read me the contents.'

It was far from obvious what it meant, though Elphick quickly confirmed it was not Borden's handwriting.

'Mr. Elphick, I am going to ask you to allow me to take this note with me and I will tell you why. Mr. Borden was at the lifeboat station last night and I have been given reason to believe he used that as a place for assignations with females of his acquaintance. I suspect this note may be from one of them.'

'Assignations?' Elphick replied, seriously blushing this time.

'At this time your senior partner is nowhere to be found and it may be, whoever wrote this note, may have some idea of his whereabouts.'

Before Elphick could respond Ben Foulkes knocked and entered, followed by a deeply suspicious-looking receptionist. She turned to the young solicitor. 'This is most irregular, sir.'

'Call from the local station, Guv,' Ben interrupted. 'There's an officer MP called in who was on duty last night. I'm told he has information regarding Major Borden.'

'May I use your phone, Mr. Elphick?'

'By all means.'

'Most irregular,' hissed the receptionist.

'Mrs. Bouvoir, please go back to your desk and put the Detective Chief Inspector through to the police station.'

The call was brief and Naylor remained silent until they were outside by the car.

'We going somewhere, gaffer?'

'Yes, Ben. Station first to talk to this MP face to face, then after, I think, we'll be going to the pub. Hope you've got some dosh with you.'

Chapter Seventy-Eight

Saturday, July 27, 4:45 p.m.

Rudi had spent an age trying to work out what to do next, but one fact was obvious. To go back through Wooton Bridge carrying a kayak was out of the question. It was bound to attract attention and he might even come across someone who knew to whom the Klepper belonged. So, he had to go in the opposite direction, on a route earlier considered as a way to the town, but discarded as unlikely to gift him what he sought.

As a way to return, it was close to perfect for what he had to do. No more than a path ran east along the creek towards the sea, then turned north into more coastal woodland running all the way up to Palmer's Brook. The kayak provided the easiest way to cross even if the tide was in, added to which, it would test the outer skin for leaks from damage he could not at present see.

Back on the north shore, hopefully sure he would not have sunk and, having collected the rest of the maps, he would be in a position to complete the mission. Waiting here for night to fall was time he could ill afford, so he must move in daylight and take a chance on being spotted.

Late afternoon, around six would be best: many English ate around then, so there would be fewer people about. Even if he was seen, would it prevent what he had planned? If he was challenged, it would have to be dealt with, which had him taking out and opening his fish-gutting knife, of more use in such a circumstance than his Walther.

How would the Scotsman react when he saw a single person craft? To convince Houston he'd have to be left ashore, to be picked up later, was not going to be easy. He would surely insist if anyone was going to paddle out to deliver the maps, it would be him. In the same manner Billy had done earlier, this had Graebner talking to himself, vocally rehearsing the argument he would need to convince Houston he had to go first and with him the maps.

'You don't speak German. How are you to relay to my comrades, who you are and the nature of what you carry. They might just shoot you.'

'Have you ever paddled a kayak, Mr. Houston? It is not as easy as it might appear. If handled badly, they can easily capsize which, given you cannot swim, would be fatal.'

Surely Houston would see the logic and acknowledge there was only one sensible course, agree he must be patient and put his trust in not just him, but the Führer! The effect of the methamphetamines was wearing off once more, while a cupped hand showed he was down to the last two pills and these he would surely need. A maximum state of alert was necessary for what was coming, so he must wait to take them. This allowed the previously experienced negative reaction to set in.

By the time he was ready to depart, and with a couple of hours having past in which he could think, Rudi Graebner had come to the conclusion nothing would convince the Scotsman he would survive to claim his reward. Thus, he would have to be kept in the dark. Any kind of confrontation might ruin everything. It might be necessary to dispose of him for, even if he had liked Houston, and he did not, the mission came first.

CHAPTER SEVENTY-NINE

Saturday, July 27, 5:32 p.m.

Arthur Craddock was watching Jeannie Milburn pour his second evening pint when the car pulled up outside the open door. Large and black, it required no ringing bells to tell the landlady it was the police and, if the first man to appear looked benign enough, she was not minded to be taken in.

'Afternoon, gentlemen,' she asked as she laid Craddock's pint on his table. 'What can I get you?'

George Naylor patted the dog, which had waddled towards him, before showing his warrant card, allowing Jeannie to examine it.

'Pity we can't indulge, it's a warm one today,' Naylor remarked cordially. 'Would I be addressing Mrs. Jean Milburn?'

'My name's above the door as the law requires.'

'Ben, ask the gentleman there to take his drink outdoors. And no more customers to enter the bar for a while. Mrs. Milburn, I need to talk to you in private.'

'I take it you're here to ask about Billy Houston?'

For all his years in the force, Naylor couldn't keep the surprise from his face. She was way ahead of him, but how? Enlightenment came swiftly as she continued,

'I'll tell you what I told our local bobby, who was here earlier asking about him. Said his inspector was going mental, with the whole force hunting for a gang of murderers.'

'I find it strange he called on you, unless your local man knew you were acquainted with him.'

Never having had much time for the village copper, a right ejit in Jeannie's view, she had no hesitation in dropping him in it by explaining how they had both come to know Billy. The talks he had given and why. After all, her politics were her own business and thoughts were not deeds, but she couldn't assess how Naylor was reacting.

Apart from the slight frown when she had mentioned Billy, his face gave nothing away. The policeman was actually thinking the local copper was an idiot and not only for attending meetings hosted by the Right Club. The man had denied him any element of surprise. Now he would get no chance of throwing this woman off balance by springing Houston's name on her.

'Did he tell you why Houston is being sought?'

'He did, though it sounded nonsense to my ears.'

'You know him well enough to say so?'

'You might as well hear it from me as from anyone else. Billy and I had a bit of a thing going. Mind, it was months past and I haven't seen him since early April.'

'Take it from me, it's far from nonsense. He's involved in a number of homicides. There's another name I'd also like to bring to your attention. Mr. Alaric Borden. You know him, too?'

'I do.'

'Well?'

'I had an arrangement to meet with him last night, but decided against it.'

'For the purposes of?'

Her eyes flashed. 'I'm a widow. Why do you think?'

'Where?'

Jeannie dropped her head, as if to hide embarrassment. Sex was one thing but the location, the lifeboat station, to her mind when she mentioned it, rendered it sordid.

'He had arranged to guard the place so we could—.' A sigh. 'I couldn't go through with it. I went for a bike ride instead. Lost track of time and didn't get back here till near midnight.'

'So, you didn't go to the lifeboat station?'

'Got close, but no.'

And you'll find no evidence I was there, you bastard. Jeannie reassured herself, staring Naylor right in the eye. He'd be suspicious for sure, but he had no proof she could see. The Black Jug had been scrubbed clean of any trace of Billy and his companions. Even in wartime they needed evidence. Contact with the Right Club might lead to the Isle of Man, which she could live with.

The questioning went on, round and round as Naylor tried to catch her out, unaware he was dealing with someone who had grown up having to hone her lies on the streets of Belfast and sticking to them. Half a dozen other policemen arrived, as well as men in civilian clothes with little Gladstone bags. They asked if they could search the place to which she just shrugged.

'I've nothing to hide. Go ahead.'

'I'm afraid that will include your personal possessions, Mrs. Milburn.'

It was hard to ignore the sound upstairs and, because she couldn't see them, she could only assume the men were looking for fingerprints. After a while one of the coppers approached the table and whispered in George Naylor's ear.

'Forgive me.' He rose. 'One of my men has found something.'

Taken out to the barn, the Scenes of Crime bod had moved barrels and the rest of the detritus. It was close to the last thing he did, carefully opening the pannier at the back of the bicycle. The Webley was brought in, swinging on a pencil, but if Naylor had expected Jeannie Milburn to be shocked, he was disappointed, albeit her mind was racing to find an excuse.

'I'm a widow, out in the country, with cash in my till of a night. Money I can't bank till morning and then going into Chichester only once a week makes sense. I've no one but a local bobby to turn to and he's no great shakes, I can tell you. By the time anyone else got here, it would be too late for them to do anything, so I look to my own defence.'

'And do you have a licence for this?'

'I do not. It's an old weapon my late husband had, left over from the Great War. I carry it in the pannier because I use the bike to go to the bank.'

Naylor took the pencil, weighing the gun curiously, before lifting it up to inspect the area below the chamber. He then called to his sergeant.

'Ben, have a look in your notebook, will you, and read out to me the number they gave you of the weapon issued to Major General Strathallan by the armoury at Chelsea Barracks.'

CHAPTER EIGHTY

Saturday, July 27, 6:55 p.m.

Billy was fretting, a feeling which intensified as the hands of his stolen watch moved way past the appointed hour. Several times he had gravitated to the edge of the western woods to look out for Graebner, only to scurry back to the shore, fearful the motor launch had returned to *Prinz Eugen*. His anxieties were not eased by its absence from view below the cruiser's gangway. Hope of getting aboard could only last so long.

The German had said he would be back long before now, but what if he had got into trouble? It was only too easy to imagine how, when in current times anyone remotely suspicious was thought to be a spy. Even though his English was near flawless, he could easily give himself away and, if he had, Billy reckoned he would be next on the list for capture. Would it be better to try to get to the ships by himself? If he could, the Germans would, hopefully, send a boat for Graebner.

He might have ditched the idea, on the grounds of the difficulties, had he not decided to look in the grip stashed in the tree. He was as aware as Graebner he lacked any German, but might there be anything in the bag that could help him to communicate with them? Shoving aside the clothing, he ogled the pouch of gold sovereigns, which might come in handy.

He had no idea what he might encounter but if he could so easily be distracted by the sight, so could others. The British passport, obviously forged, came with the German's photograph, though it might be of use. However, the other one, also with a photo, said *Rodolfo de Bázan*— diplomatic, albeit Billy didn't know—could be better, the two together even more so. At the bottom lay a bulging envelope and, ripping it open,

Billy stared in disbelief at a copy of the notes Graebner had handed over in his apartment, at which point Billy felt the red mist rising.

'Ya dirty bastard, ye've been lyin' to me from the very start.'

Thoughts flashed through his mind: Leo being left with Graebner's pistol; conversations in Spanish—morphed into threats reprising the feeling that, all along, he had been at risk. Every remark, every gesture Graebner had made since Billy had met him ran through his mind, not one of them reassuring. The German, who'd abandoned Leo Aviles, was a cold-hearted bastard who had only kept him alive because he might need him. Did he still, because if not, Billy couldn't risk what might come next?

He shimmied back up the tree, fetching down the shotgun cases. If Graebner could see how much use the maps were, the same would apply to his comrades. True, there was a risk, but in Billy's increasingly agitated state of mind, there was only one result if he failed to try. The sight of a British Army uniform could make the Germans nervous, so he stripped off his khaki and struggled back into the suit, not at all improved for being stuffed inside the kitbag.

Then, shotgun cases slung across his breast, his rifle on his shoulder, his own notes in the webbing backpack, along with the remans of a set of rations and the half empty water bottle, he headed north again, deliberately leaving a mess behind him, his discarded uniform piled beside the gaping grip and scattered notes. When he came back—if he came back—Graebner would know right away he had been rumbled.

Before he cleared the woods, Billy heard the whirr of aircraft engines, so he pressed himself against a tree, until he realised they weren't overhead but out at sea. As he moved on the noise rose and fell, but since there was no sign of a plane in the sky, he paid it little heed, concentrating on making sure he wasn't about to bump into anyone. Just in case, he made sure he had the bayonet within reach.

Always prone to let his imagination run free, he was wondering what would happen if he chose not to tell the Germans about Graebner. No boat would be sent to fetch him, which would serve the treacherous bastard right.

CHAPTER EIGHTY-ONE

Saturday, July 27, 6:40 p.m.

The flying boat, a Supermarine Southampton, was perfect for the task of searching a seascape and had already done one full circuit of the island. An out-of-date biplane, with a low flying speed, it was manned by four men in open cockpits. The engines were housed between the two sets of wings above the superstructure, which gave the crew a three-hundred-and-sixty-degree view. It could also land on water, which the pilot decided to do after making several passes over a small oil slick, sighted some two hundred yards offshore.

Swinging round for another pass, right over the glistening patch, the floating rope stretched out on the surface became visible. Static, it had to be tied to something, while just below the surface lay evidence of a shape, though the Solent was too murky to reveal more than an indistinct outline. Once landed and manoeuvring right above it, it soon became clear it was the wreck of a lifeboat, the forward mast only a few feet below the surface.

Radioing the news to HQ at RAF Castor, the message was passed to one of the people from the basement communications room of Osborne House. He immediately headed out to find Adam Strachan.

He was busy escorting the party of grim-looking Germans round the building, having found his joke regarding fascist salutes had nearly backfired. The embarrassment he felt about tractors and haycarts was evident as there were helped down and introduced. Two of the party were in grey SS uniforms, wearing caps fronted by a skull over crossed bones. Thankfully they were unarmed, or he would have been obliged to confiscate their weapons. It was clear the rest of the technical party were in fear of their good opinion of this pair; if the SS duo were not going to smile, neither were they.

Exchanges were abrupt, Avery, once indoors, translating questions regarding the uses to which the various reception rooms could be put. In every chamber they entered, a suspicious look was aimed at the light fittings, walls were tapped and door jambs fingered. Adam surmised this was only a preliminary to what, over the coming days, would be a thorough examination and a test of his department's skill at concealment.

The senior SS man spoke eventually, in decent if broken English. He'd been introduced as Sturmbannführer Schellenberg, almost his first words demanded the jetty and a cordon of one hundred metres around it be designated German territory for the duration of the talks. The security of the advance party could not be guaranteed otherwise, he insisted, and the problem would only increase once the full delegation arrived.

'Avery, just so everyone's clear,' when the request was repeated, 'translate what the major has asked for is beyond my power to grant.'

If Schellenberg was troubled by the fact Adam failed to use his SS rank, but its military equivalent, he covered it well.

'To translate there is no need.'

'Major Schellenberg, I am sure you'll appreciate there should be no confusion. Indeed, it would be better if the request came in writing and from Berlin.'

'Mr. Strachan, a word, sir.'

Adam moved swiftly to the Royal Signals operator who'd called out his name and a whispered exchange ensued. No hint of what he had been told showed on the MI5 man's face as he returned to Schellenberg.

'Something has arisen, with which I must deal. Is there anything more you and your colleagues require?'

A slim, good-looking cove, the German had an air of intelligence about him. He smiled beguilingly.

'Left alone we need to be.'

'Sorry, you may go where you wish in the main rooms without hindrance, but you will at all times be escorted.' Avery got a meaningful look. 'Now, if you will excuse me.'

Adam made for the comms room where the message was repeated to him. Frustrated because it was impossible to speak directly to the pilot, he immediately asked for the number of the Naval Diving School on Horsea Island. Having spoken to an officer there, he was assured no vessel could get across the Spithead Boom without major damage to the hull, not even a lifeboat, which was why it would be sitting on the bottom.

'I need the wreck examined.'

The request had to go to higher authority and Harker did act, this time with commendable speed. Information was passed back to say the navy would send out a team of divers in the morning to survey the wreck, so Adam was back on the phone to Horsea Island.

'If it is a lifeboat, anything you find is to be brought to me at Osborne House.'

'What is it we're looking for, Mr. Strachan?'

'Bodies.'

The comms personnel stared at him but he ignored them. If his fugitive trio were dead, the maps should be with them. If there were no bodies, he would have another set of problems altogether.

CHAPTER EIGHTY-TWO

Saturday, July 27, 7:55 p.m.

Rudi had used some cut up fishing line to tie the paddle inside the Klepper. If the kayak weighed close to nothing, it was still awkward to carry, yet to break it down into component parts would be worse. Even with the sun well past its zenith, it was hot work, his tongue felt like leather and he had taken frequent rests. He tried where possible to stay within the trees as much for the shade, ready to retreat deeper into the woods if danger arose. But the precaution proved unnecessary; few people used this route so progress was good.

Coming close to Palmer's Brook, with the sun now cut off by the height of the surrounding wood, he stopped for another rest, a feeling of exhaustion beginning to overwhelm him. Thinking about Billy Houston prompted him to take out his automatic, slip out the magazine and check the firing mechanism, before jamming it back again.

Would using it, always assuming Houston would react as expected, be a bad idea? The sound of a gunshot would carry to the ships and might alarm his comrades, putting them on guard just as he was hoping to approach. There was also the chance it would alert any unknown and land-based threats which existed. Whatever occurred, it would be best it should happen in silence.

Again, he turned to the gutting knife which, even if the blade was short, was extremely sharp. If it could be used to gut a fish, it could slice a throat, albeit he would be up against a bayonet. Certain he was cleverer than the Scotsman, a way would have to be found, but he would need to be at the top of his game with man as suspicious as Houston.

Rudi, for the umpteenth time, glanced at his watch. Time for his last couple of Pervitin. Hopefully by the time they wore off, Houston would be dealt with and he would be aboard *Prinz Eugen*. The saliva to swallow took time to produce and he nearly choked, but eventually the last one slid reluctantly down his gullet.

CHAPTER EIGHTY-THREE

Saturday, July 27, 7:38 p.m.

Billy's previous disguise had provided some cover; there was now none. He was back in rumpled civilian clothes, carrying an army rifle slung over his shoulder, as well as the twin shotgun cases and a water bottle. This turned him into the kind of sight which would make even the dimmest local curious. Luckily, despite having to make detours to avoid people working late in the fields, he encountered few other worries.

Having been assured the grounds around Osborne House were unguarded, the shock was total when, once he was within the perimeter, he saw a quartet of soldiers patrolling the pathway behind the stretch of beach where the jetty lay. There was a corporal carrying, like him, a Lee Enfield, plus privates with what looked like pickax handles, leaving him no option but to try and skirt round them.

First it meant moving closer to the shore, but here he ran up against a beach cut off by deep rolls of impassable barbed wire which ran right out into the sea. Luckily the guards didn't see or hear him, the north-east wind effectively masking the sound of his movements. Forced to back-track, he decided to try and get across the pathway closer to the main house, the risks soon evident.

A strip of open grassland lay on the far side of the path, while the few trees there had been individually planted and spaced to line to shade the route. The crossing had to be attempted because, Billy's plan, if it could be called that, required him to get into a good position.

It had to be one from which he could observe the access to the jetty, ready to move only when he was sure the German party was about to depart. Then, he needed to get into a square of forested ground, close to, but not visible, from a mapped building he assumed to be a boat house.

Heart in mouth, he strolled across the path, reckoning faster movement might catch an eye, or be noisy enough to attract attention. Only wide enough for a horse and cart, he was behind a large copper beech tree in seconds. With no sound of alarm, he was free to move fast: there would be no sound on grass. He crossed a strip of pasture fifty yards wide, to the wood on the other side, his onward progress just as hurried

He wanted to make it to the point where two paths met, one running parallel to the shore, before joining the wider lane which led down from Osborne House but another setback awaited him there. Soldiers were guarding the junction, not many and two of them armed NCOs, but enough to make crossing it unseen impossible. Cursing, Billy pulled back to a small clearing and sank down, back against a tree, to try and work out his next move.

The newspapers had said the Germans were coming to inspect Osborne House and surely, they had come ashore to do just that. If they had been and gone, there was nothing he could do about it and there was no way for him to tell without a clear sight of the jetty. If they had yet to depart, then the road junction he had just observed formed part of their route.

He would wait and, if darkness fell, he had a choice: to stay, or make his way back to the north shore of Palmer's Brook, not that he could see much appeal in the latter. If Graebner had failed to return, there was no point. If he had, it could only lead to a fight for possession of the maps Billy was in no mood to surrender.

Having not eaten since morning he was starving. It was time to eat those emergency rations, or at least the biscuits which he could butter, with a sip of water to ease them down. The butter being in a tin, it required the use of the can opener provided. A less than perfect tool, it needed both hands to work, which would have been fine, if one of those armed NCO's, a corporal, hadn't decided to use the clearing as a latrine.

As he wrestled with the army issue can opener, he failed to hear the corporal homing in on the clearing in search of a private space in which to relieve himself. Coming through the trees and spotting Billy preoccupied with the tin and opener, he whipped his rifle off his shoulder, hand automatically working to the bolt to lever it open and snap it shut. This pushed a bullet up into the chamber. It made a sound Billy knew too well. It was one of those never to be forgotten.

CHAPTER EIGHTY-FOUR

Saturday, July 27, 8:02 p.m.

Rudi Graebner got across the babbling Palmer's Brook safe and dry, proving the Klepper was watertight. He then took it as close as he dare, to the clearing where Houston should be waiting, before hiding it behind some thick bushes. When he made the spot and saw the mess, his first thought was that the Scotsman had been captured, but this was quickly replaced by the possibility he had been betrayed.

He clambered up the tree to find the shotgun cases and their contents gone, along with the binoculars and a pack of rations. The loss of the sovereigns meant little, but the missing documents were a different matter. Nevertheless, once he'd thrown down the things he might need, all he could do was gather up his notes and pray, even without any maps, he could convince his superiors regarding their accuracy.

Either way he had to keep going. There was no future for him on British soil, but the conviction all might not be lost marginally tempered his resentment. Even if Houston had found some way to get the maps to his comrades, Rudi knew, as long as he could join him, he could still claim most of the credit.

Standing on the shoreline, as twilight descended in a cloudless sky, he watched as all three ships begin to turn on their lights. To irritate the British, or a means of protection, it mattered not, for it showed him the way to go. There was still too much daylight to set out, but he began to make advance preparations. Retrieving the Klepper, he used the cutters and gloves to cut a very wide swath through the wire barricading the beach, ensuring the flimsy skin did not tear.

The idea had occurred earlier he might use the torch to send a Morse code message, to say a German officer and Abwehr agent wanted to come aboard, but he had abandoned it as too risky. The British patrol boats would be able to see the flashes and might well have translators on board. Sea water and earth made a paste he used to cover his exposed skin, which would reflect moonlight. The fishing waistcoat was light-coloured, so he streaked it with mud as well.

The eastern sky, at lower the edge, began to turn deep blue, which had him thanking providence, as well as his Führer, for his good fortune. Reckoning on still having an hour until it would be safe to leave, he sat down with the leftover rations from the general's car, sucking on a boiled sweet when he heard the first gunshot.

The corporal's rifle had been aimed at Billy, as he simultaneously demanded to know who the hell he was and what he was doing there. If he had raised it to take aim, he might have come out best, but the Lee Enfield was at his waist. From there it was hard to control the recoil, rendering it far from accurate on the first discharge. Billy had immediately spun behind his tree, grabbing his own weapon, which already had a bullet in the chamber. The corporal fired another round and took a clump of wood out of the pine, hitting high on the bark, the noise echoing through the woods.

Rolling to his left, Billy came out from cover, flat on the ground, hearing the crack as another shot went over his head. His response took place as the corporal worked his bolt again, a single shot, with the stock pressed into his shoulder and a tight grip on the barrel.

It took his opponent in the upper chest, sending him flying backwards, the rifle dropping from his hand. Billy didn't linger, he was up and running, heading back the way he had come, shotgun cases in one hand, his rifle in the other.

CHAPTER EIGHTY-FIVE

Saturday, July 27, 8:14 p.m.

Adam Strachan reacted swiftly to the sound. On his way to re-join Sefton Avery, he was in time to stop the Germans from exiting the Council Room onto the wide terrace overlooking the gardens. He ordered everyone back inside and away from the windows. Jocelyn Deveraux, showing great presence of mind, arrived within a minute with their pistols. Adam had Avery ordered everyone to retreat into the corridor running along the rear and, when Schellenberg looked set to argue, it was made plain force would be used if necessary.

'It's my job to make sure no harm comes to you. Whoever fired those shots is either an intruder or a soldier wishing for a court martial.'

Trenton came rushing in, demanding to be told what to do. He received a terse response as Adam, pistol cocked, dashed through the double doors, with the second lieutenant on his heels, issuing orders to his youngsters to make sure the Germans were kept safe. From the wide terrace, it was impossible to see what was happening in woods downhill and several hundreds of yards distant. Even this diminished as they took to the steps on the stairway, heading for the long shrub lined path that ran between the lawns.

Even if he could hear mayhem breaking out to his rear, Billy had to stop. He criss-crossed the shotgun case straps over his shoulders so he could run with more freedom, knowing his first problem was the guarded path. This time there was no looking to see if the men were still in place so, once across the strip of grassland, he plunged straight on over, hearing a shout but paying no attention. He kept going, knowing a pursuit was inevitable, seeking a possible way out and not coming up with anything which made sense.

Rudi Graebner had moved towards the edge of the trees to look north in the imperfect light, thinking the only reason for gunfire was trouble and it had to be Houston who had found it. Was he still alive or was the absence of more gunshots an indication he had been killed or wounded?

Stopping to get his bearings, Billy heard the soldiers to his rear. Who was he being chased by? Those stupid privates with nothing but pickax handles? He knew running towards gunfire was terrifying, even for the best soldiers, so he let off two rounds, not to hit anything, just for the noise and to show the pursuit what they might face.

Unseen by him, the undertrained territorials of the Royal Sussex immediately demonstrated the kind of morale which came from being chased halfway across France by the German Army. The crack of a couple of passing rounds was enough to stop them, their NCO's reduced to calling them bloody cowards. Even a threat to shoot one or two failed to get them to budge.

Thus, Adam discovered two sections of the company he'd been landed with as a milling mob, who were not going to be harangued or threatened into risking their lives with nothing but clubs against bullets. Trenton was too young and inexperienced to assert authority, so all Adam could do, once he got some sense of what had occurred, was proffer advice.

'I would suggest armed men only, Mr. Trenton. Can I suggest you get them together? I take it you were taught infantry tactics at Sandhurst?'

The affirmative was so feeble, it made the MI5 man doubt if he had. Mentally, Adam was back at school, in the cadet corps, trying to remember what the master in charge had taught them, this as another NCO caught up with the party. He loudly reported to Trenton, the corporal who had been shot was in a bad way but able to talk.

'Said it were one bloke, sir, with a Lee Enfield, same as his, an' the bugger knew how to use it.'

'Best you spread your men out, Mr. Trenton,' Adam called, 'but within sight of each other. I think it best we move forward slowly.'

309

'Including you, sir?' Trenton asked, his voice betraying real gratitude.
'I don't think I have a choice.'

Seven men, five of them NCOs, were never going to cover much ground, but Adam had a quiet word with CSM Grout, who had just joined them from the golf course. It was obvious he was the most experienced person present.

'Can I suggest, Mr. Grout, you stay close to Mr. Trenton and advise him?

'It's what people like me do, sir,' was the quiet response, as he cocked his Webley. 'It'd be Fred Karno's Circus if we didn't.'

'Then, if I'm allowed, I recommend it's time to move.'

Saturday, July 27, 8:47 p.m.

A lack of alternatives took Billy back in the direction from where he had come. In his head he tried to make up a convincing excuse for Graebner if he found him waiting, not that he could conjure up anything credible. His only hope was the German, if he was back in that clearing, would still see the need for both of them to get away.

Stood at the treeline, Rudi was struggling with the fading light, so it was only Billy's movement which alerted him to an approach, an outline he was unable to identify. Was it hostile, was it Houston and, if so, what should he do? It was hard to now consider the Scotsman an ally. The temptation to use his Walther was strong, but if it was who he thought, the swine could still be in possession of the maps. Unable to see the danger which lay to Billy's rear, he guessed it must exist, not that it provided an immediate threat.

The line was moving very slowly, weapons at the ready as befitted the risk, with Adam wondering who it was they were chasing. The report of the possible sunken lifeboat and its location had changed the game. He had been assured it was impossible the trio could get to the south coast, but they had done so. He had to consider, despite everyone's seeming certainty it was also impossible, for them to have got ashore on the north shore of the island as well.

The weapon fired at the wounded corporal was a Lee Enfield, so who could it be in possession of such? Grout's rank meant long service in the regulars, so edging a bit closer, the question was posed about what might have come from the Strathallan house.

'General's driver would have a rifle, sir. Standard issue. Being with a senior officer, it would be needed for protection in the field.'

'It's a pity not every soldier gets one.'

'If you mean the lot I've been landed with, they're more of a danger to themselves than Jerry.'

'I know we've been told we're in pursuit of one person, Mr. Grout. I think it best to say it may be three.'

There was a pause before the CSM answered. 'Be dark soon, sir. We'll have to call off the search, any road.' Then he raised his voice to address the nearby subaltern. 'Can I suggest, Mr. Trenton, in this light, we start calling to each other every twenty paces, so as not to get separated.'

'My very own thoughts, Mr. Grout.'

Billy had a pain in his chest and was breathing hard; the life he had led did not involve much actual running, so he was far from fit enough to do so without suffering. Right ahead lay the darker outline of the trees enclosing Palmer's Brook, towards which he kept going, slowly now, until aching lungs made him stop. There was another reason to do so; he had no idea where Graebner might be, so he loudly called out. This time, the 'Mein Herr' was a plea, instead of a dig.

Rudi nearly responded, to ask if Houston still had the maps but, whether or not they were with him was irrelevant, the only decision now being what to do about a man who had betrayed him. Absurdly, he recalled the book he had mentioned to Houston in the Hillman, which clarified his thinking. As an Abwehr agent, he had to escape regardless and he had the means to do so, while the fast-fading light was going to give him the required cover of darkness.

His comrades, who must have heard the gunfire, would never send a boat to rescue Houston. So, half-hidden behind a tree, he said nothing, sure his silence would bring the Scotsman on. It did, but slowly, with the rifle at his shoulder and a bullet in the chamber.

'If yer there, ah've got the maps and ah've found a way to get off the island too. There's only a few suggers guarding the big house and there's a party of your lot ashore now.'

Billy was desperate enough, but his heavy breathing made it sound despairing. 'We can blast our way through to the jetty if we work together.' A pause and a few forward paces. 'Are ye there, damn ye?'

Graebner was silently pleading for Houston to move faster, it being near pitch dark under the trees where he was standing, when he heard a series of faint shouts fill the air, unmistakeably the noise of a pursuit. These were heard by Billy, who had no doubt as to the nature of the sound and, from inching paces, he moved fast enough to force Graebner backwards. The German took a tight grip on his pistol, there being no need now to worry about gunshots.

There was going to be an element of guesswork as to the point at which Houston would pass him, so he kept going until a gap in the leaf cover provided a modicum of light from the sun, now below the western horizon, this while the voice, still seeking to persuade came closer. The oiled metal of Billy's rifle gave off a very faint reflection, which Graebner spotted, soon followed by the outline of a hunched body, one he let pass.

The butt of the automatic took Billy Houston on the back of the head, the Scotsman staggering into a tree, which stopped him from going down. The barrel of the Lee Enfield swung round, which nearly did for Graebner, but he got inside the arc of the sweep just in time to take a heavy blow on the forearm. It would have been painful if it had been given time to register.

Choosing to rely on the butt of his pistol, he swung viciously at the little he could see of the pallid face and head before him, not once but several times, oblivious to the sounds of protest, as well as to the crunch of metal on flesh. Billy, hampered by the shotgun cases and desperate to hang on to his rifle, tried to reach the bayonet stuck in his belt.

In doing so he gave the German the space to maintain his attack and so he went down, still protesting and pleading, but for what? Mercy? Understanding? Rudi Graebner didn't care as, with a grip on one of the lapels of that crumpled suit, he delivered a last blow to a man now on the ground and silent.

'Let your fellow-country hang or shoot you. You are scum and not worth one German bullet. But if you can hear me, know this. I have the means to get to my comrades, with your maps and it pleases me it will be without the burden of you.'

The soft 'Seig Heil' was followed by a cackling laugh, as Graebner tugged the maps off Billy's shoulders. That done he was quick to run through the trees to the shoreline and reach his Klepper, now sat on the narrow strand of beach and ready to launch. Stuffing the shotgun cases into the canoe, he pushed it in to the shallows and, extracting the double paddle, clambered in, immediately propelling himself forward.

He began swinging slowly and gently, right and left, to get the blades biting into the water, the prow aimed at the lights of *Prinz Eugen*. There was no need to rush, there were hours of darkness, and he could lie off until that Royal Navy patrol boat, its searchlight bright and obvious, too close for comfort now, was well out of the way.

The pursuit had reached the last of the fields which lay to the north of Palmer's Brook, not that any of them knew of such a watercourse. Adam did register, if you excluded the calling of one soldier to another, the silence, which was worrying. Had their quarry turned inland? If he had, they would never find him in the dark. And if it was three to catch, not one, where were they? Should he advise Trenton to break off and get back to Osborne House and protect it?

CHAPTER EIGHTY-SEVEN

Saturday, July 27, 9:16 p.m.

If Billy had groaned before Graebner left him, he might have got a bullet regardless. He did so now, half-awake after some twenty minutes, seeking to raise himself and struggling, a feeble hand scrabbling for his nearby rifle. He needed the aid of the weapon, as well as the tree, to get even halfway to his feet, more time to get some breath into his lungs, to then fumble for the torch he had last used at Wisley and left in the pocket.

The battery was beginning to run low, but it gave off enough light, even swinging about, to show him the path. The hand that held the rifle found it hard to keep a grip, especially staggering through and careering off trees. In compressing his fingers, Billy inadvertently pulled the trigger, the sound of the shot carrying to his pursuers, making everyone stop and think of taking cover.

Billy ended up on his hands and knees, crawling the rest of the way into the tiny glade where he and Graebner had earlier parted company, collapsing on to the pile of his own abandoned battledress as well as the canvas grip. Close enough to the shore to allow the illumination of the German warships to penetrate, this acted as a draw on his vision.

He crawled for the shoreline, finding the gap in the wire, thanks to the broken strands being silhouetted against the glaring lights out in the Solent. If it didn't tell him how Graebner had got away, it was enough to establish he had. Even with a confused mind, it seemed obvious the bastard had intended all along to leave him behind. The blood from Graebner's beating was clouding his eyes so a sweep across his face was required to clear his vision.

This time, when he looked out on the water, he could hardly believe the scene before him. In the distance was the German flotilla and, in the foreground silhouetted against the ships' lights was what had to be Graebner, paddling very slowly towards the *Prinz Eugen*.

'Gotcha ya bastard.'

That was the vocal response; the physical one was to drag forward the rifle, to grip it as tight as he could, a finger flicking up the sights and, a second later, a hand to work the bolt, with a motion drummed into him and every British rifleman. Mentally he was back in 1914, an Old Contemptible private to whom his rifle was his friend. The firing position he adopted was little different to that which he and his regiment had occupied at Mons. Laid flat, stock pulled tight into the shoulder and his left hand screwing on the wood below the barrel in a grip which supressed the recoil. The working of the bolt followed without any thought at all.

The crack of the first bullet passing Rudi Graebner was followed by a hiss as it hit the water just beyond and his reaction was immediate. From a leisurely progress, he began to paddle furiously, with no idea who was shooting, for it surely could not be Houston. It made no difference and, in truth, his only real worry was he might take a wound which would stop him paddling. He was less concerned for the Klepper, which would survive a couple of bullet holes long enough for him to reach safety.

By the edge of the trees, Adam Strachan also heard the first shot and he knew, whoever it was aimed at, it wasn't him. Grout suggested to his officer the men come together on the treeline and go forward in pairs, this added to some advice for Adam Strachan.

'Best you stay back, sir.'

Billy was too weakened to replicate the rate of fire he had once been trained to execute as an infantryman. He got off two more shots, with no idea if they had hit anything, before his head began to drop, yet the synchronised working of the bolt and trigger was carried out by habit. With head and body lolling forward, the barrel of the Lee Enfield was raised a fraction, so the next round flew well over Graebner's head, smacking into the armoured plating of the heavy cruiser's hull. Billy was near to passing out, but his hand had a life of its own now and worked the bolt again.

The German warships were already under guard, but the repeated sound of gunfire, especially with a party of their own ashore, had brought to the deck every marine aboard, officers included. The clang of a bullet on the armoured plating had them shouting to hold fire until the threat could be determined. Soon, another round smashed into the hull, followed by another, as Billy Houston fired regularly and by habit.

Unaware of what was being hit and only able to hear the crack of the bullets flying over his head, Rudi was paddling furiously towards the lights illuminating the gangway, shouting in German his name and rank. His words were lost to the roar of an approaching British patrol boat, whose searchlight began to play over the sea between him and his destination.

A burst of machine pistol fire from the foredeck of Prinz *Eugen* rent the air, a warning which Graebner was unable to heed. As he came into the cruiser's halo of its own on-board lights, he reached into the kayak, producing one of the waterproof canvas cases containing the documents, shouting to tell those who couldn't hear him Hitler would have sacrificed a whole division of his army for possession.

The shape of the case, to a young German marine peering into the indifferent glow, looked very much like what it had been made to carry. Holding an already cocked weapon, his nerves were jangling and, never having been in action, his feeling of near dread was acute.

Billy got off two more aimless shots, one hitting the plating just below where the marine was standing, the other passing over the rail to crack into the metal of the upperworks, so close to his ear he reacted instinctively and in terror on his machine pistol trigger, with a weapon already aimed. Opening fire, he raked the sea all around the kayak, tearing holes in the cover, the shot going right through the flimsy material to puncture the base in a dozen places from front to rear.

The Klepper immediately began taking in water, which did not matter much, because Rudi Graebner had ceased paddling, such an effort being impossible for a man who was a fraction away from dying of multiple bullet wounds.

317

CHAPTER EIGHTY-EIGHT

Saturday, July 27, 19:40 p.m.

CSM Grout and one if his corporals crept into the glade, with Adam Strachan close behind. Progress was one step at a time towards the shoreline, with stuttering halts, sounds reverberating as Billy Houston fired off the last of his ten-round magazine. Entering what passed for a clearing, Adam was just in time to see a silhouetted Grout taking aim with his Webley. He screamed in vain for the man to hold his fire, as the CSM put three quick bullets into Billy Houston's back.

Seconds later, stood over the prone body, Adam could see the silhouette of the British patrol boat, as it heaved to between the shore and the *Prinz Eugen*, but his mind was on Grout's victim. A search of the body by torchlight was frustrating, likewise the scattered clothing and grip, doubly so since the man carrying it out would not allow anyone to aid him. There was no sign of the maps, while written numbers on the papers Adam found scattered around were as incomprehensible to him as they had been to Billy Houston.

Exasperated, he was also conscious the German shore part were still back at Osborne House and they had to be dealt with. Since only he could handle it, he had to leave Grout and two of his NCOs to guard the clearing until daylight, then hurry back to face a seriously rattled Schellenberg. The SS man was not mollified by any assurances the matter had been resolved, nor was he afforded an explanation. He was even less enamoured when he and his party were ordered under escort to board the hay cart for the jetty and their motor launch, before being obliged to cast off for *Prinz Eugen*.

The lieutenant captaining the Royal Navy patrol boat, once he'd reported to his superiors, had been given instructions to come alongside the same landing stage, with both the shredded kayak and its dead occupant laid out on the deck. Two of the crewmen had fished the ripped Klepper out of the water with boathooks before it sank, bringing with it the dead body of the man who had been paddling.

Adam was obliged to establish both himself and his function before he could go aboard, which led to a delay, as Naval HQ had to be consulted. Having cleared it with the Admiralty and Whitehall, he was allowed to have a look, with a strong naval flashlight, which allowed him to identify Graebner. Still anxious he was presented with a waterproof shotgun case.

'We found this clutched in his hand, sir. It's full of rolled up maps. Bit wet I'm afraid.'

Rudi Graebner had held on to the shotgun case and its vital secrets in a death grip, while the second case was subsequently found inside the body of the kayak. So, the numbered copy of the National Defence Plan, taken out by de Vries, was back in the War Office safe by midday on the Sunday.

The bodies of Graebner and Billy Houston were buried in unmarked graves on the island, the body of Leo Aviles never found. The case against Jeannie Milburn, for aiding and abetting an enemy spy, as well as conspiracy to commit murder, saw her charged under the Defence of the Realm Act. In a closed court with no jury, she was sentenced to life imprisonment and incarcerated in Holloway Prison. No papers relating to the case have been released, even under the standard thirty-year rules on disclosure.

Author's Note

The activities of Tyler Kent, the US Embassy cipher clerk, are in the historical record. The cables between Churchill and Roosevelt were especially awkward for the Americans because they undercut President Roosevelt's stated intention to stay out of the war. While they contained no vital secrets, the traffic between London and Washington, to do with arms shipments and equipment orders, were highly sensitive, as were the two men's honest and private opinions.

Also implicated in the affair was Anna Wrockoff, daughter of an ex-Czarist admiral, owner of the Russian Tea Rooms in South Kensington. This was a meeting place for those sympathetic to Hitler, or so virulently anti-Soviet they would do anything and help anyone to fight Communism. The folk denouncing democracy over the samovar had no idea many alongside them worked for MI5, specifically for a counter-intelligence officer called Henry Maxwell-Knight.

There was not a right-wing organisation in the country Maxwell-Knight had not fully penetrated, all based on the fact that he was a poacher turned gamekeeper. At one time he had served as the treasurer of the British Union of Fascists. Vernon Kell had known Anna Wrockoff since she was a child and was unwilling to believe she was Kent's recruiter, insisting she was guilty of nothing other than being naïve. This had been enough to see the man who had helped create MI5 & MI6 dismissed from the post he'd occupied for over twenty years.

If it seems hard to imagine the number of fascist and anti-Semitic organisations active in Britain during the 1930s, listed over leaf, it becomes less so when contemplating the world we live in today:

Perish Judah
Imperial Fascist League
White Knights of Britain
Nordic League
Militant Christian Patriots
National Socialist League
The Link
Christian Defence Movement
British People's Party
National Citizens Union
National Ratepayers Association
The Right Club

Captain Archibald-Maule Ramsey MP was arrested on 23 May 1940 and interned without trial until September 1944. He was the founder of the Right Club, a secret anti-Jewish, anti-war organisation of which both Tyler Kent and Anna Wrockoff were members. On launching the club in June 1939, Ramsay declared that:

'Hitler is a splendid fellow with whom we should be proud to be friends.'

Two hundred and fifty others were listed in the membership book: one Prince, two Princesses, one Duke, one Marquess, two Earls, five other Lords, two Professors, two Reverend Gentlemen, six Doctors, twelve MPs, nineteen retired military officers and sundry others with 'Sir', 'Lady' or 'Hon' prefixing their names, few of whom have been publicly shamed.

Adolf Hitler subsequently selected Osborne House to be his official British residence after a successful invasion, on an island which, no doubt, would have been denuded of its inhabitants.

DD. Deal 2022